CRUZ

A DARK AND DIRTY SINNERS' MC: FIVE

SERENA AKEROYD

Copyright © 2021 by Gemma Mazurke

All rights reserved.

No part of this book may be reproduced in any form or by any electronic or mechanical means, including information storage and retrieval systems, without written permission from the author, except for the use of brief quotations in a book review.

❦ Created with Vellum

CRUZ

DEDICATION

FOR ALL THE Moms who were betrayed as little girls. For all the Moms who are doing what needs to be done to make sure their babies are never betrayed. For all the Moms who are reeling in the aftermath of a betrayal…

Those bastards, may they rot in hell, will meet their Nyx one day.

To Abby. You'll never go through what your mom did. She'll make sure of it.

And so will I.

UNIVERSE READING ORDER

FILTHY
NYX
LINK
FILTHY RICH
SIN
STEEL
FILTHY DARK
CRUZ
MAVERICK
FILTHY SEX
HAWK
FILTHY HOT
STORM
THE DON
THE LADY
FILTHY SECRET (COMING NOVEMBER 2021)

SOUNDTRACK

If you'd like to hear a curated soundtrack, with songs that are featured in the book, as well as songs that inspired it, then here's the link:

https://open.spotify.com/playlist/43E4Vq7NPvU0EQYzuvnyzK

This might not be what you're used to from the Sinners.
That's my fault. ;)

TRIGGER WARNING

FOR SURVIVORS OF SEXUAL ABUSE, approach with care.

This book was vetted by a survivor and she herself told me to tell you:

> "For people like me, Indy's story is too common. But Serena has done survivors justice with this book. I remember telling Serena that reading Cruz made me feel normal, not alone in what I had gone through, so yes, I cried, and yes, if it's too raw for you, then don't read it. But, now, Indy can finally start to heal, and maybe, you'll feel that way too."

Also, just FYI, there are BDSM elements in here.

If either of these things affect you, please, don't read this book and feel free to seek a refund. <3

PART 1

ONE

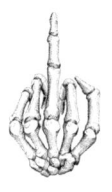

INDY

IT WAS LATE, but I was wired.

One of the downsides of not only working at, but owning a tattoo parlor, were the hours. They were long, arduous, but more than that, they were whacko too.

I'd finished working on my last client's back an hour ago, and that was at three AM. What could I say? I worked when my peeps needed me, saying screw it if it messed with my circadian rhythms.

Hey, nature was born to be fucked with.

But, the trouble was, when I'd tried to clamber upstairs, head to my own quarters, I'd just been too buzzed.

Steeler's back piece was legendary.

Shit, I'd done enough career-making tattoos to recognize one.

From the top of his shoulders, along to his hips, over the plump mounds of his muscular ass, then to his thighs and calves, when I said it was a back piece, I meant it. Every inch of his back half was covered.

By my work.

Talk about a fucking honor.

Flames licked at his heels, and along to his lower thighs where a body soared out from the fire. A woman stood there, a heart in her hands, her face lowered to the organ that dripped blood down her form.

It was, in a word, breathtaking.

The only color came from the blood and the heart, everything else was black and white, and it was beautiful.

If I could have adorned my own back with it, I would have, but no way in fuck would I trust just anyone with my body. Not anymore. I had the pieces that mattered to me now, and the rest would come with time, when I trusted another artist. When my mentor, Jimmy Laruso, had passed on, my time under the needle had come to an end. But tonight gave me as much of a high as Steeler had from the endorphins.

Sure, my shoulders ached, my spine felt like it had a permanent crick in it, my eyes were tired, and the skin beside them felt crinkled and in need of ironing out from fatigue and squinting, but aside from all that, this was about as 'on top of the world' as I ever got.

Which was why I was rolling up the driveway to the Satan's Sinners' clubhouse.

I wanted to be left alone and I didn't want to see or speak with anyone for at least eight hours.

If I did, I'd have headed into the city to go and sit with Stone, my best bud, who was in the hospital. So, avoiding David, my assistant, who'd been trailing my ass until the turn off to the compound, and seeing the Prospect who was manning the gates, were both bad enough, because I just wanted to be left alone while I cleaned.

Stone was coming home soon, and Rex had hauled in a bunch of brothers to get working on the bunkhouse where she'd be staying to recuperate. All the bunkhouses were stuck in another era and badly in need of an update—Rex had taken one, turned it into a home where Stone could heal without wanting to leave from just how gross the place was, and now I wanted to clean it.

She might be the doctor, but I was the one who was obsessed with keeping my environment clean. And when it boiled down to the people I gave a damn about, or in Stone's instance, *loved*, well, I'd go the extra length and bleach any motherfucking thing to within an inch of its life.

The night air was just starting to turn damp with the onset of early morning dew, and it was that time where, no matter the season, there was that little chill in the air. The one that got into your bones and made you shudder just that teeny bit.

I shrugged it off, grabbed the bucket I'd packed with cleaning products from the footwell of the passenger seat of my Camaro, and shifted into gear.

All my stuff was eco-friendly, but not the bleach. That was one thing I couldn't live without. It was actually kind of an addiction. My nails were wrecked because of it, had little lines running down the lengths so I always had them painted.

If the shrinks my family had seen in the aftermath of Carly's death had known what I'd done with bleach, they'd probably have held another intervention.

When I thought about how I'd scrubbed myself clean with it, I still shuddered in horror at just how badly it could have gone wrong. I mean, I had the scars, only they were buried under a ton of ink, but those marks had forged me into the woman I was today.

One who helped others cover up their scars, and who loved her baby brother. He was my ride or die because, when it mattered, he'd been mine, saving me from myself and that bottle of Clorox when he'd found me using it like it should never be used.

It was stupid. In fact, it was *fucking* stupid because I needed the goddamn bleach, but my thoughts, the memories, Caleb, all of it combined and I hurled the bottle ahead of me. As it soared through the sky, gravity had it plummeting with a nasty *thud*. The instant smell of chemicals had me wincing, and hoping there was some in the bunkhouse.

"You're an idiot," I muttered under my breath, shaking my head at my own stupidity.

My trouble was I had a quick-to-trip flip switch.

Always had. Always would.

Heaving a sigh, I trudged to the bunkhouse, wishing that my high of before hadn't just plummeted to the ground like the bottle of fucking Clorox.

That was another constant.

My life was like a helium balloon that was destined to soar only to fall.

"And that's enough self-pity for one night," I grumbled to myself, because no one had time for that shit.

The door was unlocked, because only an idiot would think to break onto the compound and steal anything, but it meant I didn't have to head into the clubhouse to grab a key which was a relief, as it was quite likely there'd be an orgy going down in there.

As I rolled in, my brows arched as I saw how hard the guys had been working because it was complete. The TV was up, the new sofa was in, and when I strolled into the bathroom, then the bedroom, there was still plastic wrap around the new mattress, as well as that plastic liner stuff they put on mirrors to protect the surface.

Dumping my bucket on the floor in the kitchen, I ran the water as I emptied it, then when it was hot, filled it to the brim.

And after I rolled up the sleeves of my Martin Garrix hoodie—the one Nyx and Caleb always gave me shit for—I got to work.

Bathroom, then kitchen, then surfaces in the living room and bedroom, and then the floor. By that point, I was sweating bullets, and as I tossed the scrubbing brush on the ground, I swiped at my sweaty forehead before tossing the hoodie off and onto the sofa.

A few minutes into my scrubbing sesh, I heard a wolf whistle, and I froze.

It was low.

Almost silent.

But I'd been a victim once, and I'd sworn I'd never be again, so even when I was busy, I kept at least one part of myself aware of my environment.

My head whipped around, and I saw him standing there, leaning against the doorjamb, his arms folded across his chest, his eyes narrowed at me.

I immediately registered that he hadn't intended for me to hear the whistle, but that didn't stop me from glowering at him. Not only for the whistle, not only for watching me and creeping up on me, but also for the fact that his gaze was fixed, quite firmly, on my tits.

Typical fucking man.

"The eyes are up here, Cruz," I snarled at him, and even though I was quite willing to go head to head with him, two things were going against me.

One: I'd had a nineteen-hour day, and was exhausted.

Two: If I carried on cleaning and just ignored him, I knew he'd carry on watching me.

Cruz wasn't like the other brothers. I didn't know much about him, and to be honest, I thought that was the case for the entire club. I didn't want to say that he was an enigma, because if I did, I'd find that attractive and I didn't have time for attraction right now.

I'd tried to fuck my past out of my system throughout my early twenties, and while I hadn't taken a vow of chastity, it was an old habit I was trying to get out of.

I could still remember the day when a fuck buddy had given my number to another guy, who'd thought I was a hooker. I'd woken up with two hundred dollars on my nightstand and—

"You're lucky I'm not Nyx."

I was grateful for the intrusion into my thoughts, just not so happy about what he was saying.

"Why? Because he'd tell me off for being here?" Goddamn brothers. Even Caleb who was younger than me, treated me like I was fucking five.

"No, because if he'd thought you were a home invader, he'd have shot you first then registered what was going on second."

I snorted. "Nyx'd never shoot first. You have met him, haven't you?"

Cruz's lips twisted. "Oh, I've met him. I've also seen him in action whereas you, I don't think, have."

"You'd be surprised." If he was taken aback by that, he didn't say anything, nor did he ask what I'd seen in particular.

Good thing, too. I wouldn't have told him the truth anyway.

"You're a treasure trove full of surprises, aren't you, Indy?" he mused, his voice soft.

I scowled at him as I reached up again and rubbed my forehead. My hair was clinging to my temples, sticking to my cheeks too. I knew my cami was drenched down my back, and was probably plastered to my front as well. I was just grateful I was wearing a sports bra or he'd be getting a real show.

When had camis stopped being a covering and turned into a flimsy piece of fabric that facilitated a perv ogling someone's chest, huh?

"I'm no one's idea of a treasure," I muttered under my breath.

"No? I think Stone would disagree." He peered around the place. "I was in here today fitting the TV. It was a mess. And it reeked of sawdust. You did this all on your own?"

"See any Smurfs in the vicinity?" I retorted, sniffing at him. "Cruz, I'm busy. I still have the floor to do and then I can get back home and get some rest."

His frown deepened, but he surprised me by shrugging, twisting around, and heading out the door as silently as he'd trudged in.

He'd given my lagging energy a kick in the butt though, so that was something. Whenever I thought about how he'd been looking at my tits, standing there as cool and as calm as anything, I'd scrub the floor harder and with more exertion than was technically necessary.

Those goddamn green eyes seemed to see everything. That dark mink hair made Loki's look blond. I'd bet this month and last month's rent that it felt like fucking silk against my fingers. And all that ink? He was exactly the kind of guy I tried to avoid.

I had an eye for men that were covered in tats. Especially good ones. I loved his hands too, which was inconvenient because I wanted no man's hands on me. They were inked black, and negative space was used to create the image of finger bones.

It was creepy, but it spoke of the man.

Everything about his ink did. It was grungy, grimy, dark. But it contrasted with that silky brown hair that belonged to an angel, the eyes that were clear like glass, and the face of a man who would be able to grace the front page of GQ.

Agitation saw me through the rest of the floor, but when I'd finished for real, I was exhausted. Too tired to drive. Too wrecked to even take a shower, which was indicative of how damn tired I was because I showered three times a frickin' day.

I felt bad, but there was still plastic on the mattress, so I tiptoed over the still-drying floor and plopped onto the bed. In my dirty cami and jeans, boots and all, I slept.

And slept.

And slept.

Only, when I woke up, there was a blanket by my feet that I'd shoved down while I rested, and I knew that was Cruz's doing because I hated being covered while I slept.

Which meant he'd come back.

And hadn't tried to hurt me.

Interesting.

TWO
CRUZ

AS I DROVE off the compound, I saluted Jaxson before I trundled down toward West Orange.

Only Jax and me were awake at this point, even Indy had fallen asleep because I'd checked in on her to make sure she was okay before I left to head to the warehouse district.

With her ride still parked, I'd been concerned. She'd looked a little frazzled. A lot on edge.

She was a puzzle I'd been trying to solve for a few years, ever since she'd come back to West Orange after a long time down in Louisiana.

I hated puzzles.

As much as I loved them.

Most of the mistakes I'd made in my life were thanks to a puzzle I just *had* to solve. Some of them were complex, some of them were chemical or structural, some of them were scientific, very few of them were human.

Which made her unusual.

I disliked the unusual as much as I disliked puzzles.

My fingers tightened around the steering wheel at the thought of how she'd looked on her hands and knees, tits swaying even with her sports bra keeping those beauties restrained, sweat on her brow, her eyes a little glazed from fatigue—it'd be too easy to strip off those clothes in my mind's eye and for her to look like she was being fucked. The way she'd rocked back and forth on her knees, swaying as she scrubbed, it was like she was being screwed doggy style. Not pounded, just screwed.

There was a distinct difference.

My dick had been aching ever since I'd gone to check in on the bunkhouse during my shift. The bar had been busier than usual as it was a Saturday night, a lot of brothers had been helping fix up the bunkhouse and everyone had been celebrating the fact that not only was it mostly complete, but Stone was on the mend and would be home soon.

With the revelry making my ears ache, my eyes stinging from all the smoke, I'd headed outside for a breather and had seen someone sneaking out of the bunkhouses where the girls were living, which, now that I thought about it, I hadn't investigated further because Indy had pulled up, dragging my attention her way. Of course, her arrival was weird, but weird was a regular occurrence around this place.

I'd figured she was maybe coming to visit Giulia and Nyx, except, she hadn't. She'd pulled out a bucket of cleaning materials, then, a few steps toward the bunkhouse, she'd tossed a bottle of bleach like she was lobbing a softball. It had gone sailing through the air before it collided with a wet thud as it exploded on the ground.

Attention thoroughly caught, I'd watched her as she slipped in, and through the windows, I'd seen she was setting up to clean. Brothers had hollered at me to get back and to serve some drinks up, so I'd done as asked, before, an hour later when things had died down, seeing she was still there, I'd gone to check on her.

I loved a woman who cleaned. There was nothing misogynistic about it. If I boned guys, I'd get off on watching them clean too. It was the act, not the gender. I just loved it. So, Indy, without even knowing it, had given me my version of a private lap dance.

Growling under my breath because I'd tap that ass of hers quick as breathing if given the opportunity, I trundled into town and headed off toward the east side where I had an appointment.

I could do this in the day time because, technically, I wasn't doing anything wrong, but there were a million laws between technicality and legality and, also, I intended to sleep when I got back. Waking up to do a chore I could have done before I slept was just impractical, and I wasn't an impractical man.

The roads were dead, the night air was still, and only the dawn birds were interested in me as I headed to the rougher part of West Orange.

When I made it there, drove along the roads of the industrial park, I turned down my radio because all was quiet around here, and finally arrived at the unit.

As I pulled in, the whirring of the mechanism of the doors sounded overly loud in the silence of the otherwise still night as the second I made it inside, they closed behind me.

It took forty minutes longer than I'd have liked to get the crates onto the back of my truck, but I wasn't about to complain when Kirill's guys did the heavy lifting. I didn't even have to get out of the cage.

A few minutes in, Kirill hopped into the passenger seat beside me, and we bumped fists as he asked, "You're going through more of this than usual. Might have to up my rates."

My lips twitched. "What can I say? Sometimes there's more trash hanging around than can be recycled."

He arched a bushy brow at me, but his smile was genuine when it made an appearance.

I'd met Kirill in college of all places. He was one of the reasons I hadn't offed myself when my life had gone down the shitter.

I was where I was because of my mother, but knowing Kirill, an old Chem professor from college, and his wife, Monique, cared about me, regardless of the bad decisions I'd made while I was a student, had been grounding. Enough to stop me from making a very foolish mistake when I'd been facing jail.

Now, he was no longer a professor but ran a cleaning business with Monique, and I took advantage of his contacts, new and old, for the Sinners' purposes.

Sometimes, it wasn't *what* you knew, but who.

Just in this instance, with both my know-how and contacts, it was both.

"Old friend, where you're concerned, recycling was never an issue."

I outright grinned at that, then asked, "Seriously though, if you need more, I'll tell the Prez."

Kirill shrugged. "It isn't the cost of the items, per se—"

"It's making sure the procurement stays under the radar. I get it."

He rubbed his chin. "You making a meth lab?"

I snorted. "What about the shit I asked you to purchase screams meth production? You've been retired too long if you don't remember how to make meth."

"Usually the body count is this high when drugs are involved."

"Don't ask, don't tell," was all I said. "Kirill, I don't want you getting involved in this crap."

He tutted. "It was only a heart scare."

"When it's to do with the heart, you need to take notice," I retorted. "And it has nothing to do with that. If Monique knew I was asking this much of you, she'd give me crap."

His smile turned fond. "True." It faded. "Are you in trouble?"

"No. Not personally, anyway. The club… well, that's different. But there's nothing for you to worry about. War isn't coming to West Orange. I'd warn you if it was."

A hand clapped on the side of the truck door, prompting Kirill to grunt.

"I've burned the last supplier. If you need more, then you need to wait or I'll need more cash."

"Thanks, Kir."

He shrugged. "More than welcome. Don't be a stranger. Monique misses you. She often complains about how close you are and how rarely she sees you."

I pulled a face. "I'm a Sinner. I don't want to bring any trouble to your door."

"That's much appreciated, son, but have you ever thought about taking off the vest and driving to us?" was his dry answer. "I know you're not glued to your hog."

I grimaced. "I mostly ride in the club's cages." Sadly—but it was the nature of my job—I had to haul a lot of heavy shit around.

"Well, then," he grumbled, clucking his tongue.

I laughed then pointed to my throat, as well as my wrists and hands. "You saying I wouldn't stick out like a sore thumb in your neighborhood even if I turned up in a Calvin Klein suit?"

His eyes were twinkling as he jumped out of the truck. "Maybe. I'm sure you know enough women who can lend you some foundation."

"Christ," I rumbled. "You want me to wear a skirt to blend in too?"

"I'd pay to see that," was all he said, but he laughed as he shut the door. "Stay safe," he told me, and I heard the warning, and accepted it.

Kirill had always cared, and I genuinely felt shitty for abandoning Monique.

During college, both of them had helped get me through when ramen noodles had started looking like luxury takeout. I'd attended school on a scholarship, but those funds didn't pay for students to eat like kings.

When the doors to the loading bay opened up again, I rolled out, saluted Kirill in farewell, then as I drove off with the truck a little more unwieldy and harder to steady now there was a couple hundred pounds of weight on the back, I slowed down. Last thing I needed was to get pulled over and for the cops to ask me questions about what I was hauling around…

See, I could tell them I was making soap, but I didn't exactly look like I was in the business of making crafts from home.

Though the compound was on the outskirts of town, I still had to drive through West Orange itself to reach it. As I pulled up at a red light, I whistled along to a Chainsmokers' song I had playing low, until I could carry on driving back to the clubhouse.

Jax, surprisingly enough, wasn't snoozing when I arrived. The creaky gates opened and I trundled in, pausing only for Jax to climb in with me as we both headed up the driveway before taking a detour that took us to the other side of the compound.

This was my real place of work, but because the brothers didn't always need to get rid of bodies, I spent most of my time behind the bar and doing a lot of odd jobs.

Before coming to the Sinners, I'd never have imagined being happy to be out of the lab, to be out of the field, but I found I had a place here, a purpose. And with Donavan Lancaster's death in the cards, well, I'd have some fun sooner rather than later.

The road to the Fridge was rough, and there were potholes of land that could sink a truck this size, so I was grateful for the dawn which shone a little light on my path. That was why I traveled at this time. The sun rose and illuminated a journey that had been taken often by the brothers in the fifty or so years of the clubhouse's existence. Blood spilled often in an MC, and it was surprising there wasn't a river of it around the Fridge, where most of it had been shed in the Sinners' history.

When we made it to the club's personal torture chamber, I grabbed my gear and directed Jaxson. Together, we managed to get the crate off the truck and we dragged it to a clearing that had a tarp over it that was dotted with leaves and shit for camo.

"Please! Get me out of here!"

The scream came as no shock to me, but Jax jolted like he'd been hit with a stun gun.

"It's just Lancaster," I muttered, used to the noise by now.

Jax winced, but otherwise, carried on unpacking the truck.

Both of us were exhausted by this point, especially after such a long shift, him on the gates and me behind the bar, so we made short work of grabbing the other, smaller crates, and loading them beside the cabin. As we worked, Lancaster continued releasing sharp screams, pleas for help, and each time, Jaxson jerked in surprise.

He had to know what was going on in there, what the MC was putting the cunt through, but each jolt told me he wasn't made for wet work. If my opinion mattered, I'd have told Rex that, but I had no right to judge another man's stomach—it wasn't like the only work around the clubhouse came with a side of blood.

By the time I got Jax back to his post, he looked like he was going to hurl, and while I was dead on my feet, when I saw Indy's Camaro hadn't gone, I frowned because I'd never known her to spend the night at the clubhouse.

Not that I'd been keeping an eye on her or anything.

I'd just noticed because she was very noticeable by nature—and if you believed that, then I could sell you horseshit.

My bed was calling me, but I made my way to the bunkhouse first. When I found her fast asleep on the plastic-wrapped mattress, I nearly choked on my tongue.

Never, in all the years I'd known her, had I ever seen her so relaxed. So carefree.

I'd always thought she was beautiful. With her heritage, how couldn't I? Her skin was like liquid gold, for fuck's sake. And her hair? I'd seen obsidian that was lighter.

But her features were stoic. Laced with a brittle reserve that was, most definitely, a defense mechanism.

She had a razor-like wit, but that was nothing compared to her tongue—capable of lashing a person worse than a bullwhip.

And I'd know, because I'd wielded a fair number of whips in my time.

She was so peaceful that I didn't want to disturb her. So restful that I knew I'd never seen her so at ease with herself, like in sleep that was the only time she was truly able to relax.

Why that disturbed me, I didn't know. It just did.

It made me wonder what put that permanent scowl on her face.

Made me wonder why her smile was so rare.

As a thousand questions plagued me, I retreated to a closet in the hall where I knew a bunch of Stone's things had been put into storage from her apartment in the city. My boots usually thudded on the ground, but I made sure that I moved with care as I rifled through Stone's gear, seeking something to cover Indy with. When I found a blanket, a soft one, I moved back into the bedroom and covered her with it.

The urge to sit beside her, to study her was an annoying one.

But chalking it down to a need for sleep, I pushed myself away. Then, just as I was about to reach the door, I heard her. Twisting around to look, I watched as she started to snag herself in the blanket, her limbs beginning to thrash, and then she sealed it.

Without even knowing it, she sealed both our futures.

"No, Kevin, no. Stop it. Unc—" Her head whipped from side to side, and her arms made shooing motions. She moved edgily, her desire to escape clear.

I'd only meant to keep her warm, but the blanket, something on top of her, had evidently triggered a memory.

We all knew that name in the clubhouse.

Kevin.

Nyx's uncle.

The blood brother of his father, Jester.

A pedophile.

A defiler of innocence.

A man who Nyx killed over and over as he went on a mission that saw him taking out child abusers all over the US.

He'd touched Indy. That much was clear. And from her fear? The abuse went deeper than I figured anyone knew, because we all thought Nyx's desire for vengeance was for Carly—their elder sister. If it was for Indy too, I thought it'd be common knowledge.

The distress on her face was even more repugnant in contrast to that serenity I'd seen before, and I knew I had my answers.

This was why she wore her resting bitch face like a shield, why she was a grade A pain-in-the-ass, why she never smiled, why she had more attitude than sense...

This.

Gritting my teeth, I stepped over to her and cast the blanket off her, dragging it to the foot of the bed. She instantly settled. In fact, it was so immediate that it stunned the hell out of me, enough so that I got out of there, didn't bother to grab the cover, just wanted to leave her to get some peace.

She deserved it.

And now that I knew, I'd do everything in my power to return it to her.

If it was the last thing I did.

THREE

CRUZ

FIVE WEEKS LATER

IT WASN'T by chance that I was heading into town and about to use the highway to get to Verona.

Verona was where Indy lived and worked, after all. Ever since that night, I'd been hanging around the town's main street where Indiana Ink was located. Not like a creep, just using the diner there to eat instead of staying at the clubhouse. Shit like that.

But what *was* by chance?

Seeing Lodestar slipping down a side street as I idled at a stop light.

A street that Dog, one of my brothers, had just sidled down.

As far as I knew, most of the guys were at the clubhouse. Or, at least, they were supposed to be.

Dog was one of those dumb fucks who partied way too hard. He was far too old for it, far too old to be living it up the way he was, but the idiot didn't recognize that he had a good thing going on with an Old Lady who was a fuck ton better than him.

I'd seen him throat fucking a couple of clubwhores before I left the compound so how he'd gotten here before me, and why, was definitely a mystery.

And I loved and loathed mysteries.

What were they if not a puzzle by any other name?

So though I was intending on going into Verona, having decided that getting Indy to work on my ink was the best pretext for starting a conversation, I pulled over and parked.

For a biker, I spent way too much fucking time in a cage, but I was glad for it because it meant my straight pipes weren't rattling, which didn't key Dog or Lodestar into the fact that I was sneaking up behind them.

Jumping out of the truck, I rushed over to the alley where they'd both gone. A quick glance around told me there was nothing around here that should've caught their attention. Not unless a closing coffee shop was their end destination, and wouldn't they have gone in through the front door and not the back if that was their intention?

Eyes narrowed as I peered into the mouth of the alley, I watched as Dog headed to the bottom of it, while Lodestar made moves toward him that were beyond suspicious.

I wasn't a soldier. *I was a scientist.* But even I recognized someone being hunted.

She headed down to the bottom of the alley where he was pacing, and though it was clear he was waiting on someone, it sure as hell wasn't Lodestar, because when she reached him, they didn't greet each other.

Nope.

She went for him.

I'd never seen anything like it.

And I'd seen a lot of random, cruel and gruesome shit in my life.

She flung herself at him like she was a fucking vampire, and as she went for his throat, it wasn't to bite the bastard, it was to grab him by the ears and to break his neck in one clean move with a crack of sound that ricocheted around the small space as loud as if she'd used a fucking gun.

Dog immediately crumpled to the ground, and Lodestar leaped back, her boots thudding hard as gravity had her colliding with the asphalt a few feet from the corpse of a man who, until a few minutes ago, was a brother.

Guilt hit me for not doing something to help, but none of this had gone down as I expected. I'd thought I'd—

"Shit, what did you think?" I muttered under my breath, so low that no one could hear it.

No. Fucking. One.

That was how I'd earned my rep—Grim Reaper. Silent.

Only, Lodestar *did* hear me.

Her head whipped around and she found me, her eyes narrowing as she pinned me in a death stare.

For all that she'd taken down Dog like the pro she was, I wasn't scared, and that wasn't arrogance talking, it was just common sense. When she'd moved toward Dog, there'd been something about her body language. The way she moved, the way she comported herself. Sure, she'd been hunting him, so stealth was important, but there was a lack of urgency about her that told me I was safe from her.

And it had nothing to do with the heat I was packing either. I had a feeling she'd have my guns out of my hands as fast as I could blink.

No, I'd definitely underestimated Lodestar, which told me I'd underestimated Maverick too. Which was interesting, because I rarely underestimated people.

"You saw nothing," she intoned as she moved toward me, striding down the alleyway. "And what you did see, you should know was deserved."

Deserved? What did that mean?

"There are cameras," I muttered, uneasy despite myself.

She cut me a look. "No one can touch me, Cruz. And if they can, then they're worthy adversaries. It's been a long time since I played, so that should be a hoot."

A hoot?

My eyes widened at her, but she wasn't interested in me. At all.

My pride wasn't exactly pricked, but I found myself hovering there like a pussy. Feeling like shit for not helping Dog pre- or post-death. I mean, it wasn't like I was picking up my cell and calling either the council or the police. I just watched Lodestar stride off, hips swaying as if she were walking down a catwalk and not on the sidewalk beside a coffee shop. She didn't look back. Her confidence clear as dust.

She evidently believed I wouldn't say a word. Why that was, I didn't know, but the need to go over there, to pat down the body, get rid of the evidence was harder than I could say. I'd settle for just emptying Dog's pockets, trying to figure out what he was doing down here in the first place—

The back door to the coffee shop opened, creaking loudly as it collided with the wall. A muttered, "Shit," told me whoever it was hadn't intended on letting the door smack into the brick as it had.

The light, which had already been dying as night fell, was close to non-existent now, but a glow spilled out of the opening, puddling around Dog like a soft, muted blanket. I saw the back of a head, hair tugged into two stubby pigtails, a waitress' pink apron dancing around slender calves, before I heard a scream.

The woman ran at Dog, nearly skidding as her knees collided with the ground. That she didn't run off, or run back into the coffee shop made me realize she knew him. And knowing what Dog was like, even though he was an ugly fuck with a belly that hung over his jeans, I had to figure *she* was the reason he was sneaking down this alley.

Shit.

People tumbled out of the back door at her scream, crowding around the corpse as I jerked into action, making my way toward the truck once more. As I did, I kept my head tucked low, just in case any CCTV picked up on me, and I leaped behind the wheel once more.

What I'd just seen, I'd never unsee. Not the death, that was a common sight in my world. But Lodestar's behavior…

Everyone knew she'd sneaked into the Fridge and had done something to Lancaster that had made him talk, that made him routinely scream like a banshee in the middle of the night.

When you looked at her, it was easy to see a pretty woman. Seemingly mild-mannered. Her features pleasant, her clothes non-descript.

But she wasn't just a woman. Wasn't just a soldier. She had moves. *James* fucking *Bond* moves.

Goddammit, I was lucky I'd made it out of that alley with my brains inside my goddamn head, and my balls still attached to my body.

Gritting my teeth as I recognized that today wouldn't be the first and last I heard of Dog's death, my truck's engine shrieked as I jerked out of my parking space and surged into traffic. My plans for the night were irreparably altered; I needed to get back to the MC, blend in. Monitor Lodestar and make sure she wasn't writing a death wish with my name on it.

But if this week was going to be my last, if Lodestar was just biding her time, waiting on a moment to get to me—I knew why she'd left now, after all. She'd known the woman was due to head out of the coffee shop—then I wasn't going to waste a second more.

Indy, while she didn't realize it, was gonna end up in my bed sooner rather than later.

No ifs, buts, or maybes.

If I only had days left to live, then those days were gonna go down in her pussy. My priorities had just shifted, as had my life expectancy.

Fuck.

FOUR
INDY
THE NEXT MORNING

I WASN'T in the best of moods, but then, I never was when I slept. Nightmares were an endless plague, and whenever I was embroiled in the past again, it was difficult to shake off the mindset of being a terrified little girl.

I was a woman.

I was strong.

I was empowered.

"If I tell myself that enough, maybe I'll start to fucking believe it," I grumbled to myself after I climbed out of the shower, and started getting ready for the rest of the day.

Staring in the steamed up mirror, I saw a not-bad face, a pretty bitching body thanks to genetics and the fact I forgot to eat when I was working, but mostly, I saw my ink.

They were the parts that defined me.

The parts I liked because I had a choice in them.

Choice meant a lot to me.

Choosing whether to remember to eat or not made my ass tight, but it didn't define me, did it?

My ink, on the other hand, *did*.

Maybe it wasn't the most original stuff, a phoenix rising from the flames, its wings and tail as well as its fire wrapping around my forearm, circling higher and higher around my bicep, then down over my shoulder and onto my front. I liked to think it signified what I was—someone constantly trying to rebuild themselves.

Never succeeding, but always trying.

Then there was the 'It Never Rains But It Pours' quote on the back of my neck, and the cross that was a work-in-progress as it wasn't complete since Laruso, my mentor, had died and I didn't trust anyone else with it. There was also the sakura, Japanese cherry blossoms, wrapped around the Sanskrit word for Nirvana on my stomach, dancing down to my hip and upper thigh.

I'd never experienced nirvana, and the nearest the cherry blossom analogy helped me was that it was my favorite flavor of mochi, but whenever I looked at myself, they were the parts I liked and that didn't outright disgust me. They also hid my scars, so they were a thing of beauty that hid something ugly.

Cruz suddenly flashed into my thoughts, because his tattoos were far more aggressive in nature than mine were. What was he hiding? What was the meaning behind his ink?

Pursing my lips as I shrugged into a black sports' bra, I jiggled my tits to make sure they were sat in each cup correctly. As I did, I couldn't help but wonder what it was that fascinated men about a rack... Well, what fascinated Cruz in particular.

Wincing at the thought, I shoved him mentally aside, then pulled on the pair of yoga pants I'd grabbed earlier, as well as a Van Halen cropped shirt, one of the only hard rock bands I liked, which promptly went on over the bra.

With that done, I swiped on the wings of cat eye eyeliner, then opened the medical cabinet where I stored my make-up and selected a green lipstick. It made my mouth look as if I'd sucked off a tree, but I liked it, so fuck everyone else.

Opinions were like assholes.

Every fucker had one, and they all goddamn stank.

Grunting at the thought, I headed out of the bathroom and slipped on my black and white Vans that were waiting on me by the door, then I made my way downstairs to my place of work.

When I unlocked the door between my private quarters and the tattoo parlor, I was surprised to see David, my assistant, wasn't there yet. He was always weird, but he'd been weirder than usual for a while.

Reminding myself to chastise him for being late again, I grabbed the landline and checked the messages before I took some notes on upcoming requests for appointments.

Humming under my breath at the nice intake of clientele, I took some money from petty cash then palmed my phone as I slipped in my earbuds and connected a call to Stone.

As I headed out of the tattoo parlor, locked up, and wandered over to the diner, she finally answered, her voice groggy, "The hell are you doing calling me now?"

Relieved she was at the clubhouse now and not in the hospital anymore, I grinned at nothing. "Says the early riser."

"I'm more of a night owl right now," she rumbled, sounding gruffer still after she yawned.

"More *something*. He dick you down, yet? That'll get you to sleep," I joked.

She grunted. "None of your business."

I sniffed. "I'll be the first person you come to if he can't get you off."

"Look at Steel and tell me he can't get a woman off."

"Men are all about the tits and the clit, but when they got 'em, they don't know what the fuck to do with them. You know that as well as I do."

"Okay, I do, but he had enough goddamn practice. Surely he knows what to do with a clit."

"I dunno," I retorted, pulling open the door and heading into the diner where I sat my butt down at my regular booth. As Wanda *wandered* over to me, I winked at her glum features which, as ever, were dour, pointed at my order on the menu, then gave her a thumbs up. "Most men think they do, but they don't."

She snickered. "Most men aren't Steel, remember?"

I narrowed my eyes at the table, unsure if they'd fucked or not now. I knew they'd been sleeping together, like, literally, but she was on bed rest which wasn't likely to put a person in the mood for sex. "You're really going to hold out on me?"

"Not for long, just for the moment. You know, when he isn't lying next to me, glaring at me. Shit like that."

Content now I thought she'd give me details, I murmured, "Good girl."

"You're at the diner, aren't you?"

"I am."

"Bitch."

I smirked. "You could come. You don't have to be in bed all the time."

"True." She heaved a sigh. "Just most of it. I miss *huevos rancheros*. Giulia's a great cook, but everything's pasta this and pasta that right now. She must be craving it, because that's all she fixes."

"Boo fucking hoo," I retorted. "What I'd give not to have to cook."

"Like you couldn't eat here every day if you wanted to."

I sniffed. "And have all those fuckers up in my business and in my face?"

"Then you don't get free food cooked for you."

"You're the one bitching about how boring it is."

"I wasn't bitching, just saying variety is the spice of life."

"Not for you it isn't, not anymore," Steel rumbled, loud enough for me to hear down the line.

Though I rolled my eyes, her giggle was so unlike Stone who lived up to her name in nature, that I'd admit her laughter made me happy for her. I loved her like a sister and she deserved a good man—I was just unsure if Steel was that for her.

The Sinners weren't exactly *good* men, after all. But I had a different qualification of the word 'good' in relation to people in possession of penises. Not because I hated all of them, but because a guy with a big heart didn't always wear a bright red, crushed velvet suit and yell, 'Ho, ho, ho.'

"I'm going before he says anything else sappy."

"You woke me up for no reason at all?" She huffed. "Thanks, *friend*."

I grinned, because even though she was casting shade, she wasn't. Not really. And this was exactly why I'd needed to hear her voice after waking up with the memory of that fucker's words ringing in my ears, of his breath gusting in my throat...

God.

My voice turned gruff. "You know you love me."

"Good fucking thing." She heaved another sigh. "When are you coming to visit?"

"Tomorrow."

"About time."

"I saw you yesterday," I sniped.

"Yesterday was a long time ago. I almost died, Indy," she whined. "I think I deserve daily visits."

I rolled my eyes. "Stop being a baby. The whole dying thing happened ages ago," I teased, even though it hadn't. Christ, we'd almost lost her.

She snorted at my joke like I knew she would. "I'll see you tomorrow, you pain in my ass."

"Stop being a stitch in my side."

"You know that's true."

Then she cut the call, leaving me smirking down at the coffee mug Wanda plunked there.

"How's it hanging, Wanda?" I asked as she poured me my first cup of the day.

She shrugged. "Boring as ever."

"Sorry to hear that."

Another shrug before she drifted off again—Wanda wasn't exactly cheerful but I liked that.

I preferred grouchy wait staff to the friendly, perky kind who never stopped fucking hovering around you while you ate.

Slouching into the banquette, I watched the world pass by as regular folk started to appear on the sidewalk, heading out from the office buildings in time for lunch.

Regular, in my opinion, sucked.

I didn't know if that was my past speaking or my upbringing, or if that was just because I wasn't made for a pencil-pushing job—not outside of drawing tattoos, that is—but the idea of living a normal life made me cringe and be grateful for weird hours and clients who called at three AM with ideas for new ink.

The diner door opened, letting in a whiff of gas from the road and the noise from the slowly building lunch crowd who were making an appearance in the diner. Grateful I'd placed my order before them because I needed to fill up for the busy day ahead, my gaze clashed with Cruz's when he walked inside.

The prick was self-assured, I had to give him that. He didn't dip his chin in greeting or smile at me, just walked my way and, without even asking, took a seat at my table.

I arched a brow at him. "Did I invite you to sit down?"

"I won't talk if you don't."

That had me frowning, because I wasn't sure if he was being rude or not. I mean, I knew Cruz, but he wasn't the most ebullient person. He kept to himself, I thought, but he never got into trouble because, if he did, Nyx would have bitched about him to me at one point or another.

Before I could tell him where to go, Wanda appeared with my breakfast and Cruz shot her the sweetest smile as he placed his order and sweet-talked her.

Fucking sweet-talked the most miserable waitress in Verona—right in front of me.

I wasn't even sure how he did it, because he didn't exactly say much. Didn't tell her she looked pretty or anything, but his smile was electric, and his eyes never left hers until, heaven above, she turned pink.

Her cheeks burned with goddamn heat!

Wanda was actually blushing.

Gaping at them both, I flickered my attention his way when she walked off to put his order in, shoving his in front of some other orders she'd put on the board first, her movements a lot bouncier than when she'd left my table earlier.

That mega-watt smile didn't exactly disappear, and I bit my lip as he turned it on me for a fraction of a second before he dimmed it down.

So, what? Waitresses got smiles but I didn't?

When I was sharing my goddamn table with him?

Huffing, I dug into my breakfast and spent the next twenty minutes with him in silence.

When he said he wouldn't talk if I didn't, he meant it.

And, when I finished and called for the check, that was the first time he spoke: "I'll pay that, thanks for letting me sit with you."

I gaped at him, not used to men paying for food without expecting a BJ after it on a damn date, never mind when he'd only shared a booth with me. "You don't have to do that," I said uneasily, not wanting him to think I owed him something.

"Sure I do. This place is full—I'd never have gotten a seat, and I was starving." No shit, considering the size of his stack of pancakes would fill a T-Rex. "Anyway, can I come in later and speak with you about touching up some ink?"

I squinted at him. "You trying to butter me up?"

"You're Nyx's sister. Don't think butter works on you."

That had me scowling. "Think that was butter I just heard."

His lips twitched, and he didn't bestow me with the mega-watt smile but definitely one that was high voltage.

Despite myself, I bit my lip because it packed a damn punch.

How had I never noticed that before?

It wasn't like I hadn't seen him around. He was a bit of a gofer, not like a Prospect who got the shittiest of jobs around the MC, but definitely the kind of guy who was at the council's beck and call...

But there was seeing a guy as a piece of furniture and then there was seeing him smile that goddamn smile.

I cleared my throat. "Sure. Last appointment ends at nine tonight, be there on time or I'll lock up and I won't open it until tomorrow."

He nodded. "Should be fine."

"Okay. I'll see you then." I climbed out of the booth, then asked, "You sure you don't mind covering my check?"

"I'll see you later, Indy."

For whatever reason, that had me gulping.

Because instead of sounding like a farewell, or just a throwaway comment that didn't mean anything, it sounded like a promise.

And something, I wasn't sure what, told me Cruz never broke a promise…

FIVE
CRUZ

GETTING some ink touched up was an act of subterfuge, but if that was the means of getting closer to Indiana, I'd do it.

My initial worry Lodestar was about to kill me had died a small death. Mostly because, soon after I'd returned to the clubhouse, I'd heard her and Maverick arguing in the attic about the original MS-DOS, and I didn't think that was a likely debate if she was homicidal.

Of course, I was pretty sure that, yesterday, pre-Dog's murder, she'd been hollering something at him about tracker bugs… maybe that was her way of working herself up for the kill?

Either way, when I'd headed into Verona this morning, I didn't feel like I had a set of crosshairs on my nape, so, breathing easier, I'd carried on. Making it into the neighboring town, I'd seen her sitting at that diner booth, and the instant urge to bone her had disappeared.

Reconciling myself with her past, well, it didn't make her less fuckable, not when she was a walking wet dream, but it meant that I couldn't just treat her like another piece of ass. Of course, she made it worth my while too.

The second I sat down, she'd given me shit.

After being fawned over by clubwhores, call me a masochist—which I wasn't—but I liked a woman with bite.

I'd promised her we wouldn't speak, and had felt her distrust and discomfort throughout her meal and mine. Not unsurprisingly, she had trust issues, and rather than feel like an insurmountable task that wasn't worth my time and effort, not for a one-night-stand, instead, I was pretty sure there was gold in them there hills.

That was why I was here, at nine as promised.

The assistant, a guy called David, glowered at me like I'd done something wrong, and while I usually had, as far as I was aware, tonight I'd done shit so I ignored him. He was a weirdo, one that Nyx often complained about, and I understood why.

A creep, he was probably in love with Indiana and was pining from afar.

"You're not down on the schedule."

I shrugged at the accusation. "I talked with her earlier."

"She never told me."

I shrugged again. "Not my problem."

His jaw tensed, and I saw irritation flash behind his eyes before he hid it as the door to the back office opened and Indy walked out with her client. Her gaze connected with mine, just for a second, and sweet fuck—it was unguarded, and as a result, loaded with fire.

She was pumped from her work, probably tired after a long day, and all that was written into her features, but she'd forgotten about me, so seeing me sitting here had stirred something up in her mind.

Something I liked.

Fire.

I'd hoped for that, but hadn't expected it.

I moved over to the flash racks and started to leaf through her designs. She worked alone, so all of these were her pieces, and as she finished up with her last client and sent the creep home—much to his distress—I looked through her art, stopping at the phoenix I recognized from her arm.

It was beautiful.

Majestic, and regal, empowered and loaded with hope.

Which was interesting as the first three, I'd say, described Indy, but not the last.

Knowing what I did now, I understood more than she could say.

Tattoos were a chance at rebirth, at redefining who and what we were. In my case, they covered up scars, as well as grounded me in a new reality where people wanted something from me and I embraced that rather than hope for more. In Indy's, I could see that she wanted to forget the past, didn't want to cover up her internal scars, more like sideswipe them and focus on the future.

Which I found interesting.

Me—so focused on the past, her—pinning so much hope on the future.

The thought had me smiling because I wanted that for her. Genuinely, I did. Not because she was a victim or because she was Nyx's baby sister, but because she deserved for tomorrow to be brighter than yesterday.

"Thought you only wanted a touch up."

Her brusque comment told me her walls were back up. I'd had a brief glimpse into something she hadn't meant to reveal, so I understood she needed to reconfigure things.

It was a testament to how much I'd learned about the woman through her art, through the calming and delicately detailed mandalas to the charming black and white portraits that were hyperreal to her own ink, that I didn't joke about wanting to touch *her* up.

Indy wasn't a clubwhore.

She was more than that.

Only a moron would fail to see that—which was the last thing anyone could describe me as.

"You're very talented," was all I said, prompting her to clear her throat.

The air was charged for a moment, and I wondered what she was wrestling with as she muttered ungraciously, "Thanks."

Her grouchy reply had me shooting her a smile, and when our eyes clashed, she bit her lip.

Always a good sign.

"Which ink do you want touching up?" she asked, her tone almost dogged.

"The negative tattoo on my chest."

Her gaze dropped to my cut and the Henley I wore beneath it. I felt her stare like a laser, and wished it'd have the soft jersey fabric disintegrating into dust beneath the power of her glance.

I got the feeling Indy was attracted to me, but rather than be comfortable with that, she was the exact opposite.

Could her past have fucked her up that much?

Nyx had never mentioned her having boyfriends, and I'd been wracking my brains over any conversation I'd had or overheard about her, and didn't remember hearing about her having a partner or a lover. The only guy he complained about was her assistant, and they definitely weren't together. Not with him giving her puppy eyes and her brushing him off and telling him to go home with a kindness that let me know she was aware he had feelings for her, and wasn't interested.

Even as I thought about that and wondered why she kept him around, I murmured, "Want me to take it off?"

Her nostrils flared, eyes flashing with something I didn't think she recognized in herself—lust—and she took a step back, even as she moved toward the back office. Then, freezing in place, she moved over to the desk instead, and pressed a button which had a bunch of blinds flowing down to hide the building's interior from the outside world.

So, she didn't want me in her studio, her private workspace.

Interesting.

Taking that for a positive, I watched as she folded her arms against her chest then said, "It's okay. I'm too tired to do it tonight, but I can check it out, see how much time I think it'd take, then I can give you a quote."

"Money's inconsequential."

Her brows snapped up at that. "Aren't you lucky?"

"Not really. Don't have many bills, and don't have many vices. Apart from my ink."

She grunted, then wafted a hand that told me to move things along. Her bossiness amused me, enough that I obeyed when usually it'd get my back up. With care, I shrugged out of my cut and draped it over the flash rack I'd just been glancing through. Dragging the Henley over my head next, I heard a sharp inhalation that had me smirking into the folds of fabric.

Apparently, Indiana liked what she saw.

Fisting the material in my hand, I pointed to the tattoo in the middle of my torso, one that spanned around my side toward my back. She bit her lip—again—and mumbled, "You went to Lance Black, didn't you? Only he could pull off that kind of negative ink."

"I did, just in time before the cancer got him." I nodded. "Sad to lose a talent like that, even sadder when you think how young he was and how small his kids were."

She winced, nodding. "I didn't know him that well, just of him."

"No?"

"Rep only," she confirmed. "I did my apprenticeship down in Louisiana. If I'd stayed in the City, we'd probably have crossed paths." Indy tilted her head to the side, which had her hair drifting over her shoulder and falling like a cascade into the curve of her neck—a neck I really wanted to fucking bite. "My style and his don't gel if you were interested in more ink."

"That's not a concern. I don't want more negative tattoos. I just want these touching up and, in the future, I'm ready for something different."

Her chin tipped up, and I watched her visibly steel herself as she moved over to me. I'd never seen a woman so confident be so suddenly ill-at-ease.

If I was anyone else, i.e not a brother to Nyx, I'd think she was scared of me, or that I was behaving in a predatory manner. But I *was* a brother, and I wasn't being predatory. If anything, I was working hard not to think about sex, because just being around her, with those goddamn blinds closed, thoughts of her on her knees cleaning, well, I was gonna get a boner.

She was reacting like I was a tiger that had been baited though, and it made me glad that I knew of her past because I'd probably think she was just plain weird for her response to a guy, a potential client, taking off a shirt.

Instead, I sensed that she liked me, and didn't know how to handle that.

I couldn't be the first guy she'd been attracted to, though, could I?

I mean, it was great for my ego to think otherwise, but ego meant bupkis. I preferred the whole truth, and I just couldn't see a woman like her—

What?

A woman like her not having men chasing at her heels?

Sure. But that didn't mean *she* liked the men who were chasing her, did it?

Because that was food for thought, I watched as she approached, then stopped a good four, impractical, feet away from me. It meant she had to tip forward to touch me, which she technically didn't have to, but I wasn't about to say no to having her hands on me. Did I look like a dumbass?

I watched as her fingers swiped over my rib cage, like she couldn't help herself, and though my chest was pretty nice, I wasn't sure it was worthy of her turning to ice.

Gooseflesh swirled into being over my skin at the gentle brush of her fingers, and I murmured, "Everything okay, Indy?"

She blinked at me. "Why did you put that blanket over me?"

Because I hadn't anticipated that question, I blinked back.

"That night at Stone's bunkhouse. You put a blanket over me. Why did you do that?"

"You looked cold."

She gulped. "You came back. You checked on me. Why?"

"Because you looked exhausted, and I saw your car was still there. I wanted to make sure you were okay."

Her bottom lip was sucked between her teeth again. "I must have been if I didn't hear you walk in. I'm a light sleeper."

I shrugged. "I was careful not to disturb you."

"Why? Why didn't you send me home?"

Confused, I asked, "Would you have preferred that?"

She didn't answer, instead, rested her palm on the ink and murmured, "It's beautiful."

"Thank you," I told her, aware my voice was husky.

"You're beautiful."

I hadn't expected that compliment. "Are men ever beautiful?"

"Sure they are." She peered up at me. "Why am I only just seeing you?"

Before I could answer that, she was there, right in front of me, reaching up on tiptoe, her mouth connecting with mine, and even though I was pretty fucking sure she wasn't ready for whatever *this* was, I was also pretty fucking sure that I wasn't either.

Still, a coward was the last thing I could be described as being, so I dove headfirst into the chaos this woman promised, hoping along the way that, even if it was for a short while or a long while, I brightened up her future some.

SIX

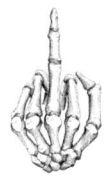

INDY

I'D SEEN beautiful men before. I'd even drawn them, had inked plenty.

But it was like a veil was dragged from my eyes as I saw Cruz standing there, so confident, so self-aware, yet so un-cocky with it.

He knew what he was, but he didn't shove it in my face, and with guys this hot, I knew that was a rarity.

There was knowing someone was cute, and then *feeling* it.

Actually feeling it.

It was only at that moment that I realized I'd spent three decades never feeling *it*.

Was that possible?

Sexual attraction was an enemy of mine. I saw someone hot, wanted to fuck them to fix *my* body into behaving normally, and of course, that never worked. But seeing Cruz effortlessly take off his shirt had the breath jerking from my lungs.

Maybe it was the artist in me. Maybe that was it.

Taking comfort in that reasoning, I'd moved closer to get a better look, and then I'd smelled him.

Sweet fuck, what a scent. I couldn't even describe what it was, had no real idea, but he just smelled clean and manly and warm. So fucking warm. Then I'd had to touch him. And I'd seen his visceral response, and knowing he was affected too, made this strange swirling sensation inside me seem normal.

Because this was how arousal felt.

This was what lust felt like.

I wasn't a coward, so rather than hide from it and deny myself, I wanted to explore it. Maybe Cruz would help me fix myself. If I could just have sex once where I liked it, maybe that would give me what I needed to feel normal. To feel like a regular woman, instead of one always chasing sex, trying to fit in, trying to force myself to feel things that everyone felt.

So I kissed him.

And he tasted better than I could have imagined. His taste reminded me of whisky—without the alcohol. Peaty and earthy, warm and musky. I could drown in his flavor, suffocate in it. I thrust my tongue against his, unsurprised when his met mine, but he didn't drag me into him.

Didn't pull me into his arms.

Didn't he want me?

The way his tongue was moving told me yes, but why didn't he haul me closer?

Unsure of myself, because that was what men usually did, I moved into him, sliding my arms around his firm waist, appreciating the hardened stack of muscles against my stomach. My hands moved to his back, running up and down the strong ropes that bisected his spine into two halves, and still, he didn't move to hold me.

He was kissing me. Actively. If anything, he was leading the way now, my tongue no longer in his mouth, his in mine, and God, what he could do with that tongue was enough to have stars floating behind my eyes and doing a little dance. This was, I registered, the first kiss where I wasn't pondering the mechanics of the act, where I wasn't making an internal grocery list. Instead, I'd dived headfirst into this, like it was a pool and I was more than happy to do some synchronized swimming.

My hands moved, going higher, up to the corded strength of his shoulders, before I tucked myself tighter into him, needing to feel him, needing him to be as close to me as physically possible. Wanting him. Actually. Fucking. Wanting. Him.

Astonished and overwhelmed and turned the hell on, I felt the impossible.

A burn in my core.

Not like a UTI.

Not like *after* sex.

This came before. And it felt molten. It felt like *I* was molten.

The sensation stole my breath from me, and I lifted my leg, hitching it onto his hip, uncaring if he thought I was being forward, uncaring if I was acting like a slut. I was chasing this feeling. Chasing this sensation that I'd never experienced before.

Finally, he helped. He reached down and hauled me into him so that I was cupping his thighs and his hands were on my ass. He pulled back, and I whimpered, chasing his mouth, chasing his kiss, before he rumbled, "Where?"

I blinked, utterly dazed, and the question took too damn long to figure out and I loathed the jarring sensation that came as I started to disconnect.

"Upstairs."

He strode over to the side door marked 'Private,' which told me he knew I lived here, and I reached into my back pocket, the tiny zipper there that housed my key in the waistband of my yoga pants. He took it, unlocked the door, and peered around the corner. A light flashed on, further jarring me from the moment, and doubts began to creep in.

That molten feeling wasn't real, was it?

The way his kiss had made me want to crawl into his skin, I'd been over-imagining it, surely?

Then, we moved upstairs, slowly, slowly because his mouth was back on mine, but it was different now he was touching me. Different and I felt out-of-focus, uncertain like always, those distinct memories of being connected to him feeling as far away as France.

Inside, I wanted to weep. My head warred with my body, trying to get me back into the zone, but I just—I just couldn't do it.

Fuck, what was wrong with me?

Why was this so hard?

His tongue drove into my mouth at the same time as his boner rubbed against my pussy. The heat had gone, died, but I let him carry on because I wasn't a prick tease, and I wasn't about to be accused of offering the goods only to take them away at the last hurdle. It was easier to give it than it was to have it taken from me, so I made a mental note about what I needed to do tomorrow, a check list of colors I needed to order in, all as he moved me into my apartment, and somehow guided us to the bed.

I let him do it, let him kiss me and touch me. Feel me up. I let him undress me. Let him lay me on the bed. I just let him do it all.

As I stared up at the ceiling, refusing to think about what might have been, studiously concentrating on the design I'd be drawing up tomorrow for a pop-in client, he moved into me.

It didn't hurt like it usually did, was my initial thought. I wasn't bone dry like normal.

Then, he started to move, and I zoned out once more. I'd just redecorated the studio, and I—

He pulled out.

Pulled off me.

Stood up.

Started to fasten his zipper.

I gaped at him, leaning up on my elbows before I rasped, "What are you doing?"

He shrugged. "I'm not a rapist."

I blinked at him. "Huh?" The words jerked me into sitting up, and I reached for the fly he'd just fastened and struggled with the zipper. "Come back to bed," I commanded.

"You weren't into it, Indy. It's okay. It's all good."

Stunned that he'd noticed, bewildered that he had, I just gaped at him. And as I did, I saw how fucking beautiful he was again.

His hair rumpled now because *I'd* rumpled it. His face free from resentment and the bitterness men presumed to get when they weren't getting their way in the sack. He was like…

I released a shaky sigh, suddenly feeling that molten heat blanket me once more.

It was weird, so weird, but I stopped reaching for his dick, and instead, moved over onto my knees and crawled to him. A grunt escaped him like I'd started sucking him off and I felt his eyes on every inch of me as I moved nearer. When I was close enough, I straightened up then pressed my naked torso against his, the denim rubbing against my lower half somehow grounding me rather than jarring me, and I reached for him. Kissing him once more, I moaned as his tongue thrust into my mouth.

Why did this feel so good?

It even felt good being naked.

My nipples budded, furling into tight tips as they rasped against his chest, and I could feel that heat starting up. Even though my hands moved on his back, sliding over firm, warm skin, his stayed off me, and that had that heat flickering into live flames.

I whimpered into his mouth, needing more of this, needing more of him but... why had it stopped before?

Groaning as I writhed against him, feeling like I was going crazy with want even as I knew I didn't *want* him inside me, I felt the disconnect start again when his hands appeared on my waist. Only, they weren't there long. He moved me into a similar position as earlier, but his tongue continued dancing with mine as he hauled me higher against him so that he was carrying me again.

I expected to feel the hard thrust of his erection soon, but I didn't. Instead, he turned us around, carefully lowered us so that he was on the bed and my knees were pinning him in place. Then, he tore his lips from mine and rasped, "Come on, Indy, give me some of that honey."

Disoriented, my mouth sore from our kisses, my brain mush from them too, I rumbled, "Huh?"

He didn't let me think, didn't let me act, instead, he hauled me up so that I was riding his face.

Even as my eyes flared wide in surprise, his tongue moved like it had when he'd been kissing me, only he was flicking it against my clit.

And Cruz knew what to do with it once he found it.

Even better, his hands, his fucking hands, stayed on the bed.

"Oh my God," I shrieked, unable to bear what he was doing to me. It felt so good, so fucking powerful that I reared up, unable to take it, then, the sensations died and he didn't force me down, so, tentatively, I lowered myself again only for him to suck on my clit so hard I was seeing those stars once more.

I ground my pussy into his face, riding him hard, knowing that I was making his jaw wet—actually fucking wet—and I just, dear God, I enjoyed it.

I fucking loved it.

It felt so… Jesus, good wasn't the word.

Phenomenal.

The flames weren't just in my core, they were flickering higher, moving into my vision, into my heart, into my chest, taking over my hands, sinking into my feet. Where they touched, tingles of sensation burst into being, and suddenly…

Blankness.

Dark.

Only, it was filled with light too.

And it felt like pinpricks against my skin, and that moment of joy when the first spoon of ice cream connected with your tongue.

Then there was how it felt like a wave was drawing me into the ocean, sinking me into the tide.

Until I was drowning, and choking, and dying, and death had never felt so good.

Distantly, I heard my scream, but even that wasn't enough to jolt me from whatever this was.

And his tongue didn't stop.

He carried on, until I was dying again, and only then, did his hands touch my ass, and he maneuvered my limp body onto the sheets. Somehow, he lifted them so my legs were covered in them, and I let him because when he left, I could always move them off me, then I heard the rattle of his buckle and fly, and disappointment began to drift into that dazed sense of wellness that had overtaken me.

He'd want sex now.

It was only fair after he gave me *that*.

An orgasm.

I'd just…

Jesus, fuck.

I'd come.

I'd actually fucking come.

I fell asleep, my body splayed and broken and warm and loaded with fading delight, and I didn't realize until the next morning, when I woke up, and the sheets were by my feet because I'd pushed them off, that he'd spent the night with me.

That he'd spent the night with me while *I slept.*

And I hadn't woken up once.

Why had I managed to fall asleep with him?

Butterflies didn't just flitter around my belly, they gnawed at my insides. Sleep was a precious commodity for me, and somehow he'd given me that.

He'd given me so much more than any other man had.

Maybe I should be joyful, but instead, it made me pensive.

Men couldn't be trusted. Cruz was no different.

SEVEN
CRUZ
A WEEK LATER

AS SHE GROUND her pussy into my face, I grinned. I loved when she did that. I fucking loved it. I wanted to cup her ass, tilt her into me, but I'd noticed that first night that my touching her did something.

Maybe another guy would have carried on regardless, but fucking a corpse wasn't my thing. Sure, they called me the Grim Reaper around the MC, but that wasn't because I was into necro-goddamn-philia.

She'd been still, and lifeless, that heat of before, her arousal of earlier gone like I'd doused her in ice water.

It was surreal. Weird. I'd pulled out, uncomfortable with how things had turned out, but she hadn't wanted me to go. Then, she'd kissed me, and somehow, she'd been turned on again.

I wasn't ashamed to admit that if it wasn't *her*, I'd probably think it was too much hassle. That she was too much work, but even though my dick was aching like a bastard, it wasn't a problem.

She'd had her first orgasm with me, I knew that like I knew my face in the mirror, and I knew, even more, that she was orgasm-drunk, high on the experience and, as a result, me.

She loved what I gave her.

And I loved giving it to her.

Her moan reminded me of what I was doing, and I went to work, giving her what she needed, giving her what she didn't know she craved, until she screamed, loud enough to make my cock pound harder. When she came, usually I got her off again, but this time, it was different.

She was different.

After a week of going down on her, I expected her to roll off and sleep like she usually did, but she didn't. She moved off me, then crawled down the bed. At first, I thought she was going to suck me off—she'd tried to do that before, and the first time, it'd felt like a token BJ so I'd told her not to do it again—then, she straddled my hips even as she grabbed my cock.

I always wore my jeans when this went down, only unfastening my fly when I felt sure the imprint of the zipper was going to be permanently etched into my cock, but though she was dripping, the second I was inside her, I felt it.

That fucking disconnect.

It was jarring as fuck for me, so I didn't know how it was for her.

Something changed, like the click of a switch, shifting from 'on' to 'off' and I didn't know why, but I always sensed when that happened.

When her reactions turned from natural and responsive to mechanical, before morphing into passive then, quite frankly, onto *dead*.

She bounced on top of me, her eyes glassy. Both from the orgasm of before, but also because she was switched off. The sight had my arousal dying, and I'd admit, I got angry.

I was turned on like fuck. I *ached* for her. Literally ached. And for whatever dumb fuck reason, I hadn't blown my wad in a willing clubwhore, even though I knew I was making a liar of myself because she'd turned me into a masochist.

So the sight of her bouncing on top of me like a sex doll infuriated me.

I knew she was into this. I knew she was, so I did something I regretted the second I did it.

I slapped her ass, *hard*, and ground out, "Enough, Indy."

The spank had her freezing, but she tipped her head down at me, and even as I expected her to give me shit—well-deserved too, because that *hadn't* been a little love tap, it had to sting like a bitch—she licked her lips.

Jesus, this woman.

She liked it. She liked the spank.

At that moment, she shoved me toward a pivotal crossroads.

She wasn't going to change. Couldn't change, in fact. How could she change what had been set in stone since she was a kid?

The way she went through the motions of sex told me this was some kind of coping mechanism, but I didn't get why, even as smart as I fucking was, and that was the most tragic thing of all because I'd never seen a more beautiful, more sensual woman in my life.

She was glorious when she came. So surprised and shocked and overwhelmed and joyous that I got drunk on her. But... shit, there was always a but.

This wasn't going to work forever. Hell, maybe not even another week.

She liked the spank though.

I saw it with my own eyes.

Testing the hypothesis like the good scientist I was, I did it again.

Just as hard.

Her pussy clenched around me.

Fuck.

She *did* like it.

Jesus.

I'd told myself I'd stop with this shit, because the games in S and M were just too fucking complicated and, in the past, in all honesty, I'd been a crappy Dom, but, Christ, how could I back away when she seemed to like it? And I fucking *liked* her?

Two spanks did not a sub make, however, so I carried on. Pummeling her ass with the flat of my hand in time to the movement of her hips.

Her eyes weren't glassy anymore, her cheeks were flushed with heat, and her skin was dewy with perspiration and exertion. Shaky breaths escaped her, and her pussy fluttered around me, drenching me in her juices, coating me in her arousal.

Needing more affirmative proof, I reared up which had her

jumping in surprise, not enough to prompt that disconnect though, and I grabbed her hair, furling the tail around my fist before I yanked her head back.

Hard enough to hurt.

Hard enough for her to slap me.

Her pussy clenched around me so hard I didn't know how I didn't blow my load.

Her nails made an appearance in my shoulders as she dug her fingers into them, and she began grinding into me even as I tilted her throat back and went for the final experiment.

I suckled the tender flesh, priming the skin, readying her for something she couldn't have anticipated. With a final tug on her hair, I moved in for the kill.

I bit her.

Hard.

She screamed.

At first, I thought she was telling me to fuck off, to get off her, but she wasn't.

She was climaxing.

I'd never felt anything more magnificent in my fucking life. I roared with her as the pulsating pussy that was like manna from the Gods drew my own orgasm out of me. I felt like I came and I came and I fucking came, understanding that whole, 'I came, I saw, I conquered,' shit for the first time in my life because triumph surged through my veins at the same time as my orgasm did.

But nothing compared to the sound of her sobbing out her release, of the tension in her body as she experienced the first penetrative orgasm of her life.

She needed pain.

It was enough to ground me.

Remind me of what I hadn't wanted for a long time.

I didn't like that she needed it, and wished otherwise for her, but I also didn't like that I could feel the craving in her to be normal.

Some people, myself included, were born to never be normal.

Another issue was her problem with being touched. Aftercare in a scene was vital, so that was another hurdle to face but, and it was a massive but, she was worth it.

God help me, was she worth it.

I didn't know why, what it was about her sass, that heartbreak in her eyes, the face that'd launch a thousand ships, but she just was.

I slumped back in bed, my brain racing as fast as my heart, and I'd admit to being surprised when she slouched on me.

I didn't touch her, not like I wanted to. Didn't kiss her or caress her back, hug her like *I* needed to. Instead, I just got my breath back, and even though my thoughts were heavy ones, I somehow fell asleep. Her on top of me was what I needed, it seemed, to get some rest.

But tonight wasn't like the other nights. She didn't sleep the night through, resting even past me leaving her bed and her apartment, at least, from what she'd told me.

Her whimpers, pained and scared, stirred me, and I woke up, just in time to hear that fucker's name on her lips.

It killed me that this had been a trigger, and I might have walked away, knowing I wasn't strong enough to deal with this, to be what she needed, but she woke up and threw herself across the bed like I was poison before screaming, "Get out, Cruz. Get the fuck out."

I never did well with orders. Apart from with the council. It was the Dom in me, a trait that hadn't died even if my taste in the lifestyle had. I didn't like being told what to do, and I certainly didn't like it when I knew why.

She wanted to cry.

Alone.

In peace.

My jaw worked at the thought, and I knew I couldn't do it.

Not just tonight, but any fucking night.

I couldn't leave her to her nightmares. Couldn't leave her to that fucker.

If I didn't do something, if I didn't help, she'd be forever tangled in that cunt's web, and while my dick wasn't magical and didn't cure everything, I just...

Fuck, she needed *this*.

But more, she needed to trust me.

So I got out of bed.

I picked up my boots.

I headed for the living room.

Then, I moved over to the sofa and I lay flat out on it, wincing at its size which wasn't enough for my length, as I grabbed the throw over it and tucked it around myself.

"What are you doing?"

I heard her voice in the darkness, heard the thickness of her tears, heard the anger and the emotions that were out of control, knew she was raging inside, and knew I could help her control that fury, channel it where it needed to be released.

"I'm going to sleep."

"No, you're not," she snapped, irritation overtaking her sadness. "I want you to leave."

"Tough shit. I'm not going anywhere," I rumbled, making my voice sleepy even though I was anything but.

I was wide awake.

I had to be.

I was about to fight for us.

For her.

Even if she didn't understand that.

"Get out, Cruz. Get the fuck out."

Was I surprised when she came at me like a wildcat?

No.

Her nails stung like a bitch though, and her slaps were hard and fierce, but even though I let her burn herself out for a minute or so—going to high school a couple of years early primed anyone for a beating—I was quick to grab her wrists, drag them behind her back, and then, questioning myself all the while, I forced her onto her knees.

She hissed at me, spitting at me and the globule of saliva landed on my pec. I'd expected worse, a bite, hard enough to draw blood, so I wasn't angry, but she couldn't know that.

Any doubts disappeared.

And I knew this was right.

What she needed.

What I needed because, somehow, I needed her. Crazy, messed up, fucked up, screwed up, all of that. I needed Indiana goddamn Sisson.

So I gave her me.

After slapping her ass, I grabbed her hair again, pulling it hard enough to jerk her head back. My eyes were on hers all the while, even though the darkness shielded us both, and I growled out, "Clean it up." Then I forced her face toward the saliva that was dripping down my chest.

At first, I wasn't sure she'd obey, thought she'd bite me, then, I felt the flat of her tongue against my skin, and even as I gritted my teeth at the sensation, I let her carry on. Moving further down until it was all cleaned up.

Then, when she was done, I hauled her up, higher so that she was leaning into me, no longer on her knees, and dragged her over me so that she covered me. She started struggling, but I held her tight, drawing one of my thighs over hers, binding her in place, and in her ear, I rasped, "You want to cry? You cry. You want to scream? You scream. You want to rail at the fucking world? You rail at the fucking world. But you do it in front of me. All of it. I want it all."

She tensed, then muttered thickly, "Fuck you, Cruz. Fuck off. I don't want you."

"Bullshit. Your pussy juices are still around my mouth, Indy. You want me as much as I want you." A hiss escaped her, but her struggles slowed.

"Now, go to sleep."

"What?! I can't—"

I growled, "Go. To. Fucking. Sleep."

This time, the hiss morphed into a shocked breath, and I knew her thoughts were scattered to the wind. I tugged on her hair once before I let go of it, and then I relinquished my grasp on her wrists, prepared for her to dive off and run for the bed. But she didn't.

Nor did she relax.

She lay there, her breathing heavy, panting like she'd run a race, until finally she wasn't.

Until, finally, I recognized the hard truth—she'd obeyed.

She'd fallen asleep.

"Hypothesis proved," I whispered to myself, knowing, full well now, that I could give her what she craved.

Me, and only me.

And even if it took a fucking lifetime to make her see that, unless Lodestar decided to kill me—which she hadn't attempted to do thus far—I intended on giving her that.

All of me.

But only if she gave me all of her in return.

EIGHT

INDY

A WEEK LATER

THE SHADOWS on the wall moved.

That might not mean anything to anyone else, but in the deep of night, when everyone was asleep, nothing should have moved at all. Especially not when Nyx was with Caleb. The black Labrador was always glued to his side, had been ever since my baby brother had been born. We figured it was down to Nyx being hyperaware of how ill Caleb had been since he was a baby. Whenever his health was bad, Nyx was there. Like glue.

But with our dog tucked away, fast asleep on my brother's bed, the shadows definitely shouldn't have been moving.

There was no light outside, no light in the house.

It was too late at night for that.

But the door still swept open.

And my heart began to pound.

A couple months ago, I'd never have been awake at this time. But now? I knew to fear the dark. I knew to fear what the stillness of my home represented.

Opportunity.

I gulped when the floorboards squeaked as the door swept back, closing, and my bottom lip trembled when the faintest noises echoed around the growing silence.

The soft steps moved in time to the rush of blood in my ears and I huddled even tighter in my 'Hello, Kitty' comforter, wanting this to be a nightmare, but knowing it wasn't.

The bed jostled as he took a seat at the side of me.

His smell was so strong. Like nothing I'd ever forget.

A strange pine scent that reminded me of the forest but that I knew came from his aftershave. That odd smell that my eldest brother stank of after gym class, and that he called B.O. There was a tang of sweat, too, and it seemed to overwhelm the flowery essence that my mom washed my comforter in.

His hand went to my hip and he murmured, "Hey there, Indy. Did you miss me?"

I tried to swallow, but my mouth was too dry. "U-Uncle Kevin, I only just saw you at dinner."

"Well, that's a long time ago," he teased, and his hand traced over my chest and up to my hair. As his fingers tangled with the dark strands, he murmured, "And it's been at least four weeks since I was last here. I've been without my best girl since then." He tugged on my hair. *Gently.* "Were you good?" He stopped tugging, tucked the lock behind my ear before he tenderly flicked my earlobe.

I tensed at the touch. "Y-Yes. I didn't get into any trouble."

"That's what I like to hear. And you didn't tell your mom or dad about our little conversations, did you?"

My bottom lip trembled. "N-No."

"Good girl. I think you deserve a little present."

Horror whispered through me. "N-No, it's okay, Uncle Kevin, I don't want one."

"Sure you do," he purred, and his hand went to the top of the blanket, and with inexorable strength, he fought my grip on it, all with a dreamy smile on his face as he started to drag it down—

"No!" I screamed, jerking immediately awake. Horror whipped through me as fast as relief did, but it didn't stop me from howling out my terror.

I thrashed at the covers that shouldn't be on me, needing out of them, needing to get out of bed, needing to be anywhere but fucking here, and then, I felt a hand at my back and a growled, *"What the fuck?"* and twisted around to slap at the intruder.

I didn't care that, consciously, I knew Kevin had been dead for nearly twenty goddamn years, he was alive.

In bed with me.

I screamed louder, hitting out, lashing at the predatory cunt in an effort to get him away from me, and then, I registered something.

The scent of man. The scent of soap. Of musk and sandalwood. An essence that was almost like incense.

I froze, because only that smell ripped the past from my mind, and shrouded me in the present.

My skin was clammy with terror and fury, my heart was racing like I'd been doing the tango on a spinning bike, and there was a wildness to my mind that made me understand how my brother, Nyx, could go out and kill people.

But at Cruz's scent, it tore through the memories, and needing more of that smell, needing it to overtake me, I hurled myself at him.

He didn't expect it. He was tense, and I knew he thought I was going to attack him still, but when I melted into him, sinking into him like syrup into steaming hot pancakes, he relaxed too, and his arms came around me.

I didn't think I'd like that. To be touched. Not so soon after—

Only I did.

I loved it.

He held me so tightly, so fiercely, it was like he wanted to let go as little as I wanted to be released.

His mouth brushed over my temple, his lips rubbing there as he buried his nose in my hair, and I just shoved my face into his inked throat, uncaring that my breath made us both sweaty, just needing more of that 'clean man' smell in my nose.

"It's okay, Indy. I won't let any cunt hurt you."

The words should have been ridiculous. I didn't need a man to look after me, but Cruz's words were nuttier still because we were fuck buddies. Sure, he spent the night, but that didn't mean anything.

We were fuck buddies.

Nothing more, nothing less.

Only trouble was, he meant it. He meant those crazy, impossible words. He wanted to protect me, but he couldn't.

It was impossible.

I shook my head. "You can't protect me from the past."

Tension hit him, but he was slow in responding, just carried on stroking my hair in a way that should have reminded me of Kevin but didn't.

It felt... good.

It connected me with him in a way I didn't realize I needed.

"What were you dreaming of?"

"I think you know," I rumbled bitterly, because every Satan's Sinner knew the sorry tale of my family history.

Uncle Kevin messed with my elder sister Carly from a young age. When she couldn't take it anymore, when Kevin's abuse amped up after she protected Nyx from him, she killed herself, which sent my eldest brother down the rabbit hole of insanity.

Ever since, he'd been slaughtering pedophiles like they were terrorists in a mission on *Call of Duty*.

The Sinners knew that, helped out, even. And me, in the aftermath, I was the one who tattooed a skull on his back. A tag, a *trophy* of another kid fucker biting the dust. In the most painful way possible.

"I-I didn't think you were—"

When his voice waned, I started to pull away, expecting his disgust, his revulsion... only, I didn't get it. He didn't let me move away, clung harder to me in fact.

"I was," I said miserably.

"This is why you can't sleep, isn't it?"

I nodded. "The dreams... they're bad."

"You've been sleeping well with me. For the most part," he pointed out softly, not referencing the time I'd slapped him and hurt him, spitting at him like he was trash.

Fuck, I regretted that night even if it had been a turning point in our relationship.

Biting my lip as I contemplated whether to lie or not, I decided there was no point in a half-truth. This was probably the last time he'd want to sleep with my sullied self, so I might as well go the whole hog and tell him all of it.

"You fuck me too good for me to stay awake after."

He didn't preen at that, nor did he shudder with revulsion like I might have expected with this truth now between us; he just said, "This is the first nightmare you've had with me?"

No, it wasn't, but I hadn't had another since the night of the spitting incident.

A sign I was getting too comfortable around him?

The thought prompted me to try to pull away again, but he rumbled, "Where do you think you're going?" He tapped me on the ass to stop me, *hard*, and the sting was bad enough to make me hiss but he took advantage of my surprise, nudging his knee between both my thighs, and pressing it into the mattress.

I should have struggled at how he pinned me down, kept me in place. It should have triggered thoughts of *him*, but it didn't.

And that sting was too good.

Because he wasn't letting me go anywhere, because I didn't really want to go anywhere either, I settled into him, and when he murmured, "Talk to me," in a tone that would normally have gotten my back up, I relaxed into the mattress, and did as he'd commanded.

I talked.

PART 2

NINE

CRUZ

"YOU WANNA FUCK ME, BABY?"

What I wanted to do was roll my eyes... I didn't. Instead, I stared at Jingles and cracked my knuckles. She bit her bottom lip, which was a clear sign as to what was going on.

These bitches, seriously.

I mean, I knew a lot of the brothers could be led around by their cocks, but I wasn't one of them.

I'd had enough of dancing to someone's fucking song a long ass time ago, and I refused to be whipped by a piece of snatch who was shared around the clubhouse by men I considered family.

Jingles' eyes dropped to my knuckles. The tattoos looked like perfect renditions of the skeletal frame of my hands, which was fitting considering I cleaned up dead bodies for the club.

"Thought Giulia asked you to clean the staircase again?"

Her nostrils flared, and I just prepared my ears for the whining that was about to come. "But we did them last week!"

"How often do you think something that gets used as often as the staircase *should* get cleaned?" I asked, genuinely curious.

These sluts were filthy bitches. The clubhouse was enough to have my neat-freak self cringing. With this much DNA floating around these walls, the place was one big crime scene waiting to happen.

Jingles, being the dirty bitch she was, shrugged, which made her tits jiggle, which made the little nipple piercings she had jingle in turn.

Hence the name.

Wherever she went, she played a tune.

Any entrancement that particular trait had triggered in me died a death a long while back.

"I dunno. Every month?"

"It's a wonder we didn't die with you cunts cleaning this place," I grumbled under my breath, then I shook my head. "Just because you wanna waste time on your back rather than doing what you're supposed to, doesn't mean I have time to play your games."

She scowled at me. "I'm not playing games. I swear, you're no fun anymore! This place used to be a real hoot, but everyone's getting all match.com and no one wants to play."

"Stopped playing when I was eight, Jingles," I said wryly. "And you're about twenty-two years too old to be thinking about playtime. Now, go on, get. You're supposed to do as Giulia says."

"I fucking am," she groused. "Goddamn bitch should have been born with a swastika on her cheek."

I should probably have defended the VP's woman, but hell, Giulia *was* faintly Nazi-ish. Without the mass-genocide of innocents, of course. If anyone was under threat from Giulia, it was the club snatch, who were feckless and cruel to the Old Ladies, and pedophiles. Both of whom deserved to deal with her wrath.

Brothers didn't talk about it, but everyone knew Nyx had taken Giulia with him on his last crusade. There were even whispers that she'd been the one to light the last sick kid fucker on fire.

As Jingles walked away and I wasn't even interested in watching the show, I recognized that the club snatch weren't doing much for me anymore.

Been there.

Done that, and watching her storm off was one big reminder that my dick was firmly in the Indiana vice.

The thought of the last time she'd exploded around my cock had me grimacing a little as I finished up changing the keg behind the bar. While beer wasn't a popular choice for most of the bikers, we still went through a keg a day. As well as copious amounts of vodka and tequila.

As I finished up my inventory, made notes of which liquors I needed to re-stock, my cell buzzed.

The Killers, *Mr. Brightside* blared out and knowing who that ringtone belonged to, I hid my face as I dipped beneath the counter.

I reached for my cell and hit connect, lip curling at the voice I was about to hear.

Mommy Dearest.

Most people might dig receiving a call from their folks, but me? I hated it. My dad, well, he was okay. I quite liked him. He wasn't too much of a dick, and he left me alone, gave me space. It helped that he was in Arizona, of course. Couldn't get much more space between New Mexico and New Jersey, after all.

I knew why he'd moved though. Understood why he'd put distance between us.

After the divorce, Mom had been her usual insaniac self, and I couldn't blame him for heading across the country. Not when, after he'd married and gotten my stepmom pregnant, Mom had taken to showing up at their house like some kind of fucking crazy person.

Which, of course, she was.

Mom's obsession with her career and then, fifteen years ago, finding out who had killed her father and bringing them to justice were the driving forces in her life. I wasn't sure when she'd had time to get married and to pop me out, but she'd managed somehow. I was living proof of the fact she didn't eat, breathe, and shit her job.

"What do you want?" I rasped by way of a greeting.

"I need you to come visit me. This isn't a secure line."

I narrowed my eyes at the keg I'd only just changed, hoping that anyone in the vicinity would think I was having trouble with it. "I have no desire to come and see you."

"Tough shit. You owe me."

"I owe you nothing," I snarled, even though as far as she still knew, that was a lie. Couldn't make this look too easy, could I?

She fell silent, then she signed my death knell. "Your Prez will appreciate the heads' up."

Jaw clenching, I glowered at nothing because glowering was futile. Everything about Caroline fucking Dunbar was.

It was either her way or the highway.

"No wonder Dad divorced your ass and took you to the cleaners," I rumbled.

When she hissed out a breath, I was surprised, like always, to learn that the divorce was still a touchy subject.

I wasn't sure if Dad was the one who'd gotten away, or if he was simply a challenge. He'd betrayed her, so he deserved to have his life ruined.

That was how my mom worked.

Who had nemeses anymore?

Hadn't they gone by the by in the days of Sherlock Holmes?

Well, apparently not for Caro Dunbar.

She had nemeses everywhere. Saw shadows at high fucking noon.

It was a wonder she kept her shit together enough to maintain her position at the FBI. Somewhere along the line, I figured she'd started screwing someone high-up to stay as a Special Agent. One who worked actual cases and wasn't tied to a desk. But no one liked to think that kind of shit about their mom… Not even me.

Caro hadn't been cruel. She hadn't been vindictive. She'd fed me, made sure I went to school, but she just hadn't been there.

So when I was sixteen? I'd done the exact same thing—I'd left for college and I'd done it with the hope of not looking back, but some of my worst choices led to my being tied to her in ways no man wanted.

My only consolation was that I hadn't gone to jail thanks to her interference.

"Less talk of your father," she sniped. "I wouldn't have contacted you if I didn't need to speak with you."

"You always need to speak with me, and somehow, you never have anything to say." I pursed my lips as I waited on her answer, but before I did, my cell buzzed with a message in a tone I'd set for Rex—the Prez. "I need to go."

"You need to come and visit me."

I sighed. "What for?"

"It's important."

"I'll just bet." Rubbing my eyes, I grumbled, "I'll see what I can do. Things are shitty right now. Not many reasons for me to head into the city without raising suspicion."

She grunted. "Damn." A pause. "Okay. Message me when you can come. I can be patient. No longer than a week though, Darren."

Grimacing at a name I hadn't answered to for years, I muttered, "I'll do what I can."

Before she told me that wasn't good enough, like always, I cut the call.

Of all the bikers in the Satan's Sinners' MC, I was the only one who didn't have Mommy issues. There were a lot of them going around, though. Daddy issues too. But my brothers here had reasons, *justification* for being fucked in the head. Me? What could I complain about? That I'd been a latch-key kid?

Snorting at the thought, especially when I tossed Nyx and Indy's background around in my head, I clambered to my feet as I read the text Rex had sent.

Unsurprisingly, he'd asked me to go to his office.

I dumped the burner cell in my pocket, and leaving shit behind, I headed out of the bar, bypassing a very noisy '69' going down on the pool table with a brother whose face I couldn't see because it was buried in Peach's pussy. My nose crinkled at the sight, because I didn't think the brother was wearing a dental dam. Brothers in an MC weren't the dental dam-wearing type.

"You're not supposed to go down on the whores," I muttered as I passed him, but a grunt was all I got for my pains.

Rolling my eyes as I trudged past the orgy and into the hall, I found my way to the office. Knocking on Rex's door, I wasn't altogether surprised to see Mav and Nyx there.

When I cut them all a look, I murmured, "Mommy dearest wants to see me."

Rex's mouth tightened, the cloned cell in his hand. "We heard."

TEN
INDY

"DAVID, could you pass me Laura's file?"

If my tone was absent-minded, then that was because I was feeling pretty absent-minded of late. Actually, not just recently. For a while now.

My brain was all over the fucking place and I knew why.

Men. Pains in my ass.

What with my baby bro, Caleb, in prison on a sentence he didn't deserve, Nyx's psychotic self head-butting me every which way I turned, and then memories of the past, it was a wonder I had a mind left.

My life wasn't, and never had been, easy. I didn't expect it to be. But I'd like a little peace, just a little tranquility, and somehow, I'd managed to find it—I just hated that I was a cliché and it was related to a man.

Cliché aside, I also wished that once Cruz had walked out of the door this morning, and every other, that the peace lasted longer than ten minutes. Especially when I got a call from my baby bro who'd lied to me about why he sounded so gruff.

He'd been crying.

God help me. I wanted to kill someone, and knowing I couldn't protect him just made me feel a thousand times worse.

"Here you go," David chirped, his tone, as always, cheerful.

He was a weirdo, a stalker, but I liked that about him.

Stalkers were men you could trust. He knew more about me than I did, knew the exact location of everything I ever touched, and, truthfully, he was a lifesaver. If he wasn't obsessed with me, he wouldn't be such a damn good PA.

Yeah, yeah, I knew it made me a bitch to be taking advantage of him, but sometimes, you just had to make the best out of a bad situation.

I sure as hell wasn't going back to the days where he'd call me, heavy breathing down the line for a good minute before he built up the courage to cut the damn call.

Nor was I going back to the nights where he'd hover outside my shop.

This way, my stalker was a functioning member of society. He got paid well for it, had a really great dental plan, and so what if I had to handle his goo goo eyes all the time? I could deal.

Well, usually I could.

Today I wasn't feeling that good, so chirpy wasn't what I needed right now.

I needed somber.

I needed serious.

I needed eyes that looked into mine, leaving me feeling like I'd been through an MRI tunnel because he'd seen everything. Every-fucking-thing. And all without me having to say a goddamn word.

Having always avoided dominant men in the past, preferring someone who was on the same level as me, I had to admit, it was a revelation.

The white noise in my head quit some when Cruz was around, and I enjoyed that more than I could say.

A shaky breath escaped me at the thought, and the need that writhed through me was uncomfortable to handle, especially when David was looking at me like I was a walking goddess.

I was no one's idea of a goddess.

Unless you were into ink, and then, okay, I'd accept the title.

What I could do with a tattoo gun was magic. Sheer, fucking perfection. Worthy of a chef's kiss, if I did say so myself.

"Thanks," I grunted at him, slapping my shades over my eyes before I traced over the lines of the design I'd come up with twelve weeks ago.

This particular tattoo was taking a hell of a lot longer than I'd like, but not for monetary reasons. Sure, it was worth a couple of grand, but a tattoo this detailed had to be broken up into hourly slots. The trouble was that every time I worked on Laura, she cringed and tensed up like I was stabbing her with knives instead of a tattoo gun.

It was agony—for both of us.

"Here," David soothed, and I'd have laughed if I'd have been anyone outside this scenario, looking in.

He wafted a pot of coffee in front of me, literally under my nose. It was like putting a freshly baked pie in front of Yogi bear or something.

But I was me. And I did take David for granted.

"Thanks." I snatched the mug from him and, kicking my Converse-clad feet up on the desk, I sank back and started slurping.

The pattern wasn't one I'd have suggested. It was more fitting for a cushion or a set of curtains, in my opinion, nothing really original, but Laura had come to me with it, and that's what I was giving her. There were massive frond leaves that played peekaboo with tropical creatures, an expanse of greenery from a rainforest that I didn't have to get to design. What set it above a regular illustration was the detail. There were birds in the design I couldn't remember the name of, but they looked like they could fly off her tit they were so realistic.

Reacquainting myself with the overlay, and also adding a few details here and there, I switched focus as he told me, "Laura will be here in two hours. Want anything from the bakery next door to set yourself up for the appointment?"

I shook my head, not even bothering to look when he headed out of the tattoo parlor for his lunch. Sure, he cared, and it was nice, and his awareness of how exhausting the session with Laura was was touching, but I couldn't be too encouraging.

If I wasn't careful, he'd start breaking into my apartment again.

That hadn't been an issue in the past, but if he did it when Cruz came over? Fuck, he'd shoot David. I didn't want my PA to die nor my fuck buddy to go to jail, especially when it was unnecessary.

When the bell tinkled over the door, my focus wasn't disturbed, because I knew it was him heading for the bakery that made the *best* bao rolls in the area, but when it rang again, I wanted to groan because I hated dealing with pop-ins this early in the morning.

Only, when I raised my head, trying not to glare at the customer who, ya know, paid my bills, I registered this kind of walk-in was one I could tolerate.

"You look like you're in a mood."

"I am." I tipped my head to the side as I peered at Giulia, my brother's woman, marveling—and not for the first time—that Nyx had settled down.

Nyx was the coolest psychopath you'd ever come across. He was so high-functioning you'd never know he was a serial killer.

Not that *I* was supposed to know that either. I was just the person who tattooed his trophies onto his back—that was all.

Giulia wasn't what I'd have picked for him, not exactly, but the bundle of Italian curves seemed to have my brother's cock in a clamp, so who was I to argue? If she stopped him from heading down the river to Crazytown, then I was grateful.

I'd lost too much family to want Nyx to disappear as well.

Even if he did drive me fucking insane.

"What kind of mood?" Giulia asked, blinking at me as she perched her round butt on the corner of my desk. It was a scratched old thing, vintage and retro weren't words that could describe it, but I'd found it in a thrift store a couple of months back and just had to have it.

With a surge of new clients lately, I'd reinvested in the shop, replacing an Ikea-special sofa with a turquoise Chesterfield, putting a nice rug down on the floor that an old friend from school had designed for me—it had one of my mandalas laser-printed onto it—and the walls were a blank white with photos of my designs on there, some on client's limbs, others just of the initial work up process. A few were framed, articles that showcased my skills and the body art that had forged the rep that was earned through hard work and determination... A determination that was founded in my desire to not let that bastard win.

The desk didn't fit. At all. It was old and cumbersome. But I liked it.

Old and cumbersome wasn't always a bad thing.

Sometimes, comfort mattered, and on a desk, drawers were like pockets in a dress—always came in handy.

"A pissed off mood," I grumbled, frowning at her over my shades. "What do you want?"

She snorted. "Thought we were friends."

"We are." I arched a brow at her. "Being grumpy with you is a sign of friendship." And it surprised me to realize I wasn't bullshitting her. I liked Giulia. She was what my brother needed, and she didn't take fools lightly.

My kind of chick.

My reply had her smiling, and that smile told me we were on the same wavelength, something she confirmed by telling me, "I work the same way."

"Yeah? Then you'll know I'm not chirpy enough for a wasted conversation. What's wrong?"

"Nothing's wrong." She shrugged. "Just been thinking of getting some more ink is all."

"I'll always talk ink." Her words perked me up some, enough to stop slouching and to sit up. Especially when I thought she might have wanted to talk about Nyx. I liked her but I didn't want a pow wow about him before two PM. I needed coffee and maybe some Twizzlers before I could handle *that* convo. "What kind?"

"Thinking of a more effeminate version of the Sinners' logo."

"You want a different kind of patch, hmm?" My mind drifted off as I started putting pieces together.

"Yeah. Just feels right. I'm tied to Nyx in more ways than just what I feel for him."

My lips twitched. "My brother is all grown up, sounds like you are too."

"Think he was that a long time ago," she said dryly. "Me? Well, that happened before him for sure."

"I can believe that about you, but where he's concerned? Barely." I rolled my eyes. "You weren't around for the ride when he was in his twenties."

"I've heard," she retorted with a laugh. "Stone's pretty big on sharing stories of when you guys were younger."

I liked that she said 'younger' and not young. Giulia wasn't jailbait, but the age gap between her and my bro would make people curl their noses up. If noses could curl.

"Yeah, well, that's Stone. All chatty." I narrowed my eyes at her. "How's she doing?"

"You only saw her yesterday, didn't you?"

"Yeah. But today's another day, and I just woke up so haven't checked in with her yet."

When Stone had almost died at the hands of a psychotic Angel of Death who roamed her hospital ward, it had been a revelation to both of us. There was an age gap between her and me too, not as distinct as my brother and his woman, but large enough for a friendship to have failed when we were kids. Still, we were closer than sisters, and almost losing her had been a prompt for us to be outed.

Until her attack, no one in the clubhouse, on the compound, had known about our friendship.

What could I say? We were sneaky bitches.

"She's fine. She was talking about her and Steel finally getting to fuck."

Hiding a grin, I said, "Christ, she's been waiting to tap that for a lifetime. No wonder she's antsy." I kept giving her shit about how long it was taking her and Steel to get it on, but it was only teasing. Mostly, I was just relieved she was in one piece and capable of walking, never mind screwing a man she'd been pining over for decades.

"Antsy ain't the word," was Giulia's wry rejoinder.

I hummed. "Maybe I should give her a call."

"Probably be a kind thing to do. She's nervous."

"I'll bet." I peered down at the calendar, checking to make sure I had time before Laura's for a call, and then I blinked. "Huh. She's scheduled for ink today."

"She is?" She pouted. "She didn't split with the details yesterday."

"Knowing Steel, he told her to be cagey. It's a good thing I know she loves him or I'd slap that man."

Giulia grinned. "She's leading him around by the dick."

"How it should be, kemo sabe," I said sagely. "Although, I don't wanna know about my bro's dick, even if you're leading him around by it. Knowing he has a Terminator penis is more than enough."

She whistled under her breath. "I'm a lucky woman."

"Enough," I groused, but I dropped my feet to the ground and stared at the calendar. "When do you want to talk about your new design?"

"I figure I'll let you come up with it."

"You don't want any say in it?"

"Nah."

My brows rose, but inside, excitement hit me. "Seriously?"

"Seriously. I trust you." She rubbed her brand, a miniature version of one of the skulls Nyx had decorating his back. He must think I was a moron if he didn't realize I knew what each one represented—the death, by his hands, of a pedophile. "I think you get me, and you, more than anyone, understand the vibes of the club."

Studying her, I granted her a small smile. I knew how it felt to feel lost, but my reasons were totally different than hers. She was trying to make the club her family, but there was no point in that. Not that I was going to tell her she was wrong or anything.

Did I look like I had a death wish?

Cruz, in a rare display of openness, had already told me about the rumors whispering through the compound about her...but it wasn't like I hadn't figured that out either. Not when she had two skulls now, which meant she and Nyx had gone a-hunting together. That also meant Giulia had pedo blood on her hands, and she wasn't going to lose any sleep over it.

Me? I was the one losing all the sleep. Well, me and Mav. The local insomniacs. We should have started a club of our own together.

"I'll text you a design, okay?" I wriggled my shoulders. "Might not be for a few days."

"You busy?" She arched a brow. "That's great."

"Yeah." I rubbed the back of my neck. "It's great but I'm a one-woman-show, Giulia. There's only so much I can do."

"If you need help around the place, I'll gladly pitch in."

If she'd told me she shat eggs, I'd have been less surprised. "You want to help out?"

She shrugged, and I immediately sensed she regretted making the offer, which made me feel like a piece of shit. "I mean, it was just a suggestion."

I actually liked my sister-in-law. She was good for my brother, and if it was true that they'd hunted as a pair, then I figured Giulia was the kind of crazy who could take Nyx unto death. But she was delicate, more delicate than I thought Nyx knew. She'd been assaulted, attacked in the press, vilified... then it hit me.

Her assault had gone down in the new bar the Sinners had started in West Orange... where she worked.

No woman could be satisfied working around the compound. Disinfecting shit only took up so much time, and while cooking for a bunch of bikers was probably like feeding an army, I had to figure that wasn't enough job satisfaction for anyone other than a clubwhore. Which Giulia definitely wasn't.

"How would you like to help out?"

She stiffened a little. "It's okay, Indy. It was just a suggestion. I don't need your pity."

"Good thing," I retorted, "because you weren't about to get any." I shrugged when she glared at me. "You surprised me."

"Why? Think I'm only good for cooking, cleaning, and fucking your brother?"

I winced. "Well, he'd be the one who'd know about the latter, as for the rest, I didn't think so, but to be honest, I never really thought about it."

"Well, I have." She bit her bottom lip, her shoulders hunching a little as she mumbled, "I need to get out of the clubhouse. Tormenting the clubwhores has been fun, but I liked working at the bar, and every time I drive past it, I want to scream. I was thinking about the diner, and I know Steel would give me a job because they're crazy busy and need all the help they can get—"

"But that's just a continuation of what you're doing at the clubhouse. I get it."

"Yeah. Though I'd get paid."

My brow furrowed. "You don't get paid now?"

"You know how the clubhouse works," she said wryly. "It's not like I need anything, and if I did, Nyx would—"

I raised a hand. "Fuck that. No woman should rely on a man for money."

"I told you, I don't need pity."

"And *I* already goddamn told you, I'm not fucking giving you any," I growled. "Even if I can only pay you a couple hundred bucks every two weeks, it's better than depending on that bunch of jackasses."

"I don't have any bills to pay," she argued. "I don't expect a wage."

"Fuck. That," I repeated, but I was a little calmer this time. "Having to ask a man for dough to buy tampons is something no woman should have to go through."

Fucking bikers.

I swore, they got my heartbeat racing like nothing else could, and not simply because their asses looked fine in a pair of jeans.

Mind whirring, I grumbled under my breath, "You can start tomorrow."

She blinked. "Doing what?"

"I don't fucking know," I retorted, "but I ain't having my sister-in-law dependent on the Sinners forever." I glowered at her. "You were getting paid at the bar, weren't you?"

"Some."

My scowl deepened at that non-answer, which told me the tight cunts had been shafting her in more ways than just Nyx was, but she met me glare for glare so I just groused, "Well, enough of that. David pretty much runs the front of house. He has no life outside of me so—"

Her eyes widened. "What do you mean?"

"I mean, he's my stalker."

"Your stalker?" she repeated.

"Yup," I told her, tone cheery for the first time since I'd woken up.

"You're not going to explain that to me, are you?"

I grinned at her. "Nope." I even popped the 'p.' "Anyway, you can help him out…"

Her smile was sheepish and she pulled something from her pocket then shoved it at me.

When I stared at the piece of paper in her hand, I tilted my head to the side to see it all, then murmured, "Well, well, well…"

ELEVEN

CRUZ

SHE SHRIEKED when she turned around and saw me standing there, leaping a few inches off the ground in surprise before her eyes turned nasty and she snarled, "I told you I fucking hate when you do this."

I didn't grin at her, even though I wanted to.

Even though, something about this crazy fucking woman made me want to grin all the time, like a goddamn clown, the last thing I was renowned for was my cheery personality.

I was the Grim Reaper by nature as well as nurture, after all.

Instead of grinning at her outrage, I arched a brow and murmured, "On your knees."

Her nostrils flared with her irritation, and she even jerked her neck a time or two in agitation, and I allowed it.

This. Fucking. Once.

Once she walked through that door, Indy was no longer a tattoo artist, no longer a sister, no longer a business owner, she was a woman.

When I was here, she changed.

Shifted.

Became mine.

Independent women were the hardest to dominate, but the fucking best. Watching them relinquish control? Nothing hotter. And a woman like Indy was like no bitch I'd ever fucked before. In fact, calling this simply 'fucking' was sacrilegious.

"You have one minute to obey," I rasped when she just stood there staring at me like the proverbial rabbit in headlights.

The words snapped her out of her stupor like I'd anticipated, and she sank to her knees.

Things had changed between us thanks to a bad dream, and another nightmare had prompted a conversation amid pillows and rumpled sheets, while entangled in each other's arms, tucked in the deep shadows of midnight, as her whispers tore through the cracks to reveal the cold, hard truth as she saw it.

I'd already known, but it meant something that she shared it with me.

"What are you doing here?" she rasped, but she kept her head bowed like I showed her.

A part of me shuddered with longing at the sight of her. Her skin, thanks to her Algonquin heritage, was a little tawny, a lot dusky, like no other color I'd seen before—unique. That was Indy. And her hair, as a result of her ancestry, was the nearest thing to silk I'd ever touched.

It'd been shorter the first time I'd ever met her, and gradually, had grown out some over the years. Now, I'd never let her cut it. One day, she'd give me a hand job with her pony tail. It was at the top of my to-do list.

The black strands were thick, strong, and the color was the perfect contrast to her skin. I wasn't an artist, not like she was. If anything, my skills were in shit that no one really understood—not because I hadn't shared the truth with anyone, but because my brain drifted through chemical formulas that went over most people's heads. I didn't have to be an artist, though, to register how truly beautiful she was.

Her cheekbones weren't all that high, but she was too skinny and as a result, a little gaunt. It meant that her lips were framed, and she usually painted them in a lurid shade. I'd seen her wear anything from bright yellow to dark green. She suited the darker colors though. I'd come to learn that her lipstick represented her frame of mind, and knew she had a color for every occasion.

Someday, and it would be soon, I'd change that.

Until Indy, I hadn't understood that a woman, sometimes, would make herself purposely ugly.

To reflect what she felt inside.

That this gorgeous creature might ever feel that way messed with my head, and I liked logic far too much to be happy about how illogical she made me.

Truth was, Indy and me should never have been anything other than fuck buddies.

But she'd flipped my switch. Tripped my trigger. Something I could never have envisaged her doing.

In the past, I'd liked my permanent subs soft.

Delicate.

A sub I fucked could be independent, but I liked them *dependent*.

Indy was strong. Hard.

Only on the inside was she fragile.

My thoughts came to a crashing halt because they were getting me nowhere. I knew all this already, but whenever I watched her slip to her knees, it took my breath away.

This woman wasn't supposed to kneel for any man.

Yet she did for me.

That was some heady stuff.

I strode out of the shadows of her small living room and toward the doorway where she was kneeling. With each step I took, she tensed, and I knew why.

This was not a comfortable position for her.

Every time I did this, I half-expected it'd be the last time she'd allow it, and I dreaded it even as I kept on prodding the beast. It was like when you had a canker sore and couldn't stop running your tongue over it, prodding it and making it hurt worse. Human nature, sure, but it meant that every time with her could be the last, and it made her more precious to me than she probably knew.

My boots thudded against the stripped wooden floor as I wandered through the apartment toward her, passing the esthetic that came as another surprise. You looked at her and you saw a rebel. Tats everywhere beneath a facade that screamed tomboy. This place was girly. All furry rugs and shit on console tables. A million photo frames, plants here and there, small ornaments that represented something to her. She was the kind of woman who, before she slept, had to take about a dozen throw pillows off her bed, and had a dozen more furry ones on her sofa.

I slipped my hand over her hair when I reached her and, carefully, tugged on her ponytail, drawing her head back so that she was looking right where I wanted her to—my eyes.

When our gazes collided, I felt something inside me settle.

A truth.

A recognition that was undeniable.

I was pretty sure she felt it too, because her gaze shuttered, and she tried to drop her chin, but my hold on her hair prevented that maneuver.

Exactly why I'd done it.

"What's going on? You didn't text," she rumbled, her voice low and wary as she looked up at me.

"Bad day," was all I said, but I let go of her hair and stroked my fingers over her silky smooth locks.

"Gonna take it out on my ass?"

Any other woman would have said that mockingly. Indy? I almost *felt* the need.

I'd known a lot of women in my life, known plenty of subs, but something about Indy spoke to me. Called out to me in a way I'd never known before.

She needed me in a way no other ever had, and I responded to that in ways that weren't necessarily the wisest.

I was rougher with her than I ought to be because she responded. If she didn't, I'd back off, but under my attentions, she was like a flower blossoming in the sunlight.

I fought my inclinations, tempering them, but when I let loose, and she did too? It messed with my head so that I felt like I was the one in fucking subspace and not just her.

"You been a good girl today?" I asked softly, letting my fingers slip around and down her cheek to her chin, which I tipped up to maintain eye contact.

"Never," she said with a smirk, and her gaze lit with a hot flash of fire that reminded me of the whip of lightning through a clear sky.

I tapped her bottom lip once, then before she even had the chance to shriek out in surprise, I shoved her face down to the floor, pinned her there by the nape, and with her butt arching up and out, spanked her there.

Once.

Twice.

Three times.

A set on each cheek.

Then I backed off.

At least four feet away and I studied her prone form.

She was the most interesting sub I'd ever come across. At first, she didn't like to be touched. She had to warm up to that. Then, when she was 'warm,' it was like a heat wave took over her.

It was that heat wave which kept me coming back for more. Though I was working on getting her used to touch, not just for sex but for aftercare, every time she didn't outright evade me was a victory I claimed as my own.

I didn't like complications. Didn't like difficult women. One of the reasons I'd fallen into the Dom culture back in college was because my studies had overtaken my life and I needed release with, what I'd stupidly believed, were easy lays that let me take full control, let me unleash myself whenever I was in the zone. Only as I grew older and wiser, did I realize I was a prick.

Subs were submissive. *Biddable. Slaves. I could treat them however I wanted. Get off and go. Be selfish because they didn't need anything from me, just wanted me to top them...*

All of it bullshit.

The belief that subs were easy was a fallacy, because they were anything but.

I'd been a fucker back then, but I wasn't anymore. One of the main reasons I hadn't had a sub in years was because I'd realized I didn't deserve one. I'd had no right to label myself a Dom back in the day, so I'd walked away. Now, with Indy, she was changing my life in ways she didn't even know.

These kinds of relationships were incredibly complicated. So bogged down with minutiae that there was nothing *easy* about them at all. So it'd been a relief to stop when I'd gone vanilla. Most of the club-whores liked to be spanked—hell, they got off on anything that meant they had center stage for a little while so I got to be rough with them, and it ticked all my boxes.

It was only when I'd come to learn what Indy needed, that I realized she was perfect for me in ways I hadn't even known mattered, and where the desire to dominate her morphed into being. I hadn't regretted a thing this far.

But today, with this shit with my mom going down, I did a little. Not because I didn't get a thrill out of seeing Indy like this, but because I'd been around long enough to know when a storm was coming. Indy had already been through too much, and I didn't want her to be tainted by me because tainted she'd be. Just by proxy.

Thoughts like those weren't why I was here, though.

I hadn't seen her in a few nights so I knew she'd have slept like shit.

That was, I realized, when you knew you cared about someone. When their fucking sleep mattered more than you getting your rocks off.

Dropping into a squat a few feet from her, I repeated, "Were you a good girl, Indy?" because I wanted a genuine answer, one that wasn't dosed with more sarcasm than cinnamon sugar on a churro.

She was quiet for a second, like she always was once I'd taken things down a notch or two. With her sarcasm fading into a distant memory, it was a reminder of why I'd taken to greeting her this way, mostly because the Indy that the rest of the world saw wasn't the real Indy. It was an act.

A show.

I didn't want that bullshit between us.

If I was going to do this, if I was going to be *this* and if I was going to taint her, then it had to be real. No lies. Only the truth would do.

As she shed off that second skin she wore for protection, her back remained perfectly still. I'd love to strip her off, see her prostrate on the floor with her tits smashing into her armpits with the pressure of the pose, but beggars couldn't be choosers. If I'd warned her I was here, after sneaking in while David was using the bathroom and she was inking someone, using the key she'd begrudgingly given me to get out in the morning so I could leave for work before her, then she could have prepared... That was the advantage of her working and living in the same building. She could have stripped the second she hit the private area, then walked up the stairs to her apartment.

Next time...

And Christ, there *had* to be a next time because as I sat here, watching her, sweet fuck, I *needed* it as much as she did.

"It was a good day and a bad day," she said at long last.

I never could tell if my silence worked on her, or if it took her that long to cast off that other Indy.

"Why?"

"Stone came in. She had her brand inked on. I worked on Steel's back piece. He has her name tatted on him. It's old." She swallowed. "Really old."

I arched a brow at that. "For as long as he's been pushing her away, I guess?"

She hummed. "It's funny..."

"What is?"

"Stone's real name is Pierre."

My brow furrowed. "Isn't that a guy's name?"

"Yeah, well, that's Stone's Ma for you. Dumb bitch."

"Wait..." My lips twitched. "So Steel's been walking around with a guy's name inked on his back for a decade?"

"Pretty much." She smiled, and her head shifted slightly so she could see me better. It didn't work, but I liked that she tried. Enough that I got to my feet, moved closer so she could see me from her position, and I didn't just crouch down, I crossed my legs at the ankle and got comfortable by placing my hands flat to the ground and leaning back.

"You made it butch?"

"It was pretty plain before," she murmured. "I was really just refreshing it. The lines were getting blurry."

"When Stone and Steel got together, you told me you'd already designed her brand—did she like it?"

Her smile made another appearance. "She did."

"I'm glad," I told her simply.

"Giulia came in too. She wants more ink. We talked about her working for me for a while."

"Really? She has work at the clubhouse though."

She sniffed. "Relying on you fuckers for money will put her in the poorhouse."

"If poorhouses still existed," I pointed out. "We're not exactly living in a Charles Dickens' book."

Indy rolled her eyes. "You're probably the only biker in that clubhouse who knows who Dickens is."

I snorted. "You have met your brother, right? And Rex and Maverick? They're clever—"

Huffing, she muttered, "I know, I know. Just saying, is all. There are different kinds of clever. Rex could wage a world war and win but talking about *British* literature, even just mentioning it, would turn him cross-eyed."

"Watch the sass or your butt will sting some more," I said calmly.

Her nose crinkled, but said butt wiggled, making me smile at the sight. Even if she didn't want a spanking, that ass of hers did.

She'd get it too. Just not as a welcome home.

"What's she going to do at Indiana Ink?" I queried, curious, and wondering if Nyx knew his woman and his sister had plans that they definitely hadn't asked the club about.

"Help David out at first." She grunted, then like she was telling me a secret worthy of the Secret Service, admitted, "But I've been thinking about bringing a full-time piercer into the studio."

A cough escaped me. "Giulia? You want her as a piercer? Is she trained?"

"No, she isn't trained for anything, and I'd like to change that. I'll invest in her if I can tie her to the studio, and considering she suggested it, I figured she'd probably get a kick out of it. She's sadistic enough by nature."

"Exactly what you want in a fucking piercer."

She grinned, and it did something to me, something to my goddamn insides to see that smile. "True, dat."

"She can pierce your nipples when you think she's ready," I said softly, and my tone had her tensing.

"Who said I was piercing them?"

"Me? I've been thinking about it for a while. Just never liked the idea of another dude seeing your tits."

A shaky breath escaped her. "C-Cruz?"

I hummed.

"You have no say over my body."

"I have full say over your body," I returned, my voice calm.

"I don't belong to you."

"You do." I arched a brow. "You haven't moved a fucking muscle," I told her softly, watching as she registered that. Even though she didn't like my words, she still stayed right where I'd left her.

Head turned to the side, cheek touching the hall rug. Back sloping to the high angle of her ass in the air, knees on the ground, feet tucked together.

She licked her lips, but other than that, still didn't move. "What's happening? This is too much."

I reached over and stroked my hands through her hair, bunching it together and letting it fall over her shoulder so it was out of the way. "I know it is. I don't think either of us intended it to go this far, did we?"

Her eyes were glued to mine. "No."

I carried on stroking her hair, trying to calm her. "By the time you'll let Giulia anywhere near your tits, we'll be ready to process things then, won't we?"

She blinked. "Y-Yeah, I guess." My smile had her swallowing. "Why?"

"Why, what?"

"Why are you investing so much time and effort in me?"

The words took me aback. Whatever I'd expected her to say, it sure as fuck wasn't that, and they had anger rippling through me. Anger that a fucking angel like this one could think that sort of shit about herself.

"Because you're not worth my time and effort?" Me? A fucking one-percenter biker, whose mom was a psychotic FBI agent, and who I was betraying to save the family I really cared about—my club.

I cleaned up corpses for the MC, deleted the evidence so that no shit would fall back on us. I was the Grim Reaper. Too dirty to lick *her* fucking boots, and she was asking me that?

Because I was angry at her lack of self-worth, the desire to punish her was a strong one. It hit me hard, how much I wanted her to see herself for what she was, but I couldn't achieve that through castigation. It required trust.

She had to trust me, had to have faith in me, to believe anything I had to say.

She was right—that took time and effort. Time and effort I wouldn't necessarily give to a fuck buddy, but I had to face the facts.

I'd never have fucked her in the first place if being a fuck buddy was all I wanted.

Nyx was psychotic enough to kill kid fuckers for a hobby. Did that sound like the kind of twisted bastard I needed hammering on my door because I was messing with his sister?

Nope.

I'd been all in from the start, and I just hadn't fucking realized it.

My response to her interested me, enough that I knew I'd be exploring it later, when she was sleeping or I was home, and I murmured, "When you trust me, I'll tell you why."

She frowned. "That's a non-answer if ever I heard one."

I smiled at her. "It's all the answer you're going to get. Now, by the sounds of it, you had a good day. What went wrong?"

"Laura came in. It was really tough." She winced. "She screamed twice."

"Christ." I blew out a breath, well acquainted with the name of the stubborn woman who bore thick mastectomy scars that Indy was working on covering up through torturous sessions that had both women sweating bullets.

Pro, fucking, bono.

And she asked why she was worth my time and effort?

Goddamn that kid fucker uncle of hers.

If Nyx hadn't already jammed his hunting rifle so the cartridge blew back on itself, exploding Kevin's head clean off his shoulders, I'd have had to come up with some twisted ways to get rid of the sick son of a bitch.

Ways that involved acid.

Lots, and lots of acid. In fact, more acid than alkali just to really burn the fucker.

"Yeah," she whispered softly. "It was intense. Messed with my head. But it was okay when Steel and Stone came in. They cheered me up."

"I'm glad. Sounds like you were good."

"I wasn't."

I arched a brow. "Why weren't you?"

"I used my vibrator this morning."

I didn't have to see my smile in the mirror to know it was one thing and one thing only—unholy.

She registered it too and did the wise thing.

Gulped.

TWELVE
INDY

THERE WAS something strange about what I had going on with Cruz.

I didn't have to tell him the truth but somehow, I always ended up doing exactly that.

It was weird. Especially when he usually slapped the shit out of my ass or came up with different ways to mess with my head in the aftermath of such an admission, but I never felt as good as when I told him the truth.

If I was a Catholic, I'd say it was absolution and that nothing felt better than a cleaner soul.

But Cruz was the last person anyone should ever expect absolution from. Sweet Jesus, the rumor was he disposed of the bodies for the MC. I mean, I could have asked, but even if I did, what was he going to say?

'Yeah, I chop up corpses and feed them to the pigs for my brothers. You got a problem with that?'

Not exactly the kind of conversation people in a... shit. What were we?

In a relationship?

Still fuck buddies?

He thought he had the right to say what went down with my nipples.

I was sitting in my hallway with my cheek kissing the floor because of him, for God's sake.

Nothing about this was normal.

Nothing had ever made me feel better than being with him, either.

That had to mean something, didn't it?

His smile in the face of my admission had me gnawing on my lip. I recognized that smile—it usually led to me climaxing.

His hand smoothed over my nape, down the length of my spine, over my ass and straight between my legs which I, quite generously, spread slightly so he could get access to the goods.

A shaky breath escaped me as he ran those tatted fingers along the split of my pussy, and I swallowed as need walloped me worse than a fist to the solar plexus.

When he carried on moving down, down, circling my clit, I arched my back some, then grunted when he spanked me there. A hiss bellowed from me when he did it three more times.

"Where is it?"

I groaned when he rubbed my clit again, but though I was starting to slide toward that delicious space only he sent me to, I wasn't that far gone that I didn't have a clue what he was talking about.

"Nightstand."

"I didn't know you had a vibrator."

"It's new."

His fingers struck again. Making me hiss, again. "I'll introduce things like that."

Though his words triggered irritation, something about them also made me wriggle my hips some more.

He surged to his feet, shocking me until I realized he was heading for my bedroom, not the front door.

Relief hit me because he was unpredictable, enough that I never knew what he'd do next, which always kept me on edge. He was quite capable of leaving me high and dry. Not because he was a bastard, but because I frequently misbehaved. Even though being *good* felt so wonderful, complying with his every whim made me feel like a trapped dancing bear, tethered to a pole, forced to dance for food.

Not that *he* made me feel that way, more like *I* made me feel that way. But around him, I was as normal as I could be, and like a brat, I tended to act out. If that didn't make me realize I was a fool, I didn't know what would.

Hearing the nightstand drawer opening then closing, shortly after, his boots clomped toward me again. He crouched at my side upon his return, dousing the area with his clean scent. Most people assumed bikers were dirty—like their jobs necessitated they stank. Dumb fucks.

No one smelled as good as Cruz.

Not even Nyx. Even if my bro did smell a little like he'd overdosed on aftershave.

Cruz was clean, scented of male. I could stick my nose into his armpit and die and go to heaven.

Not that heaven was for me…

"Hold this."

The shocking pink vibe was shoved at me, and grabbing it, I waited for him to act. His hands moved to my waistband which he plucked. Realizing it was elasticated, he snatched the vibe from me and, tunneling his hand underneath my trunk, grabbed the waistband with his free hand and with the other, shoved the pink monster beneath it and between my legs.

"Good girl," he breathed, and I hated that I blushed.

One of his earlier 'orders' was never to wear panties. Every morning, I argued with myself when I stood in front of my underwear drawer. Being bossed around pissed me off, but there was something I liked about going commando under my clothes. Something that made me feel deliciously dirty, and not in the way I felt on the regular.

Sullied.

Used…

Cruz never made me feel that way. If anything, he took those feelings away.

Was it any wonder he was addictive?

With no panties to protect me, the vibe was situated between my pussy lips, and with a little tussle with the strong Lycra yoga pants, he managed to turn it on.

A yelp escaped me even though I prepared myself for the buzz, but when he started switching through the settings until he hit the fastest one, I tensed up as the vibration felt better than I'd like.

Which meant I was wet already.

It kind of felt like a pencil being sharpened when I wasn't—I'd tried that this morning. Then I'd watched a bit of porn, got myself lubed up and I'd tried to get off.

It hadn't worked.

It never did.

I'd had to try though. Cruz's cock wasn't charmed; there was no reason why he and he alone should be able to get me off the way he did.

At least, that had been my working theory pre-vibrator.

Now I was less certain.

Orgasms and Cruz were like mac and cheese. Destined to be together.

God help me.

"Tell me why you bought this," he rasped, his knees making an appearance in my line of sight.

It was easier to focus on the denim than it was on his eyes. Those green orbs saw far too much for my liking.

Even so, I didn't answer, just let my mind fade a little as the vibe did its job.

Like it hadn't done this morning.

A whistle warned me, and only the Lycra protected me from the sharp whack.

Shit.

The ruler.

It didn't connect with my butt though… it hit my sit spots.

"Christ!" I squealed as the sensitive flesh protested the move, sending my pain receptors into overdrive.

Jerking and wiggling moved the vibrator which was a kind of torture in and of itself. Especially as I prepared myself for two more… only, this time, he didn't stop at three. He carried on. The fucker. Up and down the backs of my thighs, only the Lycra stopping the sting but not the whack. I jolted each and every time, hating that with each jolt, it was like him moving the vibrator. My heart started to beat double time, quickening and quickening as my skin began to turn dewy in response. My mouth began to dry, my tits ached, my pussy grew wetter and emptier as the dull vibrations pounded through my sex.

I came.

It hit me out of nowhere, timed only with the regular pattern of his spanking me with the ruler he'd left in my nightstand drawer.

A howl escaped me as pleasure surged through my veins, and I writhed on my knees, uncaring that my joints were aching, uncaring that my body was starting to protest the position. I cried out when the pleasure dropped off but his spanks didn't.

I knew I'd bruise.

I was glad.

"Tell me why," he growled.

He tapped the vibrator with the ruler.

I squealed.

The pleasure turned to discomfort as my clit protested the constant vibration.

Eyes blurring, I whispered, "O-Okay." I fell silent as he hit the vibrator again.

And again.

Three times total.

A shaky breath gusted from my dry mouth and I squeaked, "I wanted to come by myself."

He stopped spanking me.

"Thought you found it hard to do that?"

He sounded confused.

I couldn't blame him.

"Impossible, not hard."

My sexuality and I were frenemies at best, nemeses at worst.

Masturbation did nothing for me. Porn got me jonesing for the normalcy of sex.

Before Cruz, I'd never orgasmed.

Not once.

And I'd slept around a lot.

A lot, a lot.

Back when I'd been apprenticing, especially.

Some could call me a slut. Some, in our world, might think me no better than a clubwhore, but when your sexuality was fucked up from childhood, taking ownership of it, retrieving it from the clutches of a predator wasn't as easy as one, two, fucking three.

He slapped the ruler against the vibrator, jolting me again, but this time, pleasure cascaded through me.

I wasn't sure if I loved or loathed that he could do this for me.

Shuddering, my shoulders bunched as I dealt with the tingles that traveled up and down the length of my spine.

"No using this without me around," he rumbled, which, even worse than the spank, sent delight rushing through me.

I didn't get how I could hate being bossed around, but when he did it, I didn't automatically want to punch him in the throat.

Something didn't make sense here, and I wasn't sure if it was him, me, or just my body. A body that, sometimes, I felt sure belonged to someone else.

Maybe, just maybe, it was his.

The thought had me swallowing nervously, but before I could freak out, I tensed when his boots appeared in my line of sight as he got to his feet, and when the front door opened, I jerked as a gush of wind bellowed between my legs.

"W-What are you doing?" I cried out, but I kept my head down.

"Figure I should let you decide if you need me or if this piece of silicone will do it for you."

He sounded cold.

Calm.

At ease.

By contrast, I was overheated, stressed, and overwrought.

Goddamn, why was he so unpredictable?

Any other man, I'd know he wouldn't walk out because he hadn't gotten his yet. But Cruz was more interested in me getting mine than he was with his own release.

I'd learned that the hard way right from the very beginning.

"N-No, I don't want you to go anywhere."
"Then why buy it?"
"Because I needed to know."
"Know what?"
"If I'd changed."
More silence. But the door didn't close.
"Have you?"
"No."
"Do you want me to help you?"
"Yes."
He hummed. "Your communication skills are lacking."
I blinked. "They are?"
"Yes." He closed the door. "You're an attention seeker."
Outrage filled me. "I am not."
"Yes. You are."
I frowned. "I'm not." I didn't care if he was holding that damn ruler or not. I so totally wasn't a fucking attention seeker.

"It's okay," he said, sounding amused. "Now I know, I can deal with you better." His hand went to my waistband and, out of nowhere, I heard the flick of a flip knife. My heart boomed in my ears as the cold metal tip pressed into my skin at the base of my back, not hard enough to penetrate but for me to feel the steel before he lifted it and ran the blade through my pants.

Within seconds, I could feel the air against my slit. And knowing the metal was so close to the molten hot heat of my cunt was enough to make me breathless.

The vibrator flopped out, falling to the floor as, with my yoga pants suddenly crotchless, he grabbed the slit he'd made and pulled it wider open. His knuckles brushed my pussy, but he didn't make a noise, didn't utter a sound as he registered how wet I was. The vibrations continued, the toy fluttering against the floor as if it was a dying fish until he picked it up and pressed it directly to my clit. It was one of those sucker ones, and how he unerringly found the right position had my eyes rolling back into my head.

"You have my attention, Indy," he said smoothly, "what are you going to do with it now that you have it?"

I had no answer, but I knew he was waiting on one. I jerked up, my hips rocking high as I tried to fuck the toy he was holding, and he let me.

God, he let me.

Until I was coming again.

The air was stolen from my lungs, a flood of heat powered through me, and as I screamed out my release, he pulled the toy away so I was fucking air and switched off the vibrator.

He loomed over me then, getting to his feet as I caught my breath. "I want you on your hands and knees, Indy. You're going to crawl on all fours into the bedroom."

I should have argued, but I didn't. Feeling drugged from the pleasure that was still rocketing around my system like a demented wasp in a cardboard box, I sluggishly righted myself, stacking my hands under my shoulders as I began crawling.

My knees ached the second they connected with the wooden floor, and I grimaced as, with each movement, my pussy lips brushed together, sending sparks through my system.

When I made it, I wasn't sure what hurt worse. My joints or my pussy from how empty it felt.

Christ, I'd somehow managed to cockblock myself. That was definitely a feat.

"Onto the bed, on your knees, face to the comforter. Pussy facing the door."

I did as bid, registering how unalike the furtive fumblings I'd had in the past this was, and when I assumed the position, I shivered when he said, "Show me that pretty cunt. Spread your lips wide, Indy."

Gulping, I reached between my legs and slipped my fingers between my labia. Carefully pulling the petals of my sex apart, I bared myself to him.

"How much of my attention do you think you can handle, Indy?"

He always said my name.

I wasn't sure if he knew how much I appreciated that.

"Indy?" he repeated.

"I-I want all your attention."

"I don't think you do. Otherwise you'd have called me instead of buying a vibrator."

"I wasn't cheating on you," I rasped.

"No? Is your pussy easily replaced with one of the pussies at the clubhouse?"

Tension whipped at me. "No." I knew my voice was stony, and for good reason. "But a vibrator isn't another man," I ground out.

He laughed, but I heard him moving about the room and it was damn hard to stop myself from twisting around to see what he was doing.

I bit my lip, feeling oddly exposed which shone a light on how liberated I felt.

There was no modesty permitted between Cruz and me.

And I fucking loved it.

When the chair opposite my bed squeaked, I tried to picture how he'd look, his legs crossed, one of his ankles hovering on his knee as he watched me.

He could do this for a while.

His patience was better than mine, and I worked on people's bodies for a living. Inking lines and forming memories on their skin for hours on end. If anyone understood patience, it was me, but Cruz was different. He was capable of putting me in the spotlight for hours at a time.

Shit, maybe he was right. Maybe I *was* an attention seeker, because even if it hurt, there was nothing better than being in his spotlight.

"You want my dick all for yourself, hmm?"

I clenched my teeth. "It depends."

"On? Whether I want your pussy all for myself?"

"Yes."

"Jingles came on to me today."

My eyes flared wide. "That bitch—"

"—was just doing her job. Especially as nobody knows about me and you, do they?"

Brow puckering because I wasn't sure where he was going with this, I just asked, "No. They don't."

"You want to stake a claim on me, Indy, then a claim needs to be staked." He sucked in a breath. "However, I want you to know something before you make a decision."

"What?" I rasped, because whatever I'd expected him to say, it wasn't *any* of this.

"Being with me means putting yourself in danger."

He didn't have to tell me that. Ever since that night when I'd had a nightmare, my heart had been in danger, and it sucked because I was that walking cliche I hated.

Going gaga for a guy, losing myself along the way. I'd always vowed to avoid that particular fate, but I'd failed.

Even worse, I'd fallen for a goddamn biker.

He wasn't wrong about the danger. Just being with a Sinner was to invite a whole underworld's worth of trouble my way. Being a sister to two of them as well? More than an invitation. I might as well have spread my legs for fate and begged it to come and fuck me now to get it over with.

"What kind of danger?" I asked. "The usual?"

"No. Very unusual."

I licked my lips. "Is it council-sanctioned?"

"Yes. It is now."

Meaning it hadn't been.

Warily, I asked, "It *is* club business, then?"

"Yeah. That's why I can't talk about it."

"Does Nyx know about it? And, if he does, would he kill you for getting me involved in it?"

He snorted. "Nyx would slaughter me if I was a missionary and was trying to solve world peace if it meant he knew about us being together."

"True," I conceded with a grimace. "But you know what I mean."

"He does know, and he'd kill me but he'd have killed me if it wasn't something I'd brought to the council's attention. As it stands… I'm not an enemy of the clubhouse."

As I pondered that, I switched gears. "You want to brand me?"

"No. Not yet. You haven't earned my brand yet."

Christ, that shouldn't have twisted up my insides, but it did. And *not* with outrage, either.

Every feminist sensibility in me should have been shrieking, but when he talked like that it hit me right between the legs.

"Do you want me to earn it?" I whispered, and the question was momentous because earning a brand was something I'd never wanted.

But Cruz's?

Christ, I could deal with his. Only his.

"Yeah. I do."

"What made you come to this decision?"

"Realized if any pussy was gonna have a say in my life, on my decisions, over my choices, I wanted it to be you."

I blinked. "Romantic."

"About as romantic as I get." His laughter, however, told me otherwise, which made me wonder if he *could* be romantic, and how that'd look—mind-blowing, probably. "Especially as we're having this conversation with you holding that pretty pussy on full display. You want my tongue on it? Sucking on your clit?"

Gulping, and knowing nothing was better than him going down on me which had gifted me my first addictive orgasm, I rasped, "I do."

"Make a decision, then. It's now or never, Indy."

"W-What do you mean?"

"I mean that tonight's the last night or the first night. The decision is yours."

I didn't even have to think about it.

A millisecond later, I told him, "First night."

"Good answer." The chair creaked as he stood up.

Anticipation washed through me, making me tremble.

I wasn't sure what I'd just agreed to, aside from coming out to the Sinners, and to be frank, they wouldn't give a fuck. Nyx would, but he was a miserable asshole anyway. Giulia had cheered him up, but that didn't mean she'd given him a personality in part exchange for a brand.

The bed jostled as he leaned on it, and without touching me, he managed to stick his tongue in my slit.

"Jesus," I moaned as he fluttered it up and down my pussy. Pushing my forehead into the comforter, I fought and failed to keep my hips still, knowing full well what would happen if I moved.

When he stopped, I groaned.

His hand smoothed over the backs of my thighs, rubbing up and down the flesh he'd whacked with the ruler before. It was surprisingly sensitive, proving that the Lycra yoga pants hadn't done much to protect me in the long run, but my skin tingled, heating up with his touch.

The knife made another appearance as he plucked the fabric away from my skin, and it made a scraping noise as he cut it from my body.

This wasn't the first time he'd done this, and I knew no matter how hard I bitched later on, it wouldn't be the last.

I enjoyed it, if I was being honest.

I liked being clothed around him. Liked him cutting it off me.

Sure, it was a waste of clothes, but I'd start going to the thrift store if it meant letting this carry on.

When my pants were in shreds, he tipped the knife backward and scraped the non-cutting side down my thighs next. I hissed at the cold metal as it brushed me there, then tensed when he scraped up. A shiver washed through me when the butt of the knife slipped between the crack of my ass, down, down, until it rubbed against my clit. My hips arched up, which instantly had one of his arms banding around my thighs and holding me in place while, with the other, he continued to rub my clit.

"Oh fuck," I moaned, my skin flushing, sweat beading, heat popping through my system as the cold handle made its presence known against my delicate flesh.

Pushing my face into the comforter, I let him touch me there, uncaring that he was holding me down now. If anything, I liked it. I liked the grounding sensation.

A whimper escaped me when he moved the knife away, and a shiver of want rushed through me when, suddenly, it wasn't the weapon but his tongue once more.

Which was capable of far more deadly force where my clit was concerned.

The second he touched me there, I felt like I lit up, like I was ground zero for a bomb. As if I was about to explode, shatter into a million pieces just from the first swipe of his tongue down my center.

My pussy was so damn wet that with each pass of the tensile muscle, a squelching sound emanated from the area, and unlike every other guy I'd fucked, of which there'd been many, he was the only one who'd ever made me wet. So that noise, for another woman, might have been embarrassing. For me? It was like heaven had a sound.

I shuddered as he slurped on my clit, sucking it between his lips, the little pearl palpated against them, before he sucked down hard, making me yelp as I was still sensitive from before. I jerked, pussy clenching, rippling deep inside from how fucking empty I was.

All my life, I *liked* being empty. With Cruz? Nope. I wanted to be full. So fucking full of him.

A keening noise escaped me when he made a smacking sound against my clit, and he took it between his teeth, carefully rubbing it there, not to hurt, just to make me feel the difference between his lips and tongue.

When he pulled back, murmuring, "You feel empty, Indy?"

"I-I do."

"You deserve my dick?"

I released a shaky breath. Christ, I wanted to say yes, but I knew what he'd think. Knew he'd punish me first, so I sucked it up and sucked it in and rasped, "N-No."

He hummed. "Good answer. Why don't you?"

"Shouldn't have bought that goddamn vibrator," I said on a hiss as he swiped down through my slit, slipping the tip of his tongue into me. Of its own volition, my cunt grasped at it, but it was to no avail.

Cruz wouldn't be captured.

I knew that like I knew I found it impossible to orgasm.

Unless I was with him.

I shuddered, my shoulders hunching, back bowing as he repeated that, swiping through my sex like I was an ice cream that was melting and that he needed to catch the drips. I felt like I was something delectable—he made me feel that way. Not something dirty, tainted. Something beautiful and delicious.

Groaning when he pulled back, I was prepared for the barrage of spanks. Didn't stop me from yelping. If anything, I spread my legs wider. The clatter of the ruler against sopping wet flesh had a keening cry escaping me as he carried on, more and more until I knew my ass had to be more than just pink. I knew it would be bright red, burning like his annoyance with me.

When he stopped, he wasn't even panting hard, but I was. My breaths drowned out the sound of my heart, my skin was clammy, my pussy was desperate, and I was running both hot and cold.

Hands clenching into the covers, I rocked my hips, focused only on one thing—him. Getting him inside me. It was a dangerous move, but I had to try. This emptiness, after a lifetime of it, was more than I could stand.

"You trying to tempt me, Indy?" he rumbled, his voice low and raspy.

I grunted. "My ass is on fire," I hissed, hoping irritation would shadow the need, hiding it from him.

His laughter was as low as his voice. Just as wicked.

Then his hand was there, rubbing over the backs of my thighs, and I closed my eyes. The second he did, I wanted to weep over how fucked up I was. I tensed, awaiting the barrage of memories, but they didn't show up. My nerves were tangled up with pain, with the agony of his spanking, too embroiled in the violence he'd just shown me to remember before.

They could only handle the now.

Just like every other part of me.

With every ounce of me standing at attention, I whimpered when he made it a point to really rub the tender flesh. I hissed, hobbling from knee to knee, but it was worth it when, a few seconds later, he stopped, and the bed jostled.

Groaning with relief, I waited, hoping he'd just take me, but he didn't. His jeans were cold against my thighs, rough and coarse against the sensitive flesh. His chest still sported a Henley and his cut. He might still have been wearing his leather boots, I wasn't sure. I just loved that he was covered. Loved it even as I wanted him bare-assed naked.

But that'd come later.

Much later.

With his knee, he parted my legs as he pushed on my shoulders, pressing me deeper into the covers so that my back arched higher. His cock was there, at my entrance. I could feel it bobbing through my folds like I bobbed for fucking apples as a kid at a Halloween party, and he covered me, all of me, his hands sliding around my waist, moving to my tits.

Kevin, for all he'd forced me, had been delicate. Gentle.

He'd kissed.

He'd worshipped.

He'd...

God, the memories.

I wished he'd been as brutal with the other stuff as he had been with the penetration, because at least that wouldn't make it so fucking horrendous when a guy tried to suck on my nipples or when he kissed my neck, his lips trailing over my flesh as he headed down south.

Gentle and tender were reminders.

The way Cruz squeezed my breasts?

Painful.

It was a shock. Such a fucking shock that I yelped again as he squeezed, bringing blood to the surface. And as he hurt me there, in contrast to Kevin, he slid into my pussy as easy as walking through a damn door.

God, everything was a study in contrast.

He was so fucking clever.

Somehow, he knew. He fucking knew, and like my knight in goddamn inked armor, he gave me what my body wanted, what my brain needed to forget.

As I focused on the pain in my tits, it took a second to process the feeling of fullness. When I did, his hands slid to my neck and as he pressed them around me there, he jerked me up so that I had no choice but to rest my weight on the tips of my fingers. I only had a second though. As his grip tightened around my throat, it began, and he raised me higher so I had no support.

Nothing but him to rely on.

Terrifying, *petrifying*, but oh, so right too.

Now he was inside, it was different. My brain had clicked onto exactly *who* this was, and he knew it. He knew because I wasn't struggling. I was compliant. I was here. Ready and waiting for anything this bastard, my fucking savior, could give me.

He choked me. There was no kinder way to describe it, but as he did, his words were in my ear, his heat all around me. His hands might have stolen my oxygen, but his body gave back to me in ways he'd never understand. His thrusts were hard, deep. He barely bucked his hips as he slid out and in, and with each pass, I could feel the fog as my deprived lungs strained.

"You need me, Indy, don't you?"

"You feel my cock inside you, Indy?"

"Whose cock is fucking you, Indy?"

"I'm Cruz, Indy. Cruz. Fucking spell it in your head."

The words had my lips trembling, my eyelashes fluttering, and I gasped out, "Cruz."

Not a safe word.

The key to the door.

He let go immediately. One hand slipped between my legs and he began to frig my clit as fast as he started to fuck me.

My torso slammed into the mattress, my body battled to right itself after being starved of oxygen, but even more than that, it struggled with the pleasure.

It hit me like he'd hit my ass—only, it smacked me in the face. A high pitched cry escaped me, so loud that, another time, I'd be grateful no one lived next door and that both buildings either side used the upstairs as storage. As pleasure walloped me like a tsunami, shadows overtook me.

Loading my mind with a blackness that tasted of sin, scented of Cruz, and felt like paradise.

THIRTEEN

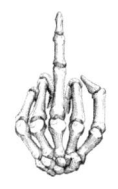

CRUZ

WHEN SHE LET GO, when subspace hit, I let myself go too. My cum slalomed into her, hard and fast as my hips bucked after I strained to reach my own orgasm. Her pussy clenched around me so fucking ferociously, it choked my cock, leaving me no choice but to slump over her in the aftermath.

Before, I'd never have done that.

I'd known she was unusual, right from the start. Things with Indy had always been aggressive. At first, it had been a turn on. The Dom in me liked that she was quick to act, willing to be violent. *At first*. Then, quickly, I'd realized she got nothing out of it.

Nothing.

She made all the right noises, then she'd turn off the second I touched her. I knew a woman's body, knew hers even more. Disarming her was the only way forward I'd soon learned, then, she'd had that nightmare, and suddenly everything made sense, and I knew what she needed. Not because I was some kind of fucking guru, but because I knew Indy. She was aggressive by nature. Could butt heads with her biker brothers. Was independent enough to have made a name for herself in a male-dominated industry, and was ferocious enough to fight the way she did pre-fuck.

I warmed her up with violence. Messed with her nerves, made them clamor in silent alarm so that she could deal with skin-to-skin contact.

I teased her with control. Made her bow to me, relinquishing all thoughts, all worries, all stresses and strains.

I dominated her with strength. Taking her weakness, owning it, protecting it. Giving her rules and parameters, letting her take ownership of the one thing she did control—her body.

Finally, I fucked her with fire. Taking what I needed, knowing full well that, once primed, she was more than along for the ride.

Pressing a kiss to her still-clad shoulders, I carefully pulled out of her. Things had stopped being playful a long while back for me, and Indy was just too fucking easy to love.

I grabbed the shirt, plucking it off her back like I had her pants, then I reached for the knife I'd dropped on the mattress and cut that off her too.

I didn't nick her bra though, because that was the one thing she hated replacing, and though she never complained about it, just sighed when she stared at the pretty bits of lace I'd destroyed, I decided to reward that by simply unfastening it until she was bare ass naked. Only then did I climb off the bed. As I stripped out of my Henley, cut, and jeans, toeing out of my boots, I studied her.

She was tense enough to stay upright, zoned enough to be insensate. I sometimes watched subs in subspace and felt envy. That freedom was something I'd crave myself if I didn't believe freedom was bullshit. Except, with Indy, I truly hoped it wasn't. I hoped for more. Because she deserved it. She deserved a break from the past, to be free of the cage of her memories.

As for myself, I was just glad I was the one holding the key to that cage.

Naked now, I headed to the bathroom. That was full of girly froufrou shit as well. Considering these buildings weren't really supposed to be residential, I figured she owned this place and had decided to live in it simply because she worked crazy hours. It was eleven at night now, but she'd only just finished up and that was because it was midweek. Weekends, she worked even longer shifts.

Still, for all this place was commercial, she'd prettied it up. The bathroom consisted of a cast iron clawfoot tub, a small shower cubicle, a toilet and a vanity that was loaded down with candles and that dried flower shit. The stuff that didn't really smell after a while and was just a dust collector. Well, maybe in other women's homes, but not this one. Indy's dried flower shit was clean. Nothing was dusty. She was pretty anal about cleanliness too. Which always made it amusing to me when I left her on the bed, cum dripping out of her pussy, dirty as fuck.

Knowing the drill, a drill we'd slowly worked into, and one that was going to pretty much be the blueprint for the future—and I definitely saw us having a future—I took a leak then started the water in the bath.

As I did, I thought back to that night where I'd seen her and wanted her. I mean, I was a guy. I'd been attracted to her for a while, but *the* night where I'd seen her for real would stick with me for years.

When I'd watched her, on her hands and fucking knees, scrubbing the floor with one of those nail brushes?

I'd been pretty sure I was about to cum in my pants.

Cleaning was imperative to me. Not because I was anal or OCD, but DNA was my enemy. Eradicating it, and evidence, was my life's goddamn work. So watching her could only have been hotter if she'd been cleaning nak—

Huh.

I scratched my chin as I thought about that as my next punishment. I'd love to watch her scrub the fucking floor, pussy and tits bare, then have it end with her sucking me off.

Christ.

I was getting another boner, and I was way too fucking old for that shit. Of course, I'd been way too fucking old most of my life.

As I poured some of the crap she liked into the tub, allowing the perfume that Indy scented of most days to fill the bathroom, I sucked in a deep breath before I twisted around and headed back toward the bed.

She hadn't moved.

That came as no shock.

If I'd ever seen anyone be fuck-drunk, it was her.

Lips twitching at the thought, I moved over to the bedside, stared at her and found myself unable to do anything other than run my fingers through the cum that was bubbling out of her slit. Fuck, I loved cream pies and I rarely got them.

That was why it was hilarious Jingles thought she could sway me with her tits and ass. You needed to double bag your dick if you approached any of the clubwhores. Where was the fun in that?

Indy had an IUD, which was a good thing because I had no intention of being a dad, not after the shit I'd done, seen, and learned, but the sight of a woman's cunt drenched in my cum…delicious.

Even better when it was *her* cunt.

She twitched at my touch, but I didn't stop. My fingers toyed with her even as I reached down and jacked off a little, not really wanting to get another boner but wanting to just enjoy the moment when Indy's defenses were down. Not in a creepy way, just in a way that meant she was allowing me in, which was hard-earned.

For the rest of the night, she'd be pliant, until she woke up, the day fucked her over, and when I got near her again, I'd have to warm her up once more.

A douche might ask if she was worth it—just like she had earlier.

But a douche didn't know what Indy was worth, period. Just like her.

There was a reason I was allowing myself back into this world—because she needed it. She needed me to be this man, to be the kind of guy who could erase her mind like I hit Ctrl+Alt and then Delete, and when I sensed her suffering, I felt like I had no alternative but to give her some relief. To give her freedom the only way I knew how.

A moan escaped her, another clue that she was coming down from her high, and she rocked her hips against my hand.

"Cruz," she said thickly, body undulating against the covers.

I clenched my jaw at how she said my name, how she always said my fucking name when she was like this. I sometimes wondered if this was the Indy she should always have been, before her cunt of an uncle had gotten to her, but there was no point in thinking shit like that.

Here and now, this was Indy, and while I wished better for her, I thought she was pretty fucking amazing as she was.

With my fingers sticky with our mingled cum, I pulled back, amused when I saw her lips twist into a pout. Her eyes popped open, and lazily, she grumbled, "Why'd you stop?"

"Want the water to run over?"

She heaved a sigh then, she made my dick harder by opening her mouth and accepted the offering of my fingers without my even having to say a word.

Fuck, I loved a smart sub and, without a shadow of a doubt, Indy was a sub. Each and every time she let me dominate her and loved it, I thought she'd never let me back in again, but she did. She needed this just as much as I did, but that didn't mean she'd want me around for good.

And that was something I had to work on.

I stuck the digits between her lips, letting her suck them clean. She moaned, the vibration throbbing through my flesh as her tongue sucked between the webbing of my fingers as she took them deep. When she was done, I thrust them a little deeper, watching her with interested eyes as she gagged. Her eyelids didn't pop open, there was no distrust or displeasure or a silent plea to stop, she just took what I gave her.

She always fucking did.

Growling under my breath, I pulled back after I stopped tickling her tonsils because I had no desire for her to puke tonight. Maybe another night, I'd be okay with it, but I really didn't want the mess. I'd had a fucker of a day, I wanted to bathe my woman, maybe come again, then sleep with one of her tits in my hand and my cock in her cunt.

Heaven.

Plus, whenever she was so compliant, as much of a turn on as it was, sometimes it pissed me off. I wasn't her uncle. I preferred her struggles sometimes, because I wasn't sure if I'd earned her compliancy. Then, she'd grumble, and my world would right itself once more.

So when I pulled away, and she pouted, my lips twitched, and my annoyance fled.

Corruption was sweet.

She slumped forward, then rolled onto her back, that skin of hers like goddamn gold against the lavender comforter. I took a second to appreciate the view, then decided I needed more than a second. Fuck the water.

Ducking down, I grabbed my jeans from the floor, then found my cell in the pocket. I took a picture of her, then grumbled, "Spread your legs." She obeyed, but her eyes were glued to me as I shuffled around the foot of the bed for the best view. Taking a shot, I murmured, "Stick your fingers inside your cunt. Show me how messy you are down there."

Again, she obeyed, but her back rippled, arching her tits up and rocking her hips down as the order flushed her with pleasure.

Such a dominant little bitch in her real life but so eager to obey when that front door was closed.

Humming, I took a couple more shots, before I dropped my cell on the bed where it bounced then I grabbed her feet, dragged her down the sheets as she squealed in surprise and hauled her into my arms.

I was a little scrawny by comparison to most of the brothers who all looked like they'd been eating steroid-laced spinach, but I was strong. I had to be. My job involved hauling dead bodies around and massive vats of chemicals to destroy evidence. What about that sounded lightweight? But when she was in my arms, she was safe, secure. I wasn't sure if that was an oxymoron or not.

I was no one's idea of a safe harbor, but I'd never hurt Indy. Every fucker else, sure. But Indy, no. She'd wormed her way into my affection, burrowing deeper than that in all honesty. So deep I didn't know what the fuck to do about it.

Rubbing my lips against her temple as she settled into the crook of my arms, I padded through to the bathroom. I placed her beside the toilet then murmured, "Go pee."

She heaved a sigh, her eyes mutinous for the first time, and I merely arched a brow and boomed the order, "Pee."

"Can't you give me some privacy?"

"No such thing as privacy between you and me," I reminded her calmly. "And for arguing, I'm gonna stand here and fucking watch you wipe when I'd have gotten into the bath before."

She grimaced but plopped down onto the seat and did her business. Her gaze was on my knees, but I watched her bowed head, seeing the awkwardness as it took her a while before she reached for the paper I already had in my hands and that I gave her.

When she was done, I flushed the toilet before I reached for her hand and said, "Bath time for dirty Indy."

Her nose crinkled. "We're both as dirty as the other."

My lips twitched. "Yeah, but I don't get a boner cleaning myself up."

She grinned at that, her eyes sparkling with glee as I helped her step into the tub. She waited, because she knew how shit rolled now—it hadn't taken long, either. We'd only been exploring this side of things for the past couple weeks, but she knew that I'd treat her like a lady anywhere but when we were playing—and I climbed in behind, then guided her down so that she was sitting between my legs, her back against my chest.

Hissing when I reached down and pulled her legs apart, she muttered, "God, I'm sore."

I hummed, unsurprised. Her back and knees would ache in the morning too from the way I'd had her posed.

Rubbing the tendons either side of her cunt with my hands, I let her wriggle around for a minute before I barked, "Stay still, Indy. I don't want to get another boner just yet."

She snorted. "Is it my fault you're always hard around me?"

"Such a fucking brat," I groused, one hand snapping up to grab her by the throat and pin her against me. She didn't struggle and stopped wriggling as I muttered, "You working up to another punishment, Indy?"

Her eyelids fluttered. "N-No."

"Then let me tend to you, hmm?" My voice was softer, and she sighed, before she buried her face in my inked throat and stayed there.

Content now she was still, pleased she sought solace in me, I carried on with my ministrations, rubbing her there, then rubbing along her thighs to her knees, manipulating her legs like she was a rag doll. Midway, I turned off the faucet with my foot, but the heat of the water worked into her bones, gradually making her limper in my hold.

It was to her detriment that her lack of appreciation of aftercare made me more intent in giving it to her. I was always careful with subs in the aftermath because it could fuck with their heads if you didn't tend to them after, once you'd messed with their minds. But Indy didn't like it.

She didn't want any tenderness from me.

Which, quite naturally, made me give her my brand of it twice as much.

I viewed Indy like a rancher viewed a fractious horse that had cost him a million bucks and that he couldn't get a fucking saddle on. Difference was, I could fuck Indy into letting me saddle her. Not that I was into pony play, but the analogy still worked.

When she was limp in my arms, her breath hot against my throat, her forehead sticky with sweat, I smiled.

There was an irony to the fact that she hated being touched, and me? I loved touching my subs. Loved smothering them in me. Loved being smothered in them.

She'd learn.

There were more ways than one to skin a cat, and Indy'd learn that soon enough.

FOURTEEN

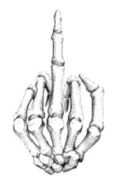

INDY

AFTER OUR BATH, Cruz had rubbed me down then, in his usual way of hauling me around like I weighed less than a bag of flour, carried me to the bed where he'd massaged me from head to toe, humming as he did so.

Though he'd gone to a lot of effort to take away the ache, the next morning I still had to dose myself up with Ibuprofen because my back was hurting like a bastard.

The massage had been nice.

And Google had already told me which song he'd been humming—that Cruz was a closet dance fan came as a surprise. I figured I could hold that against him if he decided to ever share a nude pic of me. If the Sinners knew he liked the DJ, Martin Solveig, I figured that would be my payback.

The thought had me smiling though because I knew Cruz would never do that. He was too intrinsically private. Too shielded. Plus, like any decent killer, he kept trophies. I accepted that, mostly because I was surrounded by murderers.

Death was stock in trade for the careers my brothers had decided to take.

As for myself, death wasn't as terrifying for me as it was for many. I actually liked it, had ever since good old Uncle Kevin had perished at my brother's hands, and it wasn't as if I was an innocent. I had blood on my hands too. Blood shed in self-defense didn't stop it from staining.

"Do you know how creepy it is when you smile like that?"

I cut Giulia a glance. "Creepy? I'm touched."

She rolled her eyes. "You're so like your brother sometimes it's nuts."

"He's nuts."

"You are too." She smirked at me from over the packet of information I'd had Frankie, my regular piercer, send me and which I'd printed off.

Frankie did me a favor by coming in once a week to take care of the appointments I had for piercings, but before they met, there'd be a shit ton of stuff for Giulia to learn before she could even think of starting an apprenticeship.

I grunted, then kicking my boots up onto the sofa as she spun around on the desk chair where David usually had his ass planted, asked, "I'm surprised Nyx isn't in here, giving me shit about the piercing gig."

Giulia snorted. "Indy, I know you haven't seen your brother's dick, and if I saw Hawk's, I know I'd be just as squeamish, but babe, if anything, Nyx is grateful I'm gonna be piercing."

My nose crinkled. "I've heard rumors that there ain't enough space on there for a fucking pinhead, never mind anything else."

A laugh escaped her, but her eyes gleamed with her true amusement. "Always room for one more." She winked at me when I groaned. "Mostly I think he's grateful. If anything, he'll owe you one. He knew I was going to go stir crazy at the compound."

"Imagine that... you not being so cock drunk that you weren't happy just to eat, breathe, and shit the club," I scoffed as I started flipping through the designs I had coming up the rest of the day.

"I know, right? I even talked to him about Quin."

Her voice had softened at the mention of my baby bro's name, and warmth filled me as I peered over the papers at her. "You did that for me?"

"Yeah. Course. I've been working on him for a while." She sucked her lip between her teeth. "I know it might seem like family doesn't mean much to me—"

I blinked at her. "Because you're not unhappy your abusive father is dead and because your brother was a douche who ran off with his stepmom?"

"Don't forget he's potentially a dangerous douche who maybe killed my abusive father." Her nose crinkled. "I mean, he didn't technically abuse me." She pulled a face. "I guess what I mean, he wasn't like… you know, Kevin."

Inside, I cringed, but outwardly, I just said, "Thank fuck for that."

"Yeah." She sighed. "I shouldn't compare, I guess."

I rolled my eyes. "Yeah, because we're all about the technicalities in this world."

She smirked at me. "You're right. He hurt us all. My brothers were a lot more forgiving, though."

"Idiots. Abuse is abuse, Giulia. There's no measure or set of scales that defines how bad it was and if we deserve to be screwed up over it."

"I guess so," she murmured, her tone musing. "Nuts that I think that way, huh?"

"No. Every woman does it. It's inbuilt in us. Hey, he only fingered me—that's not rape, is it? Hey, he only forced me to suck his cock, I guess I'm lucky he didn't penetrate me." I clucked my tongue. "Messed. The. Fuck. Up."

"Society sucks."

"Sure does," I agreed. "Dog was abusive to your mom, wasn't he?"

"She was abusive right back."

That had me grinning, even if, distantly, I could remember seeing Dog sporting bruises when I was younger. "Why doesn't it surprise me that your mom would be like that?"

Giulia sighed. "She used to be a lot of things. Then she changed. Got together with this secondhand car dealer and he turned her into a real Stepford wife."

"That's why you threw caution to the wind and hooked up with Nyx?"

"Nah. I did that because he's my soul mate."

She said it so matter-of-factly that I knew she didn't doubt her words. As for me, her statement had me sitting up which, of course, made my back ache. "You believe in soul mates?"

"Not until Nyx," she assured me, a small smile playing on her mouth.

"What makes you think you're... *that?*"

"Because I get him and he gets me. I know what he is and I love him anyway, and I know he feels the same way."

I pursed my lips. "Is that what love is?"

"Sounds like the start of a power ballad," she teased, and while her eyes were dancing, her voice turned serious as she said, "Acceptance is a pretty powerful motivator when there's a lot about you that many people couldn't accept."

Huh.

I frowned at that, but slowly sank back against the sofa. Then, because it felt too much like a goddamn shrink's couch and I'd been on enough of those for a lifetime, I sat up, straightened out, and murmured, "I'm glad you've found him. At least you'll stop him from losing it fully."

"Well, I don't know about that. Maybe we'll just ride into the darkness together." She heaved a soft sigh. "Fitting with a name like his."

Snorting, I murmured, "His name hasn't got anything to do with the darkness."

She arched a brow at me. "No?"

"You know Nyx was a *female* goddess, don't you?"

"Well, I mean, I haven't wiki-fucking-pedia'd his road name, Indy."

I grinned at her. "We got a dog when Quin was born. Best fucking dog ever. Calling her a pet would be doing her a disservice."

Her eyes flared wide. "You're shitting me."

"Giulia, why would I shit you," I joked, "when it'll put Nyx in the hot seat?"

She snickered. "No way. Your dog was called Nyx?"

"Nuh huh, our *epic* dog was called Nyx. She was a black lab. I swear to fuck, though, she was Cujo reincarnate." My lips formed a smile that was, in no way, forced. "I miss the shit out of her every day."

"Really?"

"Truly. She was that cool. All the council know, of course." I shrugged. "They grew up with us so they know, but it tells you how great she was that they don't give him shit for the name."

Giulia blinked at me. "I can't believe I'm only finding this out now."

"Perks of working with your sister-in-law."

Her eyes flickered with warmth. "Yeah. I'm starting to see that." She picked up the papers again, then wafted them at me. "Thanks for this, Indy."

"No worries. So, Frankie will be in on Friday, but by then, I need you to have read all that shit there." I cleared my throat. "It's from the Association of Professional Piercers. It's groundwork for what you need to know. You're lucky Frankie's studio is an APP member or we couldn't do this." I winked at her. "It's good to know people who know people."

She grinned. "Yeah, I can see that. I also saw that I'll need to register for some classes." She hummed under her breath. "I'll get that arranged within the next couple of months. Where is Frankie's studio?"

"The city. She travels this way for me. We came up together in a tattoo parlor in NOLA. She's solid. There'll come a point where you'll need to travel to gain some full-time experience or the hours you need to practice will take a fucking lifetime for you to earn. Not sure my brother will appreciate that."

Giulia hitched her shoulder. "I'm sure he'll come with."

I heard the surety, the one-hundred-percent confidence in her voice, and truthfully, I was a little jealous.

Before her, Nyx wouldn't have left the compound for any other reason than a run. I knew he'd traveled all over the States for the club, and while, when he was younger and he'd been into extreme sports that had seen him leave the country, he was pretty much a homebody.

I didn't doubt either that Nyx would commute to the city for Giulia. That was what she meant to him. My brother, who didn't like being inconvenienced, would deal with it for his woman.

Maybe she was right. Maybe they *were* soul mates.

In more ways than one if the rumors around the clubhouse were true. Maybe, in the future, I'd ask her if she really had helped him hunt… today wasn't that day, though.

"You coming to the clubhouse tonight to see Stone?" Giulia asked, evidently unaware that I was having a 'come to Jesus' moment.

"I was supposed to, but not anymore. I have some late appointments. You'll need to get used to that too," I said with a snort. "Crazy fucking hours."

"I can deal with that. It's not like I don't live that now."

The heavy throb of straight pipes made the windowpanes rattle, and if that wasn't a large enough clue that Nyx was heading our way, or at least one of the Sinners, then I wasn't as smart as I believed.

Giulia perked up at the noise which I thought was pretty fucking sweet, and a few minutes later when Nyx made an appearance, she leaped to her feet and launched herself at him. He laughed, then grabbed her by the ass and hauled her tighter into him. When he started groping her, I rolled my eyes and returned my attention to my designs.

After Giulia had been thoroughly kissed, a whisper of sensation had me looking up. I gulped when I saw Cruz was standing there, silent as ever. Licking my lips, like I could taste what we'd done last night, his soft smile was in no way soft—at least, not to someone else. He was a hard man, but I'd been raised with a hard man, had grown up surrounded by them. I knew how to sense someone's tender side, even if I didn't always want to see it.

Something about him had wormed its way into my defenses, and I'd admit that I was getting to the point where I was looking forward to seeing him.

Talk about a miracle.

Unbidden, I moved my legs restlessly, and his gaze dropped down, those enigmatic eyes of his tracing the slight motion that made me hyper aware of the area between my thighs.

He'd watched me slide into these shorts this morning. Knew I wasn't wearing panties. He'd fastened my bra for me before he'd watched me put on my shirt.

I'd say he was a voyeur, but it went deeper than that. He didn't just get a kick out of watching, he loved obliterating the walls I routinely constructed. Not just against him, but against all men.

Shit, most women too.

Only one person, aside from Cruz, knew about Kevin, and that was Stone, and she knew the palatable truth. I'd never told her the extent of Kevin's abuse. Had given her a white-washed version, and she thought I was an insomniac because I had nightmares that revolved around Carly.

I didn't.

My nightmares were—

My throat turned thick as the past invaded my present.

Like it usually fucking did.

"Indy."

His voice was calm. Enough that it didn't disturb Nyx and Giulia's make-out session at the front of my fucking tattoo parlor, but firm enough that it jolted me from ancient history.

I blinked. "Cruz."

I didn't reach for him, he didn't reach for me. So why did it feel like we were back in the bath? Him tending to me, grounding me?

"I'm going into the city with Nyx," he informed me, his voice rumbly.

Our eyes communicated what neither of us were ready to say—not in front of Nyx. Because the second Cruz told me, in front of my brother, that he'd be coming straight to my apartment once the day was done, was when we were outed for real.

Though Cruz had told me last night was the first or the final time we'd be together, I saw that now wasn't the moment to be admitting to anything.

He was antsy, bouncing a little on his toes, and I registered that he had something to do and didn't like hovering around, waiting to get it done.

If I'd learned anything about him, it was that he liked to do things on *his* schedule. No one else's. But with Nyx, as VP, it wasn't like he had much of a choice. That had to screw with his Dommy head, enough that it made me hide a smile.

I highly doubted Nyx'd bend over for a spanking... not even for Giulia.

Even as I wondered what Cruz's game plan was—not just for today, but for us—I recognized that in all my life, I'd never been with the same guy for the length of time I'd been with him. What that said about me, at my age, well, I didn't like to think about. Knowing I was fucked up and admitting to it was just depressing.

I dipped my chin, preferring to focus on the one thing that always got me through—ink. "You want me to schedule you in for some time on your back tat?"

He shrugged. "Sure."

Nyx, finally having quit with the kissy goddamn face with Giulia, muttered, "It's taken you a fucking lifetime to get that cross finished. If you weren't covered in ink, I'd say you were too much of a pussy to go under the needle again."

Cruz smirked, looking far too hot for his own good.

And mine.

Jesus.

What was it about him that got my juices flowing? Without him spanking me, scraping my skin with the back of his knife, or choking me?

I mean, I knew he was beautiful, and even though some might not consider ink to be an art, I sure as fuck did. My canvas was living, *breathing*. It moved, it had life. I didn't paint a piece of goddamn fabric and hang it on a wall. My work existed in more than just a 2D kind of way. And that was Cruz all over. Sure, he was covered in ink which was like my kryptonite, but more than that, he was just fucking gorgeous.

His hair was dark. I'd never liked dark guys, because they reminded me of my brothers, but Cruz's hair was like mink. It felt so good against my hands.

His eyes were a kind of hazel. I said a 'kind of' because they were neither blue nor green, and there were little amber top notes that I recognized because they danced around the iris on the rare occasions he smiled. Those top notes made his eyes lean toward a grassy color, but just labeling them green was underselling them. Like calling a diamond a rock.

He was, I recognized, grumpy by nature. I knew he'd classify himself as grim though. Like the reaper. He had this image of himself in his head that was worse than the one I had of myself. Why? I didn't know. What he had in his past didn't torment him. I'd have recognized a fellow survivor, someone who was drowning in the quagmire. Cruz wasn't drowning. If anything, he was surfing through life, but something drove him.

Something…

I pursed my lips as I wondered what that might be, tracing my gaze over the strong jawline, the wide set eyes, the soft brows that felt good under my thumb whenever I smoothed one down on the rare occasions I instigated the connection now and touched him. His stubble prickled the best way against my skin, and it glinted silver and gold when it was long enough.

His body was rangy. He wasn't like Nyx, wasn't a muscle-head, but his body was toned, strong. In his own way. It was like sleeping with a runner, I guessed, instead of a weight lifter.

He had the sweetest smile lines either side of his eyes which told me he'd smiled frequently at some point in his life, even if he didn't have matching lines bracketing his mouth, and his nose had been broken.

He looked like a damaged angel. With the skeleton tats on his hands and chest, the massive cross he had which was why he'd been given his road name, and then, at his throat, the big tat that was mostly black ink. I'd looked to see if it was a cover up, but I thought the negative ink was representative of something, something he hadn't, and maybe never would, share with me. There was a reason, after all, he was inked like a living skeleton.

The thought of him keeping secrets shouldn't have hurt. Not when I'd shared the bare minimum with him. He knew about my past when no one else did, but that wasn't the only part of me that mattered.

We were two bodies that came together in the night, with violence and passion, but I wasn't sure if there was more. Not yet, anyway.

Maybe two weeks ago, I'd have been okay with that.

But yesterday, something had changed.

It wasn't something he'd done, nor something I had. Even if he knocked down barriers without even trying to when he made me piss in front of him, or when he'd shoved his cum-soaked fingers down my throat.

No, Stone and Steel had done that.

In they'd walked, hand in hand. Stone stiff from riding bitch, when she wasn't supposed to yet. Steel with such an intense look in his eyes, one that had hit me with the force of a laser.

I'd known they loved each other for decades. It had been clear to anyone with eyes, even if the reason *why* was beyond any of us. I knew Steel had to have justified it to Stone, but she'd never shared the truth with me, even if she'd overcome whatever bullshit he'd used to keep them apart.

I'd seen him in the hospital, watched him watch over her night after night, week after week.

He hadn't been good enough for her. Until he'd proven himself. And sure, he'd fuck up. Bikers always did. But I figured they'd make it work. Whatever hit them in the future.

I'd seen that yesterday. When they'd come walking in for me to brand Stone, and to work on the brand I hadn't even known he had, one that declared to the world that Stone was his—for far longer than any of us had recognized.

And then, now, when I looked at Giulia and Nyx, as they tongue fucked in front of me again, as the brother who was more messed up in the head than I could ever be, as I registered Giulia's words... did I have that in my future?

Could I have that in my future?

In all honesty, I wasn't sure.

And I was even less sure if I did want it, that it'd be with Cruz.

The club's Grim Reaper.

The only man whose hands I'd been able to bear on my body.

Whose dick slid into me with no pain.

Who made me wet when we slept together.

Who knew my triggers, knew what I needed to get off, knew just what I was and why I was...

"Indy."

That commanding tone had me blinking at him, and I knew my pupils had to be blown out because his nostrils flared. Fuck, it was like he could scent my arousal or something.

Could he?

There was something preternatural about him, that was for damn sure. Or maybe I was just building into the frickin' hype about why this man had earned those bones on his hands.

I bit my lip. "I'll book you in this week."

"Where's David the Dick?" Nyx asked, peering around my shop like David was hiding under the desk.

"I gave him the morning off. He had some problem with his car," I told him, all while my eyes remained fixed on Cruz's.

"Fucking freak. I don't like how he looks at you," he carried on grumbling, and his words had Cruz's brows furrowing.

I shook my head though and grumbled right back, "He's harmless."

"That's like saying a rattlesnake won't bite."

That had me wrenching my gaze from Cruz's. "That makes no sense. Since when does David look like a snake?"

"All the time?" Nyx groused.

Scowling at him, I retorted, "When are you going to see Quin?"

My brother's mouth tightened, but he surprised me by telling me, "Next week."

Only the fact that Nyx didn't have a record was how he could get inside, because normally, someone with gang affiliations would never be allowed visitors from that same gang. So how his visit was possible was something I'd never know, even as I'd never allowed that excuse to cut him any slack. The club had deep pockets so I'd known they could either bribe someone to get Nyx into Rikers for a visit, or that they'd bribed enough folk along the way to keep my brother's hands as clean as possible. Probably most of the councilors too. Especially as they were all close to Rex, and Rex and his father had led the club for years.

That was why it was bittersweet. The council was full of murderers but Caleb, my baby bro, who'd been sick throughout his childhood and hadn't had much of a goddamn life, was doing hard fucking time now.

I couldn't say there was no justice in this world, because I didn't want Nyx or any of my club family to be inside, but it just sucked.

Big time.

"You're going next week?"

I cast a quick glance at Giulia who looked a mixture of smug and surprised which told me that she'd been working her wiles on him like she promised but hadn't expected it to happen as fast as that.

"Yeah, I just said that, didn't I?" He heaved an impatient sigh, glowering at me a second before he rumbled, "Okay, we'd better fuck off to the city. You need a ride home, sweetheart?" he asked Giulia.

"Nah, I'm gonna help Indy."

"How you getting home?"

"I'll wait on you if you want?"

His eyes gleamed. "Course I want." He squeezed her ass even as he let her down, pecked her on the lips before he rumbled, "Later."

Her smile was dirty but she just told him, "Stay safe."

His smile was all the reassurance she'd get.

Nothing about this life was safe.

As he strode out, Cruz murmured, "I'll speak to you later about the appointment."

"Sure." I bit my lip, watched as he glanced at my mouth, then he twisted around and without a backward glance, called out, "See you later, Giulia."

When he was gone, she turned to me, excitement entwining with interest. "You're banging him."

"What makes you say that?" I hedged.

"I have eyes, don't I?"

"I dunno. I thought they were rolling around in your head while my brother tongue-fucked you in my store."

She sniffed. "If you think I'm about to apologize for that when your brother's fucking my mouth—"

I raised a hand. "Spare me the details."

"The devil's in the details," she joked, making me stick out my tongue at her. Her teasing simmered down though as she wandered over to the door and closed it firmly as the wind swept in, blowing it open a little. "Seriously, Indy, you are, aren't you?"

"I don't want Nyx to know."

"Yeah, because I'd tell him." She rolled her eyes.

"Thought soul mates didn't have secrets from one another," I jibed.

"A girl has gotta have secrets from her man," she retorted. "Especially when it's with her posse."

My lips twitched. "Posse?"

She shrugged. "Yeah. My very own Sinners' posse. It's growing."

I huffed out a laugh because she wasn't wrong. "I guess it is."

"From the way you were looking at him, I'd say another one's bitten the dust."

As the straight pipes rattled down the street, I peered out the window and watched as my brother and lover headed off to the city for what ungodly business I couldn't imagine.

When they roared by, I just murmured, "More like *I've* bitten off more than I can chew."

FIFTEEN
CRUZ

HEADING into the city always put me in a killer mood, and today's visit was going to be shittier than usual. Not only was traffic a bitch, but my intent was to meet with my mom, and as luck would have it, Nyx was in a crappy mood as well. He had to liaise with a street gang who'd done us a solid, all while waiting on me to get the real goods on what my mom wanted.

Only the council was aware of any of that though. His going today was my protection for when the fallout eventually hit.

If I'd learned anything in my life, it was that the shit always hit the fan—sometimes it just took longer than others.

So, when the whole club knew about my relatives, Nyx coming today, even if he wasn't going to meet my mom, would allay suspicions about me in the long run.

I'd been born and raised in NYC, but it had never felt like home. Not like West Orange did. Crazy how it was only an hour away with terrible traffic, but the dynamic was different.

Riding to it always put me in a mood because of the congestion, but mostly, I just hated how fucking busy it was. I knew Nyx felt the exact same way because when Rex had given him this job yesterday, he'd been bitching about having spent too much time in Manhattan what with Stone having been hospitalized as long as she had, and a lot of the council heading there to be with her.

We'd all known Stone was tight with the council, but I wasn't sure any of us had registered exactly *how* much. Living was learning though.

Heading under the city through the Lincoln Tunnel always made me feel claustrophobic, so it was with relief that I headed away from the island itself and rode to one of the 'burbs where Mom lived.

It was my childhood home, but there was nothing warm and cozy about the memories I had of that place.

My parents arguing, my mom ramming my dad's manhood into him with every bitter word. The only time we'd ever been happy was when she was on the job and we were alone. Mom should never have married and had a kid, although my dad used to tell me that before the post-partum depression had taken a firm hold on her, she'd been relatively normal.

Sadly for me, that had taken over her when I was three and we'd lost my baby brother, so the mom I'd known was the nutcase who was obsessed with her father's death.

Riding through the busy streets, streets that had once been my turf, I stopped around the corner from her place, picked up my cell and called Rex. "You ready for this, Prez?"

"Go for it."

Years ago, when I'd joined the Sinners, I'd learned exactly what my mom stood for. I was many things, but an idiot wasn't one of them, so when I'd patched in as a Prospect, I'd name-dropped my mother to the council. Seemed counter-intuitive to a lot of the bikers who, at first, had eyed me with distrust. But, and it was a big but, I'd known what they'd think.

They could use me. I was a source of intel.

I was more than okay with that, but sometimes, when she went months without calling me, it was nice to forget about her, her ties.

I was an honest criminal. She was just a dirty fucking Fed, and if there was one thing I hated more than a goddamn cop, it was a squealing pig.

So, I thought nothing of betraying her because my family was back in West Orange and I kicked my hog into rolling forward, nosing down the narrow roads as I went 'home.'

Parking beside the narrow house, I became aware that she was watching for me, because the door slipped open when I took my helmet off. I strode up the short path, ducking my head so I didn't bang it on the low ceiling as I walked in.

There was something brimming inside Caroline Dunbar that made her appear a lot younger than her fifty-six years. Being objective—which was what I did best—I'd say she looked about forty-eight, because the trend of having gray hair made her look like she was trying to fit in with fashion. Mom had never given a shit about fashion. She'd always worn boxy black suits and those square-toed shoes with frickin' rubber heels so she could run.

I figured she'd believed herself to be GI Jane, and while I wasn't sexist, I had to hope that GI Jane would be a patriot and not just in the superheroine game because her sleazeball father had managed to get himself executed a long time ago. Every hero had a back story, of course, but that had to be the most pathetic of them all.

I didn't go further than the hallway, not interested in getting comfortable. The low ceiling, the side table that had the same dish I remembered as a kid with a couple sets of keys in, a coat hook by the door which had only her coat suspended from it, and the staircase which had a basket of laundry on the bottom step was all I saw as I did an initial scan of the place. I didn't sense anyone upstairs, or in the living room, and Mom's calm told me she was alone as well.

Only then did she let the mask drop and reveal the monster within.

See, it took a monster to know a monster, and she knew there was no point in hiding it from me.

"What do you want?" I asked, when she just looked me up and down with a disgust that wasn't feigned.

"I can't believe you let yourself become this," she rasped. "You had so much potential, Darren."

I smiled at her. "I'm living my best life, Mom. What can I say? I'm sorry you don't approve."

Her eyes narrowed at my sarcasm. "When I asked you to enlist with them, I never thought you'd take to the life so well. At least by being this way, you can help me out at the same time."

"I live to serve," I retorted. "What do you need this time? More information?"

I hated going into these things blind, mostly because I never knew what to shove her way to satisfy her. Thankfully, she knew I wasn't on the council so what I could pick up were only whispers, but our whispers were the equivalent of a bomb blast.

"It'd be a while ago now, but a woman was killed in your neck of the woods."

My brows rose at that. "Killed?"

She pulled a face. "It pains me to admit that the Sinners do a better job of keeping that place clean than the cops do, but yes, murdered. She was raped, too, from what I can tell. Do you know who it was?"

Genuinely perplexed by this line of questioning, I muttered, "In West Orange itself?"

"You know that new estate the Farquars were building… sounds like it was there or nearby."

"Where's this coming from?"

"That's irrelevant. I want to know who died." Her smile was wicked. "You know the game, son. Leverage."

"What's in it for me?"

That smile turned colder. "You know what's in it for you. No one will know that you built that little bomb in '13."

My mouth twisted into a smirk. "I know for a fact there's no evidence in that case."

"Yeah?" Something shifted in her eyes. "How?"

"I've got friends now, Mom. Friends who look where most people wouldn't dare. So, remind me, why would I help you when you haven't got shit over me?" Mom's language of love was leverage, just like she'd admitted.

As I looked at her, I had to admit, I didn't hate her. Sure, I hated what she stood for, but I didn't hate her. She'd made me what I was, and I was almost thankful for that.

She was also, I knew, the only person who'd ever match me. Who'd ever be my equal. There was a kind of symmetry to that that pleased me. So whenever I approached her, it was always like Garry Kasparov coming up against Deep Blue.

She squinted at me, but I only arched a brow, completely at ease with this conversation because, as my patch-in present when I'd become a full brother in the MC, Maverick had erased all the evidence in that investigation that had seen my mom become the keeper of my destiny.

I knew that made it sound like something from an Indiana Jones movie, but being indebted to Caro Dunbar was not something anyone wanted.

Sure, I was showing my hand, but I could tell... this was important to her. And there was a reason she didn't want to go running through the appropriate channels to find out who had died on our turf so it was worth burning that card to figure out her game.

"I'll owe you."

I snorted. "That's it?"

"You know I'm good for it."

Scrubbing my chin, I murmured, "I'll have to poke around. As far as I know, no one has been murdered in West Orange for a good long while. The last time was Luke Lancaster, and that wasn't exactly murder, was it?"

Something flashed in her eyes at that. Awareness? Had she been involved with the Lancasters? Took a snake to know a snake, I reasoned.

"No. I suppose not. If you have to ask around, then you're no use to me. The whole point of this conversation is for the victim to remain unknown to certain people."

I studied her, wondering what her game was, but like me, she was shielding her expression. "I'd ask which people, but I don't think you're going to tell me."

"You'd be right." She tipped her chin at the door. "You can go now."

Mockingly, I saluted her. "Nice visit, Mom."

She just grunted, turned on her heel, and headed back to the kitchen.

Letting myself out, I released a deep breath, feeling a sense of strange liberation because now she knew she couldn't play the evidence card against me, it was like a load off my shoulders. Sure, I hadn't been worried in a long time, but it was still nice for the old asshole to know the truth.

Wriggling my now burden-less shoulders as I stretched, I peered around the old neighborhood, oddly perturbed by the sight of my very middle class background. Few people in the clubhouse had a childhood as regular as mine, so in a way, I was grateful—especially after hearing Indy's horror stories—but this place was somewhere I'd outgrown, that was for sure.

As my gaze dipped around a couple of front yards, I saw the black SUV from the corner of my eye and made sure the vehicle's occupants weren't aware I spotted them.

Mom was a Fed, so I doubted she had her own people watching her unless they'd finally figured out she was dirty, but she definitely had a tail. They were purposely on the opposite side of the road to her place, and with their back to the house as well.

Still, it was no sweat off my nose if the bitch died. At least I wouldn't have to deal with those goddamn phone calls that came out of the blue. Because even though I'd removed her leverage, she'd still try.

As she'd told me all my life—God loved a trier.

Shame for her that God had turned his back on us a long time ago.

SIXTEEN
REX

IN FRONT OF MY MEN, even my council, I never allowed any weakness to show for long. If we were outside of church, talking between ourselves, maybe I would. Just as they would. It wasn't like I was running a fucking daycare here. We were men, we were bikers, we were *Sinners,* for fuck's sake.

We didn't wail about our pasts on a shrink's sofa. We dealt with shit ourselves.

But eight years ago, a woman *had* died.

She'd died and she'd changed the face of the club and my home life.

Mom.

It had seemed like a random accident. So fucking random, which was what had sent my father on a wild goose chase. Looking for answers. Looking for enemies where there were none.

She'd been found on a road. Crumpled up in a heap. Tire tracks on the tarmac where a car had braked at speed, before taking off at greater speed.

Dad had said it wasn't an accident.

He'd refused to believe the coroner's findings. Had disregarded the autopsy…

We'd been lied to.

And the lie ran deep.

Sin's hand came to my shoulder, and Maverick's gaze was steady but welling with emotions he rarely let show from behind the mask he wore to get through every fucking day. I was with family. Not all of them. But most.

Steel was at work at the strip joint, Storm was in goddamn Ohio, and Nyx had to head into the city to deal with the *Demonios Bandidos* who needed our help with a distribution problem they were having. Sin, Mav, and Link were here, watching with empathy in their eyes, and hurt in their hearts.

My mom hadn't just been *mine*. She'd mothered all these fuckers here. Even if, like with Mav, they had good moms of their own, she'd been there. For all of us. No matter what we did, no matter where we went, she'd had our back, and she'd died like fucking roadkill—

Or so we'd been led to believe.

I gritted my teeth as Sin muttered, "It might not be her."

"She said it herself," Link argued, his voice low. "We have very few murders around here."

"Hit and runs aren't murders," Sin agreed. "Not the regular kind." A grunt escaped him. "If some fucker targeted Rene, then I, as much as you, Rex, want the cunt to pay, but we only know what some nutjob dirty Fed told Cruz."

"We need more information," I concurred, my voice laced with hell.

"How do we get it? She shared shit with him."

"She told us enough. She mentioned the Farquar estate. When Rene died, that was back before any of those fancy fuckers were even living up there. They'd only just cracked the ground at that point," Maverick remarked, and he stretched out his arms, bridging his fingers together before he cracked his knuckles. "Barely any were fully constructed at that time. But I'll find out what I can, Rex. You know I will. And what I don't, Lodestar will pick up the slack."

My jaw felt like it was clamped together, to the point where I was pretty sure I'd crack my goddamn teeth if I didn't let up, but—

Jesus.

"Who'd have wanted her dead?" I rasped, even though it was a stupid question.

Our women were as much a part of the game of chess that was this life as the men sitting and standing in front of me.

We never targeted an enemy's woman, because my father had raised me with honor. Bear might not have seemed that way, but he was an honorable man. And I was too, as a result. But learning this?

What honor I had left withered some.

Because what Bear had taught me, my mom had only compounded. She was the one who'd instilled his lessons, turning me into the man I was, because she was the one who'd made me *me*.

"You know the Italians have had beef with us for a while," Sin rumbled. "That's probably why they got Tiffany's dad to build his estate here. Each house is probably owned by a *Famiglia* crony."

I couldn't argue with that, but then, I wasn't capable of much right now. There was too much white noise crackling between my ears, and before I could think rationally, I needed it to go. I needed it to abate.

"You think the Italians killed her?" Link asked softly, his voice low, like that would stop me from hearing it.

"Who else?" Sin argued. "It fits. Especially when she mentioned the estate. But why then?"

I rasped, "That's what we need to find out."

"I hate to mention it, bro, but I just got a message from Steel. The funeral director's taken possession of Dog's body."

I blinked at Sin, my brain slow to drift from thoughts of my mom's murder to Dog's.

"Fuck's sake, Sin," Link groused. "Now isn't the time."

Sin winced. "I know, but he needs confirmation. Is it okay to go ahead with the funeral by the end of the week?"

"Yeah. Whatever. Whenever," I rasped, reaching for my phone and seeing Steel had already sent me a bunch of messages about this topic. My phone wasn't on silent, which meant that it had been pinging away and I just hadn't heard it.

That wasn't like me.

But then, it wasn't every day you learned this level of shit about your mom, was it?

Scraping my hands over my face, I rasped, "I need a minute."

No one argued, no one said shit, and I was grateful for that because I didn't know where my head was at and I needed to be on the ball. For close to a decade, we'd been in a kind of stasis, and all without knowing it.

Inadvertently, we'd just set off a timer that could only end in a blast, and my ears were the only ones that could hear the ticking of the fucking clock.

I didn't look back. I didn't stop to shoot the shit like I usually did when I headed past the bar. I went straight outside and headed for my bike.

One second I was in my office, the next I was on the adjoining road that led to the only place I'd ever found any peace.

Rachel's.

I wouldn't be welcome. I never was. But she was the only one who'd be able to help, who I'd ever let see me like this.

I'd never stopped needing her, but I'd shoved that need aside because I knew she deserved better than a criminal like me. But today, I wasn't a biker. I wasn't a one-percenter. Nor was I a Prez.

I was a fucking son.

Rene's son.

And that was the only Rex Rachel had ever loved.

CRUZ

A few days later

WITH MY CALCULATIONS MADE, I grabbed the burner I'd rigged up and shoved it under the cast iron bath. It'd take a fucking lifetime for the solution to get hot enough, but I had plenty of time.

So did Donavan Lancaster.

Wasn't like the fucker was going anywhere.

Link and Lily had managed to make a real mess of a man who made a pile of rotten trash look fresh and ready to eat.

The past couple of days had been difficult.

What with visiting my mom, then Dog and Sarah's funerals... I'd admit, I'd been wondering if Lodestar would come for me, especially as I knew what she'd done. But she didn't.

Hadn't.

She'd left me alone.

In fact, she'd been tucked away with Maverick on the top floor of the clubhouse, and I'd never been happier about anything in my fucking life.

Dog's death, the subsequent investigation, all of it had felt like a waiting game where I was the one left wondering if Lodestar would come and end me.

Maybe a cold-hearted bastard would have taken her out first, but I didn't have a death wish.

I wasn't the kind of man who took lives easily—I cleaned up after those who did, which was what made me a monster.

Hence the vat of lye I was currently heating up in an old bathtub. The tub acted as a Dutch oven, and once optimal temperature was reached, I'd be dumping Lancaster's piece of shit body into it for the base concoction to do its work—disintegrate him into viscera.

With the burner on at full blast, it'd still take a while for it to heat up, so I went back to the room that had seen Lancaster's final weeks on this miserable planet, and dragged his corpse out of there.

Once his bag of bones was on the floor, with the stench of lye slowly starting to fill the bathroom, I closed the door, then I reached for some of my personal protective equipment, set the mask over my mouth and nose, shoved on a pair of goggles then dragged on a Haz-Mat suit, and started on cleaning up the rest of the Fridge.

Hauling in a power washer, I didn't sit around. Hosing it down, the initial sweep only got rid of the surface layer. Next came bleach, and then, my own personal blend. The bleach was only my being cautious, because where DNA was concerned, caution was wise. Once I dumped my own chemicals into the power washer, I let the solution disperse into the water before I hosed it down.

Twice more.

Caution favored the brave, after all.

Once the place stank like a lab, even filtering through my heavy-duty mask, I hummed with satisfaction once I'd given my boots the same treatment, before I returned to the bathroom where the large bubbles breaching the liquid's surface told me the job had taken longer than I'd hoped.

But Lancaster had subsisted in the Fridge for a helluva long time, and even though I'd made sweeps, there was nothing like a deep clean.

Switching off the heat, I moved over to the shitter where I'd placed a tray of tools. Grabbing the laser thermometer, I grumbled as I realized the lye was too hot now, so I moved outside where I knew the brothers had washed down.

The grass was scorched from where I'd ignited controlled fires in the past, but I started off with another bleach solution, followed by mine, then once that was done, I hefted sandbags into place around the patch where the Sinners all knew to stand to clean down post-beating, and dumped paper on it and set it alight.

Once the flames did more than sputter, but began to flutter and flicker in the breeze while managing to stay lit, looking no more harmless than a bonfire, I trudged back inside, tested the temperature, then hauled Lancaster's body into the vat.

With that done, and knowing it could take up to a week for total decomp, I headed outside, scrubbed my boots by the exterior faucet that was hooked up to the side wall where I stored all my gear, then I stripped down and shoved my clothes and the PPEs on the fire.

Grabbing the hose, I sprayed myself off, cleaned up with my dick swinging in the same breeze as the fire was fighting, then got changed into gear I'd left in the truck.

Once that was all done, I jumped behind the driver's seat, shoved it back as far as it would go, then reached for the brown paper bag I'd brought with me.

With a hero sub in one hand, a bottle of water in the other, I took a sip then a bite of my sandwich, and when half of both had been demolished, I rested the bottle on the dash, reached for my phone and called Indy.

I hadn't seen her that much since I'd gotten back to West Orange, which didn't sit well with me.

Even as I was trying to fight how much she was starting to mean to me, I was aware such inner turmoil was futile.

When a woman had you by the dick, you could hide it from her, but hiding it from yourself was just sheer fucking idiocy. If she'd been a regular woman, I wouldn't have hidden my feelings. I'd have been open. But the reason I felt the way I did for her was because she was anything but regular.

Complicated, see?

The second she connected the call, I murmured, "Be ready tonight."

She sniffed, which made me laugh. "I was born ready."

"Since when?" I retorted, my lips quirked up in a wide grin as I watched the flames sputtering as the paper burnt out, leaving behind the grass that I was trying to clean up.

"Since forever."

I didn't snicker, because I knew she'd be offended at that, so I just said, "I don't think you're ready for this."

"No?" For the first time, her voice was shaky, which let me know that she'd read my tone.

I might sound amused, but I was also wired.

I'd had a hard day's work, and I had no intention of spending the night alone.

"No," I told her, aware it was more of a vow than anything else.

Her gulp was audible, but she didn't back out or try to postpone the inevitable which made me fall that little bit harder for her. She just murmured, "I'll be waiting, Cruz."

The perfect answer.

"Naked."

"Naked," she confirmed.

I hummed. "See you soon."

Before she could say another word, I cut the call. Though I'd prefer to be eating her pussy, I finished off my hero sub, then returned to the fire. In good conscience, I couldn't leave it burning unattended, so I stared into the flames long enough to see the fresh scorching on the grass. Once that was in place, I hosed it down to fully extinguish the fire, then sprayed another round of bleach onto it. I knew bleach didn't disinfect when heated, so on the hot grass, it'd do bupkis, but I liked the smell of it even if it made my eyes water.

Sure, it was weird, but there were all kinds of people who liked the smell of gas. This was no freakier.

With that, I returned all my tools to the tiny storage shed to the side of the building, then I headed for the truck.

Indy was waiting, and that was a priority that went to the top of my list.

SEVENTEEN
LILY

"HOW MUCH DO YOU HATE ME?"

I stared at the love of my life in the vanity mirror, through the steam from the too long shower I'd had in an attempt to get clean. Sure, the guys had hosed me down, but that had made me feel like a Labrador Retriever who'd gotten busy in a muddy puddle.

It had dispersed excess dirt, but it hadn't left me clean.

The towel around me scented of jasmine, the vanity was made in an Italian marble that probably cost more than Link's hog, and my skin gleamed with moisturizer that cost over two hundred dollars a liquid oz.

I was rich.

Filthy, stinking rich.

And the key word there?

Stinking.

Some days, I felt like that stench went soul deep, but only Link made me see the light at the end of the tunnel. I knew he'd done some terrible things in his time. Knew he'd probably done a lot worse than what I'd done tonight, but somehow, his soul remained golden.

I felt that.

Every time he touched me, every time he looked at me, I felt that. As well as his love for me. It was clear in his patience, evident with every measured touch, and every day he was supportive of me.

"I could never hate you."

The words were simple, but the context was anything but.

My father was dead.

At Link's hands. Not mine.

"I couldn't let you do it," he rasped.

I should have known he wouldn't. Should have prepared myself, but instead, I'd let my father get into my head, had let him worm his way inside when I should have acted instead of dithering.

As a result, Link had made the kill shot.

A shot I'd been planning since the first time my father had abused me.

The steam misted over the mirror, but I didn't bother to wipe my hand over the glass. He stepped toward me, so big and so strong that he should have scared me. Should have had my shoulders cowering, my body twisting away from him as I tried to escape, but escaping Link was the last thing I wanted.

Link was my soul mate.

His hands moved to cup the balls of my shoulders, and I tilted my head to the side, letting my cheek rest on one of them. He released a sigh at that, and I could sense his relief.

It always amazed me how this man, this big, rough and ready biker, could be so careful around me. After the car crash, he'd treated me with kid gloves for a while, especially with my cut lip, broken bones, and whiplash. Ever since, he looked at me like he knew he could lose me. Which killed me.

For weeks, months even, we'd been pussyfooting around things, and I knew that was more my fault than his.

I'd let things go too far.

That he thought I might hate him was indicative of the truth.

"I'm ready."

My words had his brows arching. "Huh? For what?"

Carefully twisting around, because I knew I'd strain my neck otherwise, I moved so that I was no longer facing the vanity but facing him. He reached up, cupped my chin, so completely in the dark that I knew I couldn't love him more.

People would criticize me for keeping him on the line this long, for daring to be traumatized by what had happened in my past, but this man was the only person's opinion I gave a fuck about.

He'd given me time to heal, time to recognize that he was like no other man on God's green earth. His patience, his honor, his respect, all of it made me love him even more than I'd thought was possible.

He was a gift.

It was time I showed him that.

Staring up at him, I reached for the rosary around his neck, tangling my fingers up in it as I told him, "For you. For us."

His eyes flared wide, and it almost amused me when he shook his head. "No way. Not now. Not after…"

"Yes way. Yes now. Yes after," I told him calmly.

"You hate me," he rasped, pain in his eyes.

Confused, my brow furrowed. "Huh? I feel the exact opposite of that."

"You're punishing me for taking your father out."

When he took a step back, I'd admit, I'd never foreseen *this*.

Blinking at him, I took a step forward, and carried on moving toward him as he moved away, out of the bathroom and into the bedroom.

"Don't do this," he pleaded.

"Don't do what?" I countered huskily, his level of 'torn up' taking this whole thing to another level.

I'd thought I loved him before. Now? This turned into outright adoration. "Don't love you? Don't need to take this to the next phase? I want you, Link. I've never not wanted you, but…" I couldn't say a burden had been taken off my shoulders now my father was dead, but I couldn't deny that I felt lighter somehow. Definitely felt like I could breathe a little easier.

Knowing my boogeyman was gone, for good, it made the next couple of steps in my future seem all the more joyful.

I was free of his taint.

At long goddamn last.

Because he was a visual creature, I unknotted the towel from around my breasts and as it sank to the ground, I knew how deeply he was buried in his head because he didn't even look at me, didn't smirk and say, "There are those sugar tits I love so much."

He was frozen.

In time and place.

So it was my duty, I figured, to defrost him.

I moved toward him, not stopping until I could slide my hands around his waist, not stopping until I was bare before him, as naked as the day I was born while he was dressed.

The imagery suited me.

I felt like I was supplicating myself before him, thanking him for everything he'd done for me.

Maybe I'd wanted to be the one to pull the trigger, but knowing Father was dead without me having to sully myself was something I was infinitely grateful for.

I just wished his soul wasn't bearing the burden, and I knew he needed to hear me tell him that.

As I pushed into him, I whispered, "I love you, Link. I'm not mad at you. I could never hate you. I'm grateful. For everything you've—"

"Fuck, you're breaking up with me."

Okay, that was taking shit too far.

I pushed away from him, just moving back enough that I could shove at his chest, not stopping until he was falling back onto the bed. Before he could get up, scowling all the while, I crawled up on him, not letting him scramble off the bed. I pinned his shoulders down, glared at him, and then and only then, did I see it.

A kernel of amusement.

"You prick!" I shrieked.

His lips twitched. "A little."

"No, you fucker. You almost had me going there." I scowled harder. "You thought I wanted to break up?"

Around that kernel of amusement was a glimmer of truth. I knew he was covering up his insecurities, and the truth was, I knew exactly how insecure my man was. You'd never know it, would never see it, but I wasn't just anyone, was I? I knew him better than anyone else, and that I'd inadvertently fed his insecurities when he worked so fucking hard to shore mine up, just about killed me.

When he reached up, rasping, "There are my sugar tits," just like I'd known he would, my heart stopped pounding like crazy.

That alone told me, somehow, things were back on track.

I blinked at him, then bit my lip as he fondled my nipple. When penetration was off the cards, you got to know somebody's every hot spot, and I knew his as well as he knew mine.

But today was going to be simple.

Today my man was going to pop my cherry and claim me as his in the only way he hadn't claimed me yet.

When his fingers slipped up to my throat, and he cupped the back of my neck, I wasn't surprised when he asked, "You were joking, weren't you?"

"What about any of this is funny?"

"The timing is weird—"

"The timing is perfect," I countered, and because we were talking too goddamn much, I reached down between us and shaped his dick. "I want this. Inside me. I want you. Inside me."

"Want that more than I want my next breath, sugar tits."

"Then what are you waiting for? I want to be yours."

"You already are, Lily." His voice turned urgent. "You know that, don't you?"

"You showed me every single way you could," I agreed. "But I know you're a caveman too from time to time."

Confirming that, I shrieked when he spun us around, and the bed bounced as he was suddenly on top of me and I was flat on my back. The rough leather of his cut, the soft fabric of his Henley, the coarse denim of his jeans... all of it felt like heaven and hell against my naked flesh. It wasn't the first time I'd felt them, of course, but it was the first time I'd felt it in this situation.

A situation I knew was going to end a certain way.

I gulped, but he saw my nerves and his eyes softened as he reached down and joined us in the sweetest, most loving of kisses imaginable. I could feel tears prickle my eyes, could feel emotion choke me as our mouths connected just as our hearts did.

Everything about us was in sync. That was why his earlier reaction had surprised me. He knew me better than he knew a combustible engine... Christ, I needed to show my man what he meant to me.

Even though the leather and the denim were rough against my skin, I hitched my legs on his hips and tugged him closer to me. My arms slipped around his shoulders as I clung to him, holding on with every ounce of strength in me as he thrust his tongue into my mouth, languidly making love to me that way, stealing my breath, taking my heart with him along for the ride.

My nerves bled away, my anxiety and the day's adrenaline buzz disappearing with it. When we were together, nothing else mattered. Nothing.

I groaned as his pace sped up, and I knew that even if he'd felt unsure about my motives before, he recognized my intent, recognized what I needed from him even if I wasn't altogether certain.

He pulled away, letting his lips drop down to kiss the corner of my mouth, over to the crest of my cheekbone, my eyelid, my temple. He anointed them all with a kiss as he rasped, "Ah Lily, what the fuck do you do to me?"

My smile, when it came, was smoky and overwhelmed. "Love you?"

He shuddered at that, before he rasped, "I wake up every day wondering if today is going to be the day you realize what you've let into your life."

My brow puckered, and my smile faded. "Why would you think that?"

"Because I'm no good, and today proved that."

"Today proved that you'll fight for me when I'm too weak to fight for myself. I'm not going anywhere, Link. You're true to me, and I'm true to you."

"I see all those preppy fuckers around town eying you up—"

"Like the club snatch doesn't eye you up?"

He sniffed. "What kind of fool wants a burger when he's got a steak at home?"

"Paul Newman, eat your heart out," I retorted. "You're my steak, Link. How the hell don't you know that?"

He pushed his forehead against mine, once again stunning me with his vulnerability.

Earlier on, he'd nearly carted me from Sarah, one of my family's victims, and his brother's funerals, then he'd turned Captain America on me, letting me have at my father but taking over when doubt had crept in, and when my dick dad had made me think shit about my soul that I didn't know I cared about.

Link had taken the burden onto himself, well, it was time for me to share it.

"Link?" I rasped, my hands digging into his back, kneading his cut as much as the supple leather would allow.

"What?"

"Will you marry me?"

He stiffened at that, then his eyes flared wide as he pulled back. "Huh?"

"You heard me."

He shook his head. "No, I'm sure I didn't."

I heaved a sigh. "You got water in your ears or something?" I grumbled. "Where's my cocky lover, huh? My pain in the ass—"

His mouth was on mine again, this time it was Link. Not the man who'd shown a side of himself I saw rarely, one that made me want to cosset him because I wanted to know every aspect of his nature, his personality.

But this was the man I knew well.

He took my mouth like the rampaging Viking he was, thrusting his tongue against mine like he'd be thrusting into my pussy soon. Rather than scare me, it filled me with fire. I couldn't be scared of Link. I just couldn't. I knew his body too well, mine knew his weaknesses and strengths, and he knew my triggers so I didn't have to worry about him overtaking me. Not that I thought he would. Just, my insecurities were as overwhelming as his.

The weight on me was one I recognized, the kiss I knew, the dick that burrowed into my softness was one I'd held and touched and stroked and sucked.

Every part of this man was registered and filed in my brain, and there was no fear to be had. No fear whatsoever.

He pulled away from me, harder this time, and when he flung himself off the bed, I gaped at him, but not for long. My gape turned from confused and concerned to hungry as he stripped down within seconds, baring every delicious muscled inch of him to my gaze.

When he was naked, he crawled back on the bed, and this time, when he settled into me, his hardness met my softness for real.

It wasn't the first time he'd done this, wasn't the first time he'd rocked his hips, letting the tip of the glans burrow into me, rock against my clit. Maybe because I knew him so well, this all went so easily. I'd expected to be scared, for the memories to hit me. I'd expected for terror to flood my veins, for the past to shadow the present, but it didn't.

If anything, I could only focus on him.

Focus on us.

That was all I knew, all I saw.

I sucked in a breath as he nipped my bottom lip before he moved down to my tits, sucking on the nipples, moving further down, kissing my stomach, making my skin quiver, before he veered toward my pussy.

This was safe ground, solid ground. I lifted one leg, raised my foot and rested it on his shoulders as he started to eat me out. I groaned as his mouth worked its magic on me, sucking on my clit with the expertise of a virtuoso, one who specialized in me. I groaned again as he slurped on me like I was a feast, thrust his tongue into me, reminding me of what was going to happen today before he retreated to my clit and sucked down on me hard and fast.

Two fingers slipped into my gate, and though I flinched at first because he surprised me, I settled in for the ride. He'd been scissoring his fingers inside me for a while, getting me used to a presence there, and I moaned when a third made an appearance, and the stretch was a little more intense than I expected.

I dug my hips into the bed, letting him have at me, letting him taste me and prepare me, ready me for him and what he was going to gift me, before he gave me no choice but to come.

His endless licks and flicks to my clit had me shooting off like a rocket, and I soared high and hard, shrieking loudly as he raked his fingers upward, touching the front wall of my pussy, jerking me into sensation that was ground we'd covered long ago.

His fingers carried on scissoring, his mouth carried on tormenting me, and I let him, I let him do what he wanted, do what he thought I needed because he knew my body better than I did.

I'd come to him ashamed and embarrassed, uncomfortable with myself and sex. Fumbled jilling sessions under the sheets was how I'd gone to him, but now? I was open and proud of my body, unashamed and capable of glorying in what we did together.

When he took me to the edge, yet again, I moaned when he stopped. I didn't even have it in me to be scared when he positioned himself, his dick at my pussy, the thick, blunt tip pushing into the small, soft slit that belonged to him.

His eyes were on mine, narrowed and fierce as I opened up to him, and I didn't let go of the connection, made sure he saw what I was feeling and thinking, made sure he sensed my lack of panic.

And in the grand scheme of things, the terror I'd expected wasn't there.

Because it was Link.

Because I was his.

And because he was mine.

I sucked in a breath when it grew a little painful, but the pain wasn't a trigger. If anything, I was relieved when he pushed through, thrusting into me until I could feel him all the way inside me.

Gulping at the sensation of fullness, of thickness, I watched his eyes close, his head tip back, and his face grow tense. I knew why too.

Heaven.

He was in heaven.

A heaven I gave him.

I bit my lip at the sight, needing him on top of me, needing to be closer, but also needing to give him this moment. He'd been waiting on this for months, waiting and waiting, never knowing when I'd be ready, so if he could be patient with me, I sure as hell could be for him.

Then, his head rocked forward and he moved atop me, like he'd read my mind. He hitched my legs higher around him, rocking my pelvis up so that I could take him better. The position changed things, I wasn't sure what, but suddenly, he was deeper and there was no pain.

I blinked up at him, mouthing the word, "Wow."

He didn't laugh, didn't tease, if anything, he was unlike Link. A nerve ticked in his temple, in his jaw too, and the strain on his face told me just how hard this was on him.

Just how much this was affecting him.

Which was the cherry on the cake for me.

This meant the world to him, because I meant the world to him.

I felt honored and cherished and loved.

Sensations I'd never expected to feel at this moment.

I reached up, joining our mouths, before I breathed into him, "I need you, Link. I want you. I love you. Please, be mine?"

He brought our foreheads together again, but it was so unlike earlier that it was like night and day. He rocked his on mine before he started to move his hips. His whole body was tense, the exact opposite of my playful lover, and I registered how much it was taking out of him to hold back. Not to give into his desires.

Well, I couldn't have that.

I dug my hands into his butt, wanting to give him everything he needed from me, and I knew I'd made shit real when I grabbed his cheeks and spread them, my fingers digging toward his butthole—my man's true hot spot.

But he shook his head. "You're too small," he ground out.

"No. I'm not." I rocked into him, forcing this, forcing him to move, to claim what he needed when I slipped the tip of one finger inside him.

And when I did, he lit up.

I truly knew what a rocket flight felt like.

He'd taken me to the moon and back more than Elon Musk ever could, but sweet fuck, that was nothing to now. He whipped us up into a storm, into a frenzy that was impossible to match, and through it all, he grounded me, filled me with him, until I didn't know where he started and I ended.

Our skin was cleaved to each other, the heat and intensity overwhelming and overpowering and exactly everything I'd ever needed without knowing what it was that my body urged from me.

The orgasm took me by surprise. I hadn't thought about coming, had just focused on him. But when I recognized that with each grinding of his hips, he was rubbing my clit—smart man—it all fit, and it let me break apart, shatter into a million pieces because I knew he'd be there, would *always* be there, ready and waiting to pick me back up again.

When his hips moved faster, rockier, his thrusts less measured and more imperfect, his roar of delight had me groaning with wonder as he came.

Inside me.

At long last.

He shuddered atop me, his entire being shaking as he fell down to Earth, but all the while, our foreheads had been smushed together. All the while, we'd been united as one.

And it was so fitting, so perfect, after he kissed me, and he whispered, "Thank you."

I gulped. "You're welcome."

"The answer's yes, by the way," he rasped, pecking the corner of my mouth again, moving so close that the brush of his eyelashes against my cheek sent shivers down my spine.

"The answer?" I groaned, my mind elsewhere as I felt him and me, united and joined in this way.

His laugh was smoky. Pure Link—he was back in the building. My cocksure lover who loved me for all my flaws. "You forgotten your proposal already, sugar tits?" Then he smirked before he kissed me again. "You beat me to it. I was saving asking you for when I got inside you the first time."

I blinked at that, then grinned at him, so fucking happy at that moment I wasn't sure what felt better—the two orgasms I'd just had or this feeling. "Really? You'll be my husband?"

"I'll be anything and everything you want me to be, Lily," he rasped, his voice turning serious and somber, but deep in his eyes, I saw the truth of it.

He meant it.

He'd be my anything, my everything.

Just like I'd always be for him too.

EIGHTEEN
LINK

"WHERE'S MY RING, SUGAR TITS?"

NINETEEN

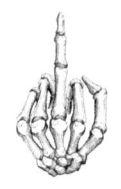

INDY

IT HAD BEEN A LONG, arduous week.

Stressful and tiring.

I figured it was fitting that things had ended with a funeral, even if I hadn't had to go. I'd never liked Dog. I'd always thought he was a jerk who thought with his prick. Sarah, one of Lancaster's victims, I felt bad for, but not enough to attend. Maybe I should have gone for Stone and Giulia's sakes, but I preferred to get lost in work, and my clients had helped by clamoring at me for appointments.

If anything, it had been such a shitty seven days because I hadn't had the chance to see much of Cruz in that time, and a little like a junkie needing their next fix, I knew he was what I needed.

I didn't appreciate needing anyone, certainly not someone I couldn't depend on, but either my heart was a goner or I was just a fool. For some reason, I'd taken to trusting Cruz, a man I barely knew, over someone like Stone who knew me better than anyone on God's green earth.

Of course, she didn't know everything.

But neither did Cruz.

Secrets, so many of them, shrouding me in their depths, covering me in shadows. Was it any wonder I slept like shit? Was it any wonder nightmares haunted me?

David had gone for the day, and while I had another client scheduled for ten PM, I'd canceled it the second Cruz had called me because, as much as it pained me to admit it, I needed tonight more than he could know.

More than I needed the five hundred bucks Grace was supposed to pay me after I finished up her tattoo, at any rate.

As I stared at the paper Giulia had given me, one that was dog-eared from her handling and now mine, I tried to transfer her crude drawings into reality. She'd said it was down to me to handle the design, but she'd still had some ideas.

The Satan's Sinners' MC logo was simple. A skull with a short set of flared wings. Brisk. Masculine. It was what it was—a sign. You got in their way, they'd send you to the devil with wings on your back and your brain blown to smithereens.

But the idea that Giulia had conceived surprised me because it had flowers on it. *Flowers.* On a skull. Not like a *calavera* or anything like that. If anything, the skull was harder. Meaner. The lines a tad fiercer, with the promise of death in the eye sockets. Somehow that made for a sweeter contrast with the wings that were spanned fully. Some sweeping down with a feminine line, other feathers bristling with flight. There were flowers dotted at the jaw, around the teeth, above the head like a fascinator of all things, but the promise was still the same.

Death.

To anyone who fucked with a Sinner.

Which made it quite clear that Giulia believed she was one of them.

Which made her a fool. A fool I liked, but one nonetheless.

Women were good for a few things in the MC, and being a brother wasn't one of them. Cock-sucking, cleaning, cooking—the three 'C's. None of them appealed to me, which made it all the more galling that Cruz had managed to get his hooks into me.

I grimaced at the thought, then as I lowered my head to the desk so I could make the tiniest of final strokes to the petals of the flowers decorating the skull, I decided that it was perfect.

For the moment.

I'd be seeing Giulia in the morning, so I could show her then. We'd work on the final design until she was pleased with it, and then I'd be tattooing her declaration on her skin—even if it was a silent declaration that no one on the council would ever sanction.

As my cell phone buzzed, I arched a brow when I saw who it was.

"Thought you'd be in an orgasm-induced coma by now."

Stone snorted out a laugh. "I would be, instead I'm just in the afterglow."

I made a gagging noise. "Stop being such a pussy."

"Why? Steel loves it."

"I'll bet," I said dryly. "Why you calling me if he's all up in that puss-puss of yours?"

"Ewww."

I grinned, well aware of what she'd think of that question. "Come on, spill. You're calling for a reason. Is it the funeral? Did something happen?"

Stone released a breath. "You don't want to know, and what I can tell you is that I shouldn't say shit over the phone."

Brows furrowing, I asked, "Is everything okay?"

"It's fine. Now." A note of glee entered her voice. "Guess who had to hit the road tonight."

My mouth dropped open. "Someone left the Sinners?"

"Nope. They didn't leave, they were pushed."

"Who?" I demanded, dread filling me because...

Shit, this was why I didn't like getting involved with people.

When you got involved, they started to matter to you.

Before, I couldn't have given two shits about whether or not someone was tossed out of the clubhouse. But when it was a brother, they didn't leave by choice. Usually it went down with a bullet between the eyes.

It wasn't Cruz.

It couldn't be—

"Tink."

At that, my eyes flared. "No fucking way."

"Yeah. Some shit went down after the service, and I was pissy at the wake. Steel went upstairs to his room, and I followed him. Only found the slut trying to wander into the bathroom, stripping off. We got into a fight. I let her win."

I rolled my eyes. "Yeah, yeah. You *let* her win. You're still fucking injured, Stone. You couldn't shove a butt plug up Link's ass if he spread his cheeks for ya."

"Ewwww. Why are you being so gross tonight? I don't want to think about Link's butthole."

"Only Steel's?" I mocked, chuckling when she grumbled.

"Shut the fuck up about my man's ass."

"Well, you can't deny that it's fine."

"I don't deny it, but you shouldn't be thinking about it."

"No, I guess not. Not if you'll have me run out of town," I said with a laugh. "What happened?"

"I'm not going to lie, I was weak, but I knew if the guys caught her beating the crap out of me, she'd be tossed out. Not very fair of me but—"

I huffed. "Fair? When she was beating the shit out of you after you've been so sick? Yeah, she was really worried about fair too."

She hummed. "This is very true."

"Don't feel guilty. You know what they're like."

"Cunts?" she asked sweetly, making me laugh.

"Exactly." I grunted. "So, we're one skank down. What with you and Giulia making their lives miserable, they'll be pouring out like flies soon enough."

She giggled. "That's the plan."

Chuckling as well, I picked up my pen and added a few tweaks to the drawing. "It's good to hear you laugh, Stone. I mean, I'm not saying you were a miserable bitch before, but…"

"You're all heart."

"I know," I teased, but then curiosity hit me. "Aside from Tink, everything else go okay?"

"As well as a funeral can go. I'm surprised they're not angrier about Dog's death. From what I can tell, they're not even going after his kid and ex-wife."

"That's some funky shit right there. The Sinners have always been incestuous, but seriously? Banging your dad's wife? How skeevy is that?"

"Verrrrry," she drawled. "I get it though. You've seen North. Why would you fuck Dog when you could have North instead?"

A mock gasp escaped me. "My, my, and you so recently branded, Stone."

She pshawed. "Not saying that I want to tap it, just that I get the reasoning behind it." She heaved a sigh. "You were lucky to get out of the funeral."

"Lucky? Ha. I ain't a Sinner, sweetheart. You're the one who's neck deep in the MC again, not me. I can still do whatever the fuck I want."

"You and I both know that kind of freedom is BS," was her retort. "They'll let you go so far before they start reeling you in."

"Bear let me go to Louisiana," I pointed out.

"And Rex hauled you back in again, so don't pretend your ties are cut. Plus we both know the lengths you'll go to for Caleb. You've already pulled some ninja moves for him and the MC, so you're not as untouchable as you like to think."

I blew a raspberry down the phone.

"Very adult, Indy, very mature," she joked.

"That's me. Known for my maturity." I grunted. "Will I see you tomorrow?"

"I don't know. I have my first full shift coming up. I'm already exhausted."

I pursed my lips at that. "Pretty sure if Steel knew that he'd tie you to the bed or something."

"I wouldn't argue."

"Kinky," I said with a laugh, but it wasn't like I could fucking judge, not with the shit Cruz did to me. I got the feeling that the rest of the brothers were pussycats in comparison to him. "Anyway, I'm not asking you to go for a goddamn hike with me, Stone. Just feel like binge-watching some Netflix together is all."

"Oh, that sounds like fun. You come to mine though, right? So I can crash after? I get tired far quicker than I'd like, and even though it was totally worth it, Tink did pull some moves tonight that've made me sore."

"Course. You bring the snacks though."

She scoffed, "When don't I? Your tiny ass is shit at bringing junk food."

My lips twitched. "Yours is tiny now."

"Seems there's an advantage to almost dying. Insta-diet."

"Yeah, well, don't feel like you have to do it again. I'd prefer your ass to be the size of Lady Liberty's but for you to be hanging around, yanking on my chain all the goddamn time."

"Aww, Indy, I didn't know you cared."

"Shut up, bitch."

She snickered. "Takes one to know one."

I straightened up once I set my pencil down, then wriggling my shoulders where the strain of bad posture made them ache, I got to my feet.

A slight movement in the corner of my eye registered with me, and I whipped around, jerking in surprise when I saw David standing in the doorway. How he'd managed to open the damn door without me knowing set me on edge, and I scowled at him, before I said to Stone, "Honey, I gotta go."

"Okay. I'll see you tomorrow, you pain in my ass."

God, I loved this woman. She always remembered my anal-retentive farewell, and it was doubly important now, considering it had saved her butt when that psycho fucker had kidnapped her. I'd only known something was wrong because Stone had hung up the phone without our habitual farewell.

"Takes a stitch in my fucking side to know one," I retorted with a smirk, but the second the line cut dead, I grumbled at David, "Thought you were on your way home."

His narrow face puckered with nerves as he looked at me, he even started wringing his hands in his agitation.

"What's wrong?" I asked with a sigh.

He swallowed. "He isn't right for you."

My brows surged at that. "Excuse me?"

"You heard me," he rasped, but when he repeated himself, his voice was stronger, a tad more strident. "He isn't right for you."

"Who isn't?" I snapped, not pleased with the direction this conversation had taken.

As far as I knew, he'd been making his way home. Why the hell he'd come back again, I'd never know…

Unless.

Had he tapped my phone again? Bugged it so he knew Cruz was on his way over?

Or was that just me being paranoid?

David's shoulders hunched at my annoyance, making me wonder what on earth it was about me that made him stalk me. I wasn't someone who'd ever make him happy. Even if he was deranged, he had to know that.

We were like apples and oranges. Nothing about us fit. I'd never questioned things, never threatened the status quo though because being obsessed with someone didn't have to make sense, did it? But I didn't understand what it was about me that was like moths to a light.

I was independent, bossy, strident. Rude, most days. Angry all the time. I had a massive chip on my shoulder…

What about any of that would appeal to a mild-mannered *man-boy*?

But appeal to him I did.

He'd never confronted me like this before though, had always used underhanded methods of keeping an eye on me. Some of them had been creepy, and I'd gotten in his face over them, but this was different. Which meant he was either concerned or escalating and neither prospect put a smile on my face.

I didn't need his concern.

As for escalation, the last time that had happened was when I'd moved from New Orleans to West Orange. At first, he hadn't followed me. He'd just sliced his wrists open. Guilt had me visiting him in the hospital, and offering him a position at my new tattoo parlor—Indiana Ink.

He'd come with, and had been relatively normal ever since.

As normal as a stalker could be, at any rate.

Reaching up, I rubbed my eyes where exhaustion was hitting me hard. The last thing I needed was to get spanked tonight—more than anything, I just needed to sleep. Unfortunately for me, sleep came with a dose of orgasms.

Huh.

Maybe not so unfortunate, after all.

Trying not to smile at the thought, I heaved another sigh and grumbled, "David, don't spoil things."

"Spoil things?" he repeated, the pitch of his voice surging high at that. "I dedicate my days to you, Indy—"

"That's your choice, David," I retorted, trying to stay calm. "You want to be here. I don't make you do anything you don't want to." When hurt creased his features, I told him, "I'm grateful for you, David. I'm grateful for all you do for me, and to help me, but you have no right to dictate to me. You're not my brother, father, or lover."

"What am I then?" he snapped, temper making his eyes flash with a light I didn't like.

"You're my friend." I tried to temper that with a gentle smile, because I knew being a friend wasn't what he wanted from me.

In all the years he'd been stuck to my side, I wasn't sure what he wanted. He never seemed to look me up and down and strip me naked, never seemed to be sexually attracted to me. If anything, he looked at me with yearning. Like I was a favorite treat he wanted to savor but had been denied it by his mother.

I wasn't sure what got his rocks off, and to be frank, I didn't want to know.

I figured I'd been kind by letting him hang around me, but if he thought I was going to let him lay down the law, then he was wrong.

No one did that to me. Not even Cruz. He might think he did, but only because I let him. Only because I trusted him and let him inside.

In more ways than one.

And that only happened when we were upstairs. Outside of my quarters, I didn't need someone taking charge of my life. I was a successful businesswoman, and I didn't need a man for anything other than orgasms.

"I'm more than a friend," he rasped. "I do more for you than anyone else around you."

"You do," I agreed. "And I'm grateful."

"You never show me that," was his petulant retort.

I narrowed my eyes at that, not appreciating his words or his tone. Hitching my hip against the desk, I folded my arms against my chest and decided to call his bluff. "How would you like me to show you that, David? Would you like me to sink to my knees and—"

A mixture of horror and disgust flashed over his face. "No!" He even backed up a step.

"Then what do you want from me?" I replied, trying to puzzle what on earth he got out of this arrangement if the thought of sex with me was that repugnant.

"I just want to love you. I want to look after you. Is that so wrong?" The step with which he'd retreated, he surged past, taking four more to get closer to the desk. The beseeching look did nothing for me, because I hadn't asked for any of this.

Never had. Never would.

I hadn't asked for Cruz's attention either, even if, now, I was grateful to be in the epicenter of his focus.

I wanted no man to look at me the way David did. In my opinion, it wasn't right, to be the air someone breathed, to be the reason they got up in the morning. And definitely not with someone like me. Not when I was who I was.

Because the truth hurt, I rasped, "You deserve someone better than me, David."

My candor had his mouth gaping. "There is no one better than you."

Tilting my head to the side, I murmured, "You know what my family has been through, and how it changed me."

His face turned puce with rage. "I'm just glad he only hurt Carly and didn't touch you."

My eyes flared wide at his remark, a remark that felt like a slap to the face.

"Carly's suffering was okay then, was it?" I snapped, straightening up, my hands furling into fists.

"N-No, I didn't mean that!" he denied, retreating once more. "I just meant I-I'd kill your uncle if I could."

So many men willing to kill Kevin, it was just a shame no one had been around when it was happening.

What use was all this *after* the fact?

They were just words.

Not a promise.

If Nyx knew what I'd gone through, he'd want to kill Kevin all over again, and would probably go on the rampage a thousand times more until his soul bled black.

David uttered those words like they could help me, like they meant something. When they meant nothing. They were just letters that were scrambled together to form *his* emotional reaction to something *I'd* gone through.

It was the same with Nyx. Of course, if I told him that, he'd shout me down. Tell me that everything he did, he did for Carly, our elder sister. But that was bullshit. She was dead. A bag of bones that had rotted away a long time ago... Me, I was alive. Living. Breathing. Somehow getting through what that bastard had done to me. Maybe not always achieving it, but I considered it a win that I hadn't tried to hurt myself for a very long time.

I couldn't say how grateful I was that Cruz, though he knew the full story, had never said anything like that to me, had never made me feel lesser for what I'd gone through.

"The threat has long since gone, but the stain inside me hasn't, David."

His brow puckered. "You're not stained. C-Carly—"

"I am." I shot him a dead-eyed stare. "I'm dirty."

His eyes flared wide again, like he registered what I was saying. Like he understood. But rather than empathize, rather than tell me again that he'd kill Kevin if he could, and rather than wish me all the happiness in the world, instead he snarled, "And being with that filthy biker—?" His head whipped from side to side in confusion. "I don't get it. Why *him*?"

"That you even know about me and Cruz tells me you've been looking at the security footage or doing something I told you not to do again, David." My mouth tightened. "If I find a camera in my apartment that will be the end of things. Of *everything*, do you hear me? I've been violated one too many times, but I trusted you. Don't make me regret that trust," I rasped, watching as his eyes shuttered.

"I've seen him leaving here at all hours of the night," was all he said.

A likely fucking story.

"What I do with him is my business," I spat.

"I'm trying to keep you safe."

"I am safe with him, David," I snarled. "I *sleep* when he's around."

His reaction to my words was like I'd hit him with a saucepan. His eyes rounded as he jerked back, but even as dismay laced his expression, there was a desperation too.

"No," he whispered.

But I nodded. "Yes, David. *Yes*."

"You can't feel safe with him. He's a liar," he snapped, before he started digging through his pockets. When he produced his cell phone, he swiped it open then tossed it at me.

As I stared at the photos on the screen, I shook my head as I moved through the gallery. "What is it? What am I looking at?"

"That woman is a Fed."

"You know this how?" I scoffed, scowling at him over his phone.

"Because I made it my business to know." He tightened his mouth. "She's a Fed and he went to her. Sneaked off the other day."

I narrowed my eyes at him. "When you just had to have the day off?"

He shrugged. "I had things to do."

Things like stalking my—

Shit.

My, what?

I hated that I needed a frickin' label when I loathed goddamn labels.

Boyfriend? Lover?

Cruz felt like more, but the words that described 'more' weren't ones I could handle right now.

As I dealt with the repercussions of what he was saying, I murmured, "If you knew that Cruz had plans that day, and you had to because you left before he even turned up, and you also know about

Cruz coming here at all hours, I'm going to assume that you haven't just kept an eye on me but somehow, you've managed to get into the clubhouse." When his glance flittered off mine, I knew I was right. Knew he'd learned about Cruz a long time ago. Maybe he'd known from the very beginning? "You stupid prick, David," I snapped. "What the fuck do you think you're playing at?

"Do you think the Sinners are just joking around at being an MC? Christ, they're one-percenters! They don't just wear cuts because it's a fashion statement." Swiping my hand over my hair, I didn't stop until I could rub the back of my neck where tension was gathering like I'd been plunked dead in the center of the eye of a hurricane.

I had to believe that Maverick kept the clubhouse swept clean of tracking equipment, but somehow, David had gotten inside—

As I stared at him, questions hitting me square in the face, I took in the man who'd committed a grievous sin against my family, who had picked up on only God knew what as he spied on them as a means of spying on *me*, and I reasoned that, even if he wasn't my type of guy, he *was* handsome.

Maybe a little skinny, a little too nerdy, but someone in the clubhouse had helped him, and the only person I could think of, the only *people*, were one of the clubwhores.

Not only would David be gentle where the bikers weren't, but I knew there was a lot of resentment floating around among the sweetbutts. Not only because a lot of the council were slowly picking up Old Ladies like they were souvenirs on a trip to Greece, but because those councilors weren't cheating on said Old Ladies. Throw in the fact that Giulia was making their lives hell by forcing them to clean, it was all a disaster just in the early stages of brewing.

Processing that wasn't easy. I'd thought David was harmless, but I should have known he'd get jealous of Cruz. It was stupid, even worse, *shortsighted* of me, not to realize that and act accordingly, yet neither was it exactly my fucking fault. I didn't ask David to be obsessed with me. I didn't want this level of attention aimed my way.

This was on him.

All of this was.

And the trouble was, what he knew, he could leak.

Would leak if I wasn't careful.

He'd hurt them to get to Cruz, to get to me, which made him dangerous.

I'd known that for a while, but I'd thought I could handle him. Now, I learned I couldn't.

He was out of control, and he'd taken things up a notch.

In the periphery of my line of sight, I registered that the streets outside were empty. It was past ten and the bars were at the other end, not near my storefront because I'd wanted to be away from the action. Close enough for the drunks to trickle in, but far away enough to avoid bar brawls.

The roads themselves were quiet too, and the only light in the vicinity burned from my building.

There'd be cameras somewhere. I knew Big Brother was always watching, but... Would it look suspicious if I shut the blinds?

Before I could say a word to mess things up, I strode away from the desk, away from David. He growled under his breath, demanding, "We're not done, Indy."

Oh, we were more than fucking done.

I ignored him, well aware that would agitate him further, and stalked deeper into my studio where there was no line of sight to the street.

With barely a few seconds to spare, I headed for my work station that was clean from my earlier appointment and ready for the one I'd canceled so I could be with Cruz, and ducked down to grab a pair of scissors from one of the drawers in the medical cabinet where I stored some basic First Aid.

Palming the handle, I twisted around when David snarled again, "We're not done, Indy," and compounded his foolishness with the cocking of a gun.

It'd have sounded overly loud in the charged atmosphere if not for the rushing in my head, the burning in my ears of my pulse as it surged like a geyser, deafening me to everything, including his shriek as I twisted around and threw the scissors at him.

My aim was true.

Exactly like Nyx had taught me years ago, and unfortunately for me, it wasn't the first time I'd had to protect myself this way.

Somehow, knowing I was cursed, I knew this wouldn't be the last time either.

The handle turned over in a straight line, folding over and over itself as the blade writhed around during its catapult across the way. The gun fired, but his inexperience with the weapon had the bullet shooting wide as he sank to his knees, the scissors sticking out of this throat.

I gulped, watching the blood bubble around the wound, before it started to trail out of his mouth, down the corners. The light in his eyes began to fade away as he started to sputter. He toppled forward, and I shoved my fist to my lips as he gurgled when the move had his chin tipping down, ramming the thin blades in further.

Expecting to see the tips of the scissors through his nape, I studied him a little too hard for comfort. Then, a shaky breath escaped me, because though I'd done many things in my life that I was ashamed of, I'd never stooped to murder. Self-defense, sure. Yet, here I was, killing for the Sinners.

Fuck.

Although, he'd waved a gun at me... Did that make this self-defense too? Even if, when I'd drawn him in here, I'd known exactly what I was going to do—eradicate a threat against the people I loved?

As I stared at David, at his stillness, where the only movement from him came from the blood pooling around him, trickling out into an ever-growing puddle, I wasn't sure what I was feeling predominantly.

Was it fear?

Terror?

Rage?

Uncertainty?

I knew I should feel ashamed, but mostly, it was just relief. God, how horrible did that make me sound? I was relieved someone had died, and at my fucking hands.

Gulping, I flopped down against my stool, which skittered backward because I gave it no purchase. As I jolted into the client chair, the cabinet loaded with tools rattled, and I jumped like another bullet had gone wide.

My mouth trembled as reaction set in, but still, I felt no shame. No guilt.

David had always been a concern. Maybe not an active one, and he sure as shit wasn't the reason why I was losing sleep, but I'd known he was delicate. That he had to be handled.

That he was gone was a weight off me, a burden that disintegrated into dust that I no longer had to carry on my shoulders.

But my biggest concern was what he'd done.

What he'd learned and who the fuck he'd told.

And who he'd used to infiltrate the clubhouse.

Christ.

I sucked in a breath, unsure of what to do. *Who to call.*

Did I want the Sinners involved in this? Did I just call the cops and plead innocence, tell them it was self-defense?

My instinct was to call Cruz, but what David had said blew that all into question.

Cruz had gone to a Fed.

A fucking Fed.

And David had learned that because he had to have been boning a clubwhore. Someone on the inside who'd given him that information.

All the while my brain raced through options, time ticked on, as it had a habit of doing, until it eventually ran out because the front door opened and I heard boot steps.

Ever since Kevin, I'd learned to listen to people's steps, and to use them as a means of identifying whether or not someone was friend or foe.

That, and the fact I knew it had been long enough for him to find his way here, was proof enough that Cruz had just walked through my door.

Was he a traitor?

And if he was, what did I do with that information?

He'd betrayed the Sinners. I already had one brother in prison. I couldn't deal with Nyx being in there too, and never mind the council, most of whom I'd grown up with. Steel and Stone had just found each other, Link was happy with Lily for the first time in forever, then there was Sin and Tiffany, and Nyx and Giulia—all of them lost souls that had found their other halves in each other.

My mind whirred at that, because I couldn't let them be torn apart. I just... fuck, I just couldn't.

Scrambling off the stool, I raced over to David's side. Grabbing his gun, I held it in my shaking hands as I started to back away from the door that led to the reception area.

"Indy? Are you down here? You shouldn't have left the place unlocked," Cruz called out, his grumble clear.

If this was any other night, he'd have spanked me for it. I could hear it in his voice. There was anticipation as well as annoyance. Need, too.

For me.

And I wanted that. I wanted *him* so much.

God, how had this situation derailed so terribly? How had things exploded in my face when I'd only just been saying to Stone that I wasn't involved in the MC? She'd called me out, said that was a steaming pile of BS, but this was a thousand times worse than anything she could have hurled at me.

"In here," I hollered, and I cringed because, even to my own ears, I sounded shaken.

Cruz was getting more and more used to reading me, to sensing my non-verbal cues so when I gave him verbal ones, I knew he wouldn't fail to recognize that something was wrong.

The door kicked inward, but as it did, it slammed into David's body.

"What the fuck?" Cruz muttered, before he shoved harder, forcing the corpse decorating my floor like it was some kind of messed up art exhibition to slide across the tiles.

The blood dispersed, running into the cracks of the tiles, and I bit my lip, trying to use the pain as a means of keeping myself grounded, of not letting panic overwhelm me.

Now he was here, the timeline had shifted, and I had to act.

The question was, it had been easy to take David out of the picture.

As for Cruz, even if he was a traitor, it might not simply be *difficult* to take out the rat, it might very well be impossible.

TWENTY

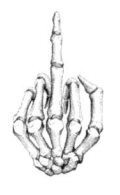

CRUZ

I KNEW something was wrong the second she called out, but when I saw the dead body on the floor, I'd admit, I hadn't expected that.

My interest caught, I kept my focus on the corpse, trying to figure out who it was. Definitely a guy, from his clothes and stature, but with his face kissing the floor, I couldn't make out the man's identity. Then, I looked at her, and found myself staring down the barrel of a gun.

A *shaking* gun at that.

Attributing that to nerves, I murmured, "Indy, it's okay. You took out the threat. Well done." I had to assume that whoever this fucker was, he'd tried to attack her, because Indy wasn't violent. She was a brat, sure, and had more attitude than frickin' hair, but she wasn't a danger to other people. And I'd know, because I lived with a shit ton of guys who *were* dangerous to the general pop.

At my words, however, she didn't respond. The gun stayed pointed at me, quivering as it wavered in her grip.

"Indy," I intoned, trying to imbue her name with a bark she'd be used to hearing by now, "put the gun down."

Only, she shook her head. Not just once, but twice, three times even. "N-No. Who the hell are you?"

Surprised, I blinked at her. "What do you mean? I'm Cruz." Jesus, was she heading into some kind of fugue state? She was more fragile than people knew, but I'd never have thought she'd crumble—

"Liar," she spat, and though her vitriol was out of place, I didn't let it stop me from dropping down so that I could turn the body over.

When I did, she let out a soft cry, and seeing David, her assistant, as well as the scissors that were burrowed in his throat, I knew that, whatever he'd taught her, Nyx had made sure Indy knew how to handle herself.

I'd figured that, to be honest, but had just never thought I'd be seeing it firsthand.

"I'm not a liar," I told her calmly. "I'm Cruz. You know this."

She stopped bracing the hand that held the gun and blindly sought something out on her worktop. I caught a glimpse of the phone, but the next second, it was flying through the air at me. Catching it, I peered at the screen, then sighed when I recognized where I was.

And with whom.

A couple of swipes into the gallery and I saw that I'd not only picked up a tail but the fucker had caught me with my mom.

Shit.

No wonder she was quaking like a fucking leaf.

"I can explain," I told her calmly, even as I was deleting the images on the phone. It wasn't Indy's iPhone, but a Samsung, so I had to reason that it belonged to David. "But first you need to tell me what the hell happened here? Did he try to hurt you?"

"He's been spying on me. Spying on us, and…" She sucked down a breath. "The MC."

Tension hit me. "No way. That's not possible."

"Isn't it?" she rasped, but she jerked the gun at the cell in my hands. "How do you think he knew to catch you there, huh?"

"David took the photos?" I asked, because though I'd assumed it, confirmation would come in handy. I thought back to that black SUV that'd been hovering in my mom's street—had that been David?

"Which part of 'he's been spying on me,' didn't you understand?"

"I'm not you."

"No, but you've been fucking me. That means the same thing to

David." She pressed her hand to her mouth, took a shaky breath, then corrected, "*Meant* the same thing."

Frowning, I asked, "What's that supposed to mean?"

"David's been my shadow since the last year of my apprenticeship in New Orleans," she whispered. "He was obsessed with me. That's what this is about. He was trying to show me that you couldn't be trusted." She swallowed. "Apparently he was right."

"No, he wasn't," I countered, annoyed as hell that she was questioning me. "For fuck's sake, Indy, are you going to take a goddamn stalker's word over mine?"

"Apparently he's been listening in to shit that I'm not able to hear… He said the woman in the photo is a Fed. Is that true?"

"It's true," I confirmed, regret hitting me when she released a pain-filled gasp. "But, what he didn't tell you, is that she's my mother."

Her eyes rounded. "No. No way. The Sinners would never have let you in if you had ties to law enforcement."

"Well, I'm a brother, and I'm privy to a lot of their secrets, so I can tell you, categorically, that's not true." I gritted my teeth when her hands clenched around the gun. "Indy, put the damn gun down. You're not going to shoot me."

A shaky laugh escaped her. "No? Aren't I? You've seen what I can do—"

I eyed David's body, unable to feel sorry for the fucker when he'd been spying on us.

Only the council had known about my mother, only they'd known where I was going that day. So unless David had just followed me to NYC, and it had been luck or a coincidence, that meant someone had told him where I was going.

I believed in neither luck nor coincidences, however, which meant there was someone definitely on the inside.

It wouldn't be a brother. We knew the risks of turning rat, and a bullet hole between the eyes or a pair of scissors to the gullet wouldn't be the end. No, those fates would be relatively pleasant in comparison to what happened to men who betrayed the MC.

That meant it was a woman.

I discounted the Old Ladies because they knew shit about the place,

Lodestar—well, she seemed a likely option considering I'd seen her break Dog's fucking neck. There were the clubwhores who fit the MO better, though. I highly doubted Lodestar would work with someone like David, whereas clubwhores were like rats abandoning a sinking ship—they always tried to find dry ground before anyone else and didn't care how or who they screwed to find it—and they not only had more access but knew the place like the backs of their hands because the clubhouse, depressing though it might seem, was the center of their universe.

Had to be one of them.

While I needed to inform the council of the threat, more than anything, David's body was the priority. And Indy's safety.

"I need to dispose of the body, Indy. I'm not about to get the police involved in this. I don't particularly want the Sinners to know he's dead either—"

"Why? So you can keep the truth from them? That you are really a fucking narc?"

"No, because I don't want them to know we have a leak. At least, not the lower ranks." I reached up and plucked my bottom lip. "I'm going to get my cell phone. It's in my left jeans' pocket." Then, because I'd be pissed if she did, I groused, "There's no need to shoot it out of my hand. I'm going to call Nyx."

She blinked at me. "What? Why? Nyx? What can he do?"

"Confirm everything I've said, all while keeping this shit under wraps."

Her mouth trembled. "You're really going to call Nyx?"

I scowled at her, not appreciating her lack of faith when I'd gone out of my way to prove that she could trust me over our time together. "Yeah, I am."

A shaky sob escaped her, and within seconds, the gun was on the bench, and she was flinging herself toward me. At first, I wasn't sure if she was going to hit me or hug me, then she burrowed into me, her arms coming around my waist in a chokehold that spoke of her distress.

Indy wasn't affectionate by nature, something that made complete sense to me now, but apparently after killing someone, she was.

Who knew?

Unashamedly taking advantage of the rare embrace, I hugged her back and murmured, "The council knows about my mother. I swear to you, Indy. I have no need to lie to you about that."

Her sobs echoed in my head, and the fact I'd promised myself to protect her, to keep her safe, only for shit to turn around like this, was an ice pick to the skull I wasn't sure I'd ever heal from.

"Why did you kill him?" I whispered, my arms tightening about her when she froze in my arms.

"He backed me into a corner." She pulled back to stare at me with tear-sore eyes, her eyelashes bunching together in tiny triangles that glistened with droplets. "No man will ever back me into a corner again."

The vow came from an adult, but I only heard the whisper of a little girl who'd been betrayed by someone close to her, who swore she'd never let herself be vulnerable again.

I wasn't the most emotional of men. I preferred cold logic, reason, and hard science to feelings. But for that little girl, I almost started crying too.

Palming the back of her head, I shoved her face into my throat, turned mine into her hair and just held her.

"Cruz, what do I do?" she whispered rawly. "I-I wasn't thinking, not really. I grabbed the scissors before he pulled the gun on me, but when he cocked it, I just reacted. I wasn't thinking," she repeated. "But then, he was threatening us all. I knew he'd put the MC in danger—I couldn't let him—"

I hushed her. "It's okay. I'll sort it out."

She shook her head, making the silk of her hair brush against the prickly stubble on my cheek. "That isn't fair to you."

"Fair? Indy, this is what I do. This is my job." Not just getting rid of corpses, but protecting *her*. Tangling my fingers in her hair, I stroked them along the short length of black silk, comforting us both as I murmured, "You forgot that, didn't you? When he was spouting shit in your ear?"

"I never knew for certain that was what you did, though," she reasoned dully. "No one ever said it out loud."

"And I'm not now. But you know what I'm saying, don't you?" In her ear, just in case David's spying involved listening devices, I whispered, "I've cleaned up messier scenes for punier reasons." I kissed the crown of her head. "Everything will be okay. I want you to go upstairs, get a shower, clean off—"

"He didn't touch me," she argued.

"No?" Something settled inside me. I mean, I wasn't fucking happy about any of this, but at least the fucker hadn't tried something on.

"No."

"Well, good. Then take a bath. Just relax, okay? I'm going to sort this out. Nyx will as well."

She peered up at me with terrified eyes, but her words weren't scared, they were strong. God, this woman, *my* woman, was such a fucking fighter. "Look, you don't have to get involved in this. I'll go to the cops."

"And be vilified like Giulia was?" I shook my head. "That's not going to happen. I won't allow it or anyone else to hurt you, do you hear me?"

"I-I hear you," she whispered, a welter of emotion in her eyes that I wasn't used to seeing.

Christ, I felt it too. Like a mirror image.

I patted her ass, not hard enough to hurt but a sharp tap that would stir her into moving.

It worked. Like I'd known it would.

We'd never had the usual negotiations where it came to a Dom/sub relationship, didn't even have a safe word. For anyone else, that'd be a red warning sign that flashed, but I'd kill myself before I pushed Indy too far. She hadn't cared enough about herself to think about a safe word, but now, with the trust between us, I knew it wasn't necessary.

And getting rid of a body was only one way in which I could prove how much she meant to me...

With regret, she pulled back, the way she lingered telling me she didn't want to be anywhere but my arms, then she bit her lip as she looked down at David. Seeing the play of emotions in her expression, knowing the sight of him had frozen her in place, I grabbed her shoulder and steered her out of the room, pushing her toward the door.

Only when I heard her Converse trudging up the stairs did I pull out my phone and call her brother: "Nyx? I need your help. Maybe Maverick's too."

TWENTY-ONE
KEIRA

"HONEY? DO YOU WANT SOME POPCORN?"

Silence.

Deadly. Silence.

I sighed, reached up and rubbed at my tired eyes before I twisted around and returned to the kitchen.

All those years ago, when I'd shacked up with Storm, I'd never have imagined that I'd be living on the compound of the MC I loathed, with an eleven-year-old daughter who hated my guts, or that I'd be bunking with a woman I was pretty sure was a criminal who'd kidnapped her foster daughter.

Shit, there was so much wrong with that sentence that I didn't even know where to start.

To be fair, everyone on the compound was into something illegal. Except me, of course. I was too boring by half to be anything other than the goodie two shoes I was. Just call me goddamn Pollyanna.

As for Lodestar and Katina, if I had to bunk with anyone, they were really nice. Friendly. Gave us space, and we gave them room too. Although it was a little different for us.

Lodestar spent most of her time in the main clubhouse, tucked away with Maverick in his attic. Katina seemed to float around between this bunkhouse, the clubhouse kitchen, and the bunkhouse where her sister was living with two others—women, or girls really, who'd experienced things no woman wanted their daughter to ever go through.

Unlike Katina, Cyan, my little girl, rarely budged from the bunkhouse unless I took her to gymnastics or to her babysitter's place, because even though her daddy was now the Prez of a Sinners' chapter, we'd never really been brought around the clubhouse all that much so the brothers didn't know her. They didn't know me, either.

To them, I wasn't Keira. I was just Storm's Old Lady. Because even though I was his ex, to them, I'd still be his Old Lady until he got another one. Which I doubted would be happening any time soon. Maybe never. Storm wanted me back, after all. Plus, he had no need to be saddled down with another bitch. He was more than happy with the clubwhores who sucked him off without expecting him to do chores on the rare occasions he *was* home.

Unlike Giulia, Tiffany, and Lily, I wasn't a part of the Sinners. I was just an add-on. Cyan was too. Yet even though I'd always been disparaging about them, they'd opened the gates for us, and put a roof over our head and food in our stomachs. I wasn't sure whether to be surprised or simply grateful.

"She'll come around."

I jolted in surprise, twisting so I could see Lodestar standing in the doorway. "I didn't hear you come in."

Her smile was unnerving. "That was my intention."

My nose crinkled. "Do you try to be creepy?"

The smile blossomed into a wry grin. "Nope, but I usually manage it without trying." She winked at me. "I'll have some popcorn."

Taken aback because, thus far, Lodestar hadn't really taken much notice of me, I murmured, "Oh! Well, I was going to watch something on TV. Do you want to join me?"

"Gladly."

Pleased that this wouldn't be another lonely night in front of the TV with no one but myself for company, I dumped the bag of cheesy popcorn into the microwave, then grunted when my cellphone rang.

The ringtone was 'West End Girls' by the Pet Shop Boys. Why? Because I was a West End girl and Storm was an East End boy.

Not literally, of course, but life didn't have to be literal all the damn time, did it?

Cyan, recognizing the song, practically skidded as she rushed out of her room and into the hall, her hands outstretched for my cell. I gave it to her, wondering what had happened these past couple of months to make her so broody and moody. I knew Storm leaving had upset her, but this change had been a gradual thing. His departure had been the opposite of that. One second, he'd been pleading with me to uproot Cyan and myself once more, the next he'd already been in goddamn Coshocton.

"Daddy!" she squealed, making my heart melt and harden at the same time which made it a frickin' miracle I didn't flop around on the floor with a coronary.

She was so excited to hear from him, and after her endless moods, it was a relief to behold. Then I felt guilty. But no one ever told you that you could love your kids, but you didn't always have to like them. I'd go to frickin' war for Cyan, but I'd pay a million dollars, I didn't have, just for this dearth of grumpiness to dissipate.

With one step toward the bedroom we shared now, she muttered, "Huh?" then twisted back around to face me, a glare marring the beauty of the smile she'd just bestowed on a father who...

Ugh.

I couldn't say he didn't deserve her love. He did. He was a good dad, just a shitty husband.

"Daddy wants to talk to you."

The word Daddy came out like she was talking about Justin Bieber, and the 'you' was more like she was talking to a pile of dog turds.

Out of nowhere, her shoulders straightened though, and her eyes widened as she bit her lip. "Sorry, Daddy." She blinked a few times, then, after swallowing, peered at me and whispered, "Sorry, Mom." The phone was shoved at me, and she took off like a rabid dog was nipping at her heels.

Lifting the cell to my ear, I murmured, "Thank you for that."

"There's no need," he said gruffly, and just the sound of his damn voice had me closing my eyes as I turned around to face the small kitchenette so Lodestar, who was watching on with interest, couldn't see my expression.

I didn't need her to know the truth—that I was still head over heels in love with my jerk, manwhore of an ex.

It was a truth I wished *I* didn't know, so sharing it with someone else was just too shameful for words.

"She shouldn't be talking to you like that."

I cleared my throat. "She's just going through a phase."

"Doesn't mean she gets to be rude to you." He released a sigh. "It's good to hear your voice, Keira."

My brow puckered at that, because he sounded genuine. As genuine as a liar like Storm ever could be. I'd say that he could sell bullshit to a rancher, but I was used to hearing those lies. Used to sensing the half-truths he couched in every word he uttered, except, here and now, I didn't hear anything amiss.

And as far as I was aware, there was no reason to have my guard up. What could he do to me while he was all the way over in Ohio?

Aside from rupture the vows we'd made to each other time and time again, of course.

"Are you okay?" was all I asked in response to his comment. I couldn't tell him the truth, that it was good to hear from him too, but I could make sure the father of my baby was doing well. "How's the transition going?"

"It's a clusterfuck," he admitted gruffly. "It's always difficult making shit right, but this is harder than I thought."

"Means it's worth fighting for," I murmured, my eyes on the microwave plate that was spinning around and around as popcorn kernels started to pop. "You know how bored you were here."

"Yeah, I do," he agreed. "I'm pretty sure boredom was the reason I always got into so much goddamn trouble."

I narrowed my eyes at that. "Everything you did here—" It went unspoken that I was talking about his inability to keep his cock in his pants. "—you'd have done whether you were VP or Prez, Storm. You're kidding yourself if you think otherwise."

He grunted. "Maybe."

"No maybe about it."

Silence fell, then he rumbled, "I miss you."

"Did you miss me when I was a twenty-minute drive away?"

"You know I did."

"So why didn't you come for me?" I retorted, brows pinching as I already knew the answer.

"I tried."

"You tried to worm your way back into my bed, sure. You never tried to stop doing the stuff that broke us up in the first place." I jerked my chin up. "Look, I have plans tonight. I don't want to rehash old stuff. Is there a reason you wanted to talk to me? I know Cyan must be bursting at the seams to speak with you."

"I miss her as much as she misses me." Half expecting him to ask me to let her visit him, I was about to argue when he murmured, "I miss you as much as you miss me, Keira. Why do you fight this shit?"

My eyes widened at his words, words he'd never uttered when we were together, never mind now we were apart.

For a few seconds, I'd admit to being speechless, simply because I'd never anticipated him telling me anything like that. Storm had never been one to use words to woo me. He'd just used my body against me, a body that responded to him like gas did to the flame from a lighter.

When you had that on your side, soft words, wooing... neither were exactly necessary.

I gritted my teeth though, unable to fathom that he truly missed me because he'd never missed me before, and as stupid as it sounded, as much as I hated that Lodestar could hear this conversation, I whispered what had been my initial reaction to his remark: "You never missed me before."

"That's where you're wrong. I always missed you. I was just too much of a dumb fuck to accept that what I felt for you wasn't a weakness."

Anger surged inside me. "I'm sure that's exactly what you were feeling when you were fucking clubwhores when I was pregnant," I snarled, the rage spilling out of me in a way that it never had before.

Even when I'd left him, packing up mine and Cyan's things and slipping out of the house in broad daylight because I knew he wouldn't be there to stop me, not when he hadn't come back home in days already, I hadn't been angry. I'd been resigned.

My mother and father's dire promises that he was bad news, that he was scum, that he was a Sinner, and in more than just the club he rode for... all the trash they'd spoken about him over the years had echoed in my head.

I'd felt dumb.

So fucking dumb.

But that was nothing to now.

Until my house of cards came tumbling down because Lodestar muttered, "Keira—"

And when I twisted to look at her, I came face to face with Cyan.

Torment was etched into her eyes, and I knew she'd heard every miserable, damning word I'd never, *ever* meant for her to know about the father she idolized.

TWENTY-TWO
MAVERICK

WHEN SOMEONE GRABBED my arm while I was asleep, I jerked up, ignoring the soft shriek of surprise as my spare hand went for the fucker's throat.

A strong fist around my wrist, followed by the gentle caress of some fingers on my stomach had me blinking, waking up to the fact that I was choking Nyx, and that Ghost was stroking me while crooning into my ear like I was a baby in need of a lullaby.

Although, granted, with her voice, God, she could command anyone to do anything she asked of them. I'd never heard a voice like it. I might stop taking the Valium on the worst nights and just have her lull me to sleep. The combination of that ghostly whisper and her ability to carry a tune was close to angelic—as much of an angel I'd ever get to meet with all my sins darkening my soul, at any rate.

Shaking off the shadows of the past, the screams that littered my ears, the memories that were more turbulent than a tsunami roiling around my head, I focused on Nyx as he shook off my grip and asked, "Haven't I told you fuckers not to disturb me while I sleep?"

If I sounded like I'd been chewing on nails, well, so be it.

"It's urgent," he rumbled, his voice deeper too, thanks to my squeezing on his throat like he was a ripe orange in need of juicing.

"It always is with you bastards." With one hand, I patted Ghost's thigh, and the other I used to wipe at my eyes.

"Ghost, I need some privacy—"

"No. She stays," I barked, my hand tightening about her leg. Not to the point of pain, but in warning. I didn't want her to leave, not so Nyx could bring club business to me.

Nyx heaved a sigh. "Just a few minutes' privacy, Maverick. For fuck's sake. Please?"

I grunted, but directed at Ghost, "You need the bathroom, sweetheart?"

She hummed and scampered off the bed, barely jolting the mattress as she did so.

"Lives up to her name, doesn't she?" Nyx asked, watching her until the door closed behind her before he perched on the side of my mattress. "Almost as bad as Cruz the way they whisper around the place."

I grunted. "Yeah."

"Didn't think she was sleeping in here with you."

"Well, you know what thought did, don't you?" I snapped, then with annoyance, I spouted, "If you tell anyone, I'll gut you like a fish."

He snorted. "Like I'm going to talk smack about your woman. I'm just surprised is all. I'll tell Giulia because it will give her comfort to know you're there for Ghost. You know the women have a soft spot for her."

That was because Ghost was pretty fucking lovable.

Tatána and Amara were nice enough, but Ghost was easier to connect with because her English was close to perfect.

"What do you want?"

"I need to know if you have some kind of device on hand that'll sweep for bugs and monitoring devices."

Scowling at him, I queried, "Why would you ask that?"

His jaw worked. "I need to use one. And I think you might need to sweep the clubhouse."

"I have the equipment, and I run sweeps every week."

"Trust me, it might be wise to scan the clubhouse now."

I narrowed my eyes at him. "Where's this coming from?"

"This isn't council business," he rasped, but I could see he wanted to share.

"Brother, I ain't going to tell anyone shit."

"Good," he ground out, "I don't even need Rex to know this yet. I wouldn't have involved you if it weren't for needing your help. Indy... well, she killed her assistant."

Thoughts flashed through my brain like it was a lightning fast processor. "David? That guy who works with her? The creep?"

"Him," he confirmed, his mouth tightening.

"She killed him?" I repeated, confusion lacing the word. His nod gave no answers, save for a confirmation—it looked like he was just as confused as I was. "Why the fuck did she do that? Didn't David come with her from New Orleans?"

"He did. Cruz—" His jaw hardened. "Cruz went to visit her and found David there on the ground."

"Cruz and Indy?" I asked, brows surging in surprise because Indy's distaste for Sinners was renowned.

"Apparently," he grated out. "He's going to clear up the body, but from what she told him, David's managed to get eyes and ears around the clubhouse."

"Impossible," I grumbled.

"*Not* impossible," he countered. "According to Cruz, the fucker followed us to the city. Took pictures of him with his mother."

"Jesus," I hissed.

"Yeah, you see my problem." His mouth tightened. "We have a rat in our midst, because I haven't seen David around this place, and I'm pretty fucking sure you haven't, or if you had, you'd have told me." He rubbed his chin. "Do you think Lodestar kept the fucker from us?"

I shook my head. "No. She has no interest in our personal security."

Nyx rolled his eyes, but his temper was dramatically reduced at my less than sterling words.

Only a fool would mistake Lodestar's reason for being here.

She was on the hunt while running from someone, and we could keep her safe. At the same time, we could protect Katina, she could get to know her sister, Ghost, and I was here—with a battalion of brothers who were willing to fight to bring down her enemies.

Why wouldn't she stick around?

And though I didn't put it past her to have some kind of listening device on any of us, and was well aware she was capable of spying on us because she'd somehow found out about Cruz's Mom being a Fed—hadn't that been a fucking joke talking her down from shooting his ass?—this just didn't have her scent. I knew her too well. As much as anyone *could* know Lodestar, because I'd known her back before this goddamn world had ruined her.

Had ruined me, too.

Sorrow for us both hit me square in the chest, but I'd long since stopped feeling pity for either of us. What was the point? It changed nothing.

Nothing whatsoever.

"If it isn't Lodestar, then it's either a brother or one of the bunnies," Nyx was saying, drawing me from my thoughts like he knew where they'd taken me when that was impossible. His mind was on the breach in our defenses as well as his sister's welfare.

I reached for him, grabbed his arm and said, "Don't worry about this. It's my job and Sin's. I'll wake him up. You're the VP now, you don't have to deal with this shit, and you have a sister who needs you more than we do."

He grimaced. "Is it shitty that I'd prefer to handle the security?"

"Probably," I confirmed, surprised by the admission though I didn't show it.

"I've never been able to get through to Indy. I doubt she even wants me there."

"You're her big brother, aren't you? When shit goes wrong, when it hits the fan and splatters everywhere, don't you want a psychopathic relative on your side?"

Though his mood was turbulent, his lips twitched at that. "Maverick, you're so good for my ego."

"Just saying it like it is."

"I'm sure." Ruefully, he smiled at me before he rubbed his chin. "I want to help her."

"Then help her."

"I don't know how."

"At the moment, I think she just needs to get rid of a body, and hey, that's something we do on the regular."

"Yeah, in the grand scheme of things, I guess she isn't asking for too much from us, is she?" was his dry comment.

"Nope." My grin died. "You've spent all your life fighting for the sister who died, Nyx, maybe it's time to start fighting for the one who's alive, hmm?" I spoke with caution, not because I was afraid of him or his reaction, but because I didn't want to trigger something in him.

His uncle, his sister's death, all of it had fucked Nyx up. But he'd never seen how his uncle's abuse and the fallout had affected Indy, or Caleb for that matter. I highly doubted Caleb, AKA Quin, would even be a Sinner if it weren't for Nyx. As it was, the kid was in state lock up and all because he'd been trying to impress his brother.

Uncle Kev had a lot of sins to lay at his door, but that didn't mean Nyx had to compound them.

He cleared his throat. "Shit, you don't really think that, do you?"

"Rarely say what I don't mean, brother," I told him softly, clapping him on the shoulder again. "Go on. Go and dig a metaphorical grave for your sister's enemy. That should put you in a good mood."

Laughing, he shook his head. "You're a prick, Mav."

"You and I both know it," I agreed, smirking at him, but I watched as he got off the bed and started toward the door. He veered to the left, though, first, and I watched as, before his hand connected with it, he murmured, "I hope she makes you happy, Mav. You deserve that." Then he tapped, and called out, "Thanks, Ghost. You can come out now."

She didn't obey, not until the outer door to my room closed and then she peeped out, staring at me with those big fucking eyes of hers that I felt certain could see into my goddamn soul.

To me, she was like an angel. While I was no monster, I was well aware that she deserved a man far better than me. But few would slay her demons like I would, and I had to take comfort in that. Take refuge in the fact that I could give her what few else could.

Sanctuary.

A home.

I held out my hand for her, even as I asked, "Can you grab my chair?"

"Is everything okay?" she queried as she hustled over to it, then pushed it my way.

As I clambered into the wheelchair, I murmured, "Everything's fine, baby."

It wasn't.

A witch hunt had just begun, but I always worked at my best when I was under fire, and with her to protect, as well as Katina, under fire was an understatement.

TWENTY-THREE
CRUZ

I EXPECTED him to smack the shit out of me the second he saw me, and I was prepared for it, even if I didn't have time to be dealing with a fistfight, not when David was leaking evidence all over Indy's fucking tiles.

It was my job to get rid of bodies, but this time it was personal.

Indy was going to jail over *my* dead body, so I needed to get moving.

Maybe Nyx registered my concern, my level of dedication to this particular cause because when he tapped on the back door and slipped inside, he didn't say shit, just stared straight ahead at the body on the floor.

Donavan Lancaster had been much worse, and I knew, for a fucking fact, what my brother put his victims through was a lot grodier than this, but he still blanched.

Murder was murder, after all.

And with Indy's past and ties, who the hell knew what could go wrong.

See, for most white folk the cops were a comfort. To others, they weren't, and while Indy hadn't done a damn thing wrong in her life, in their eyes, she was still the 'red-skinned bitch' who'd be judged and found wanting by those wearing a badge simply because her daddy had been a Sinner and her brothers were too. Throw in the fact that Quin was in fucking prison? That was just another nail in her coffin.

Suddenly empathizing with Steel because Stone had been in a similar situation, and look what had happened there? I knew someone had beaten the shit out of one of the detectives working her case because he'd treated her like crap…

"The sheriff is on our side in this town," Nyx rumbled, like his thoughts and mine were entangled.

"You trust him with her?"

Our gazes clashed, and he ducked his head, which gave me my fucking answer.

Reaching up, he rubbed his eyes before he muttered, "What went down?"

"As far as I can tell, nothing that would necessitate this level of force."

He scowled at me. "What's that supposed to mean?"

"That he didn't rape her. But he did pull a gun on her."

That had him snorting. "Then this level of force was exactly right. No one holds a gun on my fucking baby sister."

"I'd ordinarily agree if it didn't mean she was under threat. If she'd done this on the compound, I wouldn't give a shit, but we ain't on the compound. We're in the middle of fucking Verona, and while the West Orange sheriff *is* on our side, who the hell knows if Verona PD is?

"Even with the law in our pocket, Giulia was still slated in the press by the Lancaster family, and I ain't about to have Indy go through that, not when she's already—" My words waned, dropping off before they had a chance to tumble on because I realized, then and only goddamn then, that Indy had never told Nyx the truth.

Not about her past. Not about that cunt. Not about anything.

Fuck.

"She's already what?" he rumbled.

I shook my head. "Nothing. It doesn't matter. I'm just not willing to let her go through that kind of scrutiny, not after this shit with Stone. Not when we've seen what the cops'll do to our women because of their ties to us."

There was a malevolent entity in his eyes as he stared me, and I'd swear to fuck, he was possessed as a tidal wave of hate was leveled my way. "Our women?"

I tipped my chin up because I wasn't scared. Maybe it took one monster to dance with another monster without one of them pissing themselves, but I'd been dealing with cunts since I was born.

Thanks, Mom!

"Yeah, *our* women."

"You staking a claim?"

"Not staking shit without her say so."

"We're Sinners, we ain't equal opportunity when it comes to our Old Ladies."

My top lip quirked up to the side. "Yeah? Then Giulia is a lot more chill with you than Indy is."

"Either that or you ain't keeping a handle on her."

I snorted. "You met your sister? I have plenty of a handle on her, just like she does on me. I'm not just doing this because you're her brother, I'm doing this because she matters to me. We're wasting darkness with a pissing contest that makes no sense because in three weeks' time, she could decide to end shit because that's what she does."

"Yeah, she does. A commitment-phobe that's my sis, but when it happens, are you gonna grow a pussy and start whining about what you've done for her?"

Maybe he saw that he wasn't the only person with malevolence in his soul, because when *I* leveled a look *his* way, his eyes narrowed. "She's safe with me."

And that was all I was willing to say on that matter.

He got it, too, because he shut the fuck up and we got to work.

Both of us with the same task in mind—keeping Indiana Sisson's ass firmly out of jail.

Him, because she was his baby sister.

Me, for more complicated reasons. Not just because I was boning her, or because she was turning into my sub—neither of which even quantified how much she meant to me—but because Indy would die in jail. I wasn't talking about being shanked or shit like that. Nothing to do with her gang affiliations.

I was talking about her soul.

She'd die without freedom. Her spirit would wither away, and when someone came along like her, a woman with a soul as beautiful as Indy's, it'd be a tragedy not to do everything in my power to keep her safe.

TWENTY-FOUR

INDY

I DIDN'T WAKE up with Cruz that following morning, which, I'd admit, made my heart sink.

More than when I realized *why* he wasn't here. I mean, there were one of two reasons. He was still working on getting rid of David's body, or he was disgusted by me.

For obvious reasons, I preferred the original train of thought.

Dealing with Cruz's repugnance was as hard as dealing with the potential truth that he was a rat.

As I lay in bed, staring up at the ceiling as light flickered through the dreamcatchers I had hovering over me while I slept—dreamcatchers that didn't work, I might add—making shadows on the walls, I tried to process just how evil I was if I didn't care that David was dead, but I cared that Cruz hadn't come to bed.

David had been a part of my life for a long time. A *loooong* time. Not of my choosing, obviously. Thing was, I'd always just dealt with him. Just let him hang around, never really thinking about him as a person, just as a *thing*. Like an accessory I didn't want but had to have on me at all times.

That was David.

I'd met him when he came in for a tattoo. He'd surprised me because this weedy little guy had just stared stoically up at the ceiling tiles as I inked a sleeve on him, one that was dedicated to his mom. I'd pretty much read between the lines, seen that he was a Momma's boy and that, likely, she'd died.

A strange memoriam for a man who looked like he worked an office job, never took one foot off the normal path, always doing the supposed 'right' thing. I'd been kind to him at the end, and that was when it had started.

An act of kindness.

He'd come in four times to finish off the ink, and that fourth time, he'd cried as he looked at the complete image. His mom and him in an ornate oval photo frame, and this was no word of a lie, on a tattoo of a wall in his house. He'd even brought the picture in, where it had markings of him getting taller, and pictures she'd framed that he'd drawn over the years.

I'd had weirder requests in my time, and it had been quite a challenge getting the shading on the wall right without it just looking like his skin was dirty, but after, when it was done, I'd hugged him, and I'd been paying for that hug ever since.

Nyx always said that it didn't pay to be kind, and he was fucking right.

The blankets were tangled about my legs, speaking of another fretful night, a night that I'd anticipated ending with me having at least one goddamn orgasm after which Cruz made me hug him, and instead it was the beginning of a living nightmare.

I'd killed a man.

Another one.

And I felt nothing for him.

Nothing at all.

No guilt or shame, at the moment. I wasn't even feeling relieved like I had yesterday.

I guessed, in all honesty, I was just numb.

Rolling my head on the pillow, I winced when I saw the time was eleven. I'd have to be up soon, and while the shop always opened late on Thursday's, the prospect of putting on a blank mask and pretending nothing had happened was an annoying one.

I clambered to my feet, rolling out of bed because I was just getting more and more maudlin as I trudged over to my bedroom window to peer out at the street.

I liked Verona. It wasn't as incestuous as West Orange, somehow. Not as rich, not as well situated, but great for me. Close to my brothers when one of their asses wasn't in prison, and even then, Caleb wasn't far away, I could visit as I chose, and it had a small-town vibe. I'd missed that when I was in NOLA, and that was pretty much why I'd set up shop here. For the vibe. It fit me. Fit where I was in my life right now.

With the memory of last night at the forefront of my mind, I had to wonder if I was as much of a crazy person as my brother because David's death didn't taint things for me like I'd imagined it would.

I wasn't feeling like I needed to run away.

If anything, and maybe the relief was starting to bleed through me now I wasn't groggy with sleep, but I felt like there was a lighter weight on my shoulders.

No more worrying about him catching me with other guys.

No more heavy breathing down the line when he didn't like something I was doing, but was too chicken shit to confront me over it. Of course, the first time he'd confronted me, I'd hurled a pair of scissors at him, so maybe there was something to the whole heavy-breathing thing.

No more him being aware of every single item in the tattoo parlor —which, with my sloppy ass down there, I could admit might be a pain.

And no more wondering sick things.

I mean, I had no proof, but I'd be stupid not to *think* about it, wouldn't I?

He was sneaky, and it wouldn't be the first time he made it into one of my *locked* apartments.

Had he put cameras up here?

Had he seen me rushing from the bathroom into the kitchen bare-assed naked because I'd forgotten to pull a towel out of the dryer?

Had he watched me watch a movie?

Seen me cry into my pillow before I fell into an exhausted sleep?

Had he seen what Cruz asked of me?

That last question resonated.

It'd explain why he thought he had to be the big man all of a sudden. He'd be thinking he could be my white knight, never imagining that the things Cruz wanted me to do were what *I* needed to feel real.

For reality to remain firmly in my grasp for the first time in forever.

Cruz and I had been the trigger.

Which meant he did have video-recording equipment up here. Just like I'd accused him of. Just like I knew he did at the Sinners' compound.

Shuddering with revulsion at the thought, I didn't bother glancing around the place, wondering if there were glass eyes watching me. Instead, I stared sightlessly down at the street, well, I did until a small face cropped up in my line of view. I didn't know Storm's daughter, like, at all, but seeing her smile Storm's cheeky smile, I recognized it was Cyan from that alone.

Curious as to why she was out of school, I trained my gaze on her, trying to see if she was with friends. It was eleven on a school day, for fuck's sake. That had to mean she was cutting class, which made me feel like the responsible person in the room because I knew she shouldn't be doing that.

Yeah, yeah, who was I to judge? I'd just murdered someone and here I was, worrying about Cyan's school record, but ya know, *priorities*.

Storm's daughter meant a damn sight more to me than David did, so I was concerned.

Expecting to see a gaggle of girls wandering down the main street, everything inside me froze when I saw her slip her hand into a man's clasp.

Especially when that man turned around and I didn't recognize him.

It'd be creepy enough as it was if she'd been with a Sinner, but at least they were family. Not that family was much protection sometimes, but everyone knew to fear Storm.

I mean, he came across as one of the most mild-mannered brothers, the admin asshole who could rule over a kingdom he pushed pens so hard, but that didn't mean he wasn't deadly with a knife. I wouldn't want to get in his face over scratching his goddamn bike, never mind laying a hand, be it in violence or sexually, against his baby girl.

And shit, she *was* a baby too.

A little older than me when I'd been targeted, but still so fucking young nonetheless.

I watched as they stopped, her tugging on his hand in a way that was playful as she stood outside the ice cream parlor.

Her lack of fear indicated so much, but that didn't make any of it right.

Who the fuck was he?

As far as I remembered from Storm's wedding ceremony, Keira had been an only child, and her parents hadn't shown up because they were prudish pricks who were against the marriage. There'd been no family there that day, none save for Sinners, so that meant he was a stranger.

Well, to me, not to Cyan though, evidently.

I didn't even bother tugging on pants or a sweater, just grabbed some panties then shoved my feet into my Converse, and on the way out of the door, dragged on a coat from the closet that was way too hot for the season, but I didn't give a damn. It just needed to cover my ass.

As I dashed out, I hurried down the stairs, almost falling as I did so. Grumbling to myself, I struggled with the lock next, then managed to burst through the front door. Leaving it open, uncaring what the fuck happened to my shop, I ran down the block to the ice cream parlor, terrified that, by now, they'd have left already.

But fortune was on my side.

They were there, sitting in the window, looking almost like father and child with the way he was staring down at her with an adoration that couldn't be feigned, and the way she looked up at him with stars in her eyes.

There was so much wrong with the tableau that, for a second, I wondered if Keira had brought another man into her life. Was this guy a boyfriend? But, surely not. She was staying at the clubhouse, so why would a man who loved Keira's daughter so much let her live on a bikers' compound? I doubted it.

With a million things running through my mind, I started to dash inside. A second before I did, I smoothed a hand over my hair, and tried to calm myself down.

There had to be an explanation. It was only my past that was making me see shadows at high noon.

So, I sucked in a calming breath and then, as I walked through the door, Cyan's eyes collided with mine, they widened, then she ducked her head and quickly looked away.

Fuck.

Fuck.

Panic started to whirl out of control inside me, but I forced it down, forced myself to smile as I wandered over to them both.

"Cyan, is that you?"

Both the stranger and the little girl, because that was exactly what she fucking was, tensed up.

Bringing Cyan to the next town over was dumb, but if he was grooming her, it'd make sense. What better way than shopping and ice cream to get a child on your side?

Especially one who was messed up over her mom and dad's break up, and the fact that her father had just moved hundreds of miles away—she was perfect prey for a predator.

And when I looked at the guy, whose face was as soft as David's, who looked as goddamn mild-mannered as he had last night, I saw, deep in his eyes, the truth.

Just like I'd seen in Kevin's goddamn eyes.

Struggling to hide my disgust, I murmured, "Cyan, baby, what the heck are you doing out of school?"

"Indy, oh, nothing. I just have a doctor's appointment."

"You do, huh? Where's your momma? Is she parking the car?"

Cyan licked her lips as her shoulders started to bunch up around her ears. "She's working at the diner. Her shift doesn't finish until nine tonight."

I heard the resentment there, but I ignored it, and instead, turned to the man. While it creeped me the hell out to hold out my hand, I had to play nice.

"Indy. I'm a friend of Cyan's father." I smiled at him. "I don't think we've met."

Unease slipped into his mask, but he returned my smile with a pleasant one of his own. "I'm Martin. Keira asked me to help out, so help out I am."

"Oh?" I tipped my head to the side. "You're friends?"

Cyan burst in, "Yeah, Indy, we're friends."

Her rebellious tone had me frowning at her, but I just said, "I don't think your daddy would like to hear you talking to one of his friends like that, do you?"

Her mouth turned mutinous. "Don't care what Dad wants or doesn't want," she snapped, and her hand reached for the guy's. Only, he dumped it like it was as hot as burning coal.

Dismay graced the small features, followed by acute distress, and sensing that this situation was derailing, I murmured, "This is actually good timing, Cyan, because I have a gift for you."

She scowled at me. "You do?"

I knew why she was confused. I barely knew her, had never talked to her, so why the hell would I have a gift for her?

"I do. But it's in my store." I cut Martin a look. "I'll make sure she gets home safely."

He started to protest, but then he said, "Okay, I'm sure that'll be fine. I'll check in with Keira later—"

I'd just bet he fucking would. *The liar.* The stench of the untruth polluted the air around us.

I reached out for Cyan's hand and murmured, "Come on, honey."

She shot Martin a look, but he was shooing her away with a smile that held the tinge of a warning—something I remembered too well from my own past. The tenderness that was couched in a selfish desire. The pervasive command that told a small child *they* would get what they wanted, no matter if the kid was scared or unhappy—their wants counted for nothing in this dynamic.

The past choked me, shadows flooding me to the point where I could have blacked out, but knowing I had to keep her safe, had to protect her like no one had protected me, I tugged her into moving, and when we reached the counter, Pearl, the server, called out, "Indy, I've got her ice cream here."

I paused, waited for Pearl to pass Cyan her treat, then tugged her out onto the street.

As the ice cream started dripping down her hand, I got the feeling that today hadn't turned out how she'd expected.

Nor had it for Martin.

Brightly, I asked, "Where did your mom meet Martin?"

Cyan scuffed her toe into the ground, and that goddamn ice cream carried on dripping down her hand. Splat. Splat. Splat. We left a trail of breadcrumbs back to my store of molten orange sherbet.

"He's a volunteer with the gymnastics' team at school."

My throat felt tight. "Huh. I didn't realize you were into gymnastics."

"Well, no, you wouldn't know that, would you? You don't know me."

And that begged the question why she'd come with me, why Martin had allowed her to go, if they were supposed to be together. If they weren't trying to hide something.

When we made it back to my store, I saw Cruz was waiting there, scowling at me, but his scowl dispersed when he stared down at Cyan's wan face.

I flared my eyes, trying to get him to back off, and he seemed to get it because he retreated to the backroom without Cyan catching notice of him.

As I locked the door behind me, pocketing the key so that she couldn't run off, I murmured, "Take a seat. You need to eat that ice cream or more of it will be on you rather than in you."

She flung herself down on the sofa and did as I asked. No enjoyment to it, just mechanical in motion like she wanted to obey to, once again, quell my suspicions.

Unfortunately for her, my suspicions were at an all-time high, mostly because I knew from what Stone had told me that Cyan had been acting up like mad, giving her mom a lot of shit. But also because of my past.

She was a prime target for someone like Kevin. I could almost stamp his face onto Martin's features.

Animals all looked the same.

I had a small table over in the corner with a Keurig on there and some cups along with a tray of pods, and desperately in need of the caffeine and the sugar, I started brewing a cup before I murmured, "Martin looked kind."

Cyan peeped a look at me before she muttered, "He is."

"Were you really going to the doctor's office?" I asked, throwing the question over my shoulder.

"Of course. I said I was, didn't I?"

"You did, but girls lie." I winked at her. "You looked like you had a fun day ahead of you, not an appointment to get a shot."

Her mouth tightened. "It was supposed to be fun. We were going to go to the park next."

"You were, huh? So the doctor's was a lie?"

"Maybe."

"I'm not sure your mom would be happy to think of you cutting school to hang out with your friends, Cyan, do you?"

She shrugged. "Mom doesn't care about me. All she cares about is work."

I snorted at that bullshit, because no woman left a Sinner like Storm without reason. And that reason? Self-respect and the need to imbue it into her daughter.

As Storm's woman, Keira wouldn't have had to work a fucking day in her life. Yet, here she was, slogging away at the diner, working hard for little pay, and barely any gratitude from her kid.

My reaction had Cyan scowling. "Are you laughing at me?"

"You bet your ass I am."

"Why?" she snapped, her eyes flaring wide with agitation. "You have no right to laugh at me."

"I have every right, because you just proved to me how young you are because no one, no one, loves working at a damn diner more than they love their daughter. She isn't exactly saving lives, is she?

Ain't finding a cure for cancer in the bottom of a pot of coffee... what on earth made you think she cares more about her shitty job than you?"

Tiny shoulders hunched. "She's never around anymore."

"Probably because she's working hard to put food on the table."

"Dad sends money."

"Yeah? Does he also send self-respect?"

That had her peering at me, her eyes round. "What does that mean?"

The Keurig hissed and spat as coffee sputtered from the spout, and I kept my attention on it, rather than her, as I asked, "You know when you ace a test, and it feels good?"

"Yeah."

"If you'd cheated, if someone else had done the hard work, would it feel as good?"

"N-No."

"That's self-respect. Your mom can take your dad's money, or she can work hard to show you that you don't need a man to put food in your belly.

"Sure, it sucks that she isn't seeing you as much, and I'm sure that hurts her as well. But I bet it hurts her more that you're so upset with her when all she's trying to do is prove to you that she's worth more than just the pennies your father lays in her hand.

"What's she supposed to do with the rest of her life? Just let him keep on providing for you both?"

"At least I'd see her," was Cyan's grumbled retort.

"You could go to the diner, you know? You could sit there, it's kind of what you do in a diner. You could do your homework there, and when she's between orders, she could talk to you then."

"It isn't the same."

"Why? Because you don't get all her focus? Grow up, Cyan," I said with a snicker. "You don't even want her full attention, because if you did, then I doubt you'd have been able to skip school to hang out with Martin."

I turned around just in time to see her cheeks burn a bright red. "He's my friend. He's interested in me."

"Yeah? I'm interested in you too. Tell me, what do you and he do together?"

"We just hang out."

I hummed. "That all?" I raised my coffee to my lips and took a sip even though it was scalding hot. Then, deciding to throw whisky onto the flames, I asked, "Does he kiss you? It feels nice when a man kisses you on the lips, doesn't it?"

Eyes widening, she sputtered, "He doesn't do anything like that!"

"No? What do you do then? Does he hold your hand?" I knew he did. I'd seen that on the street.

"No," was the belligerent retort, which meant I couldn't believe a fucking word she said.

At least I could see she had a tell. The more mutinous she was, the closer I was to the truth.

I just hummed. "When I was younger than you, I had someone who showed me a lot of attention. It feels nice, doesn't it?" The lie burned inside me like acid tearing into my organs. "It's strange at first, because, when I was that young, I used to think all boys had cooties, but I liked the way he treated me like I was so grown up." I cast her a look. "Is that how Martin makes you feel?"

She twisted her head to the side, her mouth pursed into a flat line, and I knew I'd lost her.

I didn't say another word, just strode over to the phone, picked it up and placed it to my ear.

"Who are you calling?" she demanded, her voice morphing into a squeak.

"Your mom. So she can come and pick you up. I have an appointment soon."

"Y-You said you'd take me home. That's why Ma-Martin let me leave."

Well, wasn't that an interesting turn of phrase?

Why Martin let her leave.

I turned it over in my head, then said, "Well, I need to tell her how upset you are. She needs to know so she can make things better."

"I-It's okay. She doesn't need to know. You're right. She's working hard to make sure I have self-respect—"

"What does he do with you, Cyan?" I asked, sliding the question in with all the finesse of a batter sliding into base feet first.

"Nothing," she rasped. "Nothing." And just when I thought she wasn't going to tell me anything, she tacked on, "I mean, not yet, anyway."

And my heart both soared and sank.

TWENTY-FIVE
NYX

MY BLOOD LUST WAS HIGH.

What with helping Cruz dissemble a corpse in my sister's workstation, then watch as he shoved it into a vat of goo where another corpse was already being broken down into gunk, the monster in my soul was beyond ready to party.

I wasn't made to be the VP.

It wasn't a role that was natural to me. Leadership wasn't something I could ever be comfortable with, but I'd only just killed a sick fuck and usually, with Giulia riding me harder than the monster in my soul, things stayed calm for a mite longer than this.

But knowing there was a pedophile working in the town neighboring mine?

Knowing that he'd targeted my brother's kid?

I was more than jonesing for this kill.

It was only by chance that I overheard. Cruz and I had just finished our final clean-up of her shop, when she'd gone storming out before storming back in again.

When I'd tried to go after her, Cruz had held me back. I didn't appreciate that, and I'd showed him my lack of appreciation with a punch to the gut, but he'd still stopped me from going after her. Just in time too. He'd shoved me back into the studio when the door had slammed open yet again, but she was no longer alone.

I didn't know Cyan that well. It wasn't like I was interested in kids, even my brother's, but she'd been hanging around the place with Katina, the two of them getting into all kinds of shit on the compound, so I'd recognized her voice.

I'd also recognized what she was saying, what Indy was drawing out of her with girl talk... *Cyan was being groomed.*

Right under my fucking nose.

A hand slapped me on the shoulder, jerking me from my thoughts. I flinched, not expecting it, which told me how deep inside my head I was.

Twisting to look at Cruz, I rumbled, "Best not to touch me when I'm in this mood."

He shrugged. "The only person who's under fire right now is that sick fuck." His mouth tightened. "I want in."

My brows rose. "Huh?"

"You heard me. I want in. When you catch him, I want to be there."

My lips snagged up in a snarl. "You think you can handle—"

"Bro, I melt corpses down for the club. I think I can handle the shit that goes down beforehand." I knew he thought he believed that, but I eyed him skeptically. "You ever killed someone before?"

He snorted. "Think I'm little orphan, Annie? Yeah, Nyx, I've killed someone before."

"Who?" I jeered, watching his scowl make a swift appearance. "And I'm not talking a long-distance kill either."

"Because that takes away from the act?" he snapped, glowering at me. The glower, however, made me let up. Not because I was frightened of the fucker, but because I got it.

I saw it.

Death changed a person, and if you killed enough people, it left a stain on your soul. The eyes were the windows to that, after all, so, deep within that glower, a frown that was burrowed into his eyes, I saw the truth.

"You never told Rex," I remarked.

"Some shit you don't share."

I shrugged. "You'd probably be doing more than pouring tequila if he knew."

"Doubt it. Not with my mom around."

"True." I winced. "Think you've proven yourself by now though."

"It's okay. I never asked to be on the council, and I'm not asking for anything more than what I'm already doing. I like keeping my hands dirty, and you guys give me the opportunity."

"Is it true what Maverick says?"

"What does he say?" was Cruz's wary retort.

"That you used to be a scientist? Wore a white lab coat and everything?"

His smile was twisted. "Yeah. I even had a pocket protector and a little lanyard just to tie it all up in a neat bow."

My brows rose at that. "Legit?"

"Legit." He just hitched a shoulder. "Not like it's something to brag about."

"In a place where half of us didn't bother to get our high school diplomas, I'd say that I respectfully disagree."

"Never known you to be respectful, Nyx, so don't feel the need to start now."

His insolence pricked my temper, but he'd done Indy a solid. My baby sister knew what it was to kill someone now, but this man, this brother of mine, had helped make things right. Had covered it up.

That was the joy of the law.

No body.

No crime.

Was there anything more beautiful than that?

I leaned my arm against the door, peering through it as Indy and Cyan sat together, their shoulders hunched as they talked about things I didn't really understand, or want to.

After Carly, Mom had done her best. She'd taught Caleb and Indy how to protect themselves, what to watch out for. But it wasn't like Stranger Danger was a thing here when your fucking uncle was the viper in the nest.

Just thinking about Kevin made my blood boil, and normally, I wouldn't let it. I'd force myself to calm down because if I killed too often, then shit would come raining down on me.

Before Giulia, I'd always thought I'd either end up dead before forty because no way was I going to let the cops take me in willingly. I'd imagined a blaze of glory with the boys in blue shooting my ass before I ever got to jail. Or, if luck wasn't on my side, then I'd end up in an orange jumpsuit and I'd die on the inside.

I had no intention of heading toward either future. Not now. Giulia needed me. More than she knew. And I was very okay with that. I needed her to need me. It kept my head on straight. Stopped me from losing my shit on the regular.

Like now.

I had the wherewithal to reason that I couldn't piss in my own backyard, which was where this fuck, who thought he could groom a Sinner's kid without retribution, was.

Well, he'd learn otherwise soon enough.

I reached for my cell and flipped through for Maverick's number, before I hit connect, Cruz murmured, "She's already called Keira."

"She isn't who I'm ringing." When the call connected, I murmured, "Mav, I need you to do a search for me."

"Sure. Who?"

"No surname, not yet—"

"Jesus, I swear you think I can find a needle in a farm of needles."

"Stop bitching, you know you love a challenge."

Mav grunted. "Go on, give me details."

"Martin's a volunteer at Cyan's gymnastics' class."

He hesitated. "Huh?"

"Cyan—Storm's kid."

"I know that, dumb fuck, but what the hell am I—" He broke off, then a hiss escaped him. "No."

"Not yet," I soothed, but there was no soothing either of us.

"Storm needs to know."

I blew out a breath because Mav was right, but this couldn't happen here. It was bringing too much shit to our door.

There were already whispers about the guy who killed kid fuckers, who made them pay for their sins. They roamed around the States because I usually did my hits when I was on a run, but if I pulled a stunt here, it could lead things directly to our front door. We'd already had an issue back in Coshocton, at our sister chapter where Storm was the new Prez, because Giulia had inadvertently blown up the warehouse where we'd been torturing the last guy on our shit list.

The police were dumb fucks, but they weren't that goddamn dumb.

"Let's just find shit out first. I need confirmation, you know that."

Maverick grunted. "I'm on it."

"Whatever you do, don't tell Lodestar. This kill is mine. And if not mine, then it's Storm's, you hear me?"

"Loud and clear. You have any other information?"

"No. I don't want to ask Cyan, either."

"Understood. I'll figure shit out."

He cut the call, and I shoved my cell back into my jeans' pocket, wondering at my next move.

With Maverick on the case, working to find evidence that Martin deserved my wrath and wasn't just an overzealous parent—it hadn't happened once in all the time I'd been doing this, but fuck, you never knew and I wasn't about to kill someone who didn't deserve my attention—I had some choices to make.

First things first, Storm needed to get his ass back home so he could make things right with his woman and his kid.

Once the threat was out of the picture, that was the priority.

My parents had been torn apart by what had happened to Carly. My mom blaming my dad for not figuring out that his brother was a pedo, dad unable to cope with not only Carly's suicide, but the fact that Kevin was who he was.

Dad, while never overly demonstrative, had been torn to shreds by the fate that had befallen our family, and had drunk himself to death long before his time.

By that point, it'd been a relief for him to pass over. Not only was he a mean fuck, Carly needed someone to protect her in the afterlife, and that was all Dad had wanted.

To be reunited with his baby girl.

I scraped a hand over my jaw as an innate refusal hit me. Whether

Storm and Keira liked it or not, the Sinners, as a fucking whole, were going to get them back together again.

I didn't give a fuck if it took a vat of Gorilla Glue or if we had to chain their asses together for a week.

They were going to be a family again. Because Cyan needed that. She deserved that. And I protected kids in more ways than just seeking out predators who sniffed around them.

That was the promise I'd made to Carly a long time ago, and it was one I'd never break.

Ever.

TWENTY-SIX

INDY

KEIRA'S PANIC, her frantic terror, all of it resonated with me on another level.

This was love.

This was what it looked like.

I was sure my parents had looked at me like this too, at one point. Back in the day, we'd been pretty close before our worlds had come crashing down around us, and everything had gone to shit.

What had been a pretty tight home life, at least, for a family in an MC, had suddenly begun crumbling down around our ears.

Trouble was, it hadn't been a safe space for me to reveal anything that I'd gone through. With Mom and Dad ricocheting through their lives like they were a pair of cannon balls that had gone wide, arguing and hating on each other, casting blame left and right, I'd just never been able to tell them what I'd gone through.

It was the first time that I realized how special Cruz was.

How much I trusted him to keep me safe, how much I believed in the protective circle he had around me.

We'd made no vows to each other, had basically agreed that we'd start dating out in the open, for all the world to see, which wasn't exactly the equivalent of a marriage proposal, was it? Not that I wanted that, but still, there was no commitment between us.

But trust and commitment were not the same thing.

I trusted my body with him, when I'd never trusted anyone with it before.

And that had let my mind unlock, had let me find my way to opening up to someone for the first time in my life.

I knew when he slipped behind me, when his arms moved around my stomach as I stood, watching Keira and Cyan talking in the front seat of her car.

They hadn't moved since they'd left, and I wasn't sure why she hadn't taken advantage of my offer to stay in the parlor, especially when I'd closed up for the day, my mind definitely not ready to handle the brush with the past as it morphed into the present, but watching them, seeing her talk, trying to get through to Cyan, it made me realize how much my mom had let me down.

"She never asked me if Kevin touched me," I said softly.

"Your mom?"

I nodded. "Never."

He hesitated. "Because she didn't want to know?"

"I think so. Or maybe because she was just so devastated that she couldn't handle knowing he'd touched me too."

"Which do you think?"

"A mixture of both. Things changed after Carly died."

"In what way?" One hand moved from my waist to run up and down my arm. The touch made the tiny hairs there prickle in response, and I registered yet again how my body seemed to sense this was Cruz.

Anyone else who dared touch me right now, even Nyx, maybe even Stone, I'd probably have started shrieking.

As it was, Cruz grounded me.

And I didn't think he even knew it.

"The news only came out about Kevin after Nyx killed him."

"You know about that?" he asked, his surprise clear.

I snorted. "Yeah, I know about that."

"How? I thought it was a club secret."

"I was there that day."

He tensed. "No way."

I hummed. "Dad and Kevin were going out hunting. One of Nyx's chores was to clean the guns." I shrugged. "I happened to watch him doing something to Kevin's."

"He messed with the barrel of his rifle, didn't he?"

My smile was twisted. "Yep. That's why you should always clean your own guns," I chuckled, aware I sounded bloodthirsty and uncaring of that fact.

If anything, I'd have given my left ovary to have been the one with the balls to stuff something down that goddamn barrel, but instead, I'd just watched, a little wide-eyed and in awe as Nyx did something no teenager should even be thinking of doing.

It was then, as my family crumbled around me, as my parents who loved us, started doing stupid shit that robbed them from us, essentially abandoning us, I realized Nyx never would.

He'd always be there for me. For Caleb and me.

Which was why he pissed me off when he didn't visit Caleb in prison.

Because he'd been there, a fucking thorn in our side throughout the majority of our childhood, beating up bullies, getting in teachers' faces, generally hovering until we were old enough to live our lives.

It was only now, that I saw how much he'd pulled back when we'd become old enough, that I realized how much I missed him.

Would Giulia bring him back to us? It felt like she was.

He'd been on the brink a long time. His absence not just physical, but mental and emotional.

Nyx was changing.

I knew Giulia was the reason for it.

A kiss was pressed to my shoulder, a soft one, then a little swipe of his tongue along the tendon that joined it to my throat which he nipped had me jolting to attention.

"You didn't trust me."

The flat statement was in sharp contrast to the gentleness with which he held me.

"For less than fifteen minutes," I argued, "and hey, I just killed someone. I think I'm allowed a timeout."

He snorted. "You're aware that isn't how we work, aren't you?"

I winced, even as, deep down inside of me, some part craved what he was telling me.

Why?

I'd never really know, not unless I went to a shrink, and that wasn't about to happen. I'd put myself through a couple hundred hours with a psychologist, but had come out of it feeling worse rather than better.

Self-medicating with fucking around was a lot cheaper and had made me *feel* something, even if what I'd felt was all bad. Messing with other guys to try to make my body act normally, punishing it because it wouldn't behave like everyone else's, was in the past, at least.

I knew full well that staying true to Cruz was another act of self-medication. I was too aware of my nature to fail to recognize that.

So, because he was right, I just sighed. "I'm sorry."

And I meant it.

"He showed you some things that would make anyone question," he reasoned, which countered what he'd just said because he gave me an excuse.

"The second you wanted to show Nyx, I knew everything was okay."

He hummed. "We need to work on making sure that you trust me, and not your brother's word. I get that he's always been your guardian though. The one you run to whenever shit hits the fan, but that's going to change."

The tension inside me hit fever pitch. "You can't replace him, not when you don't intend to be in my life for a long time."

"Who says I don't intend that?"

I froze, unable to believe he'd said that. "The other night, you just wanted us to come out to the club. You said I had to earn my Old Lady patch…"

"That was because I hadn't seen you kill a man with a pair of scissors yet."

I heard the amusement in his sinister tone. "This isn't funny."

"I never said it was. I'm just amused at your weapon of choice."

"It wasn't like I had an arsenal waiting out in the backroom for me."

"No," he concurred. "Still, it was nice to see you're great with improvisation.

"But, you have to bear in mind. Until now, you didn't know about my mother, and while she means nothing to me, I knew it was a chasm I'd never be able to cross without reason. The council knows about her, and that's about it. That's how they sanctioned my patching-in in the first place."

"I'm surprised they didn't shoot you between the eyes."

"I think they were hoping I'd be able to get information out of her to feed them, but in the end, I had other talents they preferred to take advantage of."

"Like getting rid of bodies?"

He hummed. "I'm not saying either of us is ready for branding, Indy, but I'm just saying, I can see a light at the end of the tunnel, and there's a shape blocking it that looks like you."

Emotion choked me, making it hard to swallow, making it difficult to breathe for a handful of seconds until, like always, I fell back on snark. "That your way of saying I have a fat ass?" I wheezed.

When he tapped my thigh, with enough force to jerk me to the side, I bit my lip.

"That your way of trying to earn a worse punishment? Just take the declaration in the spirit it was given, hmm?" He pressed a kiss to my throat once more, only this time it was an open one. As he sucked down on the sensitive skin, the tissues that were raked to life had me shuddering in his hold and turning me into a pile of mush. Any other man's kiss there would have me shrieking too, but this felt so good. A whisper of calm before the scream of a storm that was brewing. "Now, are you ready for your punishment?"

My fluttering eyelashes froze, but I released a breath. "Y-Yes."

This felt different somehow. I was used to the stern taskmaster, the man who could order me to kneel on my welcome mat and I'd obey. But his voice was a little... Crap, the only way I could think to phrase it was *odd*.

It was just odd. Not one I'd heard before.

When he turned me around, dragging my gaze from the mother

and the daughter who were trying to work things out, trying to come back from the fact that Cyan had almost trusted someone she most definitely shouldn't have, I let my brain switch off.

I had to.

The need to go to her, to tell her what it was like when an older man gave you *that* kind of attention, to reveal secrets I'd only told Cruz, was a weight on my soul.

I'd never meant to tell Cruz, dammit, never mind a little girl, but I'd see how things panned out.

Her dynamic with Martin was entirely different than the one I had with Kevin.

I'd been terrified. She, quite clearly, wasn't.

"Stop thinking," ever diligent and ever the goddamn mind-reader, he rumbled.

And because he made it an order, I found myself willing to obey it.

With my focus on my room, I saw a couple of things that had my brows rising.

"Thought you got rid of corpses, didn't think you made them."

He sniffed. "Every serial killer's tool is the same as a cleaner's tool, except the blood is shed post-mortem, not ante."

My nose crinkled, because I knew that meant a knife wasn't used to end life, but to chop up limbs.

Great.

My boyfriend.

The cleaner.

And we weren't talking toilets here.

I cleared my throat as I took in the knife which was sitting on the nightstand, then the two kind of knots of white nylon rope which gleamed silver in the light.

"Indy," Cruz barked. "I won't warn you again. Keep your focus on me."

I shot him a look. "How do you know when it isn't?" I wasn't speaking with belligerence, more like curiosity.

"Tension leaves your body, and I want you very much tense. I don't like it when you turn to ice on me"

I crinkled my nose at that. "Charming."

The quirk of his lips in a barely there smile had me rolling my eyes.

"Now, you won't like this, but you're not supposed to like a punishment, are you?"

And with that, he began.

TWENTY-SEVEN
CRUZ

THERE WAS a soothing rhythm I found when binding a woman, making loops here, knotting there, sweeping the length of cord over elegant limbs, framing bones just so.

But with Indy, it was actually hard.

With every ripe curve I unveiled, I wanted to taste it. Wanted to taste her.

Punishing her involved punishing myself, and that was one of the things I'd always hated about BDSM.

There was so much pageantry sometimes, so much effort when, some nights, you just really wanted to end the day with your cock in your woman without having to whip her ass first.

But a vanilla life wasn't something I could enjoy entirely either, so I found myself at an odd crossroads as I tied Indy into the position I wanted.

A crossroads that delved into the fact I'd only started being a little more masterful because she needed it, but I saw that I needed it too. Maybe not as much as her, maybe just as much. I wouldn't know until we'd been together for a while.

Until we were out of the closet, and the excitement of hiding behind closed doors had waned.

Not that I'd felt that way, but I knew a lot of women liked the idea of the forbidden. Knew it got some of them wet.

Speaking of...

A garbled noise escaped her as I finished my last ties, and I peered at her, saw the anxiety in her eyes, as well as the relief.

Such an odd combination.

I knew she'd expected something worse than this, but she wasn't going to get it.

As this wasn't about sex, I'd stripped her down to her panties, not even complaining about her wearing them when I'd ordered her not to—this was about trust, and with her pussy covered, she knew that from the get-go.

Leaning forward, her stomach against her thighs, I had each forearm bound to her calf, strapped there with a web of knots that ended at just above the elbow and starting in a cup I made around the ball of her foot.

One leg was already complete, the other, I was just making that cup for her heel.

The bright red ball gag stopped her from speaking, but had drool trickling out the sides of her mouth and down her chin, some of it pouring over her tits, some of it landing on the mattress or on her legs.

As I finished the final knot, I stepped back to take in my work of art.

It was good.

Very good.

I'd gone for a white nylon because I'd known the shiny white would look breathtaking against her golden skin, and here was my confirmation.

I hummed as I moved forward, and started to unravel the bun I'd put her hair in at the start. When the shorter strands tumbled loose, I sighed in delight at the picture she presented.

A picture I needed to capture.

Grabbing my phone from my pocket, I snapped her defiant eyes, the grace of her arched back, the intricate knots that made diamond shapes along her limbs, and the general submissiveness of a pose that restricted her movement to that of rolling around the bed and simply spreading her legs wide or closing them.

There was a reason this was called the crab pose.

If this was entirely sexual, I'd have fucked her like this, while she was incapacitated, unable to do anything other than take what I had to give her.

Instead, I was teaching her a lesson.

More garbled noises escaped her as I took a couple dozen pictures, focusing on little points that only I'd recognize and appreciate. The way the skin dimpled under the pressure of the rope here, how one diamond of bound flesh was redder than the next.

When I was done, I returned my phone to my pocket, and eyed the strip of material between her legs which was damp.

And not from her drool.

I shook my head at her, wagging my finger as I murmured, "Good girls get rewarded. Bad girls need to think about what they've done."

I twisted around at that, and started to walk away from the bed. Her garbled words turned higher in pitch, her panic clear. I turned back to look at her and intoned, "Calm down."

But her eyes were wide, and those gorgeous tits of hers were heaving from a combination of panicked breathing and the restrictions of her position.

If she didn't calm down soon, she'd pass the fuck out.

I stared at her, rumbling, "You will calm down, Indy, or the punishment is over and I'll be falling asleep in *my* bed and not yours."

Her eyes flared wide, but she made a choked effort to gentle her breathing.

I nodded as I headed to the door, where I toed out of my boots and placed them in the rack there. Then, barefoot, I ignored her entirely and went to the kitchen.

Thanks to the open plan nature of her apartment, I knew she could see me from the bedroom, and I made it a point not to look at her once, not now I'd taken all the pictures I needed to remember tonight.

Not that I'd forget what had gone down, not exactly, but at least this way, I'd end it with a better sight than how it had started.

Indy's wet panties were a helluva lot more interesting than her assistant's sightless eyes staring up at me.

Peering into the refrigerator, I saw she had the ingredients for roast chicken in there, which came as a surprise because as far as I knew, she didn't really cook.

Still, seeing carrots, onions, a bag of string beans, the chicken itself, and then upon further inspection, finding some potatoes, I decided that was what we'd be having for dinner.

Which fit with the timeline.

Though it was a deceptively simple position, it couldn't be maintained for long. But, because it was deceptive, in her mind, she'd be thinking I could leave her like that for hours on end.

I wouldn't do that, even if I was tempted. Which, today, I wasn't. Maybe in the future she'd piss me off enough to tie her up with the intent of leaving her there for hours, but today wasn't that day.

Today, she'd been traumatized, in more ways than one, and I was just grounding her.

Reminding her that she wasn't the kid who'd been abused by someone she should have been able to trust.

Today, she was a woman. A woman who'd helped a girl that could've ended up as twisted up inside as Indy.

Here, now, she was more than just Indy. She was a woman. A living, breathing sculpture who needed to remember that, to me, she was more than the sum of her past.

Every day was a fresh one when you had a submissive. You couldn't take bitterness over into tomorrow, otherwise you'd spank too hard, whip deep enough to bleed.

Doms were only human, and filled with foibles, but when you had a sub, one who allowed you to enact all those kinks that made you different, one whose trust enabled you to be free, you had to tread lightly. You had to forgive.

They trusted you.

You had to live up to that trust.

So, I cooked. While she watched.

I scrubbed the potatoes, peeled the carrots, chopped up the onion, and tossed them together in a little oil I placed in a baking tray. When I found some rosemary on the windowsill where she had some fresh herbs, I tossed that in too, before I placed the chicken atop the veggies, covered it with foil, then set it in the oven.

Prepping the string beans, I placed them in a pan of cold water, ready to boil them later when the chicken was done.

All that set, I saw it had taken me thirty minutes from the time on the stove, and I washed up, before I padded over to her.

She hadn't moved, and her gaze tracked me as I headed for the bed.

When I stripped off my cut and Henley, leaving my jeans on, interest lit those bronze eyes, and I climbed onto the bed, before I arranged her how I wanted her.

On her side.

It was awkward, but I was a fan of awkward.

Nothing worth doing was ever simple.

So, to the 'C' shape she made, I curved myself around her, letting my front cup her back, and my hand moved over to her front.

She was wet with drool, and I started to swirl my fingers in it. Not to soothe, just to ground.

Nothing was dirty here.

Not drool, not pussy juices, not my cum.

I wasn't into piss or scat play, but if I was, that wouldn't be dirty either.

What we had transcended the regular bounds of a relationship.

I didn't want to see her at her best.

I wanted to see her at her fucking worst, because that was trust.

That was freedom.

"Last sub I had, I was only twenty-three," I murmured, hushing her when she tensed.

It might not have seemed wise to talk about another woman when I was in her bed, but there was shit I needed to share, shit she needed to hear. I didn't need feedback, just for her to grasp the reality of the situation we found ourselves in.

"Not many subs will trust a Dom as young as that, but I found them. Usually they were older than me. A lot. I didn't mind. I kinda liked it because they settled on me for the age difference. Bored housewives with aging husbands who had pouches over their belt buckles—

why wouldn't they like a trim guy who reminded them of what they could have had when they were my age? When they were too scared to play how they wanted to?

"The reason subs don't trust young Doms isn't just because of a lack of experience, it's the lack of wisdom. It took me a long time to realize that I had a lot of disdain for subs, especially the ones who were eager to obey.

"That was why I stopped. I backed off, because that wasn't, and isn't, how this dynamic should work.

"I was a disrespectful asshole, and I actually apologized to the women I dominated. They didn't understand, because I hadn't mistreated them, so they didn't get why I'd be annoyed at myself, but it was a point of honor for me to apologize and for me to move on with my life because no Dom should ever feel that way.

"Submission is something a man earns. It isn't something he deserves."

A noise escaped her, but the gag did its job. I cast a look at my watch, registering I had another twenty minutes max to keep her like this. That was edging it, but Indy liked to push boundaries and I knew she'd tell me if she was in outright pain.

Trust worked both ways.

I tapped her thigh, just above the webbing, and murmured, "Just listen. No talking." A sigh heaved from her, a disgruntled one, and even though I grinned, I murmured, "Now, at the clubhouse, there's a glut of pussy, and I won't lie, I took advantage of it. But the second I saw you on your hands and knees, scrubbing the floor in Stone's bunkhouse, well, hell, all those old urges came tumbling back.

"I realized that I wasn't just a Dom to get easy pussy, because as a brother, I have access to that all the time.

"Naw, I was a Dom because I like to see a woman stripped bare, and I ain't talking clothes.

"I don't like bullshit, and you're the Queen of Bullshit, Indy." She tensed. "You are. You're a liar. You wear a mask. You hide from the truth because you don't want people to know what you are. Who hurt you.

"You've let men into this beautiful cunt of yours to punish yourself.

To make yourself feel something." I reached up and rubbed my fingers over her mouth. "I've seen these sexy lips that look perfect stretched around my cock in all kinds of colors, none of them sexy. You were made for reds and golds, Indy. Not greens or blacks. I've seen you with thick make up, and while that's your choice, and you can wear whatever the fuck you want, it's *why* you wear it that disturbs me.

"Because you, sweet Indy, are beautiful. You can't hide from it. And you don't have to anymore.

"Covered in saliva, a gag straining the seams of your mouth, sweat on your limbs and beading at your temples... you're beautiful.

"And this beauty is mine. I'm not ready to brand you, and maybe neither of us will ever be ready for that, but we both know, that whatever happens, once that door is closed, this is the real you." I pressed a kiss to her temple. "And I see that real you, and I understand that you, and I want *that* you. No one else. No other shade of Indy. *This* Indy. Do you understand me?"

I let the words sink in, let her process them before I asked for an answer to my question, but then I got it.

In sobs.

They wracked her slender frame, poured out of her like a burst of rain in a summer shower. They made her heave with them, her body, already tethered, shuddered with reaction to the outpouring of emotion she hadn't expected to shed.

That *I* hadn't expected her to shed, in all honesty.

I hadn't said any of this to decimate her.

I'd said it for her to know her fucking worth.

This woman was a fucking queen, and it was time she started living like that.

With nothing else to do, I held her. Until the sobs stopped, until her breathing grew raspy, I was there for her. And then, I pulled out the knife I'd stored with my cell in my pocket, and I started to pop through the taut bindings. Releasing her flesh from the diamond webs, not stopping until she was free.

And when she was, she twisted around and huddled into me, so tightly that it was a struggle to release her mouth from its bondage too.

But I got it.

I did.

And this was honest.

Real.

Exactly what I'd asked for.

So I held her in my arms, gave her what she needed, and let her be the Indy she was born to be.

Mine.

TWENTY-EIGHT

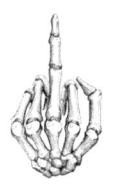

INDY

WITH THE EMOTIONAL wreckage laying around me, I didn't even notice the pins and needles in my hands and feet that came with liberation, I just noticed *his* hands and *his* feet. They pressed into me, rubbing my calves and my back, holding me tight, so tightly that I felt like he'd never let go.

And I wanted that.

I wanted him to keep me.

I wanted him to be there. Always. To hold me when I fell. Uncaring that I was a mess, uncaring that I wasn't perfect and pretty.

Wanting me raw and open.

A soothing hum escaped him as he touched me, and though I could feel his boner, and I knew I was wet, this wasn't sexual.

It went deeper.

So deep that I didn't understand it, but found a curious freedom in realizing that I didn't need to.

It just was.

Earlier, I'd watched him head for the door, certain he'd leave me like this, only to watch him untie his boots. It was then I realized how wrong it was for me to trust him so little. He'd never leave me like this.

Ever.

Then, I'd seen him in my kitchen, preparing dinner, and after, I'd listened to his experiences in the lifestyle when he was younger. In the white space he'd left me in from when he cooked, my mind had been curiously adrift. My one focus him.

It wasn't buzzing with thoughts of today or last night. It wasn't buzzing with worries or fears.

Just him.

That was all I saw.

All I heard.

All I breathed.

All I needed.

With my lips pressed against his throat, in my favorite position of them all, he grunted when the timer went off on the stove.

I clung to him harder in response, knowing he'd be getting up soon, and he didn't chide me. Didn't slap my ass like I'd thought. Instead, his embrace turned fiercer, and he asked, "Who do you belong to, Indy?"

My mouth trembled, my eyes darted from side to side behind my closed lids, my breasts heaved with shaky breaths, and my body ached from the enforced position he'd put me in.

And while, emotionally, I was more tied up than I'd been with the rope restraining me, I felt curiously free as I whispered, "You."

"Me."

I heard the vow there, knew it represented so much that neither of us had agreed to. He said he didn't want to brand me yet, that we might never be ready for that, and he could be right, but brands weren't always visible.

Brands could be made on a person's soul, and I knew I wore his name etched on mine.

Now, I just needed to make sure mine was etched on his.

He kissed my temple again, then when he started to make a move to let go of me, I didn't struggle. I stopped clinging and watched as he went to the kitchen, peered into the stove, pulled off the foil, then shut the oven door again.

When he set the timer, I thought he'd come back to me, but he didn't. He set the string beans on to boil, before he finally returned to my side.

Then, he surprised me again. He ran his hand over my legs, testing here and there, his touch firm as he looked at me, trying to see if I was uncomfortable. His fingers trailed over my thighs, up my abdomen, and to my arms, where he did the same thing, squeezing each finger, making sure I was okay.

Just when I thought he'd tell me to get dressed for dinner, his hand snapped between my legs, and he yanked my panties off me.

I yelped in surprise, then groaned when his fingers delved between the lips of my sex, unerringly finding my clit.

Even as he stroked me there, he thrust three into my cunt as he started to fuck me, hard and fast. He scissored those fingers, wide and wider, before raking them up against the front wall of my pussy.

It took me no time at all to scream out my orgasm, no time at all to be rolling on the bed again, falling onto my side as he carried on, not stopping fucking me with his hand even as I reduced his access, as he played with my clit and drove me wild as he gave me what I hadn't known I needed.

Release.

I howled when the second orgasm hit, but the third had me shuddering on the bed like I'd been tazered.

When the slight break inside me happened, I didn't feel it. Just knew something was different. Strange.

Then he moved his hand off my clit, pushed down on my stomach, and I yelped as he fucked me harder, harder, harder still, until he didn't.

Until he pulled his fingers free, and I came.

Liquid trickled out of me in a short, pressurized mass, and I groaned as the pleasure was painful when it ricocheted around my being, darting off the joints that ached from being restrained, off the mind that was tired of thinking.

"Open your mouth," he instructed, and I didn't think to disobey as he slipped his fingers between my legs, touching the mess he'd made before he shoved them between my lips.

Like always, he wasn't tender. I didn't need that. He was rough. Hard. And he made me gag before he pulled back.

Before he left me, a wreck on the bed, he pressed a kiss to my dirty mouth and whispered, "Get your breath back."

Who the hell was I to argue?

I lay there in my stupor. It could have been for five minutes or five hours for all I knew, but the scents of roasted chicken, baked veggies and a tangy sauce caught my interest.

He didn't call my name, didn't tell me to get ready for dinner, so I didn't move.

I didn't have the energy to.

I just lay there, a little insensate, a lot blurry, and waited for his next order.

Not that it came.

He moved to the bed once more, and bundled me into his arms. When he carried me out of the bedroom and toward the living room, I saw the TV was playing *The Goldbergs*, and there was a dish on the coffee table. A large one. No knives or forks though.

A little perturbed, my brow puckered as thoughts intruded, but I should have known he had it handled.

Cruz had everything handled.

Always.

He seated us in the corner of the L-seater sofa, not stopping until my back was pressed against the cushions even as I was on his lap, still bundled in his hold.

The coffee table was, I realized, closer than usual, so he didn't even have to lean forward to grab the bowl.

He placed it on the cushion, then dipped down to grab a piece of chicken. He swirled it in a sauce I hadn't seen him make, then pressed it to my lips.

"Open up, Indy."

I obeyed.

Keeping my forehead to his throat, I kept half my attention on his fingers when he fed me and on the TV, listening to the dialogue but also to his cues:

"Chew, Indy."

"Open your mouth, Indy."

It was freeing. Not to think, not to even feel, just to do.

And when he placed his sticky fingers on my chest, coating me with sauce, I thought nothing of licking his fingers clean, of sitting there, dirty.

He wanted me like this?

That was how he'd get me.

And I was more than okay with that.

TWENTY-NINE

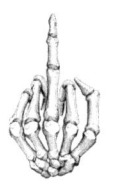

BEAR

"HEY, KID. WHAT'S UP?"

"A lot."

Rex had written the playbook on not only a poker face, but a poker voice, but I heard him loud and clear.

He didn't have to say a word, I just knew.

"Need me to come back?"

Silence.

Then:

"I swear, I'd think you were a goddamn mind reader if the idea of that didn't freak me the fuck out."

My smirk made an appearance, not that he saw it, and most of it was wasted on the side of a warehouse where I was watching a couple of DEA agents pull a deal with a Colombian cartel that was trying to make a go of it just off the Florida/Georgia border.

They'd already managed to sweep through Arkansas, peddling coke that had more goddamn rat poison in it than coca leaf, and were trying to merge into the upper eastern seaboard.

I knew NYC was safe thanks to that lunatic Aidan O'Donnelly, but I'd never liked the Colombians on principal. They were nasty sons of bitches. Always willing to come in, slice throats first, ask questions later.

Not that they were my reason for being here.

The DEA agents were.

See, they weren't wearing their little Kevlar vests emblazoned with the alphabet, but that didn't mean they weren't here without being under the radar.

Something stank worse than horse shit, and I knew I needed to get a level on it before things derailed even further.

"I'm no mind reader, kid, I just know my son. What happened?" It hadn't been that long since I'd seen him in West Orange. I rode up there every now and then to visit my Old Lady's grave, and he always seemed to know and would join me out by the MC's cemetery. "You don't normally call."

"This a secure line?"

I snickered. "Mav gave me the phone, Rex. Yeah, I think it's secure."

"Just checking." He sucked in a breath, which keyed me into the fact that he was trying not to lose his shit.

And probably failing.

On the outside, I didn't doubt he'd look calm. His men wouldn't know he was falling apart, because that poker face of his was world class.

But I knew my boy. Better than he knew himself.

"What is it, Rex?"

"It's about Mom."

Rene.

The love of my fucking life.

A woman I'd under-appreciated throughout our marriage, and who I spent more time worshipping now she was fucking dead.

There was no justice in this world, I knew that already, but I wished I'd known that before I lost her.

"What about her, son?"

"She was murdered."

The words didn't hit me as hard as I knew he thought they would.

"Dad? Did you hear me? She was murdered? We think it was the

Italians." He grunted. "Scratch that, we know it was the fucking Italians. It had to be."

"I know, son. I know."

"What?" It was a soft whisper of confusion at first, but it morphed into a boom of outrage. "You fucking knew?"

"Of course I did. But I paid to cover it up, because I wasn't about to have your mother sliced and diced in a second autopsy that'd tell me the only truth I needed to know—she was dead, and someone paid a lot to cover it up."

"You're fucking messing with me, Dad, you have to be."

"I ain't. Wish I was. Why do you think I left, boy? Why do you think I've been on the road all these years. I've been trying to find answers. Trying to find a way to get justice for her."

"You should have told me," was Rex's stony retort.

"Maybe I should have, maybe I shouldn't have. All I knew was I needed you right where you are now, not joining me on the road with some fucked up vigilante plan in mind, half-cocked with no real chance of success.

"I knew I needed you to rule over the men who are like family to us. Who need us to rule over them so they can feed their flesh and blood.

"What use would you being with me, here and now, serve?"

Silence hit the other end of the line, and I wasn't mad. I got it. For a second, I wasn't even sure if he'd put the phone down on me, but I didn't hear a click, and slowly, I heard a soft soughing breath.

"She didn't deserve to die."

"No, son, she didn't. Not for my sins." The pain was still as acute as ever it was. Just as strong, just as numbing and soul-destroying, all at the same goddamn time.

I'd thought I'd known loss in my life, but until Rene had died, I'd never truly understood it.

And now that I'd pissed years away on playing at Prez, preferring to be with my brothers than her, that stupidity smacked me in the goddamn face every day.

She was supposed to be here, riding bitch as we traveled down to Florida to winter there. We were supposed to be regular goddamn snowbirds, with me getting bored off my fucking rocker while she sunned herself and I took full advantage of her having an all over tan.

I wasn't supposed to be sitting here, watching a bunch of corrupt agents doing a deal with some Colombian assholes who were bringing poison into my fucking country.

I wasn't supposed to be hearing the heartbreak in my son's voice as he learned about his mother's end.

Nothing about this was ever supposed to have happened, yet here we were, dealing with hard truths.

Because reality fucking sucked.

"Do you have any answers?"

"Some. Not enough." I cleared my throat. "What I can tell you is that you'll think your old man is losing it."

"Right. Like that's going to happen."

His derision wasn't much comfort. "Rene died because I was sniffing around in places where I shouldn't have."

"What do you mean?" I heard his tension. "You were—"

"I'm not talking about cheating, Rex. Dammit. You know I stopped doing that a long time before she died." I was still ashamed about it though. Even more so now when I'd fucking kill to be climbing into my Old Lady's bed tonight, no other bitch's. "I'm talking about some dirty pigs who managed to smear me with their shit."

"What are you talking about?"

"I'll be home in a few days, son. I'm in Florida now. It'll take some time to get back. I don't ride as long as I used to but I'll tell you when I'm home."

When he didn't joke about me being an old man, I knew my kid was hurting. And who the fuck could blame him?

"I don't think I can wait that long, Dad."

"Eight years is a long time to wait," I agreed, reaching up to pinch the bridge of my nose. "There's a kind of organization within an organization. They work like specters, because they dump their crimes on people who look like they fit the bill."

"They stitch ex-cons up?"

"Yeah."

"Who'd do that?"

"Law Enforcement," I said gruffly. "But, look, I don't want to talk about this anymore on the phone. Safe to say, I got us into this shit and I'm working hard to get us out of it."

"You'd have gotten further if you'd just cut me and the rest of the Sinners in on this, Dad. For fuck's sake, what Mav can do—"

"I don't want to argue with you," I said firmly. "I've done what I had to in order to keep you safe. Wasn't about to lose you as well as your mother. I'll be there in a few days," I repeated.

He grunted under his breath, the noise one of exasperation. I was used to that though. "Stay safe," was all he said, before he cut the call, and prevented himself from saying anything else.

My lips curved a little at his bullheadedness which was definitely my fault, and I put down my binoculars, rested them on the handlebars as I tried to process what had just happened.

Rex learning the truth hadn't changed anything, not in the grand scheme of things. I needed to be here, keeping my finger on the pulse, but Rex was the only thing I had left that mattered to me.

If he needed me, that was more important than a vendetta that was years in the making, and years away from even a hope of coming to fruition.

I turned away from the shady deal going down, touched the kickstand with the toe of my boot, then rolled down the hill where I'd set up my position to watch the deal unfold.

Letting myself freewheel in neutral, I didn't kick the engine into touch until I was a few minutes away from the scene, and then, and only then, did I let my hog ride free.

But without Rene at my back, freedom didn't taste as good as I'd once dreamed of.

THIRTY

CRUZ

A FEW DAYS LATER

"SINCE WHEN DID you tap Indy's ass?"

For a second, I thought he meant literally, so I froze when Link posed the question, before I realized he just meant fucking.

The last thing I needed was Nyx to think I was beating his sister up, for Christ's sake. And having seen how vicious the bastard could be with a goddamn hacksaw as he helped me chop up David's corpse, I didn't need that level of rage anywhere near my face.

That depth of insanity deserved respect, and I was more than willing to respect a man who'd kill me to protect his sister.

After what that sister had been through, I was fucking glad for it too.

"You gonna answer or just gonna stare at me? You look like I could land a golf ball in that open trap of yours."

I narrowed my eyes at his joke before I poured him some tequila. "I'm sure you'd like it if someone asked you the same fucking question about Lily."

Link smirked at me. "That's the difference between you and me, Cruz, I want the fucking world to know she's mine."

I rolled my eyes at him. "Since you put a ring on her goddamn finger, do you know how much of a prick you've been?"

"He's sharing it around verbally because she's got his dick in knots," Rex grumbled, and while I understood that this wasn't as big of a celebration as it usually would be, because patch-in parties were no joke, he made a beggar at a feast look cheerful.

Link guffawed. "You know what, Rex? You're right. Absolutely right on the fucking money. She's got my dick in knots, but..." he whistled under his breath. "What she can do with those knots beats that handiwork of yours, Cruz."

That had me frowning. "What handiwork?"

Rex eyed me, and apparently reading between the lines, murmured, "The way you tie up the trash. How you wrap stuff up. He ain't talking about anything dirty."

"I wasn't, but I sure as fuck am now." Link leaned into me. "You for real? Indy seriously lets you tie her up?"

Steel perked up at that. "What's your poison? Cuffs or rope?"

This was not how I'd imagined my shift going down behind the bar tonight when, after waking up wrapped around Indy, I'd gotten a text, warning me that we were patching in Jaxson and Hawk tonight as well as swearing in a couple of Prospects.

The council, for whatever reason, were hanging around me, and while I was the one wielding the bottles of liquor, that was unusual. Rex normally held court on one of the sofas by the pool table, and the others tended to mosey around in circles.

Although, now that I thought about it, the last time we'd had a party like this, not one of these fuckers had been tied to an Old Lady.

I guessed it figured that they didn't know what to do with themselves when their cocks were, as Link had so charmingly phrased it, in a knot for their Old Ladies.

Normally, they'd have been boning anything that moved, well, apart from Nyx who'd always been particular, but I'd seen Link and Steel's bobbing asses more than I'd ever seen my own, that was for sure.

Sin, whose back was to me, his gaze on the crowd of wild animals that had taken my brothers' place for the evening, murmured, "The Old Ladies are heading outside."

"Did Giulia show you that sketch?" Rex asked Nyx, who'd popped up from out of nowhere.

With his attention twisted between the women and the Prez, Nyx murmured, "Which sketch?"

"Indy's tat. Giulia wants an MC brand."

I blinked at the notion, then Link groaned. "Oh fuck, that would be so hot. We need all of them to get one. Jesus, I'd bust my wad every time I looked at Lily with my MC's brand on her."

Rex snorted. "You're a fucking pervert, do you know that? Since when did you jones after ink?"

"Since I got a woman I want the whole world to know is mine?" He shook his head. "Jesus, Rex, ain't you listening? I'm not like Cruz—"

I shot him a warning look, then cast a glance at Nyx who was still watching the women as they retreated through the crowd.

He grinned at me, but made a zipping motion with his hand over his mouth.

"I'm interested in the idea, to be honest," Rex said, surprising me because women were good for fucking or wifing, nothing in between.

I never said this world of mine wasn't misogynistic.

"You are? I'm surprised," Sin commented, evidently on the same mental path as me. "I didn't think you'd like the idea."

"Tiff showed you too, huh?" Rex retorted. "And you like the idea?"

Sin's eyes lit up, but his grin was sheepish. "It's hot."

"I want it as a tramp stamp just above Lily's ass." Link groaned, then jacked himself. "Fuck, my eyeballs just came."

Steel shoved him in the shoulder. "Dirty fucker."

"You know it," Link agreed, totally unabashed by his actions.

Which was how it should be.

When it boiled down to it, we were all just shooting the shit with family. Especially the guys in front of the bar.

They'd grown up together, had come up together through the ranks of the MC. Me? I was an outsider, but with my ties to Indy, it surprised me to realize that, if only by proxy, I'd be considered family as well.

If I branded her.

I wouldn't do that just to get access to the council, but the idea of being included, of being a part of a bigger whole did something to me.

Nothing like what the woman herself did. A woman who wasn't here.

Who'd fucking refused to come.

I swore, that woman of mine didn't know when to quit. Her ass was going to be sore in the morning for her insolence, that was all I fucking knew.

"They're all doing more for the club than any of our moms ever did," Rex was saying, and I tuned back into the conversation, interested by his take on things. "Seems only fitting they should get some representation."

"Only councilors' women?" I asked, curious for obvious reasons.

Rex shrugged. "Haven't thought past that, especially because all the new Old Ladies belong to councilors. But I guess we could see on a case by case basis. Not every woman would want a club patch." He pulled out his phone when it buzzed, his brow puckering as he read whatever was on the screen.

One second, the party was going down, the council was shooting the shit and Rex was handling business on his cell, the next, a blast tore through the clubhouse, bursting the windows, prompting thousands of shards of glass to soar through the bar.

I ducked, it was only instinct, but when the boom sounded next, ricocheting in my head, pushing us all backward, I hit my head on one of the kegs, and that was the last I fucking knew about anything.

THIRTY-ONE
LODESTAR

I'D NEVER LIKED WORKING as a sniper, but just because I didn't like it, didn't mean I wasn't fucking good at it.

I'd always been a good shot, and that was something my daddy had cultivated in me after momma had died.

We'd gone hunting together since the time I reached his knee, and I'd grown up hunting and butchering our own venison.

Death was a constant companion of mine, and that was why, after he died of a heart attack when I was sixteen years old, I found myself enlisting.

I'd lost my family. I needed a new one.

Death wasn't something I was scared of. And I loved my country.

What better career path than that of a soldier?

They never told you you'd do shit that even someone who wasn't squeamish would find hard to handle.

They didn't tell you it would fuck with your head, being turned into a killer.

Hunting and killing were two very different things.

But when you became a hunter of humans? That changed you. Twisted you. Fucked with your head and made you a ghoul.

I'd been a ghoul for a long time, and that was why I could see the scene playing down around me with a cool head.

Anyone else, except maybe Mav, who was resting on the clubhouse roof, watching shit unroll, would feel the need to warn the men and women under me.

But I didn't.

Death was the casualty of life.

I respected that, just as much as I knew that if any of my *new* family died, I'd kill the bastards behind this attack, and I'd do so with a smile on my face.

That was why I hovered the laser sight on the biker who'd just rolled up.

My finger caressed the trigger as I held my breath, calmed my heart. I took note of wind speed, calculated the variables even though it was a close shot, and used the discomfort of my position to ground me as I made a decision whether to end the man's life or not.

Then, I heard Stone gasp, "It's Bear!"

Bear.

Rex's father.

Not a threat.

I struck him off my list even as another gun went off, only it wasn't aimed at Bear, but at his bike.

And I wasn't the one behind the hit.

Quickly, scanning the environment, I happened to see the piercing red light of another's laser sights, and just as I took the shot, all of this taking place within a second, the blast struck.

As glass shattered, and screams soared, I was pushed back off my precarious perch on the roof and hurtled into the darkness of the back yard.

The screams, the fear, the pain, all of it took me back to another time, another place, where the heat of the desert was unending, the scent of terror polluted every breath of air I took, and the promise of freedom could only be found in death.

As I collided with the ground, I wasn't sure what I hoped for when I closed my eyes.

For this to be the end?

Or the only thing that had kept me going for the past five years —*vengeance*. Because my enemies had made a fatal mistake tonight.

The Sinners wouldn't take this lying down.

And neither would I.

THIRTY-TWO

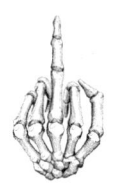

RACHEL

IT WAS QUITE by chance that I saw it.

I wasn't the kind of woman who took a seat on the deck, resting her feet on the railing as she took in the view, the otherwise silent night, and an aria from Madame Butterfly that surged through the house's smart speakers.

But tonight, I was that woman.

I'd had a bitch of a week, a bitch of a six months if I was being honest. Just sitting down, taking a moment to smell the damn roses was something I deserved. Something I'd earned.

I was, I'd admit, a complete workaholic. I loved my job, and even though my employers were a bunch of criminals, it enabled me to donate a large chunk of my time to the charities that mattered to me.

And, though I'd never admit it to Rex, the overbearing prick, I liked my work with the Sinners.

They presented me with a daily challenge, much like a newspaper provided a daily Sudoku puzzle.

They also paid all my bills.

Generously.

In fact, generously was an understatement. That wasn't to say I didn't earn every goddamn cent, because they kept me more than busy, but it enabled me to do what really mattered—my NGO work.

With the state of the world as it was, that had kept me up at night too, so just sitting here was a blessing. Something I didn't take advantage of often.

"Do you have to have this trash on so loud?"

I squinted at my brother, whose head had just peeped through the screen.

"You're going to let bugs in."

He snorted. "That all you have to say?"

"Sorry to disappoint," was my dry retort, but I kept my face averted from him lest he see my smile. "But you and I both know I'd flick your nose if I was closer. As it stands, I'm too damn tired to get up."

He huffed. "You need to take a break. When was the last time you went on a vacation..." Before I had a chance to answer, he answered himself, "Wasn't it when you went to Vancouver? With Jesse?"

I cut him a look. "Niagara Falls, and yes, for his wedding."

Rain rolled his eyes. "Always the bridesmaid, never the bride."

That had me laughing. "You trying to make me feel good about myself tonight, kid?"

"Not a kid anymore. I'm officially an adult," he retorted.

"When you call Madame Butterfly trash, that's when I know you're a kid."

"So I'll be a kid until I'm ninety? Because I'll never like that—"

Before the two of us could carry on bickering, the explosion seemed to tear through the airwaves. We were two miles down the road from the Sinners' compound but, unerringly, I knew that was where the blast's epicenter would be found.

Not only because the Sinners were the only people in the local area who would ever get their asses blown up, but because they were my only neighbors for miles around.

I jerked onto my feet, the bench skidding backward in my haste and Rain rushed forward, his hands and mine coming to the railing as we stared at the clouds in the sky, rosy red, a luminescent orange.

My mouth trembled as I whispered, "Rex."

Rain, sounding like the kid he'd just vowed he wasn't, whispered, "He'll be okay, won't he, Rach?"

I bit my lip. "There's only one way to find out." Turning to him, I grabbed his arm and said, "Call the cops, but stay here, Rain. I need you to stay here because I won't be able to help if I'm worrying about you."

"I can help too!"

I shook my head. "You know I don't want you involved with the Sinners, dammit."

Rain pulled a face, but we both knew why I didn't.

It still surprised me when he didn't argue anymore though, and he kept his teenaged butt silent as I rushed inside, grabbed my keys, hauled ass out into the yard and jumped into my SUV.

Within five minutes, I was barreling down my driveway, out of the gates, and was resenting every minute's distance between me and the Sinners.

It wasn't like there was anything I could do when I got there, but I just needed to know.

I just... shit. I just needed to know.

What with Giulia and Luke Lancaster, then the Farquars, and Stone's legal situation recently... I did my job for more reasons than the salary Rex put into my bank account every month.

As much as I denied them, as much as I'd cut ties with them on a social level a long time ago, they were my family.

And my family was under attack.

I drove too fast, which meant the bushes either side of the SUV on the thin track that was the road to my property probably scraped the shit out of the sides, but I didn't care. Didn't give a damn.

I raced harder, faster, and when I reached the gates, I happened to see a set of taillights barreling down the road toward the town.

Squinting, I failed to register the license plate, so I took a mental note of the make and model. I was mad at myself for not grabbing the plates in time, but I forgot about everything, even Madame goddamn Butterfly, when I saw the gates were blown off at the hinges, and the level of force of the blast had me wondering if anyone could have survived that kind of bomb.

"Jesus, what the hell have you gotten yourself into?" I whispered under my breath, annoyed and agitated and anxious all at the same time.

In fact, that no way summed up just how panicked I felt.

It was real. *This was real.*

All the years I'd shoved him away, rightfully so, but shoved him I had, and it all boiled down to this.

To a blast that could have stolen him from me before we even had a chance to be more than just—

"He's not dead," I reassured myself, refusing to believe that the massive force that was Rex, the Sinners' Prez, could be vanquished by anything so paltry as a bomb.

It just wouldn't happen.

Rex would be the first to say that only the good died young, and even if, he'd done as I'd told him to a long time ago, and he'd gone into politics, I was no fool. He wouldn't have been a good politician. He'd have been dirty as hell, but he'd stand by his promises, and that was why I'd always wanted that for him.

So much so that when he'd become Prez, I'd refused to talk to him for a month.

Biting my lip at the time, the wasted time, the foolish moments I'd spent on trying to change a man who'd been destined to be exactly what he was—the leader of a bunch of Sinners—I pulled up on the driveway.

What I saw was enough to terrify a civilian, but I wasn't exactly that. I'd been raised on this damn compound, so it wasn't the first attack I'd had to live through, but this was just so much more terrifying than I'd expected.

The screams—Jesus, I'd never get them out of my head. I could hear the cries as women and men escaped the burning building, but they weren't as petrifying as the flames. The roar of them. The sheer power. It was almost magnetic, in fact, no. They *were* magnetizing. I felt like an electromagnet being dragged toward them, their massive fury, their beauty.

If I hadn't been shitting myself, I'd have been mesmerized.

In the near distance, I heard sirens, which told me that the explosion had been heard over in the town because no way would the emergency services have responded to Rain's call as fast as this.

The sirens shook me out of my stupor with the flames, though, and I surged forward, rushing toward the clubhouse, my phone raised as a flashlight so I didn't fall over the stupid pebbles they had lining the driveway.

Only, as I ran, moving toward the chaos of sobs and screams, of heat and fury, I found him.

The man who'd been like an uncle to me.

"Oh, Bear," I whimpered, dropping to my knees at the sight of him.

Tears welled in my eyes, and it had nothing to do with the smoke choking the air, that was hitting me straight in the face like a sledgehammer into a wall.

This man was family.

And he was gone. Dead—

"Rach..."

My name was slurred. Barely audible. Not just because of the noise ricocheting around the compound, but because his voice was so faint as to be nearly imperceptible.

Only practice at listening to my brother attempt to sneak out of the house put my ears in good stead, and I whispered, "Bear! You hang on in there—"

"No. Time." A rasping breath heaved from his lungs. "Tell. Rex. New World. Sparrows. Must remember, Rachel. Must. Remember." The last word came out as a barely understandable slur, but if those were Bear's dying words, there was no way in hell I was going to forget them.

Now, I just had to make sure that they weren't the last words the man who I loved like he was blood uttered.

Unfortunately, that was easier said than done when he wasn't in one piece.

"Oh, Rex," I moaned to myself as I encountered space where there should be limbs. "What did you get involved in?"

THIRTY-THREE
INDY

I SIGHED when Laura reached up and rubbed at her eyes, brushing away the tears that constantly flowed out of her like she was a leaky faucet.

I got the determination, I truly did—it was half of the reason she was still roaming around the world, after all. That fight, those inner flames that kept a person going, even through the pain, even through the discomfort and agony that was part and parcel of cancer treatment, made a person infinitely stronger.

Laura was exactly that.

But the scar tissue corded around her chest was so beyond sensitive that covering one inch of it on her body felt like I was covering feet of it on another person's.

"S-Sorry, Indy, I don't mean to be a cry baby."

"Shut up, girl. You're no cry baby," I soothed, championing her when she wasn't going to champion herself. "It's a little soon after the last session. Maybe we should reschedule?"

Laura sighed, but it came out around a hiccup. "I want it done."

"There's no point in rushing these things," I chided. "Look what's happened as a result."

Laura bit her bottom lip. "I didn't mean to waste your time."

"You haven't," I denied, because I'd totally have had to go to the patch-in party at the compound if Laura hadn't called in an appointment.

She wrinkled her nose. "You're a good liar, but not that good. I'm sorry." She glowered down at her chest. "I don't understand why this is so hard."

I had a hypothesis that her pain wasn't just physical but emotional, but I wasn't about to burden her with that. Not when I wasn't a shrink.

I'd often found that people responded to the needle in different ways, ways that depended on their reason for actually getting the tattoo.

Someone who came in for a vanity tat would probably moan about the pain. Someone who came in to commemorate a family member who'd passed over, would often just hiss through it and then find a kind of calm that I believed was their way of further commemorating their lost loved one.

When it was for scar tissue, there was often a lot of repressed emotions going on inside someone. Sometimes it was survivor's guilt or fear or just plain worry.

With Laura, I knew she was scared about the cancer coming back, and with good reason. This was her second time in remission. The mastectomy was the end result.

She was only twenty-fucking-eight. No age at all. No goddamn age at all.

Why was it this mother of four, who'd lived a simple life, who'd probably never hurt anyone, was dealing with this shit when my uncle had done what he had, tortured children the way he had, and had made it to middle age?

Even then, he hadn't died because it was his time to go. No, my brother had decided that our good uncle needed putting down. Maybe Kevin would still be alive, still be polluting the earth, if Nyx hadn't put a stop to him…

Life, I registered, and not for the first time, wasn't fair.

"You ready to start up again?" I asked softly, pressing my hand to hers.

The last touch of the tattoo gun to her skin had seen her jerking up like Dracula out of his coffin come dusk. She was still sitting up, her shoulders shaking, skin flushed with gooseflesh.

She shook her head. "I don't think I can, Indy. I'm sorry."

"Please, don't apologize. But next time, come when I ask you to, okay? Trust in my experience?"

She winced. "I will."

I eyed her, looking at the tat then at her, and murmuring, "I get it though. We're so damn close." My smile was kind as I continued, "But hey, when it's done, it's done. No more pain."

"No more pain," she repeated, like it was a vow. Like she really needed to believe I was speaking the truth.

I prayed, for her sake, I was.

Twenty or so minutes later, we hugged after she carefully wrapped herself into a thin jacket and darted outside like a frightened rabbit.

I watched her go before I went to the desk and picked up my phone.

My brows rose when I saw the number of missed calls and messages I had on there, and I wasn't sure whether to be concerned or not when not a single one of them was from Cruz.

I had at least a dozen from Stone, then three messages, each of them a demand for me to call her back. Giulia and Nyx had messaged and called too, as had Sin and Lily.

Unsure what the hell was happening, unease began to spread through me as I decided to call Nyx first.

As I hit the connect button, however, my phone buzzed with an incoming call.

"Indy? You need to get your ass to West Orange Hospital."

"What the hell's going on, Giulia? I have a shit ton of messages and calls from you guys at the compound."

A hiccup sounded down the line, prompting me to pull back from my phone and check the Caller ID, because this *was* Giulia, right? My tough-as-nails sister-in-law? Only, she didn't sound so hardcore right this minute…

"You're scaring me," I said softly, meaning it. Inside my head, my skull felt like it was starting to throb, just waiting for the explosion to come as she blew my frickin' mind.

"There's been a bombing."

A bombing?

I'd expected a shooting. Some kind of drive by or... Fuck, I didn't know for sure. We'd had that in the past, some dumb fuck gangs had tried to overtake the compound when I was seven or so, but they'd broached the gates like they were a useless battalion of soldiers. Some of the older Sinners still hooted about how dumb those gangbangers had been during their breach.

But a bombing?

That was new.

And, God help us, that invited the FBI onto our territory.

After what happened in this very studio, I knew the Sinners 'recycled' their dead bodies somewhere on the compound. Would the Feds do a search of the grounds?

Jesus.

David was there.

David... who I hadn't even thought about once. Not even to miss the fact he always made sure I was fed and watered, and who'd bled out on my frickin' workstation floor.

But when I thought of him, I didn't think of the guy who'd drop everything to do what I needed, or to get me what I wanted, I thought of the prick who'd pulled a gun on me.

Who'd tried to control me.

Who'd followed Cruz, who'd surveilled me.

Yesterday, Cruz had gone upstairs while I was working and had come downstairs with a brown paper bag full of *something*.

Because I trusted that he wasn't stealing my groceries, and because he hadn't mentioned *anything* to me, I knew what it was.

Equipment David had set up inside my apartment to watch me.

If I was going to cry about anything, it was that. Not that I'd killed David. But now, if the tears were gonna fall, then I was going to weep over the fact that his corpse was somewhere on Sinners' land and there'd be wall-to-wall Feds en route.

And then, I recognized how selfish I was being, how fucking horrible. My only defense was I was in shock, but it wasn't much of an excuse, was it?

For being selfish over asking about the people I loved?

Wanting to punch myself in the gut, I rasped, "Cruz?" I knew Nyx was okay, because he'd called. But Cruz's absence resonated in a way that made me feel queasy.

"He's okay. Broken ribs, couple of burns on his arms, he got knocked out by debris we think. He's unconscious, concussed. We won't know until he wakes up when he'll be out of here."

"I'll be there in seven." Seven because it took fifteen minutes, and that was as fast as I'd be able to get there.

"Okay. Just head to the ER," she muttered grimly. "We're taking up every fucking bed."

My heart skipped a beat at that. "Giulia, any deaths?" I asked even though I didn't want to know. The last thing I needed was to be driving double the speed limit while crying my eyes out, but... shit, I needed to know.

"Yeah." A shivery breath escaped her, and I knew she was on the brink of tears. "I don't know how we're alive, Indy," she whispered brokenly. "In the clubhouse, anyone near the front was fucked, but toward the back, they were okay. Most of the council, by dumb luck, were over by the bar, getting served according to Nyx.

"It's the people near the window who got torn up some, we lost Jaxson."

I closed my eyes. "He died at his own fucking patch-in party?"

"Y-Yes," she stuttered.

I hated this fucking world.

All my life, I'd done everything I could to avoid it, and when I'd headed to NOLA, it had seemed like it was doable. I'd missed Caleb, missed him like a bitch, but to be away from the clubhouse, to be away from the organized crime, had been a sweet kind of bliss.

I often asked myself why I had come back, and the only reason I had was, family.

When Mom had died, Rex offered to help set me up with a studio, and only recently had I regretted it.

This past nine months had been some of the most stressful of my life, because of the Sinners.

And here I was, giving myself to one of them? Falling in love with one of them?

Was I a fucking moron?

Why the fuck was I getting involved when I'd known since I was a kid, that I needed to back the goddamn hell away from the life?

Stone and me had always tried, especially after Steel had treated her like shit. She'd gone to the city for her studies, and until I'd been of age, I'd stuck around New Jersey until I could head for NOLA where the late, great Laruso had let me apprentice with him.

Only something like a death could haul me back, and with Rex's offer, I'd just never left. Taking comfort in being one town away when I decided where to set up my tattoo parlor.

But, I recognized, that gradually, I'd been slipping back into the life. What with taking messages into Rikers for Quin from the MC, and then the need to protect the Sinners from David... I was getting more and more entangled, and it would only worsen now that Stone was living on the compound, now that she was Steel's Old Lady.

The MC contaminated everything, and I'd been fooling myself by believing I wasn't already tainted.

I reached up and pinched the bridge of my nose, wondering how I could be so fucking stupid as to get involved in this shit once more, shit that was like poison, that could infect anything and everything within a hundred-mile span.

"Indy?"

Giulia sounded worried, and I realized she'd been talking all while the white noise in my head was taking over everything else.

I'd heard though.

Jaxson, Matty, Kingsley, Jingles, Jojo. They were the five who were dead. But there were twenty with injuries that required, as a minimum, an overnight stay in hospital.

Bear was on the brink. He'd lost limbs, and was in a coma. As for the rest, no one was totally unscraped. Anything from concussions, to perforated ear drums, broken bones and the psychological trauma of being goddamn bombed.

As for my loved ones, Giulia's shoulder was dislocated, and Nyx had burns on his arms, and his back was covered in wounds from shattered glass.

"I'll be there in seven minutes," I repeated dully, even though the second I cut the call, I didn't storm off to my car. No, I just leaned back against my desk, and tried to figure out what the fuck I was doing.

I'd opened myself up to Cruz, but that meant I was involved in the life.

Like a sticky spider's web, it had entangled me up in it once more, rolling me around in a cocoon that let me forget just how bad things could be.

It was only by circumstance that I wasn't at the compound tonight. If Laura *hadn't* called then I'd have been there, and maybe I'd be one of the unlucky ones. I mean, why not? What about my life spoke of good fortune?

I swallowed at the thought, swallowed down the tears and the misery and the goddamn hopes and dreams that were laid to waste by the night's events.

For a second, I could do no more than process what the fuck was happening, what was going down with my family—one brother who'd just been bombed, a sister-in-law who'd dislocated a fucking shoulder, and a baby brother somewhere in a prison cell while still doing jobs for the goddamn Sinners.

My legs felt like mush, but that was nothing in comparison to my head. Brain whirring with thoughts and fears, I staggered to the floor, shoving my back against the desk, trying to find support there, but there was none to be found.

As crazy as it was, as stupid and as insane, I wanted Cruz.

I wanted his arms around me.

But in those arms, there was danger. There was violence. There was the life.

Eyes darting from left to right, I knew what it felt like to be a deer in headlights, because one part of me, the part who'd been raised with those people, was urging me to get my ass in the car and to drive like the devil himself was on my heels to make it to the hospital in those promised seven minutes.

Another part?

Telling me to run.

And not toward the hospital.

I gulped, wondering if I could do it, wondering if I could get away, but...

So many buts.

In the blank void of my mind, a place I hadn't visited since that last time Kevin had visited my bedroom, and what that meant was more terrifying than I could bear, a tinny ringing sound penetrated the vacuum.

I didn't notice it at first, barely registered it. Then, the vibrations of my cell started to hit my hand, I actually started to feel them, so a little dazed, a little like I'd been the one in the bombing, I turned my cell around so I could look at the Caller ID, and I saw Stone's name, and the picture of her where she was blowing me a raspberry.

I remembered that night.

I'd gone into Manhattan so, on the rare night off she'd had back in March, we could party. She'd drunk too many margaritas, eaten way too many soup dumplings, and had barfed her way down sixth and King.

My lips quirked at the memory, which was like an ice pick to the protective walls that were growing around me.

"Indy?"

Her voice had me clenching my eyes closed. So damn hard it hurt.

With a shaky hand, I reached up and rubbed them as I rasped, "Stone, why are we doing this to ourselves?"

She released a shaky breath. "Because they're family. This is our family, Indy."

"I don't want to be involved in this," I rasped. "I don't want to be in a world where someone can bomb you because you don't like—"

"Let me just stop you there, Indy. You think the Sinners would put their women in danger? Knowingly?"

I tensed up at the anger in her voice and knew I was only going to hear shit that defended the guys coming from her.

I got it.

She loved Steel. Had loved him for a lifetime, had spent a lifetime getting back to him, but she wasn't me.

I wasn't her.

Did I have Cruz?

I wasn't sure.

He said things, all the right things that made me think I did, but...

"I know you want to run, Indy. When Giulia told me you hadn't arrived yet, I knew what would be going through your head. That's why I wanted to be the one to tell you, but I'm helping out with the staff. They're not used to emergencies like this and, unfortunately for me, I am." She released a breath. "It's bad, but there's always worse."

"That's the only consolation you can give me?" I interrupted bitterly. "That, hey, it's not 9-11? The difference is you don't know what the fuck the Sinners did to deserve this, and those people were innocent. You don't know what the Sinners have done, and the bitch of it is, because you have a pussy, you'll never fucking know.

"You could die for the goddamn MC, you could lose your fucking life, your world, everything, but they'll always treat you like you're less because you don't have a fucking cock."

Silence met my answer, and a for second, over the pounding of my heart, the panting from my lungs, I wasn't sure if she'd hung up, then, she murmured, "You're right."

"I-I am?"

"Yeah. You are. It isn't fair, but nothing about life is fair.

"I got kidnapped by a psychopath, Indy. I was almost killed because I figured out she was hurting innocent people in a place they came to for help. To be cured, or if not that, to end their days in relative peace and quiet.

"That had nothing to do with the Sinners. One thing I learned, Indy, when I was in that goddamn hospital bed, some people are just like magnets. We're that way. We attract it because we were born into it, it's all we know. It's in our fucking genes."

Eyes awash with tears, I burst out, "But I don't want that!"

"You can't avoid it, sweetheart. It's who we are."

This time, I didn't just rub my eyes, I dug my fingers into them, because I knew she was right.

Hadn't I killed David?

Hadn't I done that as easily as fucking pie?

It hadn't even occurred to me to let him corner me, to let him have information he could hold against my family. And after, hadn't I been A-okay with letting Cruz and Nyx handle things? When their version of that probably involved a nearby pig farm or some godawful way of making a dead body disappear?

Not once had I felt remorse. Had I looked at the floor in my studio and seen the blood pooling around him, fanning out like some kind of obscene art.

Any other woman would have been traumatized.

But I was a Sinners' brat.

I was made of stronger stuff.

"Indy," she rasped. "You need to come to us. We need to be together."

I knew by 'we', she wasn't just talking about me and her. But the whole Sinners' family.

Which I, somehow, was a goddamn part of.

Lord help me.

THIRTY-FOUR

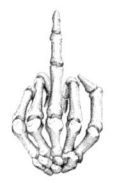

CRUZ

I WOKE UP TO CHAOS.

The green curtains that separated me from another ER bay were pulled, and I had one of those crappy blankets covering my legs. As I peered at myself through groggy eyes with a head that was banging from all the noise in the hospital, I saw I was wearing one of those wanktard gowns which always sent the worst drafts up your ass crack. From the compression bandage on my chest, I knew I'd fractured some ribs, and every breath felt like I'd swallowed a knife.

Fun.

Worse than that though was my foggy brain, like I'd been walking through clouds and instead of plummeting to the earth, I'd just started flying higher and higher.

Had I smoked weed or something tonight?

The last time I'd felt this crappy was when I'd eaten some funky pot brownies.

A groan escaped me as I finally got my eyes to stay open, and when I did, I saw her.

She sat there, tired, weary, hurting, not physically but clearly emotionally, and still, she was the most beautiful thing I'd ever seen.

Her eyes were downcast, and I realized she was on her phone, swiping left like she was looking at photos.

Amid the manic panic of the ER, she was an oasis of peace. Of calm. Something I wanted to dive in, bathe in.

Was it a crazy moment to realize that I actually loved her?

Or was it the right one? The most perfect timing of all?

Maybe.

It wasn't like I was going to tell her, but I just needed to admit it to myself.

Something drew me to her like a moth to a flame, and had done ever since that fucking night.

She'd gone from being a brother's sister, AKA hands off, to being a sexual entity. A woman who was on her hands and knees, scrubbing like it was four PM and not four AM, trying to make her best friend's place nice for her before she came back after a long stay in the hospital.

She'd been sweaty, grimy, tired, and it had all just flowed like a lightning bolt directly to my cock.

Even now, battered and some parts definitely broken, my dick responded to her. I figured when I was eighty and her tits went down to her knees and my balls hung just as low that I'd feel the exact same way.

Everything about her resonated.

It was just... *right*.

Perfect.

"I can feel you staring at me."

"Yeah? Then why haven't you said hey, huh?" I rumbled, wincing at my voice. It was dumb of me to figure out, just then, that I had a goddamn oxygen mask on, and my lungs were feeling pretty fucking incinerated.

Dumb fuck.

She looked at me though, her eyes red from crying, and I knew that not only had the worst happened, but people had died.

Family.

Brothers.

I sucked in a sharp breath, then regretted it when I started hacking my guts up and agony splintered my chest, keying me into the fact that

I'd either fractured or broken some ribs. She jumped to her feet, rushed over to my side and pressing her hand to my lower back, reached for some water that was on a small stand beside me, and hovered it in front of me for me to take when I was ready.

The pain in my chest had me cringing because I knew there'd been smoke damage. I was enough of a chemist to recognize a blast when I was in the goddamn epicenter of it, which meant someone had the audacity to bomb the Sinners' compound.

Inwardly, I reeled at the act of outright warfare, but outwardly, I knew I had to keep my shit together.

My spidey sense was telling me two things.

One, Indy was reeling from this. *Badly.*

Two, it was the kind of reeling that would see a person run away in the middle of the night.

She wasn't a runner, she was a fighter, but more than that, she had common goddamn sense.

Why, in her right mind, would she tangle herself up further with the likes of me? Not only was I a biker, I was just a lowly one. Not on the council, not pulling in the big bucks.

Throw in the fact my home had just been bombed and that someone was literally gunning for us, she'd have to have a death wish before she'd willingly tie herself to me.

I reached for the plastic cup with one hand, and with the other, I reached for her fingers. As I tangled them together, I murmured, "Means a lot to wake up with you sitting next to me."

She kept her face downturned, and I knew, just fucking knew, she was already walking out the goddamn door. If not physically, mentally.

I could feel her checking out as I sat there, tied to a goddamn gurney with all the tubes and shit coming off my body.

I had to act, and I knew I needed to key into something fast or she'd leave, on the pretense of going home and getting some rest, and I'd just never see her again.

The prospect hurt worse than the daggers ramming their way into my chest from the smoke damage.

If breathing had hurt before, that was nothing to now. Nothing to the sheer agony of contemplating a future without her.

With her fingers knotted into mine, I rested the cup on the gurney, uncaring if it spilled, and tugged down my mask.

"You need to keep that on," she chided gruffly.

"No, I need to talk to you without sounding like I'm underwater, Indy." I reached up and cupped her chin. "A smart woman would run out the door without a backward glance. We both know you're more than smart, Indy. We both know you're an incredibly intelligent woman."

"Yeah? Well, I don't feel so smart at the moment."

"I can guarantee that you don't, and I get it. Totally. One hundred percent. You'd be a fool not to be thinking about leaving and walking into the fucking sunset, but—"

When I hesitated, she looked at me. Didn't look at my chin, at my nose, at my fucking eyebrows, she looked me in the eye.

"But, what?"

"I'm gonna ask that you don't do that."

"Why?" she rasped, her jaw tensing.

"You know why."

"Maybe I do, maybe I don't. Things changed tonight, Cruz. I don't know what you guys are involved in, and I don't want to know, but the fact that it could lead a bomber to your goddamn front door tells me that I'm not safe with you."

"You are safe," I denied.

"How the fuck can you even say that?" she snarled, dragging her hand away from mine. "How can you even think that when, tonight, I'd have been there if it wasn't for Laura making a last minute appointment and me fitting her in?"

"Because I'll kill to keep you safe, and I'll die before I let anything happen to you."

"This isn't some romance novel, Cruz. This is real life. We bleed. We die. We cease to exist. This isn't Snow White. I'm not going to get hit up in a shooting only to wait for you to kiss me to wake me up.

"Once I'm gone, I'm gone, and I've—"

"You think I don't know that?" I snarled back. "What? You reckon that I believe we're living in some kind of fairy tale? No, Indy, I don't think that. I know reality bites, but I'd prefer for reality to bite with you at my fucking side than with you back in New Orleans and me stuck up here, wishing I was with you, and you wishing you were with me.

"Separated because you're too chicken shit to realize that we don't choose our time. We don't get to select an expiration date, Indy.

"One thing I've learned along the way, is that it's our day to die when someone else chooses it."

"Didn't think you believed in God," she muttered.

"I don't. I believe in something though. I have to. Or it'd be too fucking depressing to wake up every morning and think that humans are behind all the shit that goes down on a daily basis.

"It's nicer to think that someone, something, some entity, be it a God or fate or fucking... whatever... to be behind it."

"Bullshit. Never heard of free will? Every human does exactly what they want to do because they want to do it. Simple as that."

"Yeah, well, you choose to think that and I can think differently. But all I'm saying is that, whether you're right or I am, I don't want to live in this fucked up world without you."

Her eyes met mine. "You're crazy to say that. You barely know me."

I laughed. "Wow, you're full of bullshit today. I think you should be grateful that I'm not in full working order, because if I was, your ass would be bright pink for that outright lie."

Her mouth pursed into a tight rosette. "I don't need to listen to this shit."

"No, you don't, and yet you're still here. Hovering, not walking away because you and I both know that what we have is something special. Maybe we can't put words to it, maybe we shouldn't, not yet, so we won't, not until both of us are ready, but I'm telling you, waking up to this cluster fuck was a damn sight more bearable knowing that you were here, waiting on me to open my eyes."

My words had her gulping, and she rasped, "You say that like I get to be at your side. Like I can stand with you. But I've got a pussy, Cruz, so there's always shit you're going to keep from me. You're always going to keep things separate because that's how the club works.

"How does that seem fair? When you demand everything from me, my submission, my trust, my heart, and all without me knowing what kind of danger you're dragging me into?" She shook her head. "I need to get out of here. I need to get some sleep."

Knowing I was losing her, I rasped, "Indy, I won't order you to do anything, not like this, not with what's at stake, but I'm telling you, if you run... I will find you."

Her gaze caught mine. "Guess we'll have to see if you're good for your word, then, won't we?"

My nostrils flared at the challenge, and just when she started to move the curtain aside, someone, or something, blocked her.

I'd admit, my heart started racing at the prospect of her running off. Goddamn oxygen tanks and patches and tubes on my body aside, I'd be going after her whether she fucking liked it or not.

But I didn't have to.

Nyx was there.

Had he been listening?

He stared down at his sister, his face smoke-covered, black and shiny with sweat and ash, and even as he hauled her into his arms, holding her tightly, I feared the worst.

Demonstrative wasn't exactly a word I'd use to describe Indy on the regular. With her brother, even less so. That Nyx was hugging her had my stomach twisting and I started coughing, unable to stop myself as Indy ground out, "What's happening, Nyx? What's happening?"

"It's a fucking miracle," he rumbled, "but somehow, the old bastard is going to live."

She sagged in his arms, and though the words comforted the pair of them, I didn't understand. Who was the 'old bastard?'

I'd have asked if I wasn't too busy coughing up my fucking guts, but, also, I was too goddamn grateful.

Whatever, or whoever, Nyx referred to, it made her shoulders drop with defeat.

For the moment, she'd stay put.

But I had no way of knowing how long that moment would last, which meant I needed to get my ass out of this bed. Stat.

THIRTY-FIVE

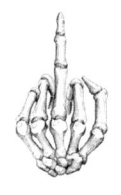

LODESTAR

"CARE TO SHARE?"

I squinted at Mav, then rolled my eyes when I saw him and Ghost sitting together on his wheelchair.

He wasn't so dirty which made sense, because I knew he'd been upstairs in the attic working on something that he hadn't seen fit to key me in on—and if I sounded pissed, that was because I was.

I hated being kept in the dark.

Sure, I kept him in the dark about plenty of shit, but Mav didn't work that way.

Usually.

Which meant it was family-oriented, which meant he didn't consider me family.

Surprise, surprise, that hurt.

Stupid of me, sure, but it did, and I couldn't help my feelings.

So, if I was pouting a little as I watched a dirt-streaked Ghost sleeping on his lap, tucked into him like she was a little girl sitting on her grandma's knee—if that grandma just happened to weigh two hundred pounds of muscle soaking wet and looked like a walking Adonis, that is.

It was only fair that Maverick didn't have any siblings, because if he did, there'd be some weird incest shit going down.

Maverick was that beautiful.

Once upon a time, I'd owned a piece of that beauty. His smile had shone for me. But we were too similar, too alike. You couldn't have two alphas in a relationship, not without going to war all the fucking time, and with our day job, we didn't need the battles to be going down in the few hours we had to ourselves.

So we'd split, and to this day, I wasn't sure if that was the worst decision I'd ever made in my life or the bravest.

Maverick would have kept me safe.

I knew that, and I'd known it before I'd even seen him with Ghost.

It was a sweet kind of torture watching them together. One that made me happy for him, even as I mourned what I'd never have.

"I know I'm pretty," he said, wading into my thoughts, "but I did ask you a question."

"You did? Mustn't have heard it."

He snorted. "I call bullshit."

"You can call it whatever you want," I told him sweetly, humming at his annoyed grunt. "If you ask again, nicely, I might answer though."

That had him rolling his eyes, which, in turn, had me hiding a smile.

"There a reason they found you in the back yard?"

I winced, realizing that I'd been flung from the roof and into the yard beyond.

Shit.

No wonder my back was hurting.

"Did I damage my back?"

"No. Broken leg, though. Bruised hip. Couple of fractures on your ribs."

"Jesus, I was lucky."

"We're taught how to land," he disregarded, "but I wanna know how you had someplace to land from. I mean, it's not like we were doing parachute maneuvers, Star."

I bit my lip at his statement, not the words, but at his label for me.

Lodestar was like my real name now. I responded to it much

quicker than I did the one I'd been given at birth. But he'd always used Star, and it always tightened the bonds between us when he did. Whether he knew it or not.

With that one comment, he was reminding us both of what we'd been through together, of the friendship we'd had that had lasted for over a decade, of the animosity between us when we fought, of the times we'd fucked, of the times we'd made love.

Whenever he called me Star, he was twisting us back in time, and he didn't even know it.

But then, his regrets were different than mine.

I'd never really gotten over him before I'd been crash-landed into hell. Mav had fallen for Dominic, and when I said fallen, I meant worse than I had tonight.

Mav had come out of that relationship a thousand times more devastated than the mere injuries of a broken leg, ribs, and bruised hips.

I'd thought Nic had broken him all over.

From what I'd heard at the clubhouse, he had.

Until Ghost.

"Is she okay?" I asked, meaning it, caring about her when I cared about few people in this world. I cared that she was well because he needed her to be, and I needed *that*, because I loved him. But I wasn't good for him, and she was. This little mouse who'd earned her own nickname because of the damage done to her voice when she was held captive by a bunch of sociopathic gazillionaires.

This tiny woman who, somehow, held a brick shithouse's sanity in her grasp.

"She's fine. Thank fuck," he rasped, peering down at her with a loving smile on his face.

It hurt, but it was good to see too.

I wanted this for him.

I wanted him to be happy.

He deserved it.

Me, not so much.

"I'm glad. No broken bones?"

"No. They were outside, all the Old Ladies were, but—" He shook his head. "I've never seen anything like it on home soil. Was more bang than blast, but still set fire to a ton of shit. Figure that's the seventies' building code to blame though."

Because I could tell he was being cautious on purpose—either to piss me off or because he didn't know the full truth—I muttered, "I'll tell you what I know if you tell me what you know."

His smirk was my first clue to the fact that I'd fallen hook, line, and sinker for his bullshit.

Those goddamn eyes of his.

Jesus.

He should wear sunglasses to protect womanhood of all ages.

Prick.

"First off, where's Katina?"

"With Lily and Link." His eyes softened a touch at me though. It always seemed to surprise him that I cared for the kid like she were my own. Which, to me, she was. "Why were you on the roof?" he repeated his earlier question, and I got it.

In the middle of a party neither of us had been bothered about attending, why the hell had I decided to go on the roof? I pursed my lips, deciding not to prevaricate.

"Intel."

"What kind of intel?"

"You know I have a lot of chatter streaming in at all times."

In this instance, it came from an unlikely source. That fucker, aCooooig.

Seeing a photo of Cruz head for the house of a known FBI agent had started me down the rabbit hole, especially after I knew what he'd witnessed me do. Then, I'd done some digging, and what I'd discovered saved his ass from me, because he'd covered up more murders for the club than Ted Bundy, but along the way, I'd learned Rex was using him as a 'double agent.'

Of course, I'd only figured that out thanks to the bug I had in his office and the tracking device on his phone.

Sure as hell couldn't tell Mav that, now could I?

Anyway, looking into Cruz had led me to his mother, who'd led me to what I'd been looking for since I'd taken back my freedom.

The New World Sparrows.

NWS.

AKA, bunch of fuckers.

"I do, and I'm going to be hella pissed if you heard chatter that indicated there was about to be a strike on the compound."

Jarred from my thoughts, I shrugged. "Chatter can be meaningless. I'm sure your brothers would have just loved me if I'd told you to cancel the fucking party because of some bullshit I might have heard on channels that aren't exactly reliable."

He pursed his lips in disapproval. "Since when don't you share intel that might be pertinent, Lodestar?"

I winced. "Ouch. I'm Lodestar again?"

"Yeah. You let my people down. We could have prevented all this."

Maybe he was right, maybe he wasn't.

There was no way of knowing.

"I was up there to protect the clubhouse. You know I'm better than most of the guys in the club with a rifle. I'm worth ten of your best shooter."

"What with Lancaster and then the shit with Dog, Jesus, Lodestar, how the fuck do you think the brothers will trust you if you keep pulling stunts like this?

"I get that you're working to your own rules, and I understand that you have plans that don't include the club and you're keeping them to yourself, but we brought you in, we sheltered you, and housed you, and we did so with no questions asked.

"How the fuck do you repay that? By getting news we're under threat and not saying a word."

Anger hit me, because I knew he was right, but, he was making out that I had a say in anything that went down around me.

"Look, I get why you're mad, but you're acting as if I took Katina and lit out of the place before the attack happened. I did nothing to save my ass over yours, and you know that's true because Katina was tucked up in bed, Mav." I refused to plead with him, but I was definitely speaking with more diplomacy than he was used to with me. "I heard that there might be a hit. I never imagined there'd be a goddamn bomb. I thought if I sat on the roof, made a nest, I'd find out if the chatter was BS.

"These lines aren't accurate," I urged him to believe. Christ, nothing about the New World Sparrows was. "Last week, they said that Kennedy was fucking alive and walking around at a Presidential rally, for fuck's sake.

"I was acting on gut instinct and thought that my being there was a preventative measure in a worst case scenario."

The stubborn set of his jaw told me he didn't want to listen, and his hands moved down to grab the wheels so he could drag his ass out of the ER cubicle.

But, as he did, Ghost murmured, "Maverick, she did what she thought was right."

His jaw tensed, and he peered down at her with such a softness in his gaze that tears pricked my eyes.

He'd never looked at me like that, though, and in all honesty, I'd never wanted him to.

I wasn't soft.

I was hard.

And that was before what had gone down in fucking Tel Aviv.

I cleared my throat and rasped, "I really did, Mav. I'd never want to hurt you or the MC. You have to know that."

His nostrils flared, but he spat, "I want to know everything. What you heard online, what you saw, what went down."

I winced. "I didn't see much. There was another gun there for sure, and I might have hit him, but the bomb struck after I took my shot.

"It was a quiet night aside from the noise of the party. Out of nowhere, this biker appeared, and I thought he might be the threat until I heard one of the Old Ladies just below me say who it was."

"Stone," Ghost uttered softly. "She identified him first of all."

I shrugged which had the pounding in my head starting up for real. "It could be, I don't really remember."

"If Ghost says it was Stone, then it was Stone." His eyes were mean as he peered at me, telling me, silently, that her word meant more to him than mine did.

I scowled at that. "Since when did you become such a prick?"

"Since my home just got bombed, and half my fucking MC looks like they've been in a fistfight with Smokey the goddamn Bear."

I hissed under my breath, because I couldn't exactly argue with that, could I?

So, hunching my shoulders, which did interesting things to my back as it pulled on my hip, which stung. Badly. And when I said badly, well, I'd been through so much in my life that I had a very high tolerance to pain.

Torture did that to a girl. So when I said this ached, it did.

Shit.

Hissing again, I winced as I processed the pain, letting it flow out of me, before, in a low and raspy voice, I said, "After I heard Bear's name, I saw a laser light on his chest before it drifted over to his bike.

"I followed the sights and took my shot, but the next thing I knew, the place was lit up like a goddamn firework."

Ghost whispered, "How is he still alive?"

My eyes widened at that. "Jesus. He is?"

Mav's mouth was tight as he nodded. "He is. Just. Lost some limbs, but he's alive."

"Fuck, it's like being back in Baghdad."

The shadows in his eyes told me he agreed even if he didn't say a word.

"Was there a Prospect on the gate?" Ghost asked, her face tilting up as she asked Maverick.

"There should have been. I'd have to ask Sin who though."

"I didn't hear the gates open," I denied, "so maybe the gates were open already?"

"So someone let in the other shooter and didn't close the gates for them to make their escape?"

"You own most of the terrain around you, but there's no way of securing that much territory," I countered. "You and I both know that, especially when it boils down to a sniper. Maybe they snuck onto your land."

"Would have to be a damn good sniper at that," he reasoned. "I know Whistler wouldn't do it, Eagle Eyes is still injured after that cluster fuck with the Italians, and that other guy, I can't remember his name, but their sharpshooter who almost took out Steel... he's no more."

I shook my head. "That's just it, they're the illegal snipers we know, Mav, but this goes so much deeper."

He frowned at me. "Explain."

I licked my lips. "You'll think I'm crazy." Hell, I'd think I was crazy too but I'd lived it. I'd been living this for years. This insanity was my reality, and it was why I trusted no one.

Because when the authorities were the ones who'd made you a sex slave. When people high up in the ranks, who vowed to keep the men and women in their command safe, sold you out?

Who the fuck could you trust?

But Maverick was right.

He'd sheltered me and Katina without much need for recompense, nothing outside of information and that was how we rolled anyway. I hadn't paid for food or lodging or electricity since I'd arrived at the compound, and I wouldn't until I left.

They'd kept me and Katina safe, when I'd brought danger to their door.

It was time I leveled with Maverick. It was just a shame that I was doing so at a moment where he'd never trusted me or had as little faith in me as he did now.

I'd always had a knack for shit timing.

It was almost comforting to see that hadn't changed even if the rest of my life had.

THIRTY-SIX

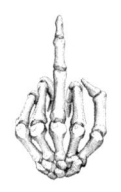

STORM

RIDING from Ohio to New Jersey in one sitting, only stopping for gas and leaks, was enough to give a man hemorrhoids, but that was the level of dedication to my brothers I had.

When Nyx had called with the news, I'd told him I'd be there, and I'd climbed onto my bike the second I'd spoken with Keira and Cyan and had assured myself they were okay.

Well, as okay as they could be after what they'd been through.

While I was tucked away in another fucking state.

I broke speed limits, laws, and pulled moves that had me crossing over farmland to cut corners on the route, because my brothers needed me. My family needed me. But as I traveled, I plotted, not just what I needed to do for the club, but for my woman and baby girl too.

The exile in Coshocton wasn't going too terribly. It was easier because I was technically single, and didn't have to deal with the female politics, but most of the guys hadn't liked the last Prez's Old Lady so they dealt well with me. But they weren't my people.

We were all Sinners, all brothers, but what I had with the West Orange chapter went deeper than labels.

We were blood.

Maybe not genetically speaking, but in the blood we'd shed for each other, with each other, over the years, tying us together in more ways than a regular family could ever imagine. But even that was nothing to the level of disconnect I felt knowing that the only women I fucking loved could have died tonight.

The Sinners were why I got onto the bike even though I was a danger to drive. My girls were why I made the eight-hour trip in just over five.

Rolling into town, I knew my people were at the hospital, but I needed to see what was going on at the compound.

Though, technically, Nyx was VP and should be leading if Rex wasn't able to, Nyx had no leadership skills in him yet. He could lead us into war but when it came down to building a new clubhouse, that was more my forte.

The guys had kept me updated and I'd read their texts while I sipped at a boiling hot coffee and had learned Bear was alive, but he'd lost an arm and a leg.

Jesus.

He'd never be able to ride again.

That loss would hit him more than the physical one, I knew.

We were born to fucking fly, and Bear had just had his wings cut off.

Maybe with prosthetics they could reap a miracle, but as it stood, with the burn damage, I knew it would be a hard won thing to get him out of bed again, never mind on the back of a bike.

That was how I knew I had to come. Rex needed me, because he'd be unable to function while his dad was in the early days of recovery.

And when I saw the state of the clubhouse, I reasoned we were lucky to have lost only five of the family because the damage was extensive.

Half of the place I'd called home was a burned-out shell. Where the bar was, all the windows had blasted inward, not just on the ground floor, but on the top floor as well as the smaller windows on the roof that let light into the attic which Maverick called home.

As I stared at the building, squinting some at the pitch black sky, the smoke that drifted lazily off the wreckage of a place that had been my respite for more years than I could count, I tried to tell myself I wasn't crying.

Only pussies cried.

But fuck.

The damage... we truly were lucky to have so few casualties.

Though chapters often rallied around in times like these, I'd come by myself because my MC was in a state thanks to the early days of my leadership. Not because I'd fucked up, but because I'd had to demote the entirety of the council and put new guys in place.

Guys the old council were constantly disrespecting.

It was a mess, bar none.

Once law enforcement had fucked off, I'd be bringing in brothers from chapters across the States to help clean this shit up. We needed all hands on deck, guys who were trained in construction who'd help bring this place back to life fast.

When a man walked up to me, his scent that of expensive aftershave, I didn't even have to turn my head.

Sure, brothers could wear Hugo Boss or Hermes, but without the scent of the road on their skin? No way.

Without looking, I knew who I was talking to.

A pig.

"You the leader of this... group?"

I arched a brow. "Group? Why, sir, we're just a riding club."

I couldn't have sounded more 'Gone with the Wind' if I'd tried.

"A riding club, my ass. Half the East Coast authorities know exactly what you are. I'm not sure how you always scrape under the radar, but it looks like someone's got to you where LEAs can't."

"Is that approval I hear?" I countered, only now turning my head to take in the bastard who was smirking at my family's misfortune.

"Maybe. Sometimes, to take down a rabid pit-bull, you have to set a rabid pit-bull on it."

My mouth twisted into a snarl, but I kept my shit together because the last thing the MC needed was my ass locked up in jail.

I could break the bastard's nose, and I'd take great satisfaction in doing so, or I could see this through, get the pigs off our property, and start rebuilding the place that housed way too many of my brothers.

More importantly, I knew we had a corpse melting into goo at the Fridge. I really didn't need the Feds to find either the body or our torture chamber.

Running a hand over my head, I was about to tell the fucker where to go, when I heard a, "Goddamnit, sir, you can't go in there."

My brow puckered as I twisted around, trying to see what was going down, who was trying to go into the clubhouse. Not seeing anything, I moved around, rushing to the side entrance, and when I saw Maverick wheeling down the corridor to Rex's office, which I had to hope one of my brothers had the wherewithal to trash before the emergency services got here, I called out, "Mav, you fucking idiot. Get your ass out of there."

He waved a hand at me, carried on rolling down the corridor toward only fuck knew where.

The basement was where he could catch the elevator to the top floor, his quarters, but surely he wasn't thinking about trying to use that now. Christ, hadn't they turned off the electricity? Something was firing the spotlights that made the place look like it was cast in daylight, but it was dark in the corridor Mav was traversing. As he rolled past Rex's door, I was pretty sure the basement was his destination, then he made a sharp turn and headed inside the office.

Angry with him for being such a fucking dipshit, I made after him. One of the arson investigators grabbed my arm, and I snarled, "I'm just going to get him." The guy tried to hold me back, and I blamed it on the fact that before the five-hour drive to West Orange, I'd been on a sixteen-hour run for my chapter. Fatigue, it had to be, that was why when he shoved me back, instead of being able to get into his face, smack the fuck outta him, I toppled onto my ass.

As I collided with the ground, sinking onto a patch that was lawn, another patch that was dirt, and another that was stone, my already aching butt hurt twice as hard.

But that was nothing to the quake it felt like my fall triggered.

A shout went down from the front, one that slipped into my ears and out again as I tried and failed to process what the team had said, but before my eyes, what was left of the clubhouse seemed to fall down like a house of cards. Snapping into a million tiny pieces as the upper floors gave way once the lower supporting walls cascaded like so much dust to the ground.

As my dazed mind registered that, I screamed, "Maverick!" Desperate, I hollered his name again, louder until my voice sounded like I'd been swallowing chalk for fun.

The fucker couldn't have survived two wars, only God knew how many battles, to die in the aftermath of a fire.

I leaped to my feet, and in the aftermath of the house settling down, the clouds of dust ceasing to boom around like noxious gas, I dove amid the rubble.

Bits of brick, snapped wood, electrical wires that sparked, pipes that spurted water, all of it bowed down to the weight of my drive.

I didn't stop until I was dashing over a cluster of particle board that snapped under my feet.

Finding stillness so that I didn't cause more wreckage, I heard the faintest of moans.

"He's over here! He's alive!" I screamed, unable to think of my brother being buried among this goddamn crap, not after the last bomb he'd been involved in had done pretty much the same thing.

Almost buried him alive.

If he stayed like this for much longer, I wasn't even sure if he'd survive mentally, never mind physically.

I could still remember the screams that escaped him as he roared out his terror in the middle of the night when he'd first come home.

It had scared the clubwhores shitless.

With dust flying, bits of ash floating and sticking to my sweaty face, and my boots slipping beneath the uneven ground that was made up of the debris of my home, I dragged shit off him. Firefighters surrounded me, working hard to free him, and even though it was barely five minutes between Maverick entering and the final crash of the clubhouse, it felt like a lifetime too long.

As we tore him out of the cocoon the drywall had buried him in, I saw the blood on his head, took note of his closed eyes, and prayed to fuck that he wasn't dead.

In the distance, I heard more sirens, and knew an ambulance was on its way.

"Why was he in a wheelchair?" someone asked as we struggled to lift him over the rubble.

"Roadside bomb in the sandbox," I answered, grating the words out from between gritted teeth. "Yeah, this dirty fucking biker was a soldier. He fought for this country—"

The sirens drowned out my voice, but I didn't care. I knew they'd only asked to make sure they didn't harm him further as we hauled him out from the wreckage, but it wasn't like we had a choice in how we got him out.

By the time we made it over the hillocks of bricks and wood, the gurney was by our side, and we lifted Mav onto it.

I wanted to go with him, but someone had to stay and monitor shit on this end.

Nyx, in that first call, had told me there was a body moldering down into soup at the Fridge. The last thing we needed was the cops or the Feds sniffing around our land.

Especially when they had a justifiable reason to search our property.

Whoever the fuck had set the bomb had known that the Feds would get involved with any kind of explosive of this nature.

Clever bastards.

Did they have a clue about whose murder we were covering up?

Lancaster had come into the country through illegal means. Steel had gone to Cambodia himself, hauling the asshole back in a crate like he was a piece of furniture. I knew we'd put him in the hold for the long haul flight too, so it wasn't like ICE had a clue about Lancaster's whereabouts in the country...

Like the prick had said, every LEA was after us for something. I was just giving it a worst case scenario as the worst possible fucking case had already happened.

As Maverick was wheeled into the ambulance, I watched him go, my mind blurring as I tried to figure out what to do next.

Lucky for me, admin was what I did best, but keeping the pigs from sniffing at our doors wasn't exactly easy when they had every goddamn right to be here.

When the bastard from before trudged over to me, I was happy to note that he didn't look as smug now. I didn't think that was anything to do with Mav almost being buried alive, especially when he'd not even bothered to help us draw him out, but he looked a little green around the gills.

"First crime scene?" I sneered, unable to help myself.

He gulped, which was an easy indication that I wasn't wrong. Or, at least, he'd seen something that was a first.

I twisted around, no longer facing the glare of the ambulance's brake lights that was drawing down the private road and back to town, and looking toward the clubhouse.

That was when I realized the firefighters were gathered around a body.

I winced at the sight, but I'd seen worse in my time in the Fridge. Still, there was no denying that the corpse they were retrieving looked like a side of goddamn bacon that had been left to burn in the pan.

I closed my eyes, wondering which brother I'd lost, even as I started making plans.

With Nyx and me at the helm while Rex was busy with his dad, we'd get to the bottom of this.

We'd figure it out.

And whoever had done this to us, we'd make them pay for daring to think they could come at us. For hurting our women. For killing our family. For destroying our home.

They'd pay.

I'd see to it.

But before then, I needed to get the pigs off any scent, and I needed a hug from my baby girl.

I didn't want it to be in that order, but lives were at stake, and never more had I felt the weight of that than I did now.

THIRTY-SEVEN

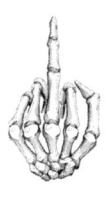

INDY

I WAS SO ready to run I was out of the damn door.

Only the fact that I wasn't a pussy, that I wasn't a runner kept my feet glued in place as I moved from brother to brother, family to family, hugging the Old Ladies, slinging an arm around the kids, trying to shore them up, make them feel better about their pops being in the ER or the ICU, injuries depending.

Such an outright attack had us all shaken, but if there was any solace to be found, it was when Storm strode in, looking normal, looking like he owned the fucking place, that something in my heart settled.

Sure, this world was messy, and Keira and Storm had a lot of fixing to do to make shit right for Cyan, but he was here, and I knew even Keira was relieved when she hauled ass over to meet him.

When Cyan didn't, my brows rose, but Storm strode over to her, kneeled in front of her, and I tuned out the rest of the world to hear him say, "Kid, you know I've done a lot of fucked up stuff in my life, but the one thing that always made sense, the proudest thing I ever did, was help make you."

Cyan's big eyes stared at him like he'd set the moon in the sky and from his words, and her behavior, I knew something had been said, something angry that was putting space between them, but tonight's events had rattled shit and when she pushed into him, squeezing him tight, I relaxed.

Things weren't right, but at least she had some comfort.

I was almost envious as I looked at her, stupid though it was. I wished my daddy was here, wished I could sit on his goddamn knee, have him tell me the world would keep on spinning even though, for some people tonight, it wouldn't.

We'd just had word that Tatána was dead. She'd survived a fucking monster, had lived through abuse that no one even wanted to contemplate never mind outright think about, but she hadn't survived the blast.

I knew there were questions.

When she lived on the compound, in one of the bunkhouses, why had she been in the clubhouse? And so late? When the other women seemed to believe her and Amara had been in their beds because the parties were too much for them to handle?

I had a feeling I knew why.

David.

Even though he was dead, she wouldn't know that, would she? No one knew. Not yet.

My throat felt thick as I thought about the next few days, and how, I'd have to sell a story to his people. I didn't think there'd be much issue though. His parents were dead, and as far as I knew, he had a cousin and an uncle left, but they weren't all that interested.

Come Thanksgiving and Christmas they might be... so I wondered if I should strike preemptively or was it wiser to wait? Wiser to let the trail grow cold?

I knew I'd have to consult Cruz, but my thoughts didn't make it any easier to stay.

I loved shows like *Bones* and *The Blacklist*, and whenever I watched them, whenever there was a regular murderer, I always wondered why they stayed around town. Why they didn't just run, leave the country, go and make a new life elsewhere.

But as I looked around the packed waiting room, where brothers stood with burnt hair and singed cuts, bandages patching them up here and there, sweat-streaked brows that were soiled with ash and grime from the fire as they hugged women and kids who were crying and shaking, this was my family.

Where else was I supposed to be?

The dichotomy of the violence of this world combined with the love and connection threw me, and it took me a few minutes to absorb that Storm had hugged Cruz, then he'd gotten to his feet and headed deeper down the corridor.

Unbidden, I followed him.

Storm was here for a reason. Not just because of Cyan and Keira, but because of Rex.

He hadn't said a word since I'd gotten here last night. Just sat there, beside Bear's room after the surgery was over.

Rachel was the only one who seemed to be able to get through to him, making him eat, go and get cleaned up in the bathroom, but even then, she'd had to clean him up some herself with a wet wipe she'd used on his face.

It was weird, seeing Rex like that. Especially because everyone knew the last thing Rex wanted from Rachel was to be babied.

She was his woman. It was a fait accompli, even as it might never actually happen.

Watching them together though, watching her stick by his side as the doctors came in and out of Bear's room in the ICU, was touching. So much so that I'd had to get out of there. I'd just needed a breather because there was more than just love between them, there was time.

It was a bit like looking at Stone and Steel, only without the animosity.

Steel had done everything in his power to hurt Stone along the way. His reasons must be big or I doubted she'd have forgiven him, but with Rachel and Rex it wasn't like that.

She was the law.

He wasn't.

I figured it boiled down to that.

But I moved with Storm, heading for the ICU Bear was in where, even though it was still early days and he was in an induced coma, the doctors had high hopes for him.

Of course, that could be bullshit. If I was a doctor dealing with Nyx, I'd tell him that too. But, then, Stone had confirmed it, and she wasn't scared of Nyx.

At least, I didn't think so.

She'd told me as well after we hugged when I got to the hospital last night, and I didn't think she'd lie to me.

I hoped she wouldn't, anyway.

As I pondered if the status reports we'd been given on Bear were BS or not, if Stone had become a better liar since we were kids, I made it to the waiting room where the council was gathered, and hovered outside the door.

Ever since Cruz had woken up, I'd left his cubicle, unable to deal with what he'd told me, with what he made me feel.

On top of everything else, it was just too goddamn much.

More than I could stand.

More than I could bear.

With my back to the partition, I strained to hear the conversation happening inside the waiting room. They spoke faintly, too faint. Made sense seeing as it was likely the walls had ears.

Then, I jerked in surprise when Giulia came out, her arm in a sling thanks to her dislocated shoulder. She studied me with surprise, then even though she looked exhausted, winked at me, then bent down with a grimace of discomfort as she pressed something to the opening.

I wasn't sure what it was, looked like a little squeegee stress ball, but when the door closed, it kept it ajar, just a tad.

She raised her good hand to her mouth and asked me for silence, but I didn't need to be told. Instead, I just listened to what I could hear, with a volume that wasn't much better but it was a little easier nevertheless.

"Rex? You got anything to say, brother?"

Silence.

Dead. Silence.

Rachel heaved a sigh. "Just leave him, Storm. He's... you know how he feels about his parents."

"I do. Yeah." Storm grunted. "What a fucking mess. What a goddamn waste."

Giulia and I had our eyes fixed on each other's, and while I knew Rachel was in there with Rex, I hadn't expected her to be allowed to stay in what was, most definitely, an unofficial church.

Giulia's eyes were pinched with resentment, and to be honest, I got it.

I did.

Even though we were MC brats, and were raised knowing how things worked, it didn't take the sting away.

She'd been bombed as well, but she wasn't allowed to listen in?

Sucked.

"We need to get some shit straight."

"Damn right we do," Nyx growled. "What the fuck was Maverick thinking of going into the fucking clubhouse?"

"I don't know," Storm answered. "I just know that it was important enough for him to go looking."

"He was talking to Lodestar earlier," Steel rasped, sounding like death. Most of them did thanks to smoke inhalation.

"About what? Anyone know?" Storm queried.

"Ghost might. She was there. You know Maverick talks around her," Link pointed out.

"Shit, we'll need to speak with her then," Storm muttered. "Fuck." He heaved a sigh. "Okay, we'll deal with that after. First things first, we need to get shit rolling. Lots of brothers lived in the clubhouse and they'll need places to stay."

Rachel surprised me by murmuring, "There's enough room for Rex and a few councilors at my place."

"Anyone else can stay with Lily and me," Link offered.

"That's great, guys," Storm added. "But while Lily is Daddy Warbucks and Rachel, your place is plenty big, it won't serve for everyone.

"I got the idea when I drove through town. How about Budget Basement?"

"The motel?" Link hummed in thought. "Bit grimy, but so are most of the men right now."

"Yeah. I was thinking, last I knew, Jamie Peters was trying to sell the place anyway. We should buy it and then we don't have to deal with any pressure while the compound is being restructured."

"Good idea," Steel said. "We have the cash. We can buy him out whatever his price."

"Don't go too high," Nyx rumbled, "we all know that fucker is a son of a bitch."

Giulia's lips twitched at that, like her man had just spoken pure poetry, and maybe to her he had.

God knew she had to be used to him talking that way.

"I'm pretty sure Mav had a file on him, back from when he used to run drugs out of that place," Link said softly. "Maybe we can access it? Or get Lodestar to access it?"

"Good thinking."

"You think she'll help?" Nyx queried. "I mean, we all know what a wild card she is. There's a reason we prefer to question Ghost about the conversation between her and Mav than the woman herself."

"I think she will," Link intoned. "She's good people. A lot nuts, but good people. And she's doing all this shit for a reason, which isn't money."

"That just makes her all the more dangerous and a bigger wild card," Nyx retorted, then an explosive grunt escaped him and I wasn't surprised when a loud crashing sound echoed around the room.

"Fuck's sake, Nyx, you trying to get us thrown out?"

In a flash, Giulia was storming inside, and she surprised me by grabbing Nyx's hand with her good arm, and tugging him around to face her.

"I get you're stressed, I am too, God knows, but now isn't the time to be losing your shit." She scowled up at him, like a meerkat telling a grizzly bear to back the fuck down. "You hear me, Nyx? Get yourself under control."

Because she'd barged in, I stepped inside the room, tucking myself small so that they wouldn't notice me and wouldn't toss me out.

I needed to know what was happening more than they could understand.

Everyone attached to the Sinners was going through the same hell, but not all of them had my past.

The need for security, the need for things to be copacetic, was an urge that might keep the wolves at bay, and that would stop me from going crazy.

Nyx's nostrils flared at Giulia's retort, and Link asked, "What's going on?"

I shot him a look, saw he was concerned, and Link didn't really do concerned. He was too cheerful, too playful. Too happy-go-lucky.

Well, as much as a natural born killer could be.

There was a reason we easily accepted the notion of killer clowns, after all.

With the grins and the chuckles, it was too easy to think they could stab someone in the neck...

Exactly like I had.

Oops.

"Giulia, well, she—"

She heaved a sigh. "For God's sake, Nyx. I don't have cancer."

He gnawed on his lip, and for the first time in my life, a long life of knowing this man, of seeing his downfalls and his vices, or knowing what made him tick, I had to admit, I'd never seen him so uncertain. So...

Jesus.

Was he nervous?

"What's going on?" Storm demanded.

"I'm pregnant. I found out after they ran some tests."

Link blinked. "Huh." Then, as the surprise faded, his grin made a massive reappearance, and like always, that goddamn smile of his was contagious.

So much so that even though shit was crazy and our worlds were tossed upside down, the sight of it had me grinning, and as the brothers swept around Nyx, whooping and hooting their congrats, I slipped to Giulia's side and carefully wrapped my arm around her waist, much like I'd done with the kids out there.

"You're going to be a momma."

She bit her lip as she shot me a look. "What a day to find out, huh?"

"Yeah, it is," I agreed, "but maybe it's the light at the end of the tunnel, no? What the fuck else are we doing all this for if it isn't for the ones we love?"

She frowned at that, then murmured, "You doing okay?"

I shook my head. "No. I've been better. But this is good news." I kissed her cheek. "You're going to make psychotic parents, but I wouldn't miss the show for anything."

She pulled me into a hug. "That sounds like you were planning on going somewhere."

"I was." But I sighed. "Now I need to be the cool aunt who remembers important things like school and shit."

Giulia snorted. "I'm not an alien. Not like Nyx."

"You're the one having his Martian baby."

"I prefer to think he's from Jupiter," she teased, pulling back to smile at me. Something softened in her gaze as she studied me, before she murmured, "You're really happy for us?"

I nodded, and I meant it. "Terrible timing, like you said, but the best kind of timing too. That's probably going to set up the kid for a lifetime."

Giulia's smile was shaky. "I didn't expect it, not really, so it came as a surprise."

"On a night of surprises."

Before she could reply, Nyx dragged me into his arms, and he burrowed his face into my hair, much like he'd done earlier.

He was the strangest kind of beast.

So strong, so fucking rabid, so dangerous, but with the women he loved? Fucking putty.

It was, I knew, one of the reasons we weren't that close. Because I meant too much to him, and what he could avoid, he would.

The thought resonated, and I murmured, "You'd better not check out on her if she's carrying a girl."

"Giulia's got my fucking soul, Indy," he growled.

"Wasn't talking about Giulia. She knows how to get through to you, but I know what you're like with the women you aren't boning but love."

"Never boned anyone I loved before," he countered.

"True. I guess this is virgin territory for us all, but you know what

I'm saying, so don't try to change the subject. You think you can pull away from your daughter because it hurts too much to love her and need to protect her, I'll kick your ass."

"That's nothing to what Giulia would do."

"Which makes her perfect for you," I teased, squeezing him tightly. "For your sake," I carried on, my voice more serious now, "I hope it's a girl. I hope she brings you peace, Nyx. I really hope so."

He tensed in my arms. "I don't deserve peace."

"No? Well, I disagree, and I know Carly would too." Much like I had Giulia, I leaned up on tiptoe and pressed my lips to his cheek. "I want you to be happy, brother."

"You going to stick around to see me fuck up as a dad?"

"Nah, I'm gonna stick around to make sure you don't." I smiled at him.

"Wasn't sure. I overheard your conversation with Cruz."

"Figured you did."

He grunted. "Don't want you to go back to New Orleans, Indy. Want you here. Right here. Might not seem like it's the safest place to be, but whoever the fuck declared war on us will pay. You and I both know it."

"I do, and that's what I don't want to get involved in."

"Cruz was right. We were born tangled up in this mess. Moving won't change shit. Just means you're dealing with it all alone. I don't want that for you, sis."

"Well, it's a good thing you knocked Giulia up then, isn't it?" I muttered gruffly. "Because I sure as hell am staying around now."

His grin was pleased even if he did look a little nauseated, and I got it.

Nyx was a murderer.

A bad man by anyone's definition.

Just not Giulia's.

They'd made a baby together, and I meant it when I said I hoped it gave him the peace he was chasing, even if he didn't know it.

With one last squeeze, he let me go, releasing me from the most meaningful conversation I'd had with my brother in years.

When I saw the councilors gently hugging Giulia thanks to her injury and ribbing her about her kid being born with horns, saw Rex who was staring at nothing like he'd heard bupkis and Rachel whose face was tight with longing, I released a sigh.

So much was up in the air, so much was wrong, so much needed to change, and yet, deep in Giulia's belly was the seed that heralded the future.

I needed to remember that.

THIRTY-EIGHT
CRUZ

THE DAY AFTER THE BOMBING, shit was still up in the air, which, I figured, was to be expected.

That damn clubhouse had housed a dozen of us permanently, which meant we had no clothes, no toiletries, no nothing.

Throw in the fact that our phones had been lost to the blast, and that it had taken out our monitoring equipment too, well, things couldn't get much worse.

Not only had we lost people, good people, we'd lost our identities as well.

None of us had any goddamn ID, except for those of us who'd been carrying their wallets on them, but if you lived at the clubhouse, you didn't often carry cash on you. It would be like going to the john in your house and taking your fucking briefcase along for the ride if you were a regular businessman.

The clubhouse was our home, and we'd just lost it.

I was grateful the bunkhouses were still standing, even if they were severely damaged, because it meant Stone and Steel hadn't lost everything, neither had Lodestar, the girls, or Ghost and the others.

That Tatána had been found where she had, well, it didn't take a brain surgeon to figure out that E equaled MC squared, did it?

Tatána and David had been mixed up together, but deciding when to slot that information in, to keep the council in the loop when the major congregator of information and intel was still knocked out in a hospital bed wasn't easy.

Triage of the clusterfucks going down in our life was something that was difficult to calculate, and for the first time in a long while, I was grateful not to be on the council, grateful that I didn't have to make the big decisions for the MC as a whole.

A part of me had been resentful about being nothing more than a gofer, but now the time came for life-altering choices to be made, I was glad to be in the backseat.

Figuratively and literally, because our bikes had gotten caught up in the blast. As far as the Feds could tell us, they were actually the major propellent in the bomb.

Sure, the boom had been big, but the gas in our tanks had just taken things to a whole other level. Making the explosion gnarlier, and just that more ferocious.

So, as I was one of the brothers who was considered closer to the council than most, I was riding with Link and Nyx in a cage toward the Budget Basement motel which, more than likely, was going to be where I laid my head for the next couple of months as we broke ground on the new clubhouse.

Thankfully, we had a lot of contractors in our ranks, so that was something, but it didn't take away from the heavy duty planning we needed to get done.

Just thinking of that was a headache, and I knew I'd be roped in because of my engineering degree.

I hated working on projects like that because making sure buildings were up to code was a migraine waiting to happen, but for my family, I'd do it. Trouble was, the brothers were dumb fucks if they didn't see the Old Ladies eying this up like rabid dogs in need of a seventy-two ounce steak. They were going to milk this situation, make shit how they wanted it.

The only consolation was that I doubted anywhere would be painted pink or papered with fucking flowers.

I'd take the flowers, of course, if they were inside Indy's apartment.

Fuck, I missed her. I missed her something goddamn fierce. And it had only been a night. But the emotional distance between us was worse than her staying on Mars, and I had no idea if I'd be able to bring her back to me.

Rubbing my chin as I watched West Orange pass me by in a blur because Link was driving too fast, I sighed and jolted when Nyx grumbled, "Stop fucking sighing."

I'd heard the news about him becoming a father, and I couldn't say that it had cheered him up any, that was for sure.

With my feet stretched out on the backseat, I settled in for the short ride, and murmured, "Got a lot to sigh about."

"You think you got problems? I have a baby popping out into the fucking world, and somehow, I gotta make a home for us."

The money wasn't the problem, it was time. I knew that.

Time was always an issue for us.

In the next couple of days, we'd been scheduled to make a run up to the Canadian border for the Five Pointers, and then with all this other shit, from David to Tatána, to the bombing to the reconstruction of the clubhouse, from Bear to Maverick… it never rained but it fucking poured.

"You can stay in the pool-house."

"Where that asshole lived?" Nyx boomed, making Link wince.

"I forgot about that."

"Well, I fucking didn't. Not having anything to do with that place. We'll stay at Rachel's like we did last night—"

"How about Sin's place? He probably wouldn't mind, what with the situation being as is."

"Tiffany and Sin have made their place there. I ain't gonna turf them out." Nyx heaved a sigh. "It's just figuring out what Giulia wants is all, and it's not like we don't know how fucking particular she is."

"She ain't that particular," Link retorted. "Not only did she settle for your psychotic ass, but she was happy living in the clubhouse."

"That was before she got pregnant. Imagine her clean-freak ass on steroids. I've already had to ban her from cleaning Rachel's kitchen because she's stressed."

I shook my head. "That's the dream, man. You want a woman

who'll clean when she's stressed." I whistled under my breath. "When they get all sweaty and they're on their hands and knees?"

Nyx twisted around in his seat to glower at me. "I'm not sure what's worse. Thinking of you getting a boner over my sister in that position, or wondering if you're dicking around and thinking of other pussy like that."

I cut him a look, one that was loaded with as much sincerity as my duplicitous ass was capable of. "I'm in love with her, man."

He pulled a face. "Fuck."

I smiled a little. "Thought that would cheer you up."

"Not exactly. Goddamnit, I don't wanna think of my brother with her."

"Why not? Not good enough for her?" I jibed, which earned myself a glower, but hell, I'd been raised with Caro fucking Dunbar. I knew that looks could kill, and if they did, I'd have been dead by five.

"Yeah, yeah, that's why. Got nothing to do with the fact you clean up corpses for the brothers for a living, nothing to do with the fact that you found your place with us because of your unique skillset..." His voice drifted off, but the warning was clear. "You fuck her around, I'll fuck you up."

"I'm counting on it," I assured him, and I meant it. "If I hurt her, I deserve to have my ass handed to me. Any time, any place."

Link huffed. "Well, hell, Nyx, that's how you know it's serious. When a man serves himself up for a whooping, you know shit got real."

"It did with me, but I don't think so with her. She's drifting away."

"I heard," Nyx said softly.

"Figured that's why you came bursting in yesterday."

He pulled a face. "I'm not having her running off to New Orleans again. Scared the shit outta me thinking of her in that godawful city."

Link laughed. "It's one of the best cities in the States."

"Not for my single baby sister who's incapable of keeping her ass out of trouble."

Link laughed. "Jesus, yeah. She was a little shit, wasn't she?"

Curious, I asked, "She was?"

Link caught my eye in the rearview mirror. "Oh yeah, she was.

Fuck, she was terrible. Something fierce. It was almost a relief to get her ass out of Jersey, give us all a break, but then news would float up about what she was doing, and then that'd set old Mad Dog over here to frothing at the mouth."

Nyx punched him in the arm, but Link just grinned, quite cheerfully dissing on our brother like it meant nothing to get in this insane fucker's face.

"She's mellowed out though now, hasn't she?" I asked, curious if they considered this version of Indy to be mellow or not.

As far as I could see, she didn't get into trouble but she had no issue with running her mouth to a lot of very dangerous men. That was either bravery or dumbassery.

"Christ, yeah," Nyx rumbled. "It's like she's on weed now. I don't know what happened, but she changed when she came back."

My brows rose. "Thought she came back because your Ma died."

"She did, but I don't think that's what changed her. Not really. By the end, none of us were very close.

"My folks couldn't get over what Kevin had done, couldn't get over that Carly was dead and why, it was just... well, it was a fucking mess.

"Caleb started getting into shit when he was sixteen. Joyriding and pulling stupid stunts in stolen vehicles." He heaved a sigh. "Me and Indy had to straighten him out."

I narrowed my eyes at that insight, and asked, "Hang on, is that why you're so mad at him for getting caught?"

"Yeah, because we both spent a lot of time, and wasted a lot of fucking energy, in getting him on the straight and narrow."

"The only way you could get that kid to be straight and narrow is if you tied him to a fucking ruler. Prison will do him good," Link informed the truck as a whole.

"Not sure Rikers is good for anyone's soul."

"I'd usually agree, but Caleb was a hyperactive little shit. He needed to go in there, get himself a pair of balls. Grow up. The MC isn't a game, you can't just play at it, and that was what he was doing. It was only a matter of time before he was going down, and I'd prefer for him to get hit now, and serve some time, when he's young because as much of a hardass as the judge was on his case, if he'd been five years older, I'd swear he'd have sent him down for life."

Nyx pulled a face. "I hate that you're right, man, but you are."

"I'm always right," Link chirped, which prompted us to both roll our eyes.

"You keep on believing that shit if it makes you feel better, Link."

"Trust me, I will." He pinned me down with another look, then asked, "What's going on with you and Indy?"

"She's wondering if she's crazy to be with a biker. I can't blame her. Not after what went down, and then with all the other shit..."

Nyx heaved a sigh. "Shit I haven't shared in church yet."

Link's brows rose. "What kind of shit are we talking here?"

"It's a long fucking story, and we're already at the motel."

"Thank fuck Lodestar got that info off her drive," Link muttered, changing the subject to the matter at hand. "Means that son of a bitch will sell the motel to keep his ass out of jail."

While he wasn't exactly wrong... "I don't know if it's all that great. It means she cloned everything on Maverick's hard drive, Link. When she probably shouldn't have done that."

"Wouldn't be surprised if Maverick already knew. He's weird with her," Nyx pointed out. "Gives her enough rope to hang herself then cuts her down. Every time."

Because I couldn't disagree, especially knowing what I did, I murmured, "Think they were boning back when they were serving?"

"Yeah," Link and Nyx said simultaneously.

"No way he'd cut her so much slack otherwise," Link carried on.

"Agreed," I murmured, nodding at him. "I don't think she leads him around by his dick though."

"No, that's firmly in Ghost's grasp now. Did you see her at the hospital?" Link pulled a face as we drove into the motel's parking lot. "If I had a pussy, I'd have cried. She looked petrified, like she thought he was gonna die."

"They're sleeping together," Nyx said softly, his tone quiet. "Not fucking, not as far as I could make out, but sleeping."

My brows rose, because everyone knew how weird Maverick was with sleeping.

He'd scared a couple of clubwhores who'd sneaked right into his room when he'd first gotten back, shoved a knife to their throats. He'd almost sliced one bitch, Lacey. She'd left soon after, thank fuck.

Maverick was the kind of guy who didn't say what he didn't mean.

He'd told the bitches to leave him alone, that a BJ wasn't going to cure his woes, but they hadn't listened.

None of us had had much sympathy for Lacey in the aftermath, which was why she'd left, but still, it was a testament to the growing bond between Maverick and Ghost that they were sleeping together like that.

In all honesty, for Mav's sake, I hoped he found some peace with her. God knew, they both deserved it.

"He'll be okay, won't he?" Link asked, twisting around to look at me.

"My doctorate isn't in medicine," I reminded him, just like I had to remind my brothers every fucking week.

"Yeah, but you know more than we do," Nyx intoned.

I pulled a face, because that wasn't a lie. I could read between the lines, but it wasn't like I was up on that shit. "The damage to his head wasn't even that bad, so they're not sure why he's still unconscious."

"Seems like the doctors are just like us—we don't know what the fuck made him think he could go into the clubhouse."

"Yeah, well, I have more answers about his medical file than I do about that," I rumbled.

"What about Bear?" Nyx asked, his voice low.

"I dunno," I told him. "It depends. And even after, if he does make it, and they seem pretty confident he will—"

"Only because the staff are terrified of Rex."

"Yeah, well, Stone agreed, didn't she?"

"True," Nyx conceded.

"The trouble will be afterward. You've seen how Maverick was. Why wouldn't Bear be the same?"

"So, what you're saying is he might make it, might pull through, only for us to lose him to depression?"

"Could be," I said grimly.

"Jesus. We need to make sure that doesn't happen."

"We're family. It *ain't* gonna happen. He'll get through this, and whatever he needs to get back to a more normal life, we're on it," Link retorted, voice firm, like if he said it a certain way, it'd be set in stone.

The three of us nodded in agreement, and when Nyx pounded his hand into his fist and murmured, "Don't know about you fuckers, but I'm ready to bust some balls," Link and I were right there with him.

THIRTY-NINE
INDY

I STARED BLANKLY INTO SPACE, not really looking at the drawing I was making, not answering the phone that was ringing and had been, off the hook, for hours on end.

Or, at least, it felt that way.

I had a lot of clients, a lot of them, and they were all trying to come in for their bi-monthly appointments, but I just couldn't deal with that right now.

I'd dealt with worst trauma in my life, but at the minute, it was all just a little too much.

When my door opened, and I found Cruz standing there, looking his regular, calm self, except for random bandages and bulges of more of them under his cut, I wasn't sure whether I wanted to scream or smile.

There was a timeless quality about him. Something that made me feel like in a hundred years, he'd still be standing there if I didn't send him away.

Shit, maybe if I even tried to send him away, he'd still be standing there.

Knowing his determination, it would fit.

I couldn't be upset about that, so, my major question was, what the fuck was I upset about?

The thought had me swallowing nervously, which he noticed, of course, raised a brow, then asked, "Thought I might be chasing your ass down in Georgia by now."

"You have my niece or nephew to thank for me being here."

He grimaced at that. "I was hoping you were going to say me."

I bit my lip. "I won't not say it's you."

He heaved a sigh. "Music to a man's ears, Indy."

"That's how I roll, you know that," I rumbled, rocking back in my chair as I stared at him. "You look like you'd fall down if I pushed you over."

"Won't most men? If you shove them hard enough?"

I gnawed on my bottom lip. "Sit on the sofa."

"Thought I was the one who was supposed to boss you around?"

I tipped up my chin. "I'm not the injured one."

"True." He arched a brow at me, then retreated to the sofa. "Guess it's a good sign you don't want to toss my ass out."

"I—" That had never been my intention. Didn't he know that? "This isn't about you, Cruz."

"That's the fucker, I know. Usually, it's me, and in this, it's my life."

I gnawed some more on my lip. "I know I'm being stupid," I whispered, my voice low.

"No, you're not," he immediately countered. "You're being rational. What woman in their right fucking mind would want to stay tied into this life unless—"

"They come from it, or if their world was already fucking bad."

He grimaced. "Yeah."

I shook my head at him. "Why are you a biker, Cruz? Why, when your mom is a Fed, and you looked to come from a real nice home."

"I did. Dad's great, Mom... isn't. It has nothing to do with her being a Fed, either. It's just she's a psycho."

"That's why you're right at home with the Sinners, I take it," I said, and despite myself, a smile danced around my lips.

"Yeah, how couldn't I be?" He pulled a face. "My grandfather got whacked by the Irish Mob about—" He hesitated. "Christ, fifteen years ago? Something like that.

"I never knew him that well, because he wasn't that happy about Caro being a pig when he was definitely up to his eyes in filthy business. Anyway, he gets his fool ass offed, and ever since, Mom's been on a kind of vigilante mission to find his killer and right the 'wrong' of his death."

"It was bound to be a wrong to her if she loved him."

He shrugged. "She's a fool, then. He was as great a father as she is a mother. My dad, on the other hand, is cool. We got along great, still do. He's normal, thank fuck."

"That makes your decision to go into organized crime even more unusual."

He tapped his nose. "Think you can learn about my past in a couple of sentences?"

Chastised enough to smile in earnest this time, I rocked my chair and murmured, "Apologies, I'm all ears."

He dipped his chin. "It's not the best of stories, Indy," he warned.

"No origin story ever is," I said dryly. "As long as you weren't bitten by a radioactive spider... oh, wait, I could deal with that."

He snorted. "Good to know, but nothing that interesting.

"I was a smart kid. Very smart. Got a bunch of scholarships when I was fifteen, and when other kids were boning their way through their freshmen year, I was handling two Bachelor of Science degrees at NYU."

"Which ones?"

"Chemistry and Structural Engineering."

"Probably shouldn't get me wet knowing you're a clever bastard, should it?"

His lips twitched. "Whatever turns you on, Indy... it's all good."

Because I loved that twinkle in his eye, I asked, "That means you can build bridges and shit. Literal ones, I mean. Right?"

A laugh escaped him. "Yeah. Technically, it does. I'd need a license though. I got one a while back but it expired. Don't exactly need one when I'm tending bar."

"No, I guess not. Why Chemistry and Structural Engineering?"

"Always loved building shit and destroying shit." He shrugged. "Even went into a doctorate program with my favorite subjects merged together—Chemical Engineering. That was ten times more fun." His nose crinkled at the bridge, like a thought had crossed his mind, one that had his eyes darkening too, but he didn't express it out loud.

Though I was curious what had drained his amusement, I only asked, "You have a doctorate?"

"I do." He scratched his throat, bringing my attention to the negative tattoo there—like I hadn't seen it a thousand times before. "Don't look the type, do I?"

"No, but that's why I love the fact that looks can be deceiving." I sat up, suddenly interested by this man I'd shared so much with and who'd, in the grand scheme of things, only shared his DNA with me.

But my words changed the conversation—his eyes narrowed on me. "Wasn't your first kill, was it?" he asked, his head tipping to the side.

"I wish it was."

"Who?"

"David wasn't my first stalker."

His eyes flared wide in genuine surprise—who the hell could blame him? "You're kidding?"

"No. Apparently, I attract a certain type." I cocked a brow at him. "You gonna turn into a bunny boiler as well?"

"Well, I boil something, just never innocent bunnies."

I smirked. "Good to know."

"I mean, Indy, don't get me wrong, you're fucking beautiful, but why do you get stalkers? One is nuts, two? Insane."

"I'm nice to people. It causes problems." Of course, Shane hadn't been like David at all.

He'd been aggressive.

Things always turned out that way, didn't they? Until I ended them.

"I knew you were too at ease with that fuck." He blew out a breath. "Of all the things that's happened today, that messes with my head the most."

Amused, despite the situation, despite the chatter about something that had caused me a lot of distress for a long time, and despite the fact that Shane had managed to hurt me, *badly*, which was why I hurt him first, I murmured, "Glad to be of service."

He studied me, a little like I imagined him studying a problem he needed to solve and couldn't. Now I knew about his education, it fit.

Cruz was a cut above. Calm, not because it was in his nature to be restful, but because, I recognized, he was analytical. Chasing answers and finding solutions when I'd just thought him to be a lowly bartender who didn't have many outside concerns.

"Nyx told me something about you today. He said your mom dying brought you home, but you were different. Changed. And he didn't think it was to do with them."

"I had to grow up a lot when they died," I corrected. "Caleb needed a sister, not some lunatic. But you're right, it happened about a year earlier. Shane..." I cleared my throat. "Died."

"Scissors again?" he queried. "Should I start hiding them from you?"

My nose crinkled. "No. A car jack."

His eyes flared wide. "A car jack?" He leaned forward at that, his curiosity clear. "What the hell happened?"

"He slit my tires and when I was changing them, offered me a ride home. I told him where to go, he tried to drag me in the car so he could... I was having an issue getting the jack in place anyway, and it was the nearest thing on hand."

"What happened?"

"He died," I repeated stonily. "But that time, I contacted the cops and told them everything. It wasn't as bad as I thought, not at first, then after a while, they started saying I was known for leading guys on."

He hissed at that, then growled, "Fuckers."

"Yeah. I was nervous with David, because I knew the cops would look at my record, at my ties which weren't well known by the cops down in the South, but I just knew it wouldn't look good.

"They'd call me a Black Widow, when it wasn't my fault." Because I couldn't deal with those memories today, blurted out, "Do you think Tatána was the one spying on the Sinners?"

He nodded. "I do. It fits. Ties shit up neatly too. I mean, if she hadn't died, and she was the one spying, there's no way the MC would have let her live."

That had me grimacing. "Such a shame. He was using her, and she was probably looking for what Ghost has found in Mav."

"I think it's more likely she was looking for a green card," he said wryly.

I winced. "I feel bad saying that. After what she's gone through, doesn't she deserve a bit of the Land of the Free?"

"Well, she got it if that was what she wanted." He pinned me in place with a look. "Just to a more canonical level than anticipated."

I scowled at him. "Harsh, Cruz. Harsh."

He shrugged. "She was spying on us, with a man who was stalking you. That isn't the behavior of someone we need to empathize with."

"She was a foreigner, tucked away in a country illegally, who'd been sexually abused, tortured and tormented for years, who'd been forgotten by her family, and lost to the world itself like she was a spirit drifting around. I think I can understand her reasoning."

A warmth appeared in his gaze that I didn't want to affect me, but it did. "Quite the advocate."

I sighed. "Yeah, well, someone has to be, don't they? And it's not like it will get Tatána anywhere, is it? She's gone now. What a horrible way to die." I shuddered, because I'd heard a diluted version from Giulia who'd overheard the conversation between Storm and Nyx.

In actuality, my sister-in-law was turning out to be a font of information. I guessed it helped she was as devious as me, maybe more so before it had been kicked out of me by life.

By the time I returned to West Orange all those years ago, after Shane, I'd just wanted a bit of peace and quiet.

Unfortunately for me, I'd attracted David before I left NOLA.

Fuck a duck.

Maybe I needed to be with a biker because that was the only thing that would keep me free from these creeps who I seemed to attract like flies around shit.

"Should I take it as a good sign that you aren't throwing me out of the door?"

I didn't necessarily have an answer to that, because I wasn't sure myself.

I had no reason to toss him out. Nothing he'd said was any worse than what Nyx had done over the years. And he was here, hadn't run screaming from the hills even though I was getting a body count of my own.

One accidental death, a thrown-out manslaughter case that a surprisingly sympathetic DA had tempered as self-defense thanks to the defensive wounds on both mine and Shane's body, was one thing.

Two?

That was when people started to get a reputation.

Running my finger along the outside of my lip, with my gaze trained on the desk, I asked, "Cruz?"

"Yes?"

"Want me to work on your back piece?"

He blinked. "I mean, not really, because of my ribs, but the bottom half... you can if you want to."

I heaved a sigh. "I do, want to, I mean. I need to clear my head."

"Sure. If that's what you need then we'll roll with it." He got to his feet, his desire to comply clear, and a sudden welter of gratitude hit me.

As well as the realization that I'd been a bitch.

He'd lost brothers, lost his home, lost his things, but he was here, consoling me, trying to bring *me* around.

I hadn't even offered to let him crash here, for God's sake.

Guilt and shame uncoiled inside me as I got to my feet, and when he strode over to me, I reached out, letting my fingers collide with his as he moved to tangle them together.

"Would you really have run?"

I knew he wanted me to say no, but I couldn't. So, instead, I asked, "If you could liken me to any animal in the world, what would it be?"

His surprise was evident, but he didn't dismiss the question as stupid. I could see the logical reasonings and rationale being deciphered before my very eyes, so I wasn't altogether surprised when he came up with, "A wolverine."

I hissed out a laugh. "Ouch."

His eyes twinkled. "Deadly when provoked, capable of hunting through frozen soil to reach their prey? Sound like anyone we know?"

"Well, you can think that, but I think of myself as a rabbit. Too scared sometimes, too stupid to live, to breathe. Never good enough, dirty, vermin—" I grunted. "Doesn't matter if you see me as a wolverine or a puma—which, FYI, I'd have preferred—but I don't see myself like that."

"I'm not strong, Cruz. I'm not."

He squeezed my fingers. "You're plenty strong, but when the cards fall, and you're left with questions that come with insane answers, you were always going to come out fighting. A puma, rabbit, and a wolverine all have the same thing in common—when they come face to face with a gun, they ain't gonna leap for the man wielding it. They're going to tuck tail and run."

"You don't know that."

"Don't I?" He smiled. "I just figure I have to give you a reason to want to stay around."

"You've given me that for a while, but that got blurred along the way."

"Only natural. After what happened."

"I-I should have asked you before, Cruz, but you must need somewhere to stay."

"I can stay with the other brothers. We just bought the Budget Basement Motel."

My eyes widened. "You did, huh? Interesting. As far as I knew, Jamie Peters wanted a crazy asking price…" He smirked at me, which gave me all the answer I needed. "Didn't know you could beat the shit out of someone with a concussion and taped up ribs," I remarked wryly.

"Nyx and Link were more persuasive than me."

"I'll bet," was my rueful retort, well aware that both brothers were injured too. "But I mean it. You don't have to stay there. Please, I'd like you here. With me." It surprised me how much I meant that.

How badly I *did* want him here.

His gaze softened. "I'm not going to push you into anything, Indy. I know how important space is to you, as well as your independence."

I'd had one foot out of the damn door before I'd found out about my niece or nephew, but that timelessness about Cruz got to me.

He was strong, stalwart enough to be there for a hundred years. To hunt me down for a hundred years.

And, to be completely frank, there was plenty I'd prefer to be doing with him than have him hunt me down when his arms were the only place I wanted to be. The only place I found peace.

The fucking MC was what had gotten between us, just like it always did. Nerves hit me, but with it, was a rush of exhilaration as I accepted a hard truth. I needed him.

Sinner or not.

"Space and independence *are* important to me, and I love that you know that, but, and I should have realized this sooner, they're not as important as you.

"I have no way of classifying this, Cruz, no way that fits or makes any real sense to me, but I just know that I don't want to lose you. And yeah, I'm aware that I'm the one who almost took us to the brink—"

"You might be, but I'd have come after you, Indy. Never doubt that."

And as I stared at the resolve in his eyes, a resolve that was like a goddamn hug on a cold night, I recognized I'd done the impossible—found a man who saw past the surface, who recognized what I was beneath the protective layers I'd spent a lifetime cultivating... and he wanted me anyway.

FORTY

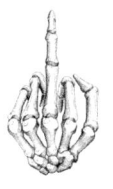

CRUZ

I WOKE up with an angel in my bed.

Or, at least, I woke up *in* an angel's bed.

As I squinted around, restricted by the way I was laying, I found her, and watched her sleep for a handful of moments.

Her breathing was soft, even, well-paced. No stressors. She wasn't having a nightmare, wasn't even having a stressful sleep.

She was calm.

And that soothed me.

Last night, over four hours of work on the lower half of my tattoo, that relentless buzzing in my ears from the tattoo gun, I'd agreed to stay with her on the proviso that I didn't mess with her sleep.

I figured it was a positive that she was sleeping at all, because I knew that had been an issue in the past.

I'd drifted off with her still awake and doing something on her phone, but I'd been too buzzed to do anything.

Even fuck.

And today, my back ached like a bitch from the extensive work but it felt good. The tenderness felt real good.

The extensive work was why I was laying on my front. Prodding hyper-tenderized flesh wasn't my idea of a good time, that was for fucking sure.

"Looks like you're staying with me, huh?" she mumbled around a yawn as her eyelashes fluttered. She looked at me once, then closed them again.

"If you slept, then I'll stay every night. Prefer to have you hooked on my cock than on Valium."

She snorted at that, and her smile appeared, making the sides of her eyes crease with it. Because they were closed, it was somehow all the more powerful. That she could look like that without even truly being awake and aware.

"You didn't feed me any cock last night."

"Since when were you a cannibal? Murdering stalkers I can deal with, cannibalism? Nuhuh."

"You getting squeamish on me, Cruz?"

"Bet your ass I am. I'm not really that fucking happy with beef, never mind eating a dude's—"

Her eyes popped open, and she eyed me with curiosity. "A dude's what?"

I scowled. "I don't know. Whichever part of the human body is appealing to cannibals. Maybe you'd know?"

Her lips twitched. "Well, it isn't dick. Don't worry. Most men don't have much meat down there."

I snickered. "Ouch."

She winked. "Feel the burn?"

"I do. Even though I don't have any insecurities about my cock." I smirked at her. "And with how you wriggle around on it when I stick it in you, I don't think you have many complaints."

When she wiggled some, my smirk grew.

"There we have our confirmation," I teased, reaching over and pressing my hand to her stomach. "Seriously though... you slept well?"

"I did." She yawned again. "Better than last night."

"Your world was in the air. I get it. You're just lucky you didn't go running, and I didn't have to chase your ass down. As it stands, you've earned a punishment but nothing too major."

Her eyes darkened. "Not sure that's fair."

Her pout had me moving my hand to trace the pucker of her lips. "Never said I was fair. Never said I was into equality where this stuff is concerned.

"You pulled away, Indy. You, not me. I thought it was men who were supposed to be scared of commitment."

That had her eyes flaring wide. "Commitment?"

"Yes. A word more terrifying than 'cunt.'"

She shoved me. "Don't joke."

"Who said I'm joking?"

Indy blew me a raspberry, but after, her bottom lip was firmly tucked between her teeth.

Even though I was glad that she'd worked on my tattoo, because the endorphin rush always made me sleep like a fucking baby, and with the headache from hell after the blast, as well as the discomfort with my ribs which there was no escaping, I needed the Zs just as much as she did.

Only thing was, I couldn't grab her hair, coil it around my wrist, and then drag her down so she was sucking on my cock. Not when said cock was currently burrowing a hole in the fucking mattress.

"You want to be with me?" she asked, her voice serious, her eyes somber, so I knew she was taking this in the spirit it was intended.

I wasn't messing around here.

Watching her waffle had cemented things for me.

Wherever she was, I'd be.

Simple as that.

I was a lot more at ease with thinking that way than thinking I loved her, but that was because I'd only ever really loved my dad and his mother, who'd died when I was young. But I'd loved her. Too much.

Love hurt.

Making a liar out of me about the whole 'not being a masochist thing.'

She twisted onto her side, and whispered, "I'm scared."

"What of?" I didn't tease her even though I could have. Not to be a prick, but just to make her smile.

I hadn't seen her this serious in, well, ever. She was taking things hard, and I got that.

What with killing a man, protecting one of our own from a fucking pedo groomer, and then a bomb blast that had taken some of our people, destroyed our world while forcing us to build it from the ground up... a lot had gone on and gone *wrong*.

When she cuddled into my side, one of her calves going over my ass as she tucked herself into me, I was a goner.

I mean, I'd already *gone* over for her, but feeling her like that, feeling her let me in, it meant more than she could know.

Jesus, it meant everything.

Her lips brushed against my shoulder, and she whispered, "Why do you make me feel safe?"

"Because you like monsters. You learned a long time ago that the people who hurt you look normal, they're what haunts you, but your personal monsters, the ones who regular 'decent' folk look down on, keep you safe."

That had her rearing back. "Huh?"

My lips kicked up in a smile. "Nyx, me?" I grimaced. "We're the same. He just has a higher body count than me."

She blinked. "You're not crazy like he is." Then, she winced. "He's high-functioning, don't get me wrong, but he's still a little batshit."

"Perfect daddy material," I joked, prompting her to shove at me again. I grinned at her, and she scowled.

"Your humor is as whacked as he is, that's for sure."

I shrugged. "I know."

"Doesn't make you a monster."

When I thought about all the gnarly shit I'd done in my life, and what I'd do in the future, without a second thought, I just hummed. "Different types of monsters out there. Predators who prey on the weak. And predators who prey on predators."

She relaxed some. "Oh."

I nodded. "I've always been wired differently, Indy, and that's why I'm surprised I feel this way for you. I've never felt this way for any other woman. And the few people I've loved have all been family.

"I never thought I wanted to feel like this. Never imagined this was how I'd feel when I first—" I broke off, because I hadn't intended on mentioning that, but it had slipped out.

Dammit.

And like I'd expect, she was on it like a fucking bulldog with a link of sausages.

"What?"

"I only saw you as Nyx's sister until I saw you cleaning up Stone's bunkhouse."

"I think you have a tendency to compartmentalize people. So maybe it's not that much of a surprise."

I blinked, because she was right. I did. People fit into pigeonholes for me, and rarely did they fly out of them and head into a different box.

Deciding I'd think about that later on, when Indy wasn't all ears, and when I thought it best to tell her something while we were still in the early days of this thing we had going on, I carried on:

"That night, I saw you and I just wanted to fuck you. It was like a hit to the dick."

"Sounds painful."

"Trust me, the way your tits were jiggling, it *was* painful."

A smile quivered on her lips. "I'll bet." She caught my eyes with hers. "I still don't get why you covered me with that blanket."

I winced. "I covered you until you started struggling."

She reached over and placed her hand on the back of my head. It swooped over the curve of my skull and played with the short whorls of hair that had grown out since my last trim. I was also in need of a shave. The past few days had been hell on my personal grooming.

"You heard, didn't you?"

"You gonna pull my hair if I don't tell you?"

She snorted. "You're not supposed to make me laugh. Stop it!" She tugged on it, just not hard enough to sting. "I wasn't going to do that but you deserved it."

"A likely story," I told her, grinning all the while.

A breath gusted from her lips as she muttered, "I—you—what did you hear?"

"You mentioned Kevin's name. Didn't take a genius, which I am, to put two and two together."

She swallowed. Thickly. "Is that why this whole thing started? Because you thought I was a pity fuck?"

Unease flashed inside me, because I knew if I fucked this up, she'd never forgive me. Ever.

And even though my life trajectory might involve me dying before I hit fifty, I wanted to spend every one of those single fucking years with her at my side.

Preferably bouncing on top of me for a lot of them.

"Nothing about you is piteous, Indy."

Her nostrils flared at my serious tone, but I could see she wasn't listening. She started to stir, uncoiling away from me as she made a retreat that was both physical and mental.

Quickly, I grabbed my cell phone from her frou frou nightstand, and as I rolled onto my side, groaning as my ribs put up a serious protest at the abrupt move, I grabbed her and kept her in place by hooking an arm over her stomach, and hauling her into my belly so that she wasn't facing me.

It happened so fast, that she shrieked, and she struggled some when I grabbed one of her thighs and hooked it over mine, only stopping when I made no move to otherwise touch her.

With one hand holding her in place, my lips brushing her earlobe, I murmured, "Open my phone. 564532 is my passcode."

She tensed at that, tensed because I knew she hadn't expected to be able to open it herself even though I'd dropped the cell in front of her stomach.

She reached for it, tapped in the code, then jolted when she came face to face with my home screen.

Her.

Legs spread wide, cum seeping from her pussy, my fingers in that delectable slit. Her face was relaxed, free because her mind was flying, her lips were slack, with just enough tension to make her look like she was moaning. Around her, the silk of her hair was like a blanket that provided the perfect contrast to what we were looking at.

Making the gold of her skin gleam harder, and my own, paler skin look even creamier.

"Does anything about that, about that beautiful woman, about that sexy fucking siren, look pitiful to you?"

She was tense in my arms, fucking vibrating so hard it hurt my goddamn ribs.

"How many times do I have to show you how you make me respond to you?" I growled the words, even as I jerked my dick into her ass so she could feel my hard-on. A hard-on I had despite the agonizing position I held her in.

"You're not pitiful. You're a fucking warrior. And you're goddamn perfect. Absolutely every single inch of you.

"I saw you that night, deep in the throes of torment, and I didn't think, 'Indy needs a pity fuck.' I saw this woman who had hidden the truth from her maniac of a brother. I had to figure it was to spare his sanity, otherwise Nyx'd know. I saw this woman who was ravaged by the past, tormented by it but still leading her best life, and I just wanted her.

"I wanted a woman that strong. That powerful. I wanted to bring her peace."

"I'm not strong. I think these past couple of days proved that, don't you?"

I shook my head, not liking the shakiness in her voice. "I told you already, so don't make me repeat myself," I grumbled. "Don't mistake caution for weakness. I don't. I respect you more for taking a step back than for throwing caution to the wind. With your past, that kind of thinking kept you safe and alive." I nudged her with my dick. "Go into my gallery."

She gulped, but did as I asked, moving to the gallery where she found *her*.

Hundreds of pictures of her, only broken up with screenshots of something I'd taken in between meeting up with her.

"Jesus," she rasped.

"You're beautiful," I told her, unapologetically, as she swiped through them all, seeing herself in various poses, various bondage techniques, sometimes asleep, sometimes drifting off, sometimes with her legs spread wide, sometimes in the middle of an orgasm.

"Tell me your pussy isn't creaming," I whispered in her ear.

She swallowed. "I shouldn't be wet, because it looks like I've picked up another stalker—"

I grinned at that. "This is the kind of stalker you'll like, I promise. This one gives you orgasms."

"Gives me, huh? So far, I've had to work fucking hard for those orgasms."

"And those pictures are proof that you love it." I pressed a kiss to the side of her head. "If you ever leave me, I will never, ever, break your trust. Those photos are mine. No one will ever see them. Ever."

She bit her lip. "And what if you leave me?"

"Won't happen."

"You sound so sure," she whispered.

"I am. Monsters mate for life, dontcha know? Just like Giulia is stuck with Nyx, you're stuck with me."

"Why do you compare yourself to him?"

"Because we're birds of a feather, only his catalyst is justified. Mine isn't. I came from a normal household. You guys didn't." I heaved a sigh. "You'll never see what makes us so similar, because I'll never let you."

"Should I be scared?"

"Of me?" I thought about that, tried to reason whether she should be or not, then I murmured, "No. You could even betray the Sinners and I wouldn't hurt you. Spank you, sure. Hurt you? No."

She tensed, and wriggled around in my hold to look at me. "Whoa."

I shrugged. "I know."

We were both aware how *massive* that was.

"You know I'd never betray them though, don't you?"

"You're not an idiot," I said wryly. "Just because I wouldn't hurt you, doesn't mean they wouldn't come baying for your blood, and while I'd do everything I could to keep you safe, they're wily fuckers."

She winced. "True dat." She waggled the phone. "Do you see me like this?"

"In my mind's eye?"

"Yes."

"Sure do. Nothing, and I repeat, *nothing* about you is pitiful, Indy."

Though she swallowed, I felt like she got it, I felt like she was listening and processing and, even more importantly, accepting.

I waited for her next question, but whatever she could have asked, it stunned me.

"Are you going to brand me?"

"Yes."

"When?"

"Don't know. When things calm down, probably." A thought occurred to me. "Can you tattoo yourself?"

She snorted. "Do bears shit in the woods."

I smoothed my good hand along her forearm, and murmured, "Here, I guess. It'll have to be." She nodded, prompting me to say, "I'll wear a brand too. But I want you on me. A pin up version of you."

Her cheeks burned hotly. "With clothes or without?"

Amused by the question, I dipped in closer, and breathed in her ear, "Which one makes you wetter?"

She licked her lips. "Without."

"Then without it is. It'll have to be somewhere no other fucker can see it though." My brow puckered as logistics hit me. "And somewhere I can cover up with clothes. Our kids don't need to see that."

"Kids?" she squeaked, her eyes rounding at the prospect.

I shrugged. "From you, adopted, fostered, don't care. Now, ten years' time, four months' time, don't care. Just figure it'll happen. It's in you, whether you see it or not."

She gulped, and her pupils had morphed into pin pricks that told me she was thinking about shit she'd never allowed herself to think.

"I-Is there damage? Did he..." Shit, I'd never thought about that before.

"Not as far as I know," she whispered.

I pressed my forehead to hers. "If I could kill him again, I would."

She swallowed. "How would you do it?"

"Tie him up and throw him into my custom blend."

"Your custom blend?" she asked, confusion making her brow pucker.

"Yeah. Chem major, remember? He'd be awake as it ate him alive." I nodded. "I think that's what he deserved."

Her eyes turned round again, and she whispered, "I think I'd have liked that."

Pressing a kiss to her lips, I murmured, "That's why you're perfect for me."

FORTY-ONE

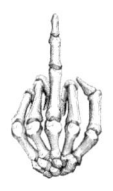

INDY

HIS KISS ACTED as a kind of seal, like he was forcing the words into me, making me believe them like they were the gospel truth.

We. Were. Perfect. Together.

I shuddered into his kiss, shivering when his good hand moved to cup me where I needed him the most. His fingers speared between my legs, and then he was there. Those clever digits sliding between my folds, unerringly finding my clit.

His movements were languid, slow, but there was an ease to them thanks to how wet I was.

So many guys had tried to finger me and found me as dry as the fucking Sahara, but Cruz always did this to me.

Always.

I was sopping wet for him, always for him.

Only for him.

Even as I arched my back, a pleasured cry escaping my lips, I started to think if he was the miracle I'd always been waiting for.

Someone who accepted all of me, who knew all my flaws and somehow seemed to think they weren't flaws. Were, instead, something to cherish.

To love.

I winced at the thought, then I burrowed my face into the duvet because, sweet fuck, what he could do with his hand was better than anything I'd ever experienced with most guys' cocks.

Shrieking when he began to frig my clit, I arched my hips, tensing my thighs as I clung to him, and when my first orgasm walloped me right in the face, I froze against him, juddering and jittering with the released pressure as the ecstasy of coming, with a man who loved me warts and all, turbocharged everything.

My entire being was shaky with the revelation, and I almost cried as the sweet torment of release drifted through my system like it was in a maze intent on seeking the way out. But the only way out was when he was inside me.

I knew this was, after all, just the appetizer.

Shivering when he thrust two fingers into me, I arched my back as he started to fuck me. He liked doing this, and I'd have been perplexed by it if he didn't always get me off. His fingers scissored inside me, thrusting hard and fast, rough with me when I needed it, hard when I needed him to ground me.

As he rubbed down the front wall of my cunt, I cried out, so close to the prize as the delirium of what he gave me was the light at the end of the tunnel.

And then he stopped.

But not for long.

His cock was there, no barrier between us, no boxers in the way as he tunneled between my ass cheeks and found my gate.

As he slipped inside, I moaned, tilting my head down so I could bite the pillow.

As he thrust into me, filling me so fucking perfectly, I wept with the sheer beauty of it.

Just the friction of him inside me was enough to make me feel like I was at a Fourth of July fireworks display.

He was so thick, so hot, filling me so full that I'd never known perfection like it.

And that was before he bottomed out. Somehow, he seemed to get deeper than usual, and the darkness of an impending orgasm hovered over my eyes, blurring everything else as he started to thrust.

Retreating almost entirely, only to thrust into me hard again, jerking me across the bed, even as he kept me clamped to him, holding me close, not letting me go.

With anyone else, the hold, the restriction, would have been a trigger.

But there was no one else in my mind. Nothing else. Just him.

Just me.

He held me tight because he needed me this tight.

He didn't let me move because he needed me right where I was.

And where I was was right where I needed to be too.

When his fingers moved to my clit and he started to thrum it in time to his thrusts, I groaned long and low as the pleasure started to bombard me. Like bullets between the eyes, the ecstasy blacked everything else out as he sent me soaring high and fast.

Taking me to a freedom that no other would ever be able to conjure, making me feel so fucking light that I knew I could soar and soar, higher than a bird, freer than one too.

As my climax hit, I screamed, unable to do anything else as the intensity of what he urged me to experience blasted me into a million tiny pieces.

Covering him in me, just as he covered me in him.

And as his cum pelted my insides, coating me and filling me up, he rumbled, "I want you to think of this, every time you start to feel wretched, every time you feel scared, I want you to remember that with me, you can fly even when you're not tethered..."

For a second, I didn't know what he meant, couldn't understand it, and then, I realized we'd just had the most vanilla sex imaginable, and I'd still gotten off.

Why that, of all the other things he'd told me and I'd told him today, had me bursting into tears, I'd never fucking know. But Cruz was there, his hard arms banded around me, holding me close, keeping me safe.

Just like he always would.

FORTY-TWO

GHOST

I WOKE up to see Maverick staring at me.

For a second, I just smiled, content that his eyes were on me and mine on his. Then, I registered where I was, and what was happening. The beeps, the scent of disinfectant, the uncomfortable chair beneath me, his injuries, it all registered.

"Mav!" I cried, relief hitting me that he was awake at last.

He blinked at me, his eyes not exactly hard, but there was definitely none of the softness I was used to from him.

In the process of getting to my feet with the intent of climbing onto the bed and snuggling with him, I froze.

There was no welcome on his face.

None at all.

The sight was jarring. I wasn't used to it. Maverick might be a hard man, might even be a killer, but he was gentle with me.

Always.

Just... not now.

I licked my lips, nerves hitting me as I wondered what was going on, then, he rasped, "Who are you?"

For a second, I couldn't understand his question. I was almost sure that I'd forgotten every single word of English I'd strived hard to learn over the years.

But then, he repeated it again, and there was no denying it. No discounting it.

"Who are you?"

Who was I?

Didn't he remember?

I was his wife. He'd married me to keep me safe, but, we were so much more than that.

Weren't we?

Why couldn't he remember?

"Where's Nic?"

I blinked. "Who's Nic?"

That, I could ask, it was just the other question I couldn't answer.

"Nic," he snarled. "Where is he?" He jerked upright, then scowled down at his chest when he saw all the different wires and things that hooked him up to the machines that were beeping away at his side, monitoring him and making sure he was safe.

He started pulling at them, and panic hit me because I knew I had to stop him, but Maverick, though he was in a wheelchair, was huge, so muscular that I didn't know how he did it. How he kept so strong, especially when he was so skinny. I knew he'd gained weight since I'd come along, which made it even less likely that I'd be able to stop him.

I got to my feet though, not wanting to watch him hurt himself, but just as he snarled, "Where's Nic?" again, he did the damnedest thing.

He shoved the blankets off his body, tore them away like they were chains binding him in place, and then he twisted around and he got off the bed.

A scream escaped me, as certainty filled me that he'd end up on his ass, but he didn't.

He stood there, and I just gaped at him.

What the fuck was happening?

Someone must have heard my scream, because I heard footsteps thudding outside the door. Just as a nurse came rushing in, so did a couple of his brothers.

All of them froze. Each and every one of them stared at him like he was a madman, which he was.

Which he had to be.

What the hell was happening?

Maverick was disabled. Had been ever since he'd been in an IED explosion overseas.

What— Why—

How?

The questions pummeled my brain even as the nurse tried to get him back into bed.

I was grateful the nurse was a guy because Maverick was rough, struggling against his hold, pushing at him when he tried to contain him, get him back into the bed, and then, finally, Steel rumbled, "Maverick? What the fuck is going on?"

Mav froze, then twisted around. "Steel, where the fuck is Nic?"

"Who's Nic?" Link asked, *sotto voce*, his confusion clear.

"I don't know," Steel muttered.

"Who's Nic?" I repeated, aiming the question at Maverick, wondering if he'd answer.

He scowled at me, his jaw tensing as he ignored me to demand, "I need to speak with him."

Link stepped forward, just as the nurse started to turn pink in the face from the exertion of keeping Mav contained.

As he approached, Mav stopped struggling, and the nurse warned, "I'll be back with a doctor and a team. You need to keep him calm or they'll knock him out."

Mav's eyes flared wide with that, and Link got there just in time to pin him down. Steel was there next, and both of them worked hard to stop his struggles.

"We don't know who Nic is," Link ground out, when Mav just carried on asking the same damn question.

Tears hit me, slipping down my cheeks as I saw this powerful man be contained by his friends. Men who were like brothers to him, who'd do whatever they could to keep him safe.

Even from himself.

That level of love was something I'd never come across until now.

They weren't bound by blood, but they might as well have been. Or, maybe that was diminishing the level of connection they shared.

They weren't blood, but acted as if they were, so didn't that mean their bond was a thousand times stronger?

I liked to think so, especially because I was living among these men, kept safe in the cocoon of their protection.

And I could say that even after their home, my home now, had been bombed.

Even unto death, they'd protect us.

I knew that.

I just... well, I didn't know my place now.

I had the nastiest feeling that Maverick didn't remember me.

I bit my lip, and the sting grounded me even as nerves overtook everything else.

Without Maverick, I...

Well, we were a...

What were we?

In all honesty, I didn't know.

We were man and wife, but we'd never consummated the relationship.

We slept together, both of us managing to get some rest in each other's arms even though sleep wasn't the respite it was for most people.

I made him eat, and he made me smile.

We were a source of refuge for each other, or, that was what I'd thought.

"We'll find out who Nic is," Link vowed, his face sweaty with exertion as both he and Steel worked hard to keep him on the bed.

But his words were like a passcode that triggered Maverick's cessation of struggling.

He stopped, just like they'd flicked a light switch.

"Until then," Steel rumbled, "Ghost is here."

Mav just stared up at him. "Who's Ghost?"

Two words.

I didn't know a heart could break with just the utterance of two simple words.

Steel and Link shared a look, but it was Link, the kindest and gentlest of all the men, who looked at me, pity in his eyes, that I knew this heartbreak went deeper.

I felt the cracks in my soul.

What a time, I realized, to accept my feelings for Maverick.

I loved him.

And he couldn't even remember me.

FORTY-THREE
CRUZ

I'D DUMPED my shit at the motel, because I hadn't actually thought I'd manage to wear Indy down, so when I drove over there to grab the bags I hadn't even bothered unpacking from Walmart, and as I pulled into the lot, found Nyx and Link heading into the first room on the ground floor, my plans changed.

Having heard about Maverick, I was curious. I knew all the brothers were.

Not only was the guy able to walk, but he'd lost his memory and was pleading for someone called Nic.

If I was closer to him, I'd have visited, because I couldn't imagine what he was going through, and he was a brother. Whether or not we were close, he was always that.

The gravel driveway sang under the weight of the truck I'd borrowed from our garage to get around, and as I parked, I peered at the MC's newest property.

The motel wasn't the best of places in town, but it would suit our purposes.

Maybe, eventually, Rex would turn the place into a legitimate business, but for the moment, it was a place for the homeless brothers to crash their heads at the end of a long night.

As expected, Storm had asked me to draft some plans for the clubhouse, and that was why I was here.

To grab my shit, but also to discuss particulars.

Any plans would need to be approved by someone who was licensed, but I was well aware that there'd be a set of drawings we knew about, and the ones that were signed off on.

I was almost looking forward to drawing those up. It would be a hoot to have secret rooms within the walls, places where we could store shit without it ever coming under threat from the Feds.

When I strolled over to the room Nyx and Link had headed into, I tapped on the door, the peeling paint coming away under the gentle force of my knuckles—hell, we'd bought a real prize, hadn't we?

"Who is it?" was hollered from inside.

"It's Cruz."

I heard some mutters, then a, "Come in."

Church was in session, that much was clear. Rex might not be here, but all the other councilors were, which told me it was bad timing.

"I can go," I told them, pointing with my thumb to the door.

"No, we need to talk with you anyway," Storm rumbled.

I blinked at him. "Sure."

Closing the door behind me, I moved deeper into the room, wondering what the issue was.

I mean, it wasn't like we didn't have plenty going on right now so I excused myself for my mind being a blur. I could be wrong, but I didn't think from the scowl on Storm's face that we were about to discuss the fucking weather. Or the construction job.

"Take a seat," Link ordered, kicking a chair out at the ramshackle table.

The rooms were grody, and were probably fresh back in the eighties, but they were relatively clean. Without a blacklight.

I didn't even want to know what kind of nasty shit was going on beneath the surface. That was more than I could probably cope with knowing.

DNA, my one nemesis.

Especially when it belonged to fucking strangers.

Inwardly shuddering as I took a seat at the cane chair which squeaked under my weight, I glanced around the brothers. They were all squeezed inside here, because this place was not built for groups. The khaki walls had old-fashioned lights on them, hovering over the bed so it felt like you were under the spotlight when you were reading. The sheets and blankets were a kind of cream that I figured, once upon a time, had been white, making me doubly grateful for Indy and her place. Then, there was the sofa whose red and green stripes hid a multitude of sins.

At least, they would when three bikers weren't squished onto it.

"What's going on?" I asked, casting each of the men a look.

"Lodestar got a hit on a couple of Maverick's searches," Nyx explained.

I blinked. "Which searches?"

"Firstly, David." He cut the rest of the council a look. "They all know what happened with Indy."

Seldom did I ever feel nervous, but for Indy, I did. "It was self-defense," I argued immediately, going with my gut because fuck, they looked grim.

Nyx waved a hand. "That isn't an issue. Mav was looking into him for me, because I wanted to make sure there'd be no bite back. As it stands, he was a good candidate for just going off grid. Then Mav found out his uncle works for the sheriff's office in Concordia Parish, down in Louisiana."

"Shit," I hissed under my breath.

"Exactly." He scraped a hand over his chin. "Now, I could tell Indy what to do, but from experience, I've long since learned there's no telling Indy shit. She'll do what she wants and when—"

"Not with this," I countered. "She's scared."

"Indy's never scared," Sin scoffed.

"She is. You give her too much credit," I retorted, pissed on her behalf at his cavalier response. "She killed someone who was threatening her, threatening the MC. She did us a favor."

"We know she did." Nyx sighed. "Mav's searches also confirmed that Tatána was the one who'd planted bugs and shit around the compound."

"Christ."

"Yeah. Lodestar found the cloud where the equipment was syncing, and she's managed to delete it, but that doesn't take away from the fact that we need to know if he shared what he learned with anyone."

"I get that."

"Good. So, what you need to get Indy to do is file a missing persons' report. It's already been, what, five days since the fucker died? She should have called in by now. We need to twist things around so that she looks like she's in the clear."

"I understand. When I get back, I'll tell her." Uneasy now, I asked, "Did the Feds ever get near the Fridge?"

"Not according to the alarms Maverick has in place," Storm rasped, cracking his knuckles. "Speaking of, don't clear the bath out until we know for sure the Feds don't have any monitoring equipment on the compound. Last thing we need is our asses hauled in on first-degree murder charges."

"Sure, I'll leave it," I confirmed, though my heart sank. That was going to be a fucker to clean up...

"Can't Lodestar figure that out?" Nyx asked, jerking his chin up in inquiry. "The monitoring equipment, I mean?"

Steel shook his head. "She's out of it, but she's doing what she can. We need Mav on this one. You know he's like a sniffer dog for this shit."

Nyx and I shared a look, but Link commented, "Guess it's a good thing Lodestar can help out, period, even if it's just a little, especially with him..." Link blew out a breath. "Well, wherever his mind's at."

"Not wherever, *when*ever," Steel corrected with a grimace.

Link winced. "True, man. Can't believe the fucker's head is back when he was in the sandbox." He rubbed the back of his neck. "You think he and Nic hooked up?"

I wasn't sure if I was supposed to be privy to this conversation, not when they were talking like I wasn't here anymore, but I wouldn't argue.

"Maybe. Lodestar never said. Just told us who he was."

Curiosity hit at Storm's answer. "Who was he?" I asked.

The ex-VP of this chapter muttered, "His battalion leader."

"We all know Mav swings both ways. I don't think he'd have been that upset if he wasn't emotionally involved with him," Nyx said, a tired sigh rushing from his lips as he scraped a hand over his head.

"Is he dead?" I queried grimly.

Link nodded. "Died in Kembesh."

"Jesus," I muttered.

"About sums it up." Sin pursed his lips.

"More fucked up that he served in Afghanistan and we never fucking knew it," Nyx grated out, prompting all of us to wince.

The lack of trust hurt me, so it had to be killing them to know how much he'd hidden from them when they were like legit family.

Clearing his throat, Sin groused, "This is the first time I've heard him mention Nic though. So, all this time, he was hiding the guy from us. What's that about?"

"I don't know, and it doesn't look like we're going to find out," Link rumbled. "Poor Ghost. She looked like Mav reached in and tore her fucking heart out."

"And with the standing up shit?" Nyx shook his head. "That bastard's been hiding that from us for a while as well. It's a good thing I love the fucker, or I'd be in his face right now.

"Who the fuck chooses to live in a wheelchair when they don't have to?"

"Someone who's psychologically damaged?" I pointed out, arching a brow at him.

Nyx huffed. "I'm psychologically damaged. You don't see me free-riding around in a mobility scooter."

"I'd pay to see that," Link said, his tone dead serious, and he earned himself the bird Nyx flipped his way.

"Children, we're getting off-topic," Storm grumbled. "Maverick has always done what he wanted to do. That tells me, for whatever reason, it suited him for people to believe that he couldn't walk."

A thought occurred to me. "You don't think he's in danger, do you?"

"From who? Aside from the *Famiglia* who are already willing to bomb our compound, you mean?" was Storm's pissed answer.

"I don't know. It just... people might think he isn't a threat if he's in a wheelchair."

"Mav's a threat when he's asleep," Nyx pointed out. "God, it's only recently that we got him to get rid of those fucking crutches." He rubbed his forehead. "I'm so fucking confused."

"Lot to be confused about," Storm agreed, "but as it stands, we got shit to get done. I asked Cruz to start drafting our new clubhouse, and I've called in brothers from the other chapters who are in construction."

Nodding, Link asked, "Cruz, you think you can handle the drawings?"

"Sure. I've built more complicated things than a clubhouse," I remarked simply, not a whisper of ego to the statement.

Link tipped his head to the side. "Like what?"

I flickered back through my mental portfolio and murmured, "Had to build a bridge once in South America."

Nyx snickered. "I think he can handle the clubhouse."

Storm grunted. "Good. We need you to deal with Indy and this situation with David, Cruz. You can handle that?"

"Of course."

"You going to brand her?" Nyx asked stonily, but his gaze didn't meet mine so I didn't take the question as a threat.

Not that there wasn't a threat brewing...

"When she's ready," I told him.

He muttered, "Good."

Storm cleared his throat. "The guys were telling me that you and your ma cut ties."

"I guess. I mean, I can call on her again. We don't exactly have a mother-son relationship that a lot of people might have, but she'll still pick up the phone if I call." I grimaced. "At least, I think she would. Why?"

"No reason." He stared at me, which made a liar out of his words because there was definitely a reason why he asked.

And then, the rest of my brothers turned to look at me, each of them giving me their attention.

"What is it?"

Half expecting for them to give me more shit over my mom or Indy, when Storm asked, "We need you to build something else for the club, Cruz."

I leaped at the chance to help my brothers.
I could just never have imagined what that 'something' would be.

FORTY-FOUR

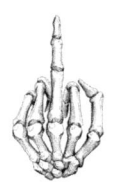

INDY

I HATED the cops in Verona. What I'd give to be dealing with the sheriff's department in West Orange, because at least they were on the Sinners' payroll. But Verona PD were a bunch of stuck up asses who, as expected, and which would probably work to my benefit in the long run, dismissed my 'missing persons' case.

They promised to file a report, especially as David had been missing for so long, but their disinterest was clear. If I'd actually cared about my ex-stalker's whereabouts, I'd have been pretty fucking devastated by their cavalier treatment.

Not that I should have expected anymore from the guys who made donut runs look like a professional sport.

Huffing at the thought, I stalked out of the small building which was probably as small as their dicks, and was a tad aggressive when I answered my phone, "What?"

I winced because that was more of a snarl than I'd been aiming for...

"Is that Indiana Sisson?"

"Yes, this is she."

"I'm so glad I managed to get through to you. I've been trying this past week but it's been hard—"

"I'm sorry about that. I've had a lot of personal issues. My family home just burned down."

Understatement.

"Wow, I'm so sorry!" the woman repeated, and it came as no surprise that she sounded more embarrassed than sincere.

"Yeah, it's been hard. Anyway," I asked, after I cleared my throat. "Is there something I can do for you, Miss...?"

"My name's Aly. I work with *City Ink*, the TV show?"

Eyes widening, I tucked the phone into my shoulder and started rustling through my purse for my drawing pad and pencil.

It wasn't the first time I'd been approached to go on TV, and each time, it had worked wonders for the parlor I was attached to.

This was the first time it had happened, though, since I'd opened Indiana Ink.

"I love that show," I told Aly. "You do great things to showcase the art."

"Thanks. My husband is the executive producer, so it's his baby."

If my eyes were wide before, they pretty much started to bug out of the sockets. "Jesus. You're Trade's wife?"

Aly laughed. "You really are a fan."

"More of his work than the show," I admitted.

"So, you wouldn't be interested in being featured?" Aly teased.

"Hell, yes, I would, but will I get to meet Trade too?"

"Yeah, you will," she said around a chuckle. "That's great you're interested."

"Let me guess, this is about Steeler's back piece?"

"It sure is. He submitted the photos himself. It's a pretty fantastic work of art, Indiana."

"Thanks. You know when you finish a piece and just get chills? That one did that for me."

"I can see why. Those chills were earned."

"So, this is a preliminary call, but if you're interested and have a lawyer we could send over the contract to, you can see what the feature entails and if you're interested, you can come into the studio and get a feel for what will go down."

"That sounds great to me." Without a second's thought, I gave her

Rachel's info, and as she made a note, I murmured, "Just so you know, she's family too, so I'll make sure she watches out for the contract but we're all still trying to piece everything together after the fire."

"I totally understand. Normally we have a two-week time limit, but I'm not going to lie to you, Indy, Trade wants you on the show. So, I'll up the time frame to four weeks, okay?"

"Wow, I really appreciate that," I replied, taken aback by the offer. "Thank you so much."

"Thank you for inspiring my husband. He's been at the drawing board ever since we got the latest set of submissions sent over to us by the studio." I could hear the smile in her voice. "I'll be in touch, and you can tell your attorney to expect an email today or tomorrow, okay?"

"I'll tell her. Thanks so much for calling!"

"No problem. Can't wait to hear from you."

As the call ended, with my heart beating a thousand rounds a second, I knew it was lame, but the only person I wanted to tell was Cruz.

But then, I had to reason, *was* it lame? Or was this exactly what happened when two people were dating?

I bit my lip at the thought, because I knew Cruz would be beyond stoked for me, and I really wanted to share this with him.

I'd never been that open to any of the few guys I'd actually dated before. But Cruz was different.

Cruz had my back.

He'd have been here today if I hadn't told him to get on with his work as he was drawing up plans for the new clubhouse with Giulia bitching at him over his shoulder.

Only the fact that she was the VP's woman, Nyx's Old Lady, stopped him from telling her to back the fuck off.

Which Giulia was using to her full advantage, of course.

With the store only a hundred feet away, I took off at a run, knowing that's where Cruz would be since I'd forbade him from joining me.

The cops saw a Sinner and instantly, things escalated.

As it was, I kept my nose clean, and the locals knew I had no real affiliation to the Sinners so they cut me some slack.

That would change, though, when people realized Cruz and I were together.

The notion should have gnawed at me, because I was losing a lot by coming out with Cruz, yet, as I headed into Indiana Ink, and saw him, I knew it was right. That it was going to be worth it.

He looked harried. His brows furrowed, his eyes stormy with temper, and his jaw was gritted even as a nerve ticked in it. He glowered at Giulia before he whipped around to look at me as the bell tinkled in the door, and when our gazes collided, his eyes softened, his frown lessened, and he inhaled sharply, like he was trying to calm down.

Not for himself, not for Giulia, but for me.

God, how I appreciated that.

I smiled at him, not a fake one, or an excited one because of the show offer, not even a warm one.

It was loving, the smile I bestowed on him. It had to be. Because my heart did the whole Roger Rabbit thing and went 'kebang' in my chest.

Seeing him, connecting with him... I wasn't sure there'd been a more powerful moment in my entire life.

"What is it?"

Giulia's question felt like it came from underwater, but I blinked a few times, and turned to her, saw from her impatient glower that wasn't the first time she'd asked.

I swallowed. "You know *City Ink*?"

"The show?"

I nodded. "The show. They asked me to be featured!"

My excitement burst out, and even as Giulia whooped, Cruz was rolling out from behind the desk he'd commandeered to work at, and making his way to me.

I leaped at him, not stopping until he was holding my ass, and as I sank my lips onto his, that sense of rightness just hit me once more.

He was a Sinner.

He was dangerous.

But he was so much more than that.

He was mine.

As I sank my tongue between his lips, thrusting against his, uncaring that Giulia could see, not giving a damn if the entire street was standing outside the storefront gawping at us, I gave him my all.

This man had my heart, and for the first time in my life, I wasn't terrified what someone would do with it, because even as I loved him, I trusted him.

And for someone like me, that meant so much more. He'd probably never understand that, but it wasn't like I needed to tell him, was it? That was the joy of this man.

He already fucking knew.

FORTY-FIVE

REX

WHEN I THOUGHT of how many of my brothers had lost their parents at a young age, I knew I'd been lucky.

I was nearing forty and my mom had only died eight years ago, and Dad was still here, barely hanging on, but still here.

The thought of losing him was crippling.

The MC didn't exactly rear kids to be Mommy's or Daddy's boys, but I loved my folks. Always had. Respect had been easy, and loyalty too. We were tight knit for a reason, and seeing him here, literally half of him left, I was so far down the tunnel to insanity that I wasn't sure how I'd get back out again if he died like this.

It was one thing for him to perish because of old age, but he wasn't fucking old. Not really. Jesus, it wasn't like he couldn't ride his goddamn bike across the country and lived at the doctor's office.

He was strong. Still as powerful as he'd been when I was younger. And if it weren't for Mom's death, then he'd have been leading the Sinners and I'd just be his VP.

"Rex?"

He couldn't die. Not like this. This couldn't be the end.

The doctors kept on telling me he'd pull through, but I wasn't sure I believed them.

I wasn't sure who I could believe right now.

Dad had been coming home with a storm cloud hanging over him, one that spoke of years' worth of cover ups. Cover ups that he'd been hiding from me.

Me.

The fucking Prez of the Sinners.

A man who wielded his own goddamn battalion of men. His own personal, private fucking army.

Of course, the second he'd shared that news with me, had told me about the LEAs who were stitching up ex-cons, this happened.

The clubhouse was no more.

The compound was a wreckage.

We'd lost men and clubwhores.

And all while a pair of corpses decomposed in a bath of fucking lye on our property.

It was a wonder we hadn't been hauled into jail. We had pull, but not with the fucking Feds. The O'Donnellys had more reach than we did with the alphabet agencies, and they could help, but—

"Rex?"

The voice was like a buzzing in my ear, and I wanted to bat at it with my hand. Shoo it off like it was a fucking mosquito, but then soft fingers squeezed my shoulder, and the scent of lilies and citrus filled my nostrils.

I felt her behind me, moving closer, turning into me, and I twisted around, unable to stop myself from burrowing my face in her stomach.

We spent half the time at odds even though we worked for the same team, but she was here when I needed her.

Just like she'd always be.

Just like I'd always be there for her.

Her hand moved to my hair, and she started stroking it, smoothing over the strands, soothing me like I was a kid.

Any other time, I'd have probably shooed her away, but this *wasn't* any other time.

"I'm being a pussy," I rasped, and my throat hurt, which keyed me into the fact that they were probably the first words I'd spoken in a while.

I wasn't even sure how long I'd been here, how long Dad had...

"You're being a son. It's always hard when family dies or gets hurt," she said sadly. "But Bear is family to all of us, Rex. You know that. We're all hurting."

I bit the inside of my cheek at that, because I knew she was right. My parents had been my council's folks too.

Theirs had mostly been a pile of shit, but mine had big enough hearts for a bunch of rag tag little fuckers who'd come to lead the Sinners someday.

I highly doubted my dad had seen that much potential in us back then, of course. If I asked Rachel, she'd say there was no potential to waste when you led the council of an MC club and not a corporation.

I made more fucking money than a legitimate corporation and paid less tax. Who the fuck wanted to be the President of an LLC when you could rule over an MC?

"The doctors are positive—"

"Positive about what? Even if he makes it, you know how hard it was for Maverick to adjust to life in a fucking wheelchair. How's a man like Bear going to deal with it?"

She cleared her throat. "About Mav..."

I frowned, peering up at her when she hesitated. "What is it?"

"Maverick's just gotten out of the hospital too."

"He has? What the fuck happened?"

"He tried to go into the clubhouse for something. Debris landed on him." She cleared her throat. Again. Never a good sign. Rachel wasn't the nervous type. "He's forgotten, well, I don't know if he's forgotten or if he's just gone back in time." She squeezed my shoulder. "Rex, he can walk."

My nostrils flared. "You're fucking with me," I rasped out.

Only, she was shaking her head. "I'm not. I know it's crazy."

"Crazy? It's fucked up is what it is. You mean to tell me that bastard has been living in a wheelchair when he didn't need to? We couldn't get him to do any of the PT—how the fuck can he walk?"

She shrugged. "You'll have to ask him. As it stands, he's mostly confused right now, so he won't even remember hiding his mobility from you. You'll need to wait for answers, I'm afraid."

My mouth firmed into a grim line. I was happy for my brother, just confused as fuck as to why he'd choose to live a lie like that. What the hell was going on in his head?

"Where's he staying?"

"Most of the council are split between my house and Lily and Link's place. The brothers who don't have homes in town are staying at the Budget Basement Motel."

My nose crinkled. "That was the best we could do for them?"

"Don't ask me. Anyway, it's in your portfolio now," she teased softly. "I had to sign off on the club's purchasing of it."

"We bought that dump? Christ." I reached up and rubbed a hand over my face. The plastic gown I was wearing crinkled with the movement, and I knew I looked anything but a dark and dirty Sinner, but I didn't give a fuck.

"It's time you got some rest, Rex," Rachel told me softly. "You haven't slept in days. He's stable. He's going to be healing slowly, and this is a marathon not a race, so you need to take some time to get some sleep, okay?"

"I can sleep here."

"But you won't," she countered my argument with a tone I was used to hearing.

It was so wrong to get a boner when I was sitting next to my father's hospital bed, but that lawyer tone got me every fucking time.

Before I could say a word, she said, "Indy is gonna sit with him for a while, then the guys have worked out a schedule so that he's never alone." Another squeeze of my shoulder. "You're needed elsewhere right now, Rex. Lots going on."

"Nowhere else I need to be but here."

"When he's awake, sure. Then he'll need you. As it stands, there's work to be done now."

I peered up at her. "Didn't think you'd approve."

"I don't," she said simply. "But even I think this level of action deserves retaliation." Her lips curved in a faint smile. "You've seen me play *Grand Theft Auto*. I'm not a pussy."

I stared up at her, surprised by the teasing, enough to rumble,

"Christ, you really do want me to sleep if you're trying to make me laugh."

"You look like shit," she murmured, and then she did the damnedest thing. She reached up and smoothed her thumb under my eyes, just along the crest of my cheekbone. "You need to sleep."

"You sure you want me at your place?"

"Nowhere else you should be," she whispered, her gaze on my lips.

I gritted my teeth at that, but I nodded, and got to my feet. My ass and back immediately protested after being stuck in this goddamn plastic seat for days on end. I'd been stuck here so long I didn't even need to piss because I'd barely drunk or eaten anything.

I rubbed my forehead as I got to my feet and muttered, "We might have to grab some food on the way back."

She nodded. "Okay."

I twisted to look at my old man and muttered, "See you soon, Pop."

The next five minutes were a bit of a blur as we headed out of the hospital. Indy hugged me, which told me I looked like a piece of shit, before she suited up for the ICU.

As Rach and I made our way to her SUV, I peered up at the grim sky, thinking that it pretty much suited my mood.

There were more gray clouds than gray streaks, and it looked like it could piss it down.

That would really fit with my jam right about now.

A tornado was something I could handle.

When she started the ignition of her swank Porsche ride, the dash lit up and revealed the date and time to me.

"Christ, has it been four days since the explosion?"

She hummed. "See why I had to come and drag you out of there? Anyway, you stank much more and it would have disturbed Bear. He needs to rest as much as he can, not be woken up by your stink."

I grunted. "Have the funerals been arranged?"

"Yeah, you know it. They should be happening tomorrow."

"Which is the real reason you hauled my ass outta there." I sighed. "Thanks, Rach."

Before she pulled out onto the highway, she cut me a look and said, "You'd do the same for me."

And I would.

I just never thought she'd look after me. Which was mean as hell, but the truth nonetheless.

We had a definite love/hate dynamic, except she always seemed to loathe me more than she loved me.

Ten minutes in, we pulled into a Popeyes, and I grabbed a couple of sandwiches, plus some extra fries because she never ordered them but always managed to eat anyone else's—she was one of those annoying females who did that. Only, on her, it was cute.

I started my feast the second we were riding back to her house, and only paused when we passed the compound.

There were construction vehicles there already. Skips and diggers as they started to clear out the site, making it ready for the clubhouse to be reconstructed.

I had no idea how it worked, but I knew Storm and Nyx would be handling shit, Steel would be pushing his nose in, and if memory served, Cruz had an engineering degree, so he'd be helping out too.

Relieved that the pressure was off me for once, I slouched into the seat and carried on eating, feeling weird to be going to Rachel's domain when I was never welcome there.

I often wondered why she lived so close to the clubhouse when she said she hated everything Sinners-related. But live close she did and that was to our benefit if she was letting us crash with her for the foreseeable future.

I had no idea how long it'd take for the clubhouse to be built again so her generosity was more than I expected.

Not even feeling guilty for thinking she'd be so uncharitable because she could be a cold bitch when she chose, I grabbed my paper bags of food as she pulled up outside the colonial-style house.

Though it was only one floor, it was massive. Built on Sinners' money of course, but I never begrudged her the crazy fees she charged.

Mostly because she earned it, and mostly because I wanted her to have what she wanted.

She was a workaholic and the expanse of this place meant she could have her office here, which meant she was safe.

So close to the compound, we kept an eye on her, and Steel and

Nyx had seen to her alarm system and the various security measures I deemed as a must for her safety.

The veranda had a couple of comfortable-looking pieces of garden furniture that I knew I'd be sleeping on today.

After being stuck inside the goddamn hospital all this time, I needed the fresh air.

So I took a seat on one of the squishy cushions that had a pattern of some palm trees printed on them, and dumped my food on the coffee table.

She didn't say anything, just took a seat, grabbed one of the drinks, and sipped deeply from it then began picking on the different items.

It was so much like when she was a kid, when she'd first moved to the compound.

She'd been tiny, really fucking small and underfed. Getting her to eat had been hard because her mom had never fed her, but if you put some food out, she'd always graze.

I'd learned to always order more so that there'd be enough for her.

Funny how old habits died hard.

We ate in silence. The only noises came from the clubhouse but even the sounds of construction weren't too loud. I could hear birds and the wind trickled the scent of the herbs she had in her garden into my awareness.

It was peaceful, nice. Until it wasn't.

When Nyx came outside, Giulia perching on his knee, then Rain, Rachel's brother, and Hawk, Giulia's, bruised like a bastard after his run in with the bomb, popped up from out of nowhere, the conversation started up like a thousand bees just starting to fly out of the hive at the same time.

And the crazy thing was, it was good.

Exactly what I needed.

They didn't talk to me, didn't ask me shit, just carried on like I wasn't there.

But I was.

I was part of this family.

A family my pop had given to me upon my birth, and whose care he'd passed over to me eight years ago when Mom had died.

These were my people.

Some of them were going to be buried in the morning, and some were still in the hospital. A good chunk of them were homeless, probably living out of Walmart shopping bags, and some of them had goddamn amnesia...

It was fucked up, one crazy chaotic pile of goo. But it was my chaos. My goo.

Mine.

And when I found out who was behind the deaths of the people I loved, they'd wish they were dead too. Because we were the Satan's goddamn Sinners, and we had Death on our fucking side.

FORTY-SIX
INDY

I BLEW out a breath as soon as I got back to the tattoo parlor. Twisting the sign around from 'closed' to 'open,' I stared around my joint, grateful that today was over.

I'd need to go back to the hospital in a day's time to sit with Bear, but now the mass funeral service was done, and we'd laid so many Sinners to rest, I knew it was the start of change.

Not necessarily good change, either.

I wasn't a fool.

We'd been in a stasis. Our home had been hit, and we needed to rebuild. The ex-Prez, a man who was like a surrogate dad to all of us, had been horrendously maimed, and we'd lost men and women whose deaths we'd mourn for a long time.

But that stasis was going to come to an end.

I'd already been warned about the 'war' that the Sinners were supposedly engaged in with the *Famiglia*, but now they'd pulled this move—assuming it was the Italians—there was no way this was the end of it.

The guys would hit back harder than Thor slamming down his hammer, and to be honest, I was grateful for it.

The people behind this deserved to pay.

With their lives.

As I slipped into the chair behind the desk, relief hit me as I toed off the Doc Martens' I'd worn to walk on the grassy marsh where we buried our dead in the private graveyard on our land, and pushed my feet into flip-flops.

Wriggling my toes once they were liberated, I sat up just in time to see Giulia pushing the door open.

"Hey!" I arched a brow at her. "Didn't expect to be seeing you so soon."

She sighed. "You're normal. I need that right now."

I blinked at that. "Me? Normal?"

Her lips twisted into a smile. "Yeah. You're more normal than your brother, that's for fucking sure." She sniffed. "He only wants me to either never leave the house or walk around with a Prospect."

I shrugged. "Makes sense. You're carrying precious cargo. You had to know that Nyx was going to make his psycho ass of before look positively Hannibal Lecter-like now."

Her nose crinkled. "Shit. You're not making this better."

I just grinned, before I peered outside and saw the Prospect leaning against a truck, his gaze on his phone.

There were some new faces I didn't recognize since the explosion had taken place on the night of a patch-in-party that had taken Giulia's brother, Hawk, and Jaxson, a brother we'd buried today, and made them full members of the MC. But a few guys had also been sworn in as Prospects, and they tended to get the shittiest of jobs.

Like guarding irate mothers-to-be.

Not a job for a faint-hearted man. Not when that mother-to-be was Giulia, at any rate.

"How's Hawk doing?" I asked, my gaze still on the Prospect.

She sniffed. "Spent most of his time pissed this week."

I grimaced. "I think a lot of the brothers have spent way too much time at the bars around here. The ones not tucked up in the hospital, anyway."

"Yeah, dumb fucks. Like that's going to do anything."

"Sometimes you just need to forget," I mused, aware I sounded wistful and not really caring that I did.

Her brows soared. "Sounds like you've been there yourself." She tipped her head to the side. "With Carly?"

I snorted. "I was only a kid."

"Like being underage stops anyone from drinking."

"Nah, I started that when I went down to New Orleans. Things weren't great for a while, then I nearly lost my apprenticeship at the tattoo parlor I was working at, because my mentor, Jimmy, was a hardass, and that sobered me up real quick.

"Too many parties, too much booze, too many guys." I admitted with a wince. "Those *weren't* the days."

"You regret it?"

"Hell, yeah. But I had to make the mistakes to figure out that I wasn't—" I broke off, unsure of what I was trying to say.

"That you weren't?"

I shook my head. "It doesn't matter."

"Doesn't it?" She studied me long enough for her eyes to soften, and that wasn't necessarily a good sign with Giulia. She was more perceptive than I thought Nyx gave her credit for. Even though I had no doubt in my mind that he knew she was a smart little shit, sometimes, you could mistake someone younger than you as not being wise.

If anything, Giulia, who was at least five or six years younger than Hawk, was a damn sight wiser than her elder brother.

As for North? He had dumb POS scrawled all over his forehead.

Not that their stepmother agreed with me, seeing as she'd run off with him.

Giulia let out a shaky breath as she moved toward the storefront and peered out onto the road. "I feel bad."

"Understandable, Giulia. We've just been to a mass funeral—"

Her brow puckered and she wrapped her arms around her waist. "I was sitting with Bear today before the service and it was, Christ, it's just so hard seeing him like that."

I grimaced. "Tell me about it."

"I can't believe he's…" She shook her head. "It's tragic. I know he's getting older and everything, but he's still so fucking vital, you know?"

I cast her a look. "He hasn't been back to West Orange for years,

Giulia. I haven't seen him in at least three. You're remembering him from when you were a kid. He's changed a lot since—"

She swallowed. "No, that's just it. I've seen him more recently."

Pouting, I demanded, "When? I always hang out with Bear when he comes back. I miss the old fucker," I finished sadly, because I did. Though I'd never liked what he stood for, never appreciated the MC and its MO, the man himself was pretty cool. And hearing his war stories was fascinating. He'd served at the tail end of the Vietnam War, and the shit he'd seen had always caught my attention.

"You know, I never told anyone this before…"

Curiosity hit me. "Told anyone what?"

"That night, when Lancaster attacked me at the bar." She bit her lip, and I realized she looked anguished. I wouldn't put it past her to start wringing her hands together. As it was, Giulia, the ice queen and chief psychopath-handler, looked to be on the brink of fucking tears. "I didn't kill him."

As the breath whooshed out of her lungs, I blinked at her. "Huh?"

"God, you've no idea how long I've been keeping that in." She pressed a hand to her chest, like she'd been holding a solid mass in place, and now with her admission, the weight had gone.

I knew how that felt, but still, she'd stunned the shit out of me. "Keeping what in?" I repeated a little dumbly.

"That I didn't kill Luke Lancaster. Bear did."

"Bear did." I gaped at her. "You're joking, right?"

"I'm not. I don't know where the hell he came from, and to be honest, I thought it was a fucking dream when salvation came walking through the door—then he killed him, and reality hit with a bang." She raised a shaking hand to her mouth, then pressed her pointer finger to her lips in the universal sign of 'silence.' "He told me to keep it quiet. So I did."

"Christ." A sigh gusted from me. "What the hell was his game?"

"I don't know."

"You didn't tell Nyx?"

"Bear saved me from that bastard, Indy. I wasn't about to repay that by letting him down. Especially when we found out what a monster he was. I could have been like the girls. He was trying to kidnap me, I know it. He didn't just want to rape me, he wanted to take me." She gulped. "B-But what if Bear's so badly injured because of me? What if this attack is related to the Lancasters?"

"Oh, sweetheart, of course it isn't because of you. Hell, you know the shit the Sinners get mixed up in. It's a wonder we don't deal with this kind of crap every-damn-day of the week." I moved over to her and tugged her into a hug. When she burrowed into my arms, it felt like she was vibrating with tension, and I realized she'd been carrying around that guilt for a long ass time. "The Lancasters aren't even a threat anymore, are they?"

"The Sinners got involved with this craziness because of me. How aren't I to blame?"

Anger hit me, and I pulled back so I could grab her by the shoulders and, baby or not, I shook her a little. A bit too hard, but enough for her to glare at me which was what I needed. "You asked that bastard to assault you?"

Her jaw clenched. "No."

"Did you ask him to try to—"

"You know I didn't," she snarled, pulling away. "I know what you're trying to do. But it doesn't stop the cause and effect, does it? Before me, the club hadn't even heard of the fucking Lancasters."

"And after you, they do, and look at what you've done. If you're to blame for all of this, then Link has met his Old Lady because of you, and Maverick, who was a fucking lost cause thanks to goddamn Uncle Sam, has Ghost." I shook my head. "I have no idea what the Sinners are doing, but I know the guys well enough to figure out that if they saved Ghost and—"

"Don't get me started on that. Not when Tatána betrayed the fucking club," she snarled. "I helped bring that bitch onto the compound."

"You saved her from starving to death in that hell-hole, Ghost and Amara too. You did good. But what I was going to say is that, however they were bought, I know the Sinners well enough to figure out they're dismantling the operation. They might be evil fuckers who have no problem with selling guns and drugs but you know what they're like with the skin trade. That matters, Giulia. That matters to so many women."

She bit her lip. "True. Tatána is still a cunt though."

"How do you know any of this?"

"I have ears, don't I?"

Amused, I tugged on her hand. "Tatána did what she did because she wanted more." I released a shaky breath, unsure whether to tell her the truth or not and feeling guilty for questioning when she was opening up to me. But secrets and me were old friends... "Cruz hasn't really mentioned it but I know David ran off because—"

"Why?" she prompted when my words tailed off.

"Remember I told you he was like my stalker?"

"No 'like' about it. You called it how it is," she rumbled gruffly.

"I think he found out about Cruz, and then got to Tatána and used her to get eyes and ears in the clubhouse. I'm not sure if he was just trying to monitor Cruz because of me, or if he had deeper motivations, but—"

"Jesus," she rasped, her eyes widening with the implications. "She was helping him spy on you?"

I dipped my chin. "I think so." That was all that Cruz had told me, anyway. Even then, he hadn't told me much, mostly because I didn't think the council had clued him in on it either. He was probably as much in the dark as I was. The last thing he'd mentioned about David was the order from the council that I head to the police to report him missing. "I can't be mad at her though. He was a pretty good-looking guy—"

"For a weirdo," she said with a snort.

"But he was kind. Why wouldn't she respond to that? And why wouldn't she want what Ghost has?" I winced. "This sounds weird, but he was never suggestive. I don't think sex—"

"You mean he just wanted to protect you, not possess you?"

I pondered that. "Maybe. I was like an object. Not a woman, you know? If he was just really sweet to her, kind and gentle, after what she'd been through, why wouldn't she fall for him? Especially when he wasn't interested in sex?"

Giulia narrowed her eyes. "How did they meet?"

"No idea. None at all."

"I didn't even know she was leaving the compound."

I snorted. "You just thought she was there twenty-four-seven?"

She shrugged. "Never really thought about it, but yeah. They were all scared of their own shadows for a long time. As far as I knew, nothing has changed much." She pursed her lips. "Granted, I wasn't spending as much time with them toward the blast. I had my hands full with the club snatch."

"Well, we know she was good at sneaking around, don't we? If she could plant stuff at the clubhouse with no one knowing?"

"Bitch deserved to burn alive."

I winced. "Ouch."

"Fucking hate traitors," she muttered, her arms going around her waist again. "I hope the brothers find that prick David and slaughter him too."

"Christ, you're bloodthirsty."

She bared her teeth at me. "Trust me, I know."

"You resent that Bear killed Luke for you, don't you?" I surmised gruffly.

"I fucking do." She tipped her chin up. "I'll never be a victim. Ever again. That's why I don't need that Prospect out there."

"In our world, a treasure unprotected isn't a treasure at all," I told her. "You know that."

Her mouth tightened, but I saw a warmth in her eyes that let me know I'd softened her up for Nyx.

Fucker owed me and didn't even know it.

"I guess."

Both of us jumped when the buzzer sounded as the door opened, and in walked a customer.

I'd been Jun's tattoo artist for years, and she wanted a quick touch up on a piece she had on her arm with the addition of her new baby's name to it.

I mocked it up for her, then when she was happy, moved it to my workstation.

Grateful Giulia was there, I left her to woman the front desk, and went to work on Jun's tattoo.

It barely took twenty minutes, and I always felt kind of shitty when a tattoo didn't take a long time. Like I wasn't giving it my all, when I totally was. But there was only so much fancying up I could do to a three-letter name.

With Mei forever inked onto her, Jun paid, now a happy bunny, just as Nyx came walking in.

"I swear, I haven't seen as much of you in years as I have these past couple months," I grumbled.

He just rolled his eyes at me, then perched his ass on my sofa.

When he spread his arm out along the back, looking like he was settling in for the night, I remarked, "Think I'm going to be borrowing Giulia more than you'd like. I need a new receptionist."

"What happened to David anyway?" Giulia asked, and her tone, to me at least, was pointed.

All women involved in the life knew there would be a lot of shit we'd never learn where the MC was concerned, but trust Giulia not to appreciate being kept in the dark.

"He didn't come in for work." I cleared my throat, shooting her a warning look. "I got the call from *City Ink* just after I left the police station to report him missing."

Now, her surprise was clear because her eyes pretty much bugged out at me. "You got them involved?"

"He's gone missing!" I retorted. "I didn't want him to be injured or something."

She guffawed. "Like they'll do anything."

"Giules, when you're not tied to an MC, it's a miracle what the cops will do," Nyx said dryly. When his cellphone buzzed, he pulled a face, and murmured, "This is why I came here." He waggled his phone, which prompted Giulia to ask:

"Who is it?"

"Cammie."

Her eyes flashed with annoyance. "Oh."

"She's left a couple of messages, but I haven't spoken with her. She's calling to make sure I'm okay. She heard about the blast. I just wanted you to be here when I answered her. She cares for me," he said gruffly. "Letting her know I'm alive is the decent thing to do."

"Since when were Sinners decent?" was her rhetorical question.

My gaze darted between Nyx and Giulia like I was watching a tennis match, which'd never happen because I fucking loathed tennis. Still, this was better than watching Federer's tight ass jogging up and down a court.

When neither of them said a word, I asked, "Why do you care what she thinks? You treated her like any other available snatch, didn't you?"

Giulia grunted. "She didn't just care for him. She loved him."

"That just makes her a fool," I mocked, folding my arms against my chest as I perched atop my desk. "No snatch ever makes it to Old Lady. It's like a law or something."

"Rachel's mom did."

"Yeah, and like a true slut, she cut and ran."

Giulia heaved a sigh. "Cammie wasn't as bad as most of them. She didn't even fight, just left."

"Heard her dad was sick."

"You keep your ear to the clubhouse ground more than the brothers realize, don't you?"

I smirked at her. "It's the only way you find anything out."

"Cruz better not be running his damn mouth," Nyx rumbled.

"As if. I've been learning shit about the clubhouse since before I got my first period, Nyx. You need to watch more Discovery Channel, get smarter, if you think half the people in that clubhouse with a pussy don't know more than you guys think."

He scowled at me, then grumbled, "Giulia?"

"You obviously want to talk to her," she huffed. "So just do it."

"I don't want to talk to her," he immediately denied, proving he was smarter than I'd just dissed him. "But I heard her message and she sounded rough. Like she was—"

"Missing the guy she loved?" I input unhelpfully.

Nyx growled under his breath. "Since you two got together, I swear to fuck, you're making my life twice as hard."

I smiled. "Good."

He glowered at me, then hit a button on his cell. Next, he put the call on speaker.

"Nyx?"

I knew Cammie from before. In her defense, she *hadn't* been like the other bitches who whored themselves out for the brothers. She'd been a little too classy to be spreading her legs for just anyone, but that was proof that we all made wrong decisions along the way. I was the last person who'd judge someone for their sexual choices, for the freedom to make those decisions, but even though I'd been around the block a few more times than I'd like, there was just something skeevy to me about the bunnies.

It smacked too much of being a hooker for my liking. I could fuck whoever I wanted, spread my legs to any guy I chose—I didn't have to do it to earn my keep.

And it wasn't like there weren't other jobs available, for God's sake.

Because I didn't like my train of thought, as I sounded a little too judgmental and it made me feel like a prick, I watched as Giulia kept her eyes trained on my brother like she could see into his chest to monitor his heart.

"Hey Cammie." Nyx cleared his throat—not that he was nervous, but having the mother of your kid stare at you like that, was enough to make any man's balls draw up into his body.

Any *wise* man, anyway.

It was nice, actually.

Nyx, in this, was normal.

Miracles really did fucking happen.

"Nyx! Thank God. You're okay."

Giulia scowled, prompting Nyx to scowl back at her.

"Since when was he nice?" Giulia asked me quietly.

"Maybe you turned him over a new leaf?" I asked, shooting him an amused smile which he returned with another grimace.

"I'm fine, Cammie. We're all..." He sighed. "Fine."

"Enya told me that the clubhouse was obliterated."

"Fucking bunnies." Giulia rumbled under her breath. "She told you that, hmm, but didn't tell you Nyx was okay as well? All goddamn liars."

Nyx pressed mute and retorted, "Thought you didn't have a problem with her."

"Yeah, well, apparently I'm all hormonal," she snarled, folding her arms across her chest. "And don't appreciate my Old Man having a conversation with some slut he used to bone."

Nyx tilted his head to the side, and there was a twinkle in his eye that had me groaning.

Jesus.

"You're jealous."

"Bet your ass I'm jealous," Giulia snapped.

"That's irrational," was the genius's next comment, as Cammie spoke to no one, "Nyx? Are you there?"

"Irrational, am I?" Giulia growled.

"Well, considering that he sampled all the goods, Giulia, and never claimed her, I guess that could be considered irrational," I said dryly, trying to stymie the eye fuck that Nyx was giving his Old Lady.

She snarled under her breath, "Thanks for the reminder, Indy."

"He wasn't a saint," I pointed out. "Not like that comes as news to anyone here."

Nyx's eyes were still brimming with heat as he turned off mute and murmured, "Thanks so much for calling, Cammie. We're all fine here."

"But, wasn't today the funeral?"

"Yeah, well, there's nothing more fine than being dead, is there? It's the living who have to clean up the mess. I'll see you around. Take care of yourself."

And with that majestic reply, he cut the call.

Giulia's jealousy seemed to disappear as both of us gaped at him.

"With magical wooing words like that, Nyx, it's a wonder you fucked anyone," I told him with a sniff. "We're fine when we're dead, are we?"

He got to his feet. "Well, it's not like anyone can hurt you, is it? It's the living who suffer."

"Words to bring a child into this world to," I grumbled, shooting Giulia a look.

She smirked. "It's a good thing you've got a Terminator dick, Nyx. That's definitely done most of the talking for you."

"Is that supposed to hurt my ego, baby," he rumbled, leaning over my desk, and somehow taking up most of it so that he was nearly in her face.

Aware some kind of disturbing courting was going down, I shoved him, earning myself a glower. "This is my place of business. Giulia's working for me now."

"I am?" Giulia asked, her surprise clear.

"Yeah, you are. Not like there's an army of brothers to feed right now, and no clubwhores to rally around and get them cleaning something that isn't there.

"You can help out here since David's AWOL."

She cast me a look then her gaze drifted over to Nyx. "What about when he comes back?" she asked, but I knew she was testing the waters.

"If he comes back," Nyx corrected, prompting another elbow in his side from me but I saw the unholy glee light up in Giulia's eyes and knew, after our conversation, she took that as Nyx declaring that David was a dead-man-walking. Even though, technically, neither of us were supposed to know shit about club business. And even though, technically, I'd already taken out the trash for the MC...

She wasn't to know that, was she?

"Either way, there's work here for you." I cleared my throat. "But I ain't about to watch you two eye fuck each other over the desk, you read me?"

"You sound just like Mom."

Giulia's brows rose at that. "That's probably the first time you've mentioned you had a mom."

"You mean, you thought he was spawned from a— Where was the Terminator spawned from?"

"I don't know. I can Wiki it though."

"Please. Do," I said sweetly.

Nyx just grinned at me. "More and more like Mom."

My top lip quirked up of its own volition at his taunt, just like he'd goddamn wanted, so I flipped him the bird and murmured, "I'd prefer to sound like Mom than sound like you... It's like listening to Dad again."

His eyes narrowed. "You take that back."

"OMG, am I about to see a brother and sister wrestling session?" Giulia clapped her hands. "I need popcorn."

"We're about twenty years too old for that," I said wryly.

"Well, you should see yourself. You look like you're about to head-butt him."

"I taught her that signature move," Nyx recounted with a grin.

I shot him it right back. "Yeah, you did. Saved my ass a few times."

He slung his arm around me. "If you'd stayed around here, I'd have saved your ass for you."

Despite myself, and even though he drove me nuts, a welter of tenderness filled me, because he meant that.

No matter if we were at war with each other, he'd always had my back. Look at what he and Cruz had done with David?

I really did have two saviors.

Reaching up, I tapped his chin. "And there you go, sounding like Nyx again."

"See why I fell for him now?" Giulia asked with a laugh.

As Nyx hauled me in for another hug, something we hadn't shared this often in far too long, I sighed into his embrace.

The Nyx of before wouldn't have given a shit about Cammie, barely gave a crap about Caleb being in fucking prison, and wouldn't have hugged me.

Giulia, did she but know it, was changing him.

"You know, if I was the kind of girl who got off on shit like this, I'd totally take a photo. This is hitting me in all the feels."

Nyx grunted. "Are you trying to make me self-conscious?"

She snorted. "Baby, the day you're self-conscious is the day I take out all your piercings with my teeth."

"Giulia, the last thing I need is to feel my brother's dick against my leg." I chuckled. "Don't be saying shit that turns him on while he's hugging me."

She grinned at me, then murmured, "Sorry!"

"Yeah, you really look sorry," I said ruefully. "What with the twinkling eyes, and all."

"Well, these twinkling eyes need to head into the bathroom. I swear, ever since I found out I'm pregnant, I've been living in there," she huffed.

Nyx let go of me as Giulia passed us by, and the way his fingers tangled with hers, not for long, just a brief connection, had me swallowing back emotion. He really was changing, and it was surreal to me because he'd been Nyx, the savior of everyone else but me, for the longest time. Since before I could even remember, he'd been this way.

When Giulia headed toward the backroom where the restrooms were, the desire hit me. It was strange, because I felt like Giulia had been edging toward this conversation, and the closer she'd edged, the further I wanted to avoid the topic.

But Nyx *had* changed. He was going to be a father. The changes in his nature that Giulia was triggering, were not enough though.

As a dad, he couldn't be riding around the States killing people. Sure, those people deserved to die. I was the last person who would believe otherwise, but his priorities needed to change.

I'd spent all my adult life trying to hide this from Nyx, and maybe it was selfish of me, because it could be a catalyst that none of us were ready to deal with, but I needed to tell him.

I needed this to be about me, and not about him.

"Nyx?"

Even though Giulia had left, I knew he'd watched her go. More like, he'd been studying her ass.

Unashamed, and I didn't blame him–if Cruz walked through the door, I'd check him out too—he turned back to me, arched his brow, and asked, "What?"

"I need to tell you something, and I know how you're going to react. I know because I've seen you react to this news before, and I'm telling you now, not because I want you to do anything, but because I want you to *stop* doing something.

"You're going to be a dad." I shook my head. "It still fucks with my head to think that, not because I don't think you'll be a brilliant father, just because, before Giulia, I didn't think you'd ever be ready for anything like that."

His gaze was pensive as he looked at me, and his beautiful face was filled with the turbulence I was accustomed to seeing. I wished things could be different for us, wished we had an easier start, and wished, even more, that Carly was here with us. I wished she'd survived to come out the other side, to live a life of freedom, one without fear, without the threat of pain from somebody who was supposed to love you, to protect you.

More than anything, I'd have liked to see the Nyx standing here, to know what he'd done for her in her name. Maybe it wasn't the best legacy, but to victims, it was as good as it got.

If our Algonquin heritage wasn't clear in me, it was there for everybody to see in Nyx. His hair made the obsidian of mine, look washed out. His skin gleamed like a precious metal, and those eyes of his reminded me of marble. They were loaded with a rainbow of striations, that probably were only visible to me because of the artistic slant with which I saw the world. To anybody else, they'd say he had hazel-green eyes, but to me, each color was an emotion.

Everybody thought Nyx didn't feel. They thought he was a monster, a killer, but he was all those things because he felt too much.

Just like now.

The charge of his emotions, his feelings, was like watching a storm brewing over the ocean.

A part of me thought about backing out, of holding my tongue, but the truth was, I needed closure.

Cruz, without even meaning to, had made me realize that. I needed for this not to be a secret anymore. I needed this to be out–the people who mattered to me had the right to know the truth, deserved to know what had made me the woman standing here today. Sure, some of that was bad, but most of it was my choice.

Mine.

Nobody else's, and that made it precious. Precious enough to share.

And so, I reached up and cupped his cheek, well aware, that even though we were never on the same wavelength, that we'd been out of sync for decades, somehow, he knew what I was about to say.

I read it in the devastation etched into every single one of his beautiful features.

But he didn't stop me. He didn't plead with me to hold my tongue. He let me liberate myself, as I told him, "Kevin raped me too."

Four words.

Such a small sentence. An object, a subject, a verb and an adverb. So tiny in the grand scheme of things, and yet, the weight of them was lifted off my shoulders.

The release was exquisite.

It was like my lungs were no longer constricted, it was like when a broken rib healed and you could suddenly take a deep breath again.

The relief was enough to make a laugh escape me. Only, this was no laughing matter. The weight that was taken off me, I could see, Nyx had taken it on himself, but the truth was, it wasn't his burden to shoulder.

I clapped a hand over my mouth to contain another laugh, because I knew it was borderline hysterical and it would get me nowhere. I needed to approach this calmly, because the next few minutes would determine my brother's future.

The doubt of before disappeared. I knew this was the right thing to do. He needed to know this, he needed to feel the same relief that I was feeling now, because he bore a weight that had never truly belonged to him.

But with the laughter having faded, the seriousness of the situation erasing my hysteria, I reached up, gripping him tightly with both hands as I dug my fingers into the tendons either side of his neck, my palm brushing the 'Carly' tattoo he had there.

Peering straight into his eyes, needing him to see my sincerity, needing him to know that every word I was about to utter was the complete and honest truth, I told him, "If there is anybody I would blame, outside of that asshole himself, it isn't you, Nyx. It has never been you."

He started to shake, and it messed with my head because I knew nothing could make him react like this, nothing other than Kevin and his sisters, and I'd done this to him.

God help me, I needed to make him see the truth.

"You weren't my father. You weren't my mother. And afterward, you were the one who made him go away. You've no idea what you did for me, no idea what you did for Carly, because she died before you could see how much better you made life for us both.

"But, what worries me, is if you're the one who's going across the country, taking these fuckers out, one by one, putting yourself in danger every single time, eventually, it's going to catch up to you.

"Maybe, this far, nobody has realized you were behind all of these vigilante deaths, and maybe people aren't looking as hard as they might because of what those bastards are, but one day, somebody will put two and two together, and you *will* end up behind bars.

"Before, I thought that might be what you wanted. As much as everybody loves their freedom, I don't think you've been free for an incredibly long time. Probably for as long as me and Carly. But now, you have so much to live for, Nyx. You're going to be a dad," I repeated. "You're going to be an amazing dad.

"And the only thing Carly and me need from you, is to keep your child safe. To do," I rasped, the words choking me as I whispered them to him, needing him to believe me, needing him to feel the truth in what I was saying, "what mom and dad never did for us. I need you to be better than them. I need your child to be safe, like I never was." Nerves hit me because what I was asking was going to be hard for him, and he could easily say no. "Big brother, can you do that for me?"

For a second, I didn't know how he was going to respond, if he'd even respond at all, and then, he slipped his arms around my waist, pressed a kiss to my temple before he pushed his forehead against mine, and rasped, "I can, little sis. I can."

Then, safe in his arms, I cried. I cried for me, for him, for Carly. I cried for Caleb, who never had a decent childhood because of the aftermath of our eldest sister's death.

And Nyx?

Though neither of us would ever admit to it, he cried too.

Somehow, his tears meant even more to me than my own, because I felt like I hadn't just liberated myself, I'd liberated him too. Allowing both of us to have a future that would forever have been denied to us, were it not for Cruz, Giulia, and the baby in her belly.

FORTY-SEVEN
CRUZ

WHEN I GOT THE CALL, I was halfway from the clubhouse to the tattoo parlor. It was hard to register that was home now, not because Indy made me feel unwelcome, but I hadn't been crashing there for long so I figured it would take a lot more than a week to get a connection with the place.

The best part about it was that Indy was there. Sure, the brothers could call me whipped, but I'd take it. Especially as if anyone was getting whipped, it was Indy.

Not that anyone would ever know that, nor should they. I was a private man, even when sparing my ego was concerned—Indy's reputation meant a damn sight more to me than my own.

The name Darren White had more black marks against it than a couple of Sinners combined.

I was ashamed of my past, even if it had forged me into the man standing here today.

I wasn't the kid of before, a kid who'd do anything to fit in, to make friends.

Taking a double major at sixteen hadn't exactly made me popular, and having always been an overachiever, as well as isolated in the aftermath of my parents' divorce, I'd made a lot of crappy decisions over the years.

Those crappy decisions, however, paved the way to Indy. I wasn't a romantic man, wasn't particularly in touch with my feelings, but I felt like everything I'd done in my life was geared toward my meeting her.

Not for my benefit, but for hers. That wasn't to say that I wasn't a lucky guy to have her in my life, but the idea of a woman like her being imprisoned in her own soul was hell on earth to me.

My body wore the scars of the bad choices I'd made along the way, and my ink helped hide them, but Indy's scars were all internal. She helped countless people cover theirs, all while hers were impossible to heal.

So, if I was here to help shine a little healing light on a woman I'd come to love, then maybe it was a means of atoning for the past.

Of course, that wouldn't be so easy if my death count increased. Nyx believed he was the deadliest guy in the MC. But what he did with his hands, in no way compared to what I could do with mine.

And I knew my brothers wanted retribution, and I knew they wanted me to build something that would give them that.

You didn't say no to the council.

You complied.

This wasn't a democracy. But even though the decision was mine to make, in the end, what I created would bring destruction. And that would rest with me and my soul.

It was why, when I saw Rex's name flash on the caller ID, I almost didn't pick up. Thus far, the council had been acting without his say-so. But for him to call me directly meant he needed something from me. Something that only I would be able to give him.

I was the most overeducated bartender on the East Coast, and somehow, I was the one who got the shittiest, dirtiest, filthiest jobs.

Old habits were ingrained so I connected the call and pulled over. Feeling more whipped now than I did when I thought about the lengths I would go to on my woman's behalf.

"Hey, brother, how are you doing?"

"Christ, man, I'm the one who should be asking you. How's Bear?" I already knew the answer, everyone in the MC did.

The level of grief ricocheting around the MC was indicative of how much we loved the old bastard. If we didn't go to war over the bombing, it would be for Bear, no word of a lie. He hadn't been my Prez, Rene had died the year before I arrived in West Orange, but I knew him, and knew I'd go to bat for him like all those who'd served under him.

"No change. But that isn't necessarily a bad thing. Look, I need your help, and I need this to stay between me and you."

My brows lowered, but Rex was good people, and if he wanted to keep something between me and him, then I wasn't about to argue.

"Sure, man. How can I help?" I asked as I watched the MC's diner in the near distance. Still in West Orange, I'd admit to contemplating whether or not to bring home take-out for Indy and me.

They said that every man thought about sex six times a second, or some crap like that, but throw in a concussion and some broken ribs, and it was a killer on your sex drive.

"Before Bear started the run back home, I called him."

Across the street, a car backfired which had me jerking in surprise, while Tiffany, Sin's Old Lady, barged her way out of the diner, giggling over something that she and Lily were talking about before they jerked like they'd been shot at the car too.

As crazy as it seemed, with half of the MC still traumatized from the bombing, laughter was the best medicine, and I resented the stupid car for ruining that moment for them. Both women were back at the compound, back to that night.

Fuck.

It was going to take a long time to get over what we'd all gone through, and I was just grateful Indy had been working, because I wouldn't want her to be going through this as well.

"Yeah, I remember," I said gruffly, watching the Old Ladies link arms and walk over to their car like they were depending on each other to keep themselves standing. "You wanted to tell him about your Ma, and what mine had to say."

"See, I thought I was keeping him in the loop, but I found out he was just keeping me out of it. He already knew."

"Shit! He knew and didn't tell you?"

"Apparently." His sigh tunneled down the line. "He told me some shit that he said I'd think he was crazy for spouting, and maybe I did, maybe I thought he was losing it. I know how hard Mom's death affected him—"

"And then we were hit."

"And then we were hit," Rex confirmed. "So now, his conspiracy theory sounds pretty fucking real to me."

"Conspiracy theory?" I scratched my chin where my stubble had turned into a full out beard—I really needed to shave—and mocked, "Let me guess, the federal government–"

"Well, partially. I know it sounds insane, Cruz, you don't have to tell me that. But this goes deeper. He seemed to think that some dirty cops were..."

"Dirty cops are alive and kicking, Mommy dearest is proof of that."

"Exactly. I was wondering if you could speak with her? Maybe offer her some information that might get her to talk? Soften her up some, you know what I mean?"

Surprise flushed through me. "You want to feed her some evidence? Shit, Rex, we just burnt the bridge with her. If we build another one, she'll come to expect it, and where Caroline Dunbar is concerned, that bridge is never-ending."

"Fuck, Cruz, you think I don't know that already? You think I'm asking this, asking you to dance with the devil without recognizing how dangerous it could be?

"I've been sitting by my dad's bedside, racking my brain, trying to think about what was said, about what we discussed. Trying to figure out if there was something I could use to piece together this fucking puzzle, but there isn't anything. The only person we know who could help is your mother.

"So, for sure, I know what I'm asking here, and I know it's a shit show, Cruz, but I just need you to cast out a net and see if anything bites. Can you do that for me?" To anyone else, it might have sounded like he was being kind of nice about it, but I heard the command, and knew I didn't really have a choice.

Neither did Rex understand what he was dragging me into. Caro would think nothing of asking me for information to use against the MC in return for casting out that net he'd mentioned.

"I will, but I want you to know that I'm uncomfortable with the request."

"Duly noted."

"And when I come to you with issues over this, because issues there will be, I need you to have my back. Especially as this is circumventing the council, which is going to put me in the shit when it gets out. And let's face it, it *will* get out."

Rex grunted. "You worry too much."

"I just know my mother." And though it was rude, I hung up on him, then threw my phone on the passenger seat. It bounced, and almost fell into the truck well, but I was past caring.

One hand on the steering wheel now, I squeezed down to the point of pain, but still, it was either that or punch something and I didn't feel like dealing with busted knuckles on top of everything else.

Inside my head, I reacted like a chimpanzee who just been dosed up with angel dust–I went crazy.

From the outside looking in, I knew I didn't look like I'd just been asked to deal with the devil again. And make no bones about it, my cunt of a mother *was* the devil, capable of more than my brothers realized. Maybe you had to grow up with it to truly see it, but I knew there was nothing she wouldn't do to get what she wanted. And Caro was greedy.

AF.

While I'd known that last visit with her wouldn't be the final time I saw her, I just hadn't thought I'd be getting in touch with her so soon.

Jaw working, I decided to bite the bullet, reached for my cell phone which I'd dumped on the passenger seat, and dialed my mom's phone.

For several minutes, the dialing tone echoed around the truck.

She didn't answer.

To say that came as a surprise was an understatement, mostly because she never made me wait, just like I never made her wait either.

We had our own rituals, our own methods of dealing with one another, and it didn't involve pissing each other around.

Unless the state of play had changed after what happened, of course... But I didn't think that was the case. Although, granted, she had to have heard about the clubhouse explosion and hadn't been in touch to ask if I was okay. Now that I thought about it, that was strange. In the aftermath, though, she'd been the last thing on my mind.

Seemed like I was the last thing on hers too now.

I'd believed, apparently incorrectly, that her ties to motherhood would extend to bombings in which her son nearly perished.

When she didn't answer, after I tried again, I grunted under my breath then shot off a text to Rex.

Me: *No answer yet. I'll keep on trying.*

I didn't wait for his response, but I took note of the read receipt and in a state of outright rebellion, against myself, I messaged Kirill next.

The guy was like a father to me, more than my own dad was anymore. He'd been there for me when the shit hit the fan, and now I had Indy, I wanted her to know him and Monique.

So I tapped out:

Me: *Kirill, I have someone I want you to meet.*

Kirill: *Someone? A contact? I told you, I'm working hard on getting you the gear. It'll take some time.*

Me: *No, you misunderstand. A woman. I've got a woman now.*

Kirill: *Don't joke about this kind of thing. Monique will have my balls if you're messing with us.*

I snorted. Me: *Don't worry, I'm not joking. I want you to meet her when things have settled down.*

Kirill: *Boy, one thing you'll learn in this life, even when you're a retired teacher, things never settle down.*

Me: *True, well, you've never had your ass blown up. I want to keep it that way.*

Kirill: *I'd prefer it in one piece as well. Monique likes it that way.*

Kirill: *I'll be in touch when I have the gear.*

Me: *Thanks, old friend.*

After I sent a message to both Sin and Link, warning them about the backfiring car that had affected their women, I set off in the truck once more.

Thanks to that conversation with Rex, and the prospect of dealing with my she-devil of a mother, even after speaking with an old friend, all of it just made me want to be with Indy again. To be close to her.

There was something soothing about her, even though internally she was all riled up, she was starting to be a haven for me. That didn't exactly put me at ease, because monsters didn't deserve havens, but for whatever reason, she had yet to turn me away from the solace she gave me by just breathing.

As I trundled down the main street of West Orange and headed over the highway to Verona, I wondered if that was what love did. If it made you feel safe, if it made you feel like you had a place in this world. Some tangible tie that kept you bound to earth.

I'd never needed that before, and it wasn't like I needed it now, but I chose that, just like I chose her, and I knew I always would. All the while, though, I would wonder if she was insane, and I would wait for the day when she realized what I was, and she tossed me out on my ass.

But hopefully, that was a day far in the future, and I had time to make memories that would give me peace and some measure of solace when I lost her. Because lose her I would.

My past was something I'd forever be running from, and while Indy was too, she was full of hope for tomorrow where I wasn't. Tomorrow brought as many problems as yesterday did.

By the time I was parking in Verona, luck being on my side as there was a space just outside the tattoo parlor– Christ, I missed my hog. Parking a truck was a son of a bitch–I saw Nyx and Giulia slouching out of the studio.

Nyx looked wrecked, and as crazy as it seemed, I wondered if he'd been crying. His eyes were kind of red, the skin around them flushed, while the rest of him was blanched, free from any color at all.

Peering at him, aware that he and his Old Lady hadn't noticed me, even though the truck I was in was a massive motherfucker, which spoke of the bastard's discomposure, I wondered—

"Shit!" I muttered under my breath as I shoved open the door and slid out of the seat, barely remembering to close it behind me, never mind lock it in my haste to get to her.

I knew of very few things that could make Nyx appear so damn wrecked, and one of those things was a woman who held my fucking heart. A woman who had a family history that belonged in a nightmare.

When I made it into the studio, I saw her, standing with her arms around her waist, her back to the front door. Her head wasn't bowed, though, and her spine was straight. In fact, as I looked at her, the strangest idea whispered through my mind.

I'd never expected her to reveal the truth to Nyx, had never thought she would feel safe enough to do that, but she had. Only, she wasn't sobbing like I might have imagined, her focus was on the wall ahead. A wall that was loaded with her accomplishments, the art she'd created, the history she'd made by etching drawings into living canvases.

Her shoulders weren't hunched, her posture was erect. Enough that I saw the 'It Never Rains But It Pours' tat, loud and proud at her nape.

I could feel her relief across the studio, and it prompted me to cautiously ask, "Indy?"

She didn't turn around, didn't even tense up. The bell above the door had clued her in to the fact that someone had entered the building, but she couldn't have known it was me.

Could she?

"I told him."

Her tone was somehow free from expression, yet loaded with it too.

"I saw him on his way out," I told her carefully.

"You should have seen him before." She twisted, so that she could look at me over her shoulder and murmured, "Telling him was never the issue. He was a big boy long before I was a big girl."

"You were just unsure about the shockwaves," I replied, understanding without her having to clarify further. Nyx, on a normal day, made a nutcase look allergic to peanut butter.

She dipped her chin as she moved to face me. "It's done now. He knows. I made him promise–"

Her voice broke off at that, and unable to stop myself, I surged forward, sliding my arms around her, encompassing her in me. Letting her know she wasn't alone. Reminding her I would do whatever I needed to in order to keep her safe.

Just like she'd said, Indy was a big girl now, she wasn't that same little girl, terrified into keeping secrets that no one should have to bear. She was a woman.

My woman.

She knew her worth.

Knew what she meant to me.

This was night and day to before.

"What did you make him promise?" I whispered, curious despite myself. Maybe that was something between brother and sister, something I shouldn't know about, but I wanted to be kept in the loop. Wanted to monitor Nyx to make sure that he didn't break a promise to Indy, something she wouldn't have asked of him if she didn't think it was necessary.

"To do what mom and dad never did for me, to be better, and to stop wasting his life on regrets that bloody the hands that will hold his child."

I rubbed my nose against the fragrant silk of her hair and whispered, "You saved his life."

She nodded, then burrowed her face into my throat. The throat that was loaded down with scars shielded by ink, flesh that bore the visible weight of the lives I'd taken, and which was cleansed by her tears.

The tears of an innocent who fell for this monster... That, one day, would have to tell her the truth.

And that day?

Had to be today.

This brave woman deserved no less than my brand, but I couldn't ask that of her, not until she knew exactly what I'd done in my life, the many mistakes I'd made, and the reason I'd been beholden to an FBI agent, who just so happened to be my mother.

FORTY-EIGHT

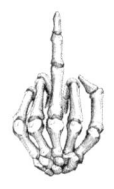

INDY

THOUGH HE HOVERED around me the rest of the day, it was interesting how I never felt as if he was underfoot. He did his thing, and I did mine.

Having never lived with a guy since my brothers, never mind co-exist, I had imagined it would be annoying. Always being in each other's faces was my idea of torture but Cruz was like living with a walking shadow.

I barely remembered he was there, that was how quiet he was, which I'd admit suited me. Just because I liked him to take charge from time to time, didn't mean I needed a pushy boyfriend getting in my face. Christ, that was the last thing I wanted.

What I *did* need?

His control, his dominance, *him* when I was at my most vulnerable. But in my studio, I was the exact opposite—I was strong. In my career, I was happy. If anything, within these walls, I was invulnerable.

Though the day could have been a shower of shit, it didn't last long. I knew that I needed the normalcy of my regular routine, and my tattoo parlor always helped.

Business was good, I had a few walk-ins ask for a tattoo, and as they weren't all that difficult, I handled two of them immediately, did a mockup sketch of the third and rescheduled them for another day as they hadn't expected the complex ink to take that much time. Several clients came in on regular appointments, and it was just a business-as-usual sort of day.

Cruz worked at the desk, grumbling and muttering under his breath as he worked on the plans for the clubhouse. Whenever I watched him use a pencil and eraser, a ruler too, it reminded me of being back at school, but what he created was a damn sight more complex than a little drawing.

It was clear to me that he knew what he was doing.

Not only was he creating a new building, there were all kinds of squiggles—and yes, that was a technical term—stuff that went over my head, that I didn't understand, but which he clearly did.

As much as Cruz felt like an open book to me, it was then I realized he wasn't.

He knew how to get rid of bodies using something he called a 'personal blend' of chemicals to do so.

And he tended bar for the MC.

As a career, it didn't exactly say much about him. And with my past, my ties to the Sinners, I wasn't totally grossed out about the body stuff. Especially when it had come in pretty handy for me.

Yet he rarely drank the liquor he served, was clean, generous with himself. He didn't use ten words when he could use three, never left stubble in the sink after he shaved, not that he had in a while and I'd admit, he was rocking that beard of his right now. He had his own soap and shampoo so he didn't steal mine, knew how to cook, and didn't leave wet towels or dirty socks on the floor—using a word like 'perfect' was dangerous.

But *could I* have the perfect boyfriend?

He didn't use my toiletries, cleaned up after himself, knew how to dispose of a corpse if I got myself into a stupid situation (which unfortunately tended to happen) and didn't have an issue with hugs or being affectionate in general. He knew how to spank me, knew how to get me wet, and my orgasms felt more important to him than his own did.

Yeah, pretty fucking perfect.

Yet the technical design that was coming more and more to life each and every time I left my workstation and returned to the front desk, was proof of him being so much more than the sum of what I'd learned. It was proof of a past he hadn't shared.

Much like with his mom.

It was quite clear to me that he had skills, skills that required a good education. So why was he the Sinners' Grim Reaper? And why was he content to just serve them tequila for the rest of his life?

These were all thoughts that whispered through my mind as I worked, and when the day was done, and I could close up, we headed to the diner that was a few doors down, and ordered a couple of sandwiches.

This was pretty much the first date we'd ever been on, which I knew sounded crazy, but when you were hiding that you were dating, and then your boyfriend's home got blown up, dating didn't exactly feel like a priority.

Was it weird that I thought people might be watching us?

Not because Cruz was covered in ink. I always expected gawkers, especially with someone as heavily tattooed, and all on visible parts like his throat and hands, as Cruz was.

Maybe somewhere else, that would be the issue.

But it was his cut that drew attention, just as I'd feared.

But that word hit me. It hit me hard.

Feared?

I was tired of being scared, and Cruz, even though he was a book of secrets, made me happy. He made me *less* scared, so that meant I had to get over myself.

Being with a biker wasn't something I'd ever intended on doing, but I was definitely doing him, and I had no intention of stopping. Reputation meant nothing, danger meant nothing in the face of something I'd been seeking all my life—peace. Which was exactly what Cruz gave me.

As we were both served our Reubens, I murmured, "You've been quiet today."

He shrugged. "It's been a long time since I made such technical plans for a building."

That gave me pause. "I didn't realize you were an architect."

He snorted. "I'm not. But I have similar training. I majored in Structural Engineering, don't forget. Even if it was a long ass time ago." He whistled under his breath before he took a large bite of his sandwich.

Toying with the pile of chips that had been served with the Reuben, I wondered, yet again, what the hell was he doing in a MC? Why wasn't he tucked away in an office in Manhattan? Earning a hundred-K-a-year and getting a bad back from a less-than-ergonomic desk chair?

He grunted. "I can hear the questions in your head without you even having to ask them," he said wryly. "It's crazy actually, tonight was the night I was gonna tell you some stuff. Just didn't think it would be the drawings that triggered the conversation."

My brow puckered at that. "What conversation?"

He shrugged. "Who I am, why I am the way I am, what I'm doing in the MC..."

"Basic shit like that, huh?"

His nose crinkled, and I'd admit it was cute as fuck. But then, even though he was covered in ink, and those he had weren't exactly warm and cozy ones what with the negative tattoos that displayed the skeletal system, he *was* cute as fuck. And anyone who didn't say that was a moron.

Saying that though, the world was full of morons.

Pursing my lips, I told him, "I realized today how little I know you."

The sudden tension in him was impossible to miss. Around his eyes, clusters of stress lines appeared, and deep inside them, the color shifted somehow.

I knew what it was like to be at the center of this man's focus, to have every ounce of his attention. But that was nothing to now.

I understood how a butterfly felt as a collector pinned it to a sheet of card before framing it on the wall.

The way he looked at me, though not aggressive, had the small hairs at the back of my neck standing on edge.

I didn't feel in danger, just like I'd stirred a beast in its den.

And even though that should have made me feel powerless,

instead, I felt alive. So filled with hyper-awareness, throbbing with life, like before I'd been dead.

A tremor whispered through my nerve endings, making them respond like his hands had caressed every inch of me, drawing me into wakefulness when I'd been asleep for a thousand years.

I'd never felt anything like it before, and definitely not outside of sex with him.

But he did this to me in a busy diner, when we were at the epicenter of a few patrons' attention.

I gulped when he broke the charged moment with a rumbled, "You know everything that matters."

"Do I though?" I dared ask, not because he scared me, but because I wasn't sure if he looked at me that way again, I wouldn't melt into a puddle of goo.

Somehow, he'd tapped into my being.

Somehow, he'd made it so that I was wet, my nipples erect, everything about me ready and open for him.

His gaze had dropped to my mouth, and a tad nervously, I ran my tongue along the outer line, well aware that he was watching the tiny move.

"Eat your sandwich," he ordered gruffly.

The command stunned me, because the way he was looking at me made me think he was about to yank me out of the booth I was sitting in, so that he could plunder me against the table. Not make me eat my damn dinner.

It bewildered me how much I wanted that.

How much I wanted him to kiss me, here and now. How much I wanted him to take control of me.

I was an intelligent woman. I was more than capable of making my own decisions. And yet, somehow, it was so wonderful when he took charge of me.

All the stupid thoughts disappeared, disintegrated into dust, and sometimes, it was just nice not to have to think.

And that was why I picked up my sandwich.

Though there were undoubtedly questions he needed to answer, secrets I needed to learn, I took a bite into the Rye bread, willingly putting off that moment, because he commanded me to.

He knew what was best for me, more than I did myself, and I accepted that with ease.

As I ate, he watched me, those eyes of his seeing everything, not missing a single movement. And I basked in it. Basked in his hyper-focus. Inside, I wriggled around with glee at owning this man as much as he owned me.

And even though it wasn't related, I came to a massive realization about myself.

All my life I'd thought about other people. I'd protected them over me. Thinking about their reaction to something that happened to *me*. I'd been tied in a cage, one of my own making, and this man had found the key.

So all of my past insecurities, every single one of them that revolved around other people's opinions, I shed them like they were a second skin.

I didn't care about the other patrons, didn't give a shit if he was a biker or not.

The danger? Fuck it.

Disapproval? Suck Satan's dick.

Freedom tasted better than the Reuben I was eating, and it was thanks to Cruz.

As I finished my sandwich, I told him that, "You're right, I know what matters."

The tension that had bracketed his mouth, causing lines to form at either side of his lips lessened some.

"I know what you make me feel."

He dipped his chin, and murmured, "You were right to question, and I'll give you answers, but first, I need you to do something for me."

"What?"

"Remember those photos I showed you? I want you to freestyle one of those onto me."

I could feel my cheeks blooming with heat at the request.

The pictures of me naked, cum all over, mine and his, my eyes dazed, like they were drugged, drugged on him.

But even as embarrassment stirred, it started to fade, because I realized what he was asking of me.

"You want me to brand you?"

"Yes." Such a man of few words.

I licked my lips. "I haven't been branded yet."

He shrugged. "Consider it a leap of faith. Either way, whatever happens tonight, I will always belong to you, Indy."

Confusion hit me, moreover, concern tangled with warmth. I wanted him to belong to me, and that he was making the declaration first, considering the nature of our relationship, it meant a lot. It was more powerful than a goddamn diamond ring.

It also meant that he expected me to reject him tonight, after he made his revelations.

But I didn't say any of that, didn't voice the knotted web of emotions his words had caused. Instead, I murmured, "Let's do it now?"

He nodded, and climbed out of the booth. He laid down enough money to cover our meal, and held out his hand for me to take as I slid out to stand beside him.

"You ready?"

Such an innocuous question, but it felt like it was studded with a million landmines.

"I'm ready."

Exactly for what, I wasn't sure, but this man had liberated me, so perhaps I could do the same for him.

FORTY-NINE
CRUZ

WHEN THE NEEDLE hit my stomach, penetrating one of the only parts of my body that wasn't covered in ink, I didn't flinch. The pain was there, acute as always, but I liked it. I almost found solace in it.

With my hands behind my head, arms flexed at either side a little stiffly thanks to my ribs, I let her work. A part of that was hesitation over sharing the truth, but mostly, it was because she was freestyling this, and I knew she needed to at least draw the outline before I wrecked her composure.

I had plans, of that I wouldn't lie.

I'd asked her to make this a nude drawing. In the future, when we had kids, if that was even possible in tonight's aftermath, I would ask her to cover up her tits and pussy with a bikini or something.

As it stood, this was for our eyes only. A visual reminder of what I could do to her, of how I could make her feel, and the trust inherent in that.

It would run low. So that her head and shoulders, her arms too, peeked above the waistband of any pants I wore. Then, along my hip and down to my thigh, that was where all the good shit would hide behind clothing, because no one else would see her like that again if I had my way.

Unfortunately for me, few men had pasts like my own. A past that a woman like Indy might understand, but, common sense would have her running for the hills.

I wouldn't blame her if she did, if she treated me like I had the plague, and that was the God's honest truth.

I'd been living with this for what felt like a lifetime, but regrets tended to fade as regular life took over everything else.

It was dangerous to hope, and that was what she'd made me do.

I'd never walked into this relationship intending on being branded. I'd never walked into it thinking there was a potential for more.

A man like me couldn't have more.

I knew that, and was foolish to think she'd be understanding. That she'd let me have a future with her at all.

A shaky breath escaped her, and I could feel her relief and knew that the outline was done.

I trusted her though, trusted in her so I didn't even peer down to look at what she'd drawn so far.

I just cast her a glance, and watched as she turned off the ink gun, and stretched her hand.

"Cramping?"

She winced. "I think I was more stressed doing that than I was the first time I tattooed somebody." She huffed. "Why you wouldn't let me draw it on paper first I'll never know."

"Because this is original, just like you."

"To look at you, you'd never realize you were a charmer."

I smiled up at the ceiling, my attention on that now and not on her. "Only for you."

"See?"

"Is that a complaint?"

"No, not exactly, but it is when I'm nervous and want to get this right. So don't get me wet." Then she tacked on, grumbling, "Again."

Despite myself, despite the situation and how nervous I actually was, I choked out a laugh, hard enough that I sat up to let it loose, uncaring that it fucked with my ribs, just joyful at her sass. I saw her eyes were twinkling though, and took heart from that.

"Did you ever imagine you'd be grumbling over that?" I queried dryly.

"Nope, but a girl can grumble when she wants, and this is one of those moments. I don't need arousal to fuck with my head. And again, I never imagined I'd ever say that either." She smirked at me. "The best kind of first world problems."

I shared the smirk with her, before I settled back down, focused on the ceiling again, and said, "I'm ready."

"Tough, because I'm not. My hand is still aching—"

"No," I interrupted, "I meant I'm ready to tell you..."

"Your secrets? Good. I'm ready to hear them. You know everything about me, or at least it feels that way. Everything that matters, everything that made me me, so while I know what counts, I think it's only fair that you share whatever it is that's making you all gloomy tonight."

Gloomy. Right.

"I agree, otherwise we wouldn't be here. Doing this," I reminded her, wanting her to know that I could have evaded this conversation for a lifetime. But she deserved more. And I wanted to give her that.

More...

She bowed her head in agreement, and murmured, "You can't look at me when you tell me this, can you?"

That she picked up on that shouldn't have surprised me. She was detail-oriented, after all.

I released a shaky breath and muttered, "I'm about to tell you something that is the exact opposite of my finest hour."

She didn't say a word, but the humming of the ink gun began, and I was grateful for the out.

"I was always an introvert," I started roughly, "always with my nose in a book, learning stuff because it was easier to do that than make friends. Surprise surprise, I didn't have many, and it made it easy to get through high school pretty fast. I had so many AP classes that getting into college at sixteen was easy.

"I took two majors at the same time, completed them in five years, drifted onto a doctorate, and all before I was twenty-five.

"It was then, when I was studying Chemical Engineering, that I met

Dean. Back then, I considered him my first and only friend, because you can't exactly count goldfish, and until then, Goldie was pretty much it for me."

A laugh rumbled from her, surprising me from the story. "Sorry, I didn't mean to interrupt, but Goldie? You weren't very imaginative, were you?"

I smiled a little. "Chemistry, Structural Engineering then on to Chemical Engineering... What about that path in college tells you that I was imaginative?"

She snickered, and her amusement lightened the stress I was under. Of course, I hadn't gotten to any of the bad stuff yet, so she wouldn't be laughing soon, but still, it made the deep breath I inhaled flow a little easier.

"Anyway, I thought Dean was like me. Just interested in learning. I was starting to turn into a career student, because I was whizzing through my doctorate, and intended on taking some classes afterward instead of heading into the real world.

"I never did well in the real world, it's probably why I do well with the Sinners. I don't feel like that world is real either. It's brutal, so in that sense the reality is hard to avoid, but it's not regular."

She smoothed her hand along the other side of my waist, as she whispered, "I know what you mean, it's okay."

It was only then I realized my throat was a little thick. Not from emotions, but from memories.

Memories of betrayal.

My betrayal hadn't been as bad as hers, there was no competition, but mine had led me down a path where there was no repentance.

"Dean and I started to hang out, we got friendly, bonded over a love of science, of cold logic and reason. I thought he was like me, but he wasn't." I swallowed nervously. "We used to sit in a local Starbucks for hours, discussing the most random shit.

"The craziest thing is that some days, I actually miss him. I miss those conversations. Nobody else my age ever gave enough of a crap about me to want to discuss anything that I was interested in, and as much as I love the brothers, the shit that got my juices flowing, well, it was just more than many could understand." I thought about how elitist that sounded, and grumbled, "I don't mean to sound like a prick."

"I get it. You're intelligent, that comes with a price. I, just, I'm not like that either, Cruz. I don't want you to feel like I'm dumb or something."

I grunted. "Don't make me spank you when you're tattooing me." She snorted out a laugh. "This was Darren, Indy. I'm not him anymore."

"You're not a split personality, and you have his brain."

"That brain got me into trouble, and what sucks the hardest, is that what I'm most ashamed of, the council wants me to repeat."

She paused at that, the needle no longer digging into my skin, creating trenches of color that would last a lifetime, but still wouldn't last as long as what I felt for her.

"You're not supposed to talk about club business with me," she whispered.

"I know I'm not, but this is me, the real me, and I..." I reached up to cover my eyes where an ache was starting to brew. "They want me to make some bombs, Indy."

"Retaliation?" she asked shakily.

"Yeah. Multiplied by three."

"So many?"

"There must be three targets." I shrugged. "I have no idea, and I don't really want to know, but I don't have much of a choice. What happened to us was wrong, but I just don't know if I can do it again."

She froze, I could feel the air around us beginning to chill, the temperature dropping dramatically as she processed my words.

"Again?"

My jaw tensed. "Yeah."

"Why?" Then she grunted. "Of course, *Dean*."

"He made me what I am today."

She pressed the flat of her hand to my stomach again. "What is that?"

"A mass murderer."

The choked breath escaped her. "Explain," she demanded, and because I needed to, I did.

"He was anti-war, to the point where he was almost rabid with it. Some days, I felt like it was the only thing that fired him. We morphed from discussions on Asimov and the Three Laws of Robotics and dark matter, to the internal politics of a peacekeeping solution in Afghanistan and Iraq."

I hadn't realized, at the time, just how our conversations had changed.

They'd gone from rousing debates on theoretical principles to hard-core anti-war diatribes.

Like a fool, I never said anything, too enamored by the idea of having a friend at long last that I let myself get swept up in a shower of bullshit.

"After Dean, I promised myself, and I know this sounds stupid, but I promised myself I'd never have friends again."

"But... The brothers?"

I shook my head. "Exactly. They're not friends. They're brothers. It's completely different. They're family by choice, and they're family that has never, ever let me down.

"Mom and Dad divorced when I was seventeen, and though I didn't blame him because she's a psycho, he moved to New Mexico when my stepmom got pregnant. My life was in the city, that was where I was going to college so I was left with her.

"Friends, blood relatives, they do that to people. They use that connection because they want something from you, and when they get it, they leave you in the lurch."

She hissed under her breath. "Cruz, I won't believe that. What Stone has done for me, and what I've done for her, that's what true friendship is. Dean wasn't a friend. I'm not sure how he made you do whatever you did, but that isn't friendship."

"Isn't it? Or maybe what you and Stone have is sisterhood?"

"Synonyms," she argued.

"My experience is different than yours, but I know that I'd go to war for every single brother in the clubhouse, and that's why I'm about to do something that I swore I'd never do again."

She pulled the ink gun back, and it switched off. Her voice was hushed as she whispered, "You're going to build them for them?"

"I have no choice. They've done so much for me, how can I let them down when this is something only I can do? Especially when it's such a dangerous job! At least I'm trained to do it. Anybody else will end up blowing their fingers or hands off. I can't have that on my conscience as well."

"And what about the people your creations kill? What about them? Can you bear to have them on your conscience?" An explosive sigh escaped her. "Goddammit, this is why I hate the MC. *This*. You guys do shit for one another, and sure, at the start, it seems like a fucking family day trip to Disneyland. That's how Caleb got involved. He saw the camaraderie, he saw the family dynamic, had grown up with the different leadership, accepted that was the price he had to pay to be a part of it, and look at his ass now. Stuck in a fucking jail cell with hardened criminals just because of the color of his skin and a racist judge." She flung the tray of inks she'd mixed up on the floor, where the metal clashed against the tiles I'd only recently scrubbed free of blood. "Goddammit, I hate this. I fucking hate it.

"They're asking you to do something that nobody should have to do, especially not out of loyalty. If you make that piece of shit, just because you're scared of the council, then Cruz, you're not the man I think you are."

Lowering my arms, I lay there in the throbbing silence, aware she was right, but feeling like a fucking pussy because I had no idea how to break away from the MC protocol without losing my lifeline to them.

"It's not as easy as that."

"Isn't it? We lost a lot of good people, and I'm pretty sure the Italians deserve their ass kicking, but for as many foot soldiers as you take out, how many innocents will there be?" She growled under her breath, more fiery than I'd seen her in a long time. "Cruz, I—"

"Don't, Indy. Just don't."

"This is why the guys don't discuss club business with their women, because you guys are all fucked in the head. Women are the only ones who are capable of rational thought. I swear to God if that's the council's solution to what happened to the clubhouse, then they're crazy."

"You said it yourself, we lost a lot of lives—those people need to be avenged."

"Maybe they do, but surely there's a better way to do it? For God's sake, your mom is in law enforcement. Can't she get involved? Stone told me that the FBI was sniffing around the clubhouse, that they were investigating. Leave this to them."

When I started to shake my head, she grabbed my hands, and said, "Cruz, you're better than this."

"Am I? I've already done it twice, God help me. What's another time?"

Expecting her to move away from me in disgust, to fling me aside like the human trash I was, she didn't. Her fingers tightened around mine to the point of pain, as she whispered, "What happened?"

"Do you remember that scandal back in 2013? When thousands of documents about the war in Iraq were leaked to the press?"

She blinked. "Should I?"

"I guess not." Ironic that something which had derailed my whole future hadn't even been a blip on her horizon. "We leaked those documents."

Her eyes flared wide. "Holy shit."

"Yeah, holy shit," I agreed sourly. "It was a coordinated effort between the US, UK, and German newspapers. Dean insisted that they receive all the documents at the same time, but could only publish the information on a certain date."

"Why a certain date?"

"Because that was the day he was going to flee to Ecuador, but he left a fuck ton of evidence pointing in my direction. Don't get me wrong, what I did was wrong—"

Infuriated, she slammed to her feet and started storming back and forth, ranting, "Son of a bitch! No wonder you have such a shitty view of friendship. He dragged you into this when it wasn't even your passion project. Motherfucker!"

Her anger, on my behalf, took me aback. I hadn't expected that. Had never thought she'd be mad for me, but then, she didn't know the half of it.

"You were arrested?"

"Yeah, by Mom. But she pulled some strings, made some moves that had some key evidence disappearing. I owed her, and she made me fucking pay every cent back to her."

"That's why you joined the Sinners?" she asked shakily.

I nodded. "But I wasn't, and never have been, a complete moron. Dean made me question that for a while, but I registered what I was. I was too young to do half of what I did, it's no justification, but going to college early, it messes with you. You never really get used to not being with your own age group.

"I was in class with kids who could drink and vote when I didn't even have a full beard. Christ, you should have seen me back then. Talk about wet behind the fucking ears."

"Don't be so hard on yourself. We all looked like dweebs when we were sixteen."

"Maybe." I shrugged. "The only people who got me through were a professor and his wife. I'd gotten close to them and I swear, I'd have topped myself if they hadn't been in my life." Her shocked gasp said it all, and I peered at her, feeling ashamed for being so fucking weak. "One day, I'd like you to meet them—I'm still friends with them." *'If we're still together'* went unsaid.

She swallowed. "What happened after?"

"Fool me once... I became a Prospect after I told Rex who I was, and why Mom wanted me there. I wasn't about to get my ass killed for her even if she had saved me from prison."

"The council has known from the beginning that you were a rat?" She winced. "Supposed to be a rat, I mean."

I grimaced. "Yeah." Sitting up, I held out my hand, gesturing at her to take it. She'd moved away, just like I'd feared she would, but she moved back toward me at my gesture, only frowning when I turned her hand palm up, before directing it at my throat.

The scars were barely there now, faded by time and care on my part. I'd had a full beard for the first few years, but even though they should be lumpy, where the tissue fused back together in a messy way, I was lucky. With the negative tattoo, the artist behind them had worked cleverly to shield the scars from view.

I directed her to where the big ones were, and at first, she frowned, before she finally felt what I was showing her, what I carefully shaved even though I was letting my beard grow out.

"You got hurt?" she asked thickly.

"I did. My throat, my chest, my arms and hands."

"How?"

"I was convinced that we needed the information the government was hiding, and Dean made sure that I was as amped up for the job as he was. But something went wrong."

It was too easy to go back to that night, the night when everything had gone fucking wrong. I could remember how I'd felt drugged, so high on adrenaline I was flying.

"The building we needed to break into was supposed to be empty, with remote security in a kind of watchtower. One bomb was set to go off to open up one of the exits, and then there was another door that had to be rigged to break through to the databanks. The area wasn't supposed to be manned by guards," I whispered, misery gracing my tone.

"But it was," she guessed sadly, her gaze softening as she looked at me.

"It was. There were about ten more security guards than we expected, or at least, than *I* expected. That was indicative of what they were guarding. What we released to the public needed to be exposed, but I never wanted anyone to get hurt. Ever.

"Looking back, I'm not entirely sure if Dean knew or not. He was so sure that what we were doing was right, just, that he didn't care about the collateral damage. Didn't give a damn that he was trying to save lives overseas but was taking them out on our own soil...

"The first bomb went off, and it was then I heard the screams. Two guards were down, and it was just sheer bad luck that they were where they were.

"I heard them, stopped to help them, but Dean didn't give a shit. He took the gear we needed toward the security door, rigged it up, but I heard the chatter on the guards' radios. They knew why we were there, or at least suspected, and were heading that way.

"I knew the layout like the back of my hand, and the guards were dead even though I tried to help them. There was nothing I could do, but I could stop the others from being hurt. So I rushed to the door, started to take the gear down, and only the fact I was wearing a goddamn visor to cover my face, stopped me from getting injured up here." I pointed with my finger, circling around my head. "I'd rigged it in a certain way—" I winced. "I won't get technical on you, but I knew that when I got to the door, it might need a larger or smaller dose of explosives, so I could adjust the strength.

"I managed to reduce it by seventy percent, but Dean, who'd run for cover, came at me when he realized what I was doing, and stopped me from deactivating it. We got into a fist fight, and I was a lot more of a wimp back then, so he managed to drag me away. The guards got there, didn't realize there was no time and..."

"How many died?"

"All of them," I said roughly. "Apart from the two who stayed in the security office."

I didn't tell her that Dean was another casualty of that night.

When I'd tracked his ass down in Ecuador, I made sure he paid for his sins, and no mistake.

"Jesus, Cruz." Her hand moved to my shoulder, while the other moved to cup my chin, tilting my head forward so that I was looking her in the eye. "You need to tell the council you're not going to build anything for them, except maybe the clubhouse."

"The Italians..." I gritted my teeth. "The MC, they're all I have, Indy—"

She shook her head. "No, they're not. You have me now."

And with that, she pressed her mouth to mine and shut me up.

FIFTY

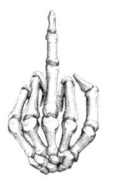

INDY

THE LAST THING CRUZ WAS, was a little boy.

I knew that, appreciated, in fact, that he was very much a grown-up, but as I looked at him while he told me the sorry tale of a friendship that had soured, of choices that took him down a path that led to me, of insane decisions he'd made that cost people their lives, in his eyes, I knew he was lost.

I'd never imagined he had a past like that. A history loaded with tragedy.

It should have repelled me. Should have made me turn him away, but the more he talked, the more I remembered.

The information leaked that year had revealed a level of corruption that had stunned the world. Even me, tits deep in trying to fuck my way free of my past, had heard the news.

I wasn't about to say that the guards' lives were worth those revelations coming to light, because they weren't, but... I'd be a hypocrite if I hadn't heard about those reports that revealed war crimes to the world and didn't think that was vital too.

My bloodline consisted of career criminals. My friends and family-by-choice were cut from the same cloth.

They made righteous kills, I knew that, knew that was how Nyx managed to get to sleep at night, but more than that, they committed crimes every day of the week. Their morals weren't like an average person's in society. Neither were mine, simply by association.

The same family wished to retaliate in a way that would kill only God knew how many. As much as I was discouraging Cruz, it was only because I didn't want him to...

What?

Didn't want his new road name to be Bomber?

Didn't want to fuck a man with so much blood on his hands?

Was it simply that I knew once he did it, there was no going back.

He would become a part of the Sinners' arsenal, and if he was cold-blooded, maybe I'd have been okay with that. Less with the fucking of said cold-blooded killer, but I could accept it.

Only, Cruz had demons.

I wasn't saying that he prayed every morning for atonement, neither was I saying that the guilt forged him into being a better man, but I knew the cross on his back, as much as the one on mine, was his hope for a better Cruz to come out of the past.

I knew for a fact his morals were questionable. He'd thought nothing of cleaning up my mess, did it on a regular basis for the club, and he wasn't wasting away under the weight of his history.

Not physically, at any rate.

But his soul?

For the first time, I'd seen it. As he revealed a secret that, to him, made him a monster.

To another woman, perhaps he was.

To me, however, he was perfect.

I was a wretched mess, my soul twisted and warped. It was selfish of me, but I couldn't deal with somebody normal. I needed someone as wretched as me. Together, two negatives could make a positive. Now, I truly knew we could be together.

But only if he said no to the council.

Which meant I had to remind him what it meant to be with me.

Needing him to know the ugliness of his past didn't deter me, that it was his future, *our* future that mattered, I lifted both my hands to cover his cheeks as I kissed him, simply at first. A gentle peck, before I edged him backward, pushing him so that he lay flat on the chair.

As I did so, I thrust my tongue into his mouth, surprised when he didn't really kiss me back, not at first. I wasn't used to him being passive, but I took advantage of it. Did what he would never allow me to do when I was tied up or cuffed to the bed.

I didn't know how long he'd allow me this level of control, of mastery, over him, but there was no way I wasn't going to let it play out.

I teased his tongue with the tip of my own, flickering it here and there, tempting him to play, taunting him into action. As his new beard tickled me, I sampled the roof of his mouth, fluttered around the root of his tongue, slid the two together, enticing him out of the cave he was hiding in.

He was slow to respond, deadly slow, but his hands moved to my hips, and gradually, the digits tightened about my ass. I could feel each one digging in, and I'd never been more grateful for the flirty miniskirt I was wearing.

The box pleats crumpled under his grip, but even they didn't protect me from the force of his clasp. And like that, I was tethered.

To him.

My nipples beaded, rubbing against the embroidered silk bra that covered them, and my pussy, that even though my skirt was a little too short for comfort, began to grow wet.

I loved that he'd ordered me not to wear panties, adored the mini rebellion.

In a society where people died, crimes were committed, homes were bombed, there were few rebellions remaining. A bare pussy was my way of flipping the finger to the world at large.

My own hands began to smooth down the rippled concoction that was his chest.

He'd said he was a wimp before, a weakling, well, that wasn't the truth anymore. He was stacked. His pecs so firm, they were as juicy as muscles could get. The need to bite them hit me, and I thanked God he was naked from the waist up, because I could ease my mouth from his, and kiss my way to them even as I was careful because we'd removed his banding so I could ink him.

Because he hadn't taken charge yet, with a final thrust of my tongue against his, I pulled back, and descended to his throat. The tendons there beckoned me like a siren song, and unable to help myself, I traced the hard lines before I found the scars with my lips.

His inked throat could be ugly to some, but never to me. His tattoos were beautiful, and I knew how hard negative ink could be so the technician in me appreciated the skill of his artist.

But what I appreciated even more was knowing the truth behind them.

Cruz thought he was a dead man walking.

A true Grim Reaper who cleaned up the messes other people made.

I found each scar, discovering them was easier with the sensitive pads of my lips, and each one, I bestowed with a kiss. Because they brought me to him. And brought him to me.

I could never be thankful for his past, but without it, we'd never be together.

He would be in an office in Manhattan like I'd mused earlier.

Either that, or stuck in a lecture hall, a geek I'd never have had the chance to meet.

My life was different now because of him. My brother knew the truth, and I was liberated from my own past because of him.

His history untangled my own, and even though I wished he'd never had to go through that, that those innocent people hadn't died, I was grateful that we were together. So I kissed his scars, the physical representations of what tainted his soul, before I started down his chest.

His torso was relatively free of ink. On his side, toward the left, he had another negative tattoo, a massive one that showed his rib cage and between them, he had a black heart forever inked onto his skin. It was, I'd noticed the first time I'd seen it, slightly shriveled, but now I knew why.

Yet if anybody had a large heart, it was Cruz.

So big that it was a wonder it fit inside his ribcage.

I made my way down there, tracing the outline, trying to kiss the 'boo-boos' better like he had mine, before I took what I needed and nicked the firm ripeness of his pec. He didn't even jolt, so I nipped the other side even harder which made him grunt under his breath.

He didn't stop me though, didn't grab my hair or drag me away as I moved to torment the other side.

Sucking on his nipple, I flitted the tip of my tongue around the tiny point, leaving it erect under my ministrations.

Nibbling on it, not nasty enough to hurt, I started my way down again, over bruised flesh, along the line of his abs, around the divots of his six-pack, enjoying just how fucking sexy this man was.

He wore just a pair of boxer briefs, having stripped down earlier thanks to the positioning of his tattoo. My brand on him. The elastic edged down at an angle, cupping the family jewels, preserving his modesty.

Although, why he bothered to preserve it, I'd never know. I'd seen every inch of him, kissed every inch of him.

The thought amused me, because I realized he had to have done it for my benefit. Still, it gave me easy access now so I wasn't about to complain.

Dragging the waist down, I found a dick that was throbbing with his own need. The sight made my mouth water, because even though he was so still that it was almost like he wasn't enjoying what I was doing, I had the proof of his response to me right in front of my eyes.

Before he could complain or grumble, I attacked. Pursing my lips, gathering saliva in my mouth, I let a long strand trail down his cock, moving my head so that the line of spit seeped down his length. Then, I pressed a kiss to the tip before I opened my lips and began to slurp him down.

He tasted like Cruz. Like the soap he used, the faint fragrance still there even though it was late, and as I made it all the way down, so my nose was buried in his groin, he scented even more like the man I loved.

He was a big man, but I was used to blow jobs, used to using them as a means of getting guys off so they'd leave me alone.

But at that moment, I cherished his dick. Gave him everything I'd never given another man, needing him to know he was special to me.

Needing him to know what he gave me, and what he'd lose if he made a dumb-fuck decision. I wasn't impatient, I savored. I enjoyed every inch of him. Reveling in my ability to please him, as arousal had him tensing, muscles bunching deliciously as I gave him what he always gave me.

Moving my hand so I could cup his balls, I rolled them in my palm, just waiting for the moment... That wonderful moment he snapped.

When it came, it was wondrous. A thousand times more enticing than anything I'd done before.

Making me realize that, as much as I enjoyed him like this, I loved the other side of him. The side that grabbed my hair, that curled it around his fist before he tipped my head back.

Every move he made took me to the brink of pain, and a slight sting did—as it always would—grounded me.

Made me feel the earth beneath my feet, an earth I shared with him.

He dragged my head back, growling under his breath, "Are you teasing me, Indy?"

I shuddered at that note in his voice, a note I recognized from upstairs. But we'd never done this at my workstation, ever, and call me stupid, but it made it just that little bit more delicious.

I rubbed my thighs together, reveling in how it pushed my pussy lips together, revealing just how wet I was.

The ache in my roots shot straight to my clit, and that bite of pain had me quivering as I whispered, "I'm sorry."

"I. Don't. Believe. You."

Each word was punctuated, and each punctuation was like his fingers attacking my clit. I groaned, unable to stop the sound from escaping me, even though I knew it would likely annoy him.

It wasn't that he didn't enjoy my pleasure, because if he didn't, he wouldn't work so damn hard to unravel me, but he didn't want it now.

He hauled me up by my hair, which had a yelp escaping me as I quickly scrambled higher, moving so that I could straddle him.

When the molten heat of my pussy collided with his equally as wet dick, I groaned again, and his hand slipped down, letting go of my hair as he cupped my throat.

I let him take the weight, let him support me, as his spare hand drifted down, cupping my breast along the way, pinching the tip, hard enough to make me squeal, before he descended further.

As his hand tunneled beneath my skirt, I tensed in preparation for the moment he would connect with me.

When he did, it didn't disappoint.

His hand tightened around me so that air couldn't flow in as easily as it should, but I didn't mind. As I gasped, ecstasy began to ricochet around inside me as he rubbed my clit. Hard. Fast. Enough to have the nerve-endings behind my eyes sparking with lights as he sent me soaring to the stars.

Just by touching my goddamn clit.

I almost melted on top of him, would have done if he didn't keep me upright with his hand on my throat, and when he grabbed his dick, and pushed it inside me, tears pricked behind my closed eyelids.

It felt so good. This was how sex should be. A smorgasbord of experiences, pleasure and pain mingling together until knowing where one ended and the other began was impossible to discern.

As his hardness plowed into me, I let my hands settle on his pecs, the tips digging into the muscles once more as I waited for his command.

The urge to ride him was powerful, overwhelming, but I knew how this worked.

He decided. Not me.

And though that gave him power over me, it was power I willingly relinquished.

I didn't want to make the decision.

My body might, but my mind didn't.

So when he drawled, "Slowly," the moan that escaped me was my response.

In tiny increments, I began to ride him. The only way I could move so slowly was to clench down on him, but as I did, it intensified the movement. Making each tiny thrust ten times more powerful.

I would have sagged against him, a molten vat of goo, only his hand tightened again, just as he moved his fingers further down, to the tightly packed slit that was already full of him.

I moaned as he prodded the tight ring of my pussy, trying to shake my head in denial at what he was about to do, but he ignored me. Carried on as he willed, not stopping until the tip breached me.

It was nothing in the grand scheme of things, but fuck, it had me speeding up slightly. Ever so slightly. But his reaction was to pull out, flip my skirt up, and just before it fell down, he slapped me on the peach of my ass.

"I'll tell you when to go faster," he growled under his breath, before his hand moved around the flesh of my butt, and found its way between it. When the tip of his finger parted my asshole, I shivered, and as he pushed in, using my own arousal against me to lubricate his path, the gentle fullness was intoxicating.

"Faster. Now!"

Relieved, excited, exhilarated, I obeyed. Riding him harder, faster, slamming down against him so that my cheeks clapped as they collided with his thighs. As he pushed down against that thin sliver of flesh that separated his finger and his dick, I squealed, well aware that a second orgasm was within reach.

Like he knew, as if he knew my body better than I did, he whispered, "Not yet. Not yet." But it was between clenched teeth, and I knew the pleasure was as excruciating for him as it was for me.

The thought set me off faster than a million fireworks. It hurled me toward the precipice because knowing that he got off on this, something that for us was pretty vanilla, just as much as me, was a sweet torment.

"Now!"

And just like that, I came.

Clenching around him so hard that I saw stars, that I knew I'd ache in the morning.

His hand moved from around my throat, denying me the grip that I needed, but he grabbed my ass, grinding me into him with a force that had me shrieking with delight.

It felt like it was never-ending, felt as if I was melting into him, merging into him until our cells were going to unite.

What we'd experienced together in the past was beautiful, but it was nothing to tonight.

Nothing could compare, not now that the secrets were bared, the truth was out there, and it made him easier to love. Not harder.

His past was grimy.

Mine was too.

Weren't we perfect for one another?

FIFTY-ONE
CRUZ

THERE WERE many things in my life that I was ashamed of. Some of them petty, some of them, quite literally, explosive.

But as Indy collapsed on top of me, her body sinking into mine without restraint, showing me complete and utter trust, I was ashamed for being a pussy.

Ashamed that I was going ahead with something simply because my peers asked me to do it.

This was the whole 'Dean' thing again, just by another name.

I didn't have to do shit.

I did plenty for the club.

I got rid of the skeletons, tended the bar, was working on the plans for the clubhouse, would literally do anything they asked of me, but this, I just couldn't do it.

And this woman, my woman, was the reason my eyes were opened.

She'd always hated regular sex. But she'd come onto me, she'd enticed me. Why? To show me that she was different? To give me hope that just because something was one way for a decade didn't mean it had to be that way for another?

Or, maybe, I was reading into it too much. What I did know was that I'd taken a seat at her workstation, fully expecting to walk out of here with a new tattoo, but no woman in my arms.

Instead, it was the opposite.

I had more than a handful of an Old Lady, I was even lying in the fucking wet spot, but the tattoo wasn't complete yet.

I was happy with that deal.

Tilting my head to the side, I nuzzled into her, rubbing my nose against her hairline, breathing in her scent, knowing that with the secret out, unless I was a complete fool, the past wouldn't tear us apart.

So I had to make sure the future wouldn't either.

She dozed against me, and I let her. I'd twisted things toward the end, knowing from the saucy glint in her eyes, that she was waiting for it. And whenever I turned on that side of myself, her pussy just gushed.

She fucking loved it, and because I loved her, because she was trying to show me that she loved me even with the clusterfuck of my past, how couldn't I give her what she needed from me?

So she was tired, and I let her rest. Maybe I even dozed a little, but I woke up to the glaring overhead light, cold from being ass-naked in the middle of the studio, still with a ripe bundle in my arms.

She was twitching here and there, tiny, minute movements that told me what was happening.

Maybe it had to be this way, maybe it needed to be this way.

For her to be here, on top of me, feeling everything she felt, experiencing it physically if not subconsciously with her.

"No, Uncle, no, please—"

Rage filled me, and I'd admit, when things were back on track, if I was still in the MC, and we weren't two computer gurus down, and we had proof, I'd go hunting for that fuck, Martin.

He'd bear my wrath against Indy's Uncle Kevin.

I didn't care if Nyx was going cold turkey, I knew how to dispose of the body. I'd do it on my own time.

Sure, I wouldn't be killing the man who had hurt Indy, the one who was behind the nightmares, but it would be cathartic, and it would make me feel a hell of a lot better.

Indy wasn't the kind to overreact, wasn't the type to misread a situation, so I knew Martin was an asshole. But I also knew the MC had rules for Nyx, knew they had to investigate a man before they put him down, so I would wait as well. Whether it was alone, with Nyx as he broke his promise to Indy, or with Storm if he found out, I'd be there for the ride.

Unable to do anything else, I simply stroked my hand down the length of her spine, wishing she was bare, wishing there were no clothes in the way. But aside from the way her legs were splayed atop me, straddling me like she was, which undoubtedly bared her peachy ass to the wall, she looked pretty normal. Normal when I wanted her naked like me.

Grunting under my breath, I murmured, "He can't hurt you, Indy, I won't let him. I'll stop him. I won't let him do this. I'll protect you. I'll keep you safe."

I whispered the words in a litany, a lullaby just for her. The tiny twitches of her muscles, the way she would lock up, her whole body clenching and releasing, started to fade. The small sounds that came from the back of her throat, petrified pleas, desperate noises, had me wanting to drop Kevin into a bathful of acid alive.

I was almost jealous that Nyx took the chance away from me, but I knew he'd had to avenge Carly, and rumor had it, that Kevin had also threatened him. If anyone deserved that righteous kill, it was Nyx, but I was still jealous.

So fucking jealous.

"Cruz, Cruz, stop him. Please?"

My eyes flared wide in response, because I realized I was in her nightmare. Having never expected that, I froze, then because this might be one way of gradually liberating her from these dreams, I squeezed her tight, and deep in her ear, whispered, "Indy, I'm here. Come back to me. I'll keep you safe. I love you. Come to me."

She didn't.

But her response made me happier still.

She relaxed against me, completely and utterly at peace, no more twitching, no more fidgeting or jerking against me, she grew slack with sleep, and stole my heart a little bit more.

Rolling us so that we were on our sides, I wasn't sure if she'd wake up, but she didn't. She stayed asleep, and I watched her for a while.

The gentle fans of her eyelashes against the upper curve of her cheeks, the way her lips would purse into a moue of annoyance, the glitter of freckles on her chest. The way her cheeks turned concave thanks to her bone structure. The silk of her hair and how it gleamed in the harsh lighting.

She was mine.

All those months ago, I'd never imagined she would be. Never imagined seeing her clean would lead me here.

But it had. And I was hers. Hers as much as she was mine.

I pressed a kiss to her forehead, and carefully untangled myself from the knot we were laying in on the narrow chair. It was awkward as hell, but I needed to do it. Needed to get to my phone.

I managed to maneuver her, releasing myself without waking her. I wanted to cover her up, stop her from getting cold, but I knew how she'd react to being covered, so I reached for the shirt I'd discarded earlier and draped it over her legs before I wandered over to where I'd dropped my jeans.

Looking down, I grabbed my cell, saw that I had a few missed calls and some messages.

Most of them were from Rex, and I knew why.

Because it was easy for me to do now, I tried to call my mom, but yet again, she didn't answer. And it had nothing to do with being late. Mom answered her phone whether it was 5AM or 5PM.

Something was going on with her, something that wasn't necessarily good. I knew that, wondered if Rex did too, but I wasn't about to say anything to him. He was already a man on the edge, and I didn't need to be the one who pushed him into a freefall.

I tried twice more, and when I got no answer, I composed a new message to him.

Me: *Rex, just tried Mom a couple of times, but still no answer. I'll keep trying.*

What the council asked of me last week, I've decided I can't do it. I won't do it. I won't be that man again.

I understand if you think that means I need to leave the club, but I'm hoping you understand that I can't be the one to reap that level of devastation again.

When I hit send, I didn't feel like I'd just started slashing at my wrists as I cut off one of my lifelines. Writing about leaving the MC left me feeling all kinds of choked though, but I didn't want to be involved with people like Dean.

Crime was one thing—I'd gone into this knowing what it would lead to. But I needed to walk away from my past, needed for my future to be different. If the MC didn't want that for me, then they were as toxic as Dean. Bombs killed too many people. They didn't disparage between innocent and criminal. I knew no weapon truly did, but a gun couldn't wreak the havoc one of my creations could in a split second. I couldn't hurt another bystander again.

My soul wouldn't take it.

A *Famiglia*-owned joint might have some pizza delivery guy driving down its road, a kid working hard to support his fam while struggling with college tuition, there at the wrong place at the wrong time, just trying to earn some honest bucks...

No. Just, no.

"Cruz?"

I turned around, and saw she was still on her side, watching me, her eyes sleepy and dazed, but somehow penetrative.

She understood what I'd done.

She held out her hand for me, leaving me no choice but to wander over to her, a little zombie-like, and to slip my fingers into hers.

"Everything will be okay," she soothed.

"The MC has been a part of my identity for a very long time," I told her, shooting her a wan smile. "I don't know what I am if I'm not a Sinner."

With her other hand, she reached out and trailed her fingers over the sore outline of her brand. "You might not know, but I do."

My lips twitched, but before I could say another word, my cell buzzed.

I sucked in a sharp breath, hating that I was nervous, hating that I was the same friendless kid again who was terrified about losing the approval of the only people who'd ever liked him.

But I was so much more than that now.

Indy was right, because Darren would never have been able to get a chick this hot. Only Cruz could do that. Only Cruz could get a woman like Indy to be his Old Lady.

So I bit the bullet, stopped being a pussy, and looked down at my cell phone.

What I saw had me closing my eyes.

"What is it? What did they say?"

I showed the phone to her, let her read the message.

Rex: *No worries. There are better ways to get retaliation anyway. Please, don't stop trying your mom. She's the only one with any answers right now. I'll speak to you tomorrow, and I'll smooth things over with the council. Night.*

"See, they're not as big a bunch of assholes as you think," she murmured, sitting up so that she could slide her arms around my waist, and press her face into my chest.

"I guess not," I whispered shakily, burying my own into her hair to hide from the world.

"Happy now?"

I squeezed her. "I don't deserve to be this happy."

She smiled—I felt the movement of her lips against my skin. "Don't worry, you haven't lived with me when I get PMS yet."

Snorting out a laugh, which was totally worth the pain in my ribs, I pulled back, relieved and glad and loving her for breaking that charged moment, before I said, "No, I guess I haven't."

"Or... did you know I hate bikes?"

My lips quirked. "Funny." Although, she never *had* ridden with me on mine before...

"I'm not lying," she told me with a small chuckle.

"You'll like riding bitch with me," I vowed. "When I get a new bike, that is." My nose crinkled at the loss of my prized hog. "Anyway, you going to finish this tattoo before I change my mind now I know you hate bikes and are a bitch when you get your period?"

Her eyes twinkled, tiny gold filaments dancing around her irises.

"Well, the customer is always right, but the tattoo artist isn't usually leaking the client's cum as she works."

"That's the perk of having one for an Old Lady then, no?"

She hummed. "It would seem so."

"Know where I want your brand?" I asked softly.

"Well, I figure it has to be somewhere I can reach," was her dry response.

I snickered at her smartass retort, then reached for her arm and twisted it gently around. "Here."

"What do you have in mind?"

I grabbed her other hand and pressed it to the tattoo on my chest, the one of a shriveled heart—how it had been for far too long, and how it would always have been. *Without her.* "This was how I was before I met you. I can't change it, you know a cover up wouldn't work on this kind of ink, but I figure since my heart beats for you anyway, you can keep it safe for me, right here..." I tapped her forearm, just above her pulse point.

A shaky breath escaped her. "You really mean that?"

"You know I do, Indy."

Her smile was beautiful, pure, innocent, joyous. Everything I needed to see to know that she felt the same way as I did about her. There were no doubts, not a single one on her face, and I knew, even though my connections might disturb her, she wasn't going anywhere.

Ever.

Unless it was at my side.

"Maybe I should be glad you want me to do it," she teased with a hiccup, "because I thought you'd want me to have a tramp stamp."

"Nothing about you is a tramp, Indy—"

"I'm no innocent, Cruz," she said, her tone slightly sorrowful, the gold in her eyes disappearing with her shame.

"What you are, is perfect. For me." And just like she had earlier, I sealed it with a kiss and shut her up, stole her breath, and erased any negativity she might have from her mind.

At least for the moment.

But I had a lifetime to work on that, a lifetime to make her see herself as the queen she was.

My queen.

The Old Lady I'd never thought I'd have.

The future I wasn't sure I deserved in the shape of a woman I knew was too good for me, but I was a Sinner, and the last thing we were, was fools. I'd take her, claim her as mine, and make sure she didn't regret it for as long as we both lived…

REX

TWO WEEKS LATER

I CRACKED my knuckles as I watched a team of ten of my brothers head for the city.

Link led the way, behind him was Nyx—they were the only show of force from the council. In all honesty, I didn't like sending them off, even though this was just a standard run. A very *late,* standard run.

They'd pick up the haul from one of the O'Donnellys' many warehouses, before taking it up to Canada for those fuckers, the Rabid Wolves' MC, to take across the border to Montréal.

I was just feeling protective. And I didn't think that was too fucking crazy of me either.

My father was in a coma, his body torn to shreds by a bomb that we still could only 'assume' was planted by the Italians. Anything he'd learned about Mom's death, and the circumstances behind it, were hidden in his memory banks as he healed.

It was crazy to think that he would have more answers than law enforcement, but surprise surprise, the Feds had come up blank. Even Cruz had. His mom was AWOL, nobody had seen her for weeks.

I had him trying her cell phone every damn day of the week, several times even, but she never answered.

In this world, my first thought was to think that she was dead, something that was most likely, but killing a Fed came with repercussions, and I knew few people who wouldn't shit themselves over that.

With her missing, though, any lead was gone. Apparently she had information about Mom too, and with her out of the fucking picture as well, I was at a loss.

I had enemies in need of killing, people who needed to pay for what they'd done to my family, both by blood and MC, but I didn't have the wherewithal to find out what I needed to know.

Maverick was no fucking use right now, and though it was hard to keep my patience with him, I tried. Normally I'd have been understanding, but the idiot had gone into the clubhouse when it was unstable, and while Lodestar was hard at work, she was at a diminished capacity too.

With both my computer geniuses incapacitated—one with concussion headaches that had her sleeping a lot of the day away and a broken leg that limited her freedom more than she was used to and made her a grumpy bitch, and the other so entrenched in his amnesia that he didn't even realize he wasn't fresh out of the sandbox—again, my hands were tied.

I'd thought I'd known frustration. Banging my head against a brick wall was par for the course in my line of work. And when you were in love with a woman who made an ass look complacent, frustration was normal.

But this was killing me. I believed the *Famiglia* was behind the bombing, but we weren't animals.

Storm had asked Cruz for a weapon to retaliate against them, but not only had he refused, I would never have allowed any kind of attack to take place without knowing full well who was behind the clubhouse's destruction.

I liked to think that we were a better class of one-percenter, but it was only common sense. You didn't bait a bear when said goddamn bear was in a cave.

I wasn't about to attack somebody who hadn't attacked us first.

We were already battered, I didn't need us annihilated.

With my hog lost to the blast, as well as many of my brothers', we were just fortunate we had Link's workshop to help with our transport issues.

Sixty percent of the guys on the run were using borrowed bikes, and none of us were happy about it.

Most of our rides were custom, tailored to our specific preferences. It was hard to bitch about that when so many people had lost their fucking lives, and with my own dad in the hospital, moaning about a bike was just pathetic. But as I cocked my leg over the borrowed hog, I grunted as I settled into the seat and kicked off.

Not even the ride could make me smile, the wind in my face, the sun on my head, the feeling of being free... It was all bullshit.

Mom was dead, knowing the whys and the hows about her death wasn't going to bring her back, but I had to know.

Needed to know.

And since the news of her murder had hit, it felt like a dozen other bullets had been fired at the same time.

I had to think that the clubhouse was targeted because Pop was coming home, which led to me thinking that Mom's passing was the catalyst. Maybe I was wrong, maybe I wasn't.

That was why I needed fucking answers.

The *Famiglia* had to be behind it, but proving that was another matter entirely.

I had already seen on the news a couple of days ago that Fieri had washed up in Connecticut, and with the head of the family now laying in a morgue, that meant the Italians were going to be at war as they figured out who would take charge.

The death of Fieri, who, if the *Famiglia were* behind Mom's hit, would have been the one to give the order, was a source of some satisfaction, but not much.

His execution had the O'Donnellys' smell all over it, not mine. I should've been the one behind his death, but if the Irish had decided to take the Italian Don out, they had a reason to.

And simply being at war with them wasn't enough of a justification. In war, foot soldiers died, they were the sheep tossed to the wolves... Leaders didn't perish.

If Fieri had pissed off the O'Donnellys, then maybe they'd have answers that would stop me feeling like I was going insane while I tried to figure out what the fuck was going on.

Sin had contacted Declan O'Donnelly after the explosion to tell them we'd be late for the run—we were even later than we'd guesstimated—but my Enforcer had never told me what the mobster had to say about the all-out attack.

Of course, I'd been with Pop in the hospital, so even if Sin *had* told me, I probably wouldn't have heard.

Brain whirring with possibilities, I made it onto the side road that would lead to the clubhouse and Rachel's compound.

It was sheer good fortune that I saw the truck at all, but when the driver saw me, he gunned the engine, accelerating at a breakneck speed down the narrow lane.

My instinct was to tail him, to chase after his ass, because his presence and his reaction tripped all my triggers, but the thought that he might have attacked Rachel had me driving like a lunatic to her place. I didn't even take the guy's plates, which pissed me off because I wasn't usually that much of an idiot, but equally, panic over Rachel's safety took priority.

When I made it to her property, however, there were no cars there. Only the truck I knew Giulia was using, and which Rachel wouldn't be seen dead in.

My tires skidded as I hauled ass off the back of my bike, and went running up the veranda steps toward the front door.

Someone yanked it open though, and I was relieved to find that it was Giulia, who, like a bandaged *and* deranged Polly Pocket, was glowering at me.

"Where's the fire?"

I grimaced. "Really?"

She shrugged then bit back a pained sigh as her injury reminded her that shrugging wasn't wise at the moment. "Felt appropriate. What's going on?" she grumbled, her voice raspy with discomfort.

"Has a truck been to the house?"

She scowled, shaking her head as she murmured, "No, we've had no deliveries."

"Shit!" I didn't wait for her to reply, just ran back to the borrowed bike, then headed to the clubhouse.

I didn't bother trying to find the vehicle because it could have hit the Interstate by now, and, if need be, when Lodestar was awake, she might be able to get a picture of the plates from any of the still-functioning security cameras—at least I hoped that was possible. Instead, I went to the gates that had just been installed as the last ones had been destroyed in the blast, my intent to head for the construction site, only, when I made it there, I saw it.

A package.

Fuck, had the Italians thought they could leave another bomb? Finish us off?

Fuckers.

But as fear hit me, the realization that the package was far too small to contain any kind of explosive sank in. I knew there were all kinds of tech on the market, stuff that was revolutionary, but this was paper-thin.

As I stared at the package, I rubbed the back of my neck, trying to figure out what the best thing to do was.

Was it likely that we'd be hit again when the evidence of the devastation of the previous attack was clear from the roadside? What else was there to destroy outside of a bunch of hired construction equipment?

We knew Pop's bike had been rigged, and that was how the bomb had infiltrated our compound, but this was a different MO.

And that truck, the way they'd been driving, spoke of panic.

They didn't want to be caught in the act.

Maybe I was a dumb fuck, or maybe I was just desperate for answers that nobody could give me yet, but I left my bike, headed over to the package, and crouched down in front of it.

I'd never handled explosives, but I knew they had to have a scent. Cruz would recognize them—should I call him in?

Or would that be bringing him into the line of fire?

If I opened the package, I was the only one who would be hurt. The brothers who were working on the clubhouse were too far away to be injured in a blast from a bomb this size.

I wanted no more collateral damage.

I needed answers.

So I reached for it.

Sucking in a breath that I held for far too long, I ripped open the package with a penknife Pop had given me a long time ago, and as I held the reassuring weight in my grip, I hoped this wasn't going to be the last breath I took.

The relief was sweet when I registered the scent of paper. Old paper. It was like when you walked into a used bookstore. There was that musty smell as each tome collected a million scents from the previous owners' homes.

Frowning, I twisted so that I was leaning against the bars of the gates, then settled my ass onto the gravel.

As I pulled out the sheets of paper, I flipped through them, trying to piece together what it was I was actually seeing.

The documents were sheathed in a brown card folder stamped with the shield of the NYPD 42nd precinct. But it wasn't somebody's record, it looked like a case file—from the beginning of an investigation to the guilty conviction the investigating officers had successfully won.

"Jason Banks," I read, repeating the name under my breath, trying to think how I knew it and where I might know it from.

But as I dug through my memory, the only thing that registered was Mom's maiden name before she'd married.

That had been Banks.

The thought was enough to trigger a wave of memories, only Banks wasn't exactly a rare name.

God, it had to be over two, maybe even three, decades since I'd heard it, though, and the age of the file was clue enough.

Banks had been in jail for a very long time, but why would somebody send this to the clubhouse?

There was no name on the package, so I had no idea who it was addressed to, but as I started reading about the case the 42nd precinct had built against Banks, I saw my mother's name and it confirmed what I'd already suspected.

Jason Banks was my uncle.

Christ, how had I forgotten that?

Scowling as I read, confused as to why this was important enough to deliver to the MC, it was only as I plowed through the different pieces of evidence the police had used against Banks that I registered the truth.

When he was supposed to be killing a drug dealer, it was on my birth date. There were pictures of Jason with us in the hospital. I even remembered when Mom had showed them to me. It was the only time she ever mentioned his name.

Racking my brain, I tried to process everything that I was reading, tried to remember everything she'd said, but there were few stories about the man himself, only the one about how miserable labor had been for her, miserable enough that they'd only had one kid. If I remembered rightly, she'd bled out, had almost died, and the birth had taken over thirty-six hours. Dad had been on a run, so Jason had been the guy who'd taken her to the hospital, and had stayed with her until Dad got back. Even then, he hadn't left.

He'd been with us the entire time.

I could remember exactly what Mom had called him—her rock.

So, while he'd been at the hospital with her, he was supposed to have headed out to murder someone, a crime with so much evidence against him, the jury had only deliberated their verdict for a half-hour...

Impossible.

A stitch-up.

"What the fuck am I reading?" I asked myself, rubbing my forehead where a headache was brewing.

And why was I reading it now? What did this have to do with anything?

Sure, it was unfair, and I was pissed off for my uncle's sake, especially as I hadn't had a chance to know him because of this fucked-up case, but why now? Why had this been dropped off at my door now?

And how the fuck had the cops managed to bang this on Jason when he had to have an alibi?

Understanding how shellshocked victims felt for the first time in my life, I reached for my phone, only as I stared down at the screen, I wasn't sure who to call.

Somebody had wanted to bring this to my attention, but why?

On the ride home, I'd been thinking about calling Declan O'Donnelly, and even though it was early days, I knew that if he had anybody in the 42nd precinct, maybe I would get some answers to questions this file brought to life.

But before I could hit dial, I got to my feet in a cloud of dust from the gravel beneath me, shoved the papers back into the file, and climbed onto my bike.

Riding back to Rachel's place, it was only then, once the gates were closed behind me, that I knew I could make the call. I wouldn't have put it past the Feds to have planted bugs during their investigation, so this call couldn't take place on clubhouse land. When Lodestar and Maverick were back on their feet, I'd have them scan the entire goddamn grounds, but until then, it was best to avoid MC territory.

Goddamn pigs.

Heading to the veranda, I sat down on one of the sofas I'd been sleeping on since Rachel had brought me here, then, and only then, did I pick up my phone again after I'd spread out the sheets of paper on the glass coffee table in front of me.

"Rex?" the Irish mobster asked when he answered the call.

"Hey Declan, I know you usually deal with Sin, but I needed to get in touch."

"Was there a problem with the run?" he asked warily.

"No, nothing like that. Ten of my men have just set off. They should be heading into one of your warehouses soon if traffic isn't shit."

"Traffic is always shit," Declan joked, but I recognized something in his tone that hadn't been there the last time I'd spoken to him.

We'd last talked back when Mary Catherine, a nice girl who was a daughter of a Five Point lieutenant, had been branded by Digger, one of my men.

He sounded, ridiculous though it might seem, gruffer. Angry. Pissed at the world.

I got it.

If anyone did, it was me.

"Sin told you about the blast, didn't he?"

Declan grunted. "Yeah, he did. Disgraceful."

"Understatement."

"Agreed."

"Thanks for giving us time to get ourselves together."

"No worries. You can't get blood out of a stone."

"Still, it's appreciated. We owe you."

He clicked his tongue. "How's your father doing? Sin mentioned that he was badly injured."

"We're hoping he'll pull through. He's a strong bastard, but that isn't why I'm calling you.

"Well, maybe it is. The situation with our mutual friends... Any chatter on the streets if it was them behind the blast?"

"Why aren't you asking your own people?"

"Because they're injured."

"Jesus." He heaved a sigh. "Lodestar as well?"

My brows rose at that. "You know of her?"

"We've known of her for a while. She's been of interest to the family, pretty much like yourself. Mutual *friends*."

"I know how that works," I grunted. "I heard about Benito. Glad the fucker's croaked."

"All over the news, couldn't have missed it."

"Definitely sends a message. Any idea what he was killed over?"

"I'm going to assume this is a secure line."

"It's as secure as this shit gets."

"Good. They went after my son."

My eyes bugged out at that. "You have a son?"

"You really don't keep tabs on us, do you?" Declan groused. "Why is that?"

"Because you're friends, tied to us through blood. Your father is insane, everybody knows he's loyal to those who're loyal to him. We're loyal, we roll no other way, so I have no need to monitor people who are friends. Not with as many enemies as we have."

"Good to know."

"I guess it is. But if I find out that you're keeping tabs on us, I wouldn't appreciate the lack of trust, understand?"

"As far as I'm aware, the only point of contact the Five Points has with you is me. And while I was injured, Brennan. There's been no need to monitor you. The Rabid Wolves are another matter entirely. I don't trust those fuckers."

I grunted. "Me either." I still had no idea why, of all the MCs north of the border, they'd picked those assholes to work with.

Still, that was their business, and I had bigger fish to fry. "Why were the Italians after your son?"

"We only found out recently, but he witnessed a murder."

As a stack of dominoes started to cascade into a free fall in my mind, I rumbled, "When?"

Declan released a breath. "When he was in West Orange and his mother was working on a piece of art for Donovan Lancaster."

Rage filled me, until I felt like my blood vessels were hyper-pressurized with it. If this was what a heart attack felt like— "And you didn't think to tell us?" I ground out. "Didn't think to ask *who* the victim might have been?"

"It's not as easy as that. The Italians started a fucking gunfight in the middle of the Coney Island boardwalk. They pinned my kid and woman in place, had a man on the inside working for them..." A snarl escaped him, and suddenly, the change in him made sense. His fury vibrated down the line. "In the aftermath, as I'm sure you can imagine, it's been crazy and you fuckers were the last thing on my mind."

Because I understood, my temper died down some as I asked, "Were you ever going to tell me?"

"Of course. I want answers. But my priorities weren't a cold case. I had active issues to be dealing with, and you said it yourself, my father *is* insane. He didn't appreciate his grandson and new daughter-in-law being targeted by our enemies."

Because I heard the truth in his words, that was the only thing that calmed me down. But my hand still tightened about my cell phone to the point of pain, to the point where I felt as if the screen would crack under the force of my grip.

"It's not like the Italians to target kids," I pointed out, knowing I sounded shaken, and not because I was distressed, but because I was seething.

"The murder Seamus witnessed, Fieri was directly involved in it."

He might as well have shoved me to the ground, then grabbed a

Mac truck and rolled over my head—that was how I felt. Like everything inside my skull had turned into soup.

"Who was it? Do you know?" I rasped.

"It was a woman, but Seamus doesn't know who. I know West Orange isn't the kind of place where murder happens every day."

Fieri had killed my mother.

And a kid had witnessed it.

I knew Declan was waiting on answers, but I didn't have any to give him right now. My brain was a blur, rapidly firing but somehow, not on what mattered most, and I grated out, "Have you heard of Jason Banks?"

His surprise was clear. "No. At least, I don't think I have. I can look into the name though..."

Who would blame him for being shocked? My uncle wasn't exactly on-topic. "If you don't mind?"

"Sure."

"Along the way, have you run into an FBI agent called Caroline Dunbar?"

A sharp intake of breath was his initial response. "What makes you ask about her?"

"I've been trying to get in touch with her."

"Why?"

I heard the wariness in his voice, but shoved it aside. We rarely admitted to trying to get into contact with the Feds, but this was different.

"One of my men is her son. She planted him here with us years ago, but when he became a Prospect, he told us the truth from the beginning."

"So he was playing both sides?"

"He plays her. He can be trusted. He's one of my best men—the stuff he does for us would get him locked up. I'm not worried about him."

"To be honest, this explains a lot. We were keeping an eye on her, and a biker visited her."

"That was probably him."

"I've sent you a photo."

Grunting, I looked at my messages, saw my man riding down a residential street, and confirmed, "Yeah, that's Cruz."

"Jesus, it would have been helpful if you'd informed us you had an in with the Feds."

Despite myself, I snorted because everyone knew the Feds were in the Westies' pocket. "Like you tell us about your ins? Yeah, I'm sure. We're friends, Declan, family, even, but let's not be ridiculous now." He wasn't to know that Caroline Dunbar wasn't exactly an 'in,' was he? She was more of a fucking albatross around our neck...

My retort had him hissing under his breath. "Why do you want to talk to her?"

"That day, when Cruz went to visit her, she asked about a murder that took place in West Orange."

"Christ. That fits. Look, Dunbar is in the hospital right now. We only just let her go."

My brows rose. "She's alive though?"

"She might wish she wasn't, but yeah, she's breathing, but a lot bruised."

"Torture?"

"You bet your ass," he said, his tone oozing satisfaction that I could empathize with. "She's the reason the Italians knew about my kid. They targeted him because of her."

It fit. All of this fucking fit. Not only had Fieri tried to have the kid killed to cover up his involvement in my ma's death, he'd fucked with my father's hog and sent him into the compound like a Trojan fucking horse.

Even though my blood sang with the confirmation, I whistled under my breath. "She's lucky to be alive."

"You're telling me. It wasn't easy," he admitted carefully. "But for the greater good, she'll make it worth our while along the way."

"How?"

"Do you know who the woman is? The murder victim?"

Because I knew this conversation required some give and take, I told him, "I do." I cleared my throat, trying to reduce some of the rasp. "It's my mother."

"Shit."

"That about sums it up."

A heavy sigh sounded down the line. "I'm sorry, Rex."

"Yeah, me fucking too. But at least I have some answers now. That's something."

He grunted. "Look, what I'm about to tell you might sound insane, but Dunbar confirmed it.

"We don't know how big, but there's a number of law enforcement officers who are dirty."

"No shit, Sherlock."

Declan snorted. "Yeah, the average dirty pig is nothing in comparison to this. These are a unit. They're all over the US, but they work together, have the same end goals in mind. What those goals are, we don't know yet, and maybe we never will. What we do know is how they operate."

I thought about what Dad had told me, my uncle's file, thought about how someone had delivered it to me, then chased off like a bat out of hell, and pieced shit together fast.

"They bring someone in, someone innocent of the crime they're investigating, tell them to do something, and if they don't, they'll send them down for what they hauled their asses in on."

"Fuck, Rex. Talk about spoiling my surprise."

I grimaced, looking down at my uncle's young face, aware that it would be old and craggy from a wasted life spent in prison for a murder he didn't commit. As I ruffled through the papers again, scanning pieces of reports along the way, I saw how they'd packed so much dirt against him that they'd convinced a jury of his guilt when he'd spent all that day with his sister who was in labor. How they'd achieved that? A forty-minute window of time where no doctor or nurse had seen him in her ward and my mom was asleep.

"Dunbar said they work behind the scenes, stitching up poor bastards into doing all their dirty work, earning them a fortune while they never get their hands bloody."

"Sounds about right."

"Seriously, how did you know that?"

I explained about the package, and the odd behavior of the driver who'd delivered it. I told him about the blast, about how we were lucky to be alive, lucky to only have lost the family we did. I told him everything. What dad told me, even though it was very little in the grand scheme of things, and I shared more. How the Feds had found nothing at the blast, about anything and everything I could think of, all in the vain hope that he would keep me in the loop in future.

After ten minutes of nonstop talking, I knew it was worth it, knew he'd taken pity on me, when he rasped, "Rex, there's going to be a summit in two days' time."

My eyes flared wide at that news. "A summit? One of them hasn't happened in at least, what is it? Fifteen years?"

A summit was where the leadership of the major crime families came together. The Italians, the Irish, the Russians, and the Chinese. The four major players who owned and ran New York like it was their personal playground.

"It's been a long time, but this situation... The families need to talk. Now Fieri is dead, even if there was protocol in place, no leadership ever transfers over that smoothly."

"If only there was a constitution in place to see this kind of shit through," I said ruefully.

"No such luck. No honor among thieves."

"Why are you telling me this?"

"Because..." He blew out a breath. "Because I have a feeling the heads of both families, the Rossis and the Genovicos, will be there, and I think you should be too."

"Why?"

"Vengeance. Trust me, it doesn't take away the pain, but it makes it easier to sleep at night."

"I can imagine," I rumbled. As my brain struggled to piece together what he was saying, to read between the lines of what he was telling me without spelling it out, I simply muttered, "I can be at the summit."

"I'll send you details of when and where. Whatever you do, don't come in through the front door."

And with that, he cut the line, and left me reeling with the possibilities of the next steps I could take.

Vengeance was my right, but did I have a death wish?

That, unfortunately enough, was the question.

REX

TWO DAYS LATER

BY THE TIME I was in Brooklyn Beach, any agitation, deep in my soul, had gone. Dissipated. Disappeared, even.

I was at peace with myself.

Whatever happened today, however it ended, I was happy with how I was going out.

I'd hugged Rachel this morning before she headed into work. I'd bumped fists with Rain, her kid brother, and I'd even slung an arm around Giulia's waist—the only woman who'd ever leveled my psycho friend out—not that she'd appreciated the gesture. I swore, the reason they both suited each other was because they were both so fucking prickly.

I hadn't texted the council, mostly because I knew they'd head out into NYC with me, and I didn't need them to sacrifice themselves for me.

What I was about to do… it might be the end of me.

For my mom, it was a risk I was willing to take.

She deserved more than she'd gotten, she deserved to rest in peace knowing that the people behind her murder were in hell. So, like the true Satan's Sinner I was, with the devil himself on speed-dial, I'd deliver them.

Personally.
And I'd smile as I did it.

THE NEXT BOOK IN THE SERIES IS NOW AVAILABLE TO READ ON KU!
www.books2read.com/MaverickSerenaAkeroyd

AFTERWORD

Just a few things, darlings,

By no means am I suggesting that a BDSM relationship is a cure-all for a survivor of sexual abuse.

In this instance, happily, it is for Indy. It's exactly what she needs. *Cruz* is exactly what she needs.

Her knight in leathers, as it were.

The cliffhangers in this book are more subtle than you can ever know… because, darlings, you might not realize it, but there are several.

I hope you're excited for Maverick and Ghost's story. I know I am. And yes, Martin dies. That won't be one of the cliffies I'll make you wait for…

Yours,

Serena

xoxo

FILTHY

FINN

Obsessive habits weren't alien to me.

They were as much a part of me as my coal-dark hair and my diamond-blue eyes. Ingrained as they were, it didn't mean they weren't irritating as fuck.

As I rifled through the folder on the table in front of me, staring down at the life of one pesky tenant, I wanted to toss it in the trash. I truly did.

I wanted not to be interested in her.

Wanted my focus to return to the matter at hand—business.

But there was something about her.

Something. . .

Irish.

I was a sucker for my own people. When I was a kid, I'd only dated other Irish girls in my class, and though I'd become less discerning about nationality and had grown more interested in tits and ass, I'd thought that desire had died down.

But Aoife Keegan was undeniably, indefatigably Irish.

From her fucking name—I didn't know people still named their kids in Gaelic over here—to her red goddamn hair and milky-white skin.

To many, she wouldn't be sexy. Too pale, too curvy, too rounded and wholesome. But to me? It was like God had formed a creature that was born to be my downfall.

I could feel the beast inside me roaring to life as I stared at the photos of her. It wanted out. It wanted her.

Fuck.

"I told you not to get those briefs."

My eyes flared wide in surprise at my brother, Aidan O'Donnelly's remark. "What?" I snapped.

"I told you not to get those briefs," he repeated, unoffended. Which was a miracle. Had I been speaking to Aidan Sr., I'd probably have lost a finger, but Aidan Jr. was one of my best friends, as well as a confidant and fellow businessman.

When I said business, it wasn't the kind Valley girls dreamed their future husbands would be involved in. No Manhattan socialite, though we were wealthy as fuck, would want us on their arm if they truly knew what games we were involved in.

My business was forged, unashamedly, in blood, sweat, and tears.

Preferably not my own, although I had taken a few hits for the Family over the years.

"My briefs aren't irritating me," I carried on, blowing out a breath.

"No? You look like you've got something up your ass crack." Aidan cocked a brow at me, but his smirk told me he knew exactly what the fuck was wrong.

I flipped him the bird—the finger that I'd have lost by showing cheek to his father—and he just grinned at me as he leaned over my glass desk and scooped up one of the pictures.

That beast I mentioned earlier?

It roared to life again when his eyes drifted over Aoife's curvy form.

"She's like your kryptonite," he breathed, tilting his head to the side. "Fuck me, Finn."

"I'd rather not," I told him dryly. "Now her? Yeah. I'd fuck her anytime."

He wafted a dismissive hand at my teasing. "I knew from that look in your eye, there was a woman involved. I just didn't know it would be a looker like this."

I snatched the photo from him. "Mine."

My growl had him snickering. "The Old Country ain't where I get my women from, Finn. Simmer down."

Throat tightening, I grated out, "What the fuck am I going to do?"

"Screw her?" he suggested.

"I can't."

He snorted. "You can."

"How the fuck am I supposed to get her in my bed when I'm about to bribe her into selling off her commercial lot?"

Aidan shrugged. "Do the bribing after."

That had me blowing out a breath. "You're a bastard, you know that, right?"

Piously, he murmured, "My parents were well and truly married before I came along. I have the wedding and birth certificates to prove it." He grinned. "Anyway, you're only just figuring that out?"

I shot him a scowl. "You're remarkably cheerful today."

"Is that a question or a statement?"

"Both?" The word sounded far too Irish for my own taste. My mother had come from Ireland, Tipperary to be precise—yeah, like the song. I was American born and bred, my accent that of someone who'd been raised in Hell's Kitchen but, and I hated it, my mother's accent would make an appearance every now and then.

'Both' came out sounding almost like 'boat.'

Aidan, knowing me as well as he did, smirked again—the fucker. "I got laid."

Grunting, I told him, "That doesn't usually make you cheerful."

"It does. I just never see you first thing after I wake up. Da hasn't managed to piss me off today."

Aidan was the heir to the Five Points—an Irish gang who operated out of Hell's Kitchen. It wasn't like being the heir to a candy company or a title. It came with responsibilities that no one really appreciated.

We were tied into the life, though. Had been since the day we were born.

There was no use in whining over it, and Aidan wasn't. But if I had to deal with his father on a daily basis? I'd have been whining to the morgue and back.

Aidan Sr. was the shrewdest man I knew. What the man could do with our clout defied belief. Even if I thought he was a sociopath, he had my respect, and in truth, my love and loyalty.

Bastard or no, he'd taken me in when I was fourteen and had made me one of his family. I'd gone from being his kids' friend, the son of one of his runners, to suddenly being welcome in the main house.

All because Aidan Sr.—though I was sure he was certifiable—believed in family.

I shot Aidan Jr. a look. "Was it that blonde over on Canal Street?"

He rubbed his chin. "Yeah."

Snorting, I told him, "Hope you wore a rubber. I swear that woman has so many men going in and out of her door, it should be on double-action hinges."

He scowled at me. "Are you trying to piss me off?"

"Why? Didn't wear a jimmy?" I grinned at him, my mood soaring in the face of his irritation. "Better get to the clinic before it drops off."

Though he flipped me the bird as easily as I'd done to him—I was his brother, after all—he grumbled, "What are you going to do about little Aoife?"

I squinted at him. "She's not little."

That seemed to restore his humor. "I know. Just how you like them." He shook his head. "You and Conor, I swear. What do you do with them? Drown yourself in their tits?"

Heaving a sigh, I informed him, "My predilection for large tits is none of your business."

"And whether or not I wore a jimmy last night is none of yours."

"If it turns green and looks like a moldy corn on the cob, who you gonna call?"

"Ghostbusters?" he tried.

I shook my head, then pointed a finger at him and back at myself. "No. Me."

Grunting, he got to his feet and pressed his fists to the desk. "We need that building, Finn."

"The business development plan was mine, Aid. I know we need it. Don't worry, I won't do anything stupid."

He snorted. "Your kind of stupid could go one of two ways."

That had me narrowing my eyes at him, but he held up his hands in surrender.

"Fuck her out of your system quickly, and then get started on the deal," he advised. "Best way."

It probably was the best way, but—

He sighed. "That fucking honor of yours."

I had to laugh. Only in the O'Donnelly family would my thoughts be considered honorable.

"If I'm fucking someone over, I want them to know it," was all I said.

"That makes no sense."

"Makes for epic sex, though," I jibed, and he shot me a grin.

"Angry sex is always good." He rubbed his chin, then he reached over again and flipped through the photos. "Who's the old guy to her?"

"To her? Not sure. Sugar daddy?" The thought alone made the beast inside rage. I cleared my throat to get rid of the rasp there. "To us? He's our meal ticket."

Aidan's eyes widened. "He is?"

I nodded. "Just leave it to me."

"I was always going to, *dearthái*r." He tilted his chin at me, honoring me with the Gaelic word for brother. "Be careful out there."

"You, too, brother."

Aidan winked at me and, with a far too cheerful whistle for someone whose dick might soon be 'ribbed for her pleasure' without the need for a condom, walked out of my office leaving me to brood.

The instant his back was to me, I stared at the photos again. Flipping through them, I glowered at the innocent face staring back at me through the photo paper—if only she knew.

Hers was a building in Hell's Kitchen. Five Points Territory. One of many on my hit list.

Back in the 70s, Aidan Sr., following in his father's footsteps, had bought up a shit-ton of property, pre-gentrification, and it was my job to either sell off the portfolio, reconstruct, or 'improve' the current aesthetics of the buildings the Points owned.

This particular one was something I'd taken a personal interest in.

See, I was technically a legitimate businessman.

This office?

I had views of the Hudson. I could see the Empire State Building, and in the evening, I had an epic view of the sunset setting over Manhattan. This office building, also Points' property, was worth a cool hundred million, and I was, again technically, the CEO of it.

On paper?

I looked seamless.

The businessman who sported hundred thousand dollar watches and had a house in the Hamptons. No one save the Points and my CPA knew where the money came from. I liked that because, fuck, I had no intention of switching this pad for a lock-up in Riker's Island.

Still, this project cut close to home, and the reasoning was fucking pathetic.

I'd never admit it to any of the O'Donnellys. The bastards were like family to me, and if I admitted to this, they'd never let me hear the end of it.

Extortion?

I usually doled that out to someone else's to do list. Someone with a far lower paygrade than me, someone expendable. But the minute I'd heard of the troublesome tenant who was refusing to sell her lot to us? After not one, not two, not even three attempts with higher prices?

Five outright refusals?

The challenge to convince her otherwise had overtaken me.

See, I liked stubborn in women.

I liked fucking it out of them.

Throw in the fact the woman's name was Aoife? It had been enough to get me sending someone out to follow her.

If she'd been fifty with as many chins as she had grandchildren, she'd have been safe from me.

But she wasn't.

She was, as Aidan had correctly stated, my kryptonite. All milky flesh with gleaming auburn hair that I wanted to tie around my clenched fist. Her soft features with those delicate green eyes that sparkled when she smiled and were like wet grass when she was mad, acted like a punch to my gut.

Now?

My interest hadn't just been piqued.

It had fucking imploded.

Yeah, I was thinking with my cock, but what man, at the end of the day, didn't?

I'd just have to be careful. Just have to make sure I put pressure on the right places, make sure she'd bend and not break, and the old bastard in the pictures was my key to just that.

See, every third Tuesday of the month, Aoife Keegan had a habit of traipsing across Manhattan to the Upper East Side. There, at three PM on the dot, she'd enter a discreet little boutique hotel and wouldn't leave until nine PM that night.

Five minutes after she arrived and left, the same man would leave, too.

At first, when Jimmy O'Leary had told me that Senator Alan Davidson was at the hotel, I hadn't thought anything of it.

Why would I?

Senators trawled for donations in fancy hotels every fucking day of the week. It was the true luxury of politics. Sure, they made it look real good for the press. Posing in derelict neighborhoods and shaking hands with people who did the fucking work . . . all while they lived it up large with women half their age in two thousand dollar a night suites.

My mouth firmed at that.

Was Aoife selling herself to the Senator?

The thought pissed me off.

I couldn't see why she'd do such a thing. Not when I'd looked into her finances, had seen just how secure she was. But maybe that was why. Maybe the Senator was funneling money to her.

The only problem was that the lot Aoife owned—did I mention it was owned outright? Yeah, that was enough to chafe my suspicions, too, considering she was only twenty-fucking-five years old—was a teashop in a small building in a questionable area of HK.

I mean, come on. I loved Hell's Kitchen. It was home. But fuck. Where she was? What kind of Senator would put his fancy piece in *that*?

My jaw clenched as I studied the Senator's and Aoife's smiling faces as they left the hotel. Separately, of course. But whatever they'd been doing together, it sure put a Cheshire Cat grin on their chops–that was for fucking sure. Jimmy being a dumbass, hadn't put the two together, had just remarked on the 'coincidence,' but I was no fool.

How did I know they were together in the hotel?

Jimmy had been trailing Aoife for four months—told you I was obsessive—and every third Tuesday, come rain or shine, this little routine had jumped out, and when Jimmy had picked up on the fact Davidson had been there each and every time, I'd gotten my hands dirty, bribed one of the hotel maids myself—and fuck, that had been hard. Turned out that place made even the maids sign NDA agreements, but everyone had a price—and I'd found out that my little obsession shared a suite with the old prick.

My fingers curled into fists as I stared at her. Butter wouldn't fucking melt. She was the epitome of innocence. Like a redheaded angel. Could she really be lifting her skirts for that old fucker? Just so she could own a teashop?

Something didn't make sense, and fuck, if that didn't intrigue me all the more.

Aoife Keegan had snared one of the biggest, nastiest sharks in Manhattan.

She just didn't know it yet.

***

Aoife

"We need more scones for tomorrow. I keep telling you four dozen isn't enough."

Lifting a hand at my waitress and friend, Jenny, I mumbled, "I know, I know."

"If you know, then why the hell don't you listen?" Jenny complained, making me grin.

"Because I'm the one who has to make them? Making half that again is just . . ." I sighed.

I loved my job.

I did.

I adored baking—my butt and hips attested to that fact—and making a career out of my passion was something every twenty-something hoped for. Especially in one of the most expensive cities in the world. But sheesh. There was only so much one person could do, and this was still, essentially, a one-woman-band.

With the threat of Acuig Corp looming over me, I didn't feel safe hiring extra staff. I'd held them off for close to six months now. Six months of them trying to tempt me to leave, to sell up. They'd raised their prices to ten percent above market value, whereas with everyone else in the building, they'd just offered what the apartments were truly worth. Considering this place wasn't the nicest in the block, that wasn't much.

Most people hadn't held out because, hell, why wouldn't they want to live elsewhere?

Those who were landlords hadn't felt any issue in tossing their tenants out on the street. The tenants grumbled, but when did they ever have any rights, anyway?

For myself, this was where my mom and I had worked to—

I brought that thought to a shuddering halt.

Mom was dead now.

I had to remember that. This was on me, not her.

My throat thickened with tears as I turned to Jenny and murmured, "I'll try better tomorrow."

The words had her frowning at me. "Babe, you know I'm not the boss here, right?"

Lips curving, I whispered, "I know. But you're so scary."

She snickered then peered down at herself. "Yeah, I bet I'd make grown men cry."

Maybe for a taste of her. . . .

Jenny was everything I wasn't.

She was slender, didn't dip her hand into the cookie jar at will—the woman had more willpower than I did hips, and my hips seemed to go on forever—and her face looked like it belonged on the cover of a fashion magazine. Even her hair was enough to inspire envy. It was black and straight as a ruler.

Mine?

Bright red and curly like a bitch. I had to straighten it out every morning if I didn't want to look like little orphan Annie.

I'd once read that curly-haired women straightened their hair for special events, and that straight-haired women curled theirs in turn, but I called bullshit.

Curly-haired women lived with their straightening irons surgically attached to their hands.

At least, I did.

My rat's nest was like a ginger afro. Maybe Beyoncé could make that work, but I sure as hell didn't have the bone structure.

"I think grown men would cry," I told her dryly, "if you asked them to."

She pshawed, but there was a twinkle in her eye that I understood. . . . She agreed with me, knew it was true, but wasn't going to admit it. With anyone else, she might have. She had an ego–that was for damn sure. But with me? I think she figured I was zero competition, so she felt no need to rub salt in the wound, too.

I plunked my elbows on the counter and stared around my domain as she bustled off and started clearing the tables. It was her last duty of the day, and my feet were aching so damn bad that I didn't even have it in me to care.

This owning your own business shit?

It wasn't easy.

Not saying I didn't love it, but it was hard.

I slept like four hours a night, and when I wasn't in bed, I was here. All the time.

Baking, cooking, serving, and smiling. Always smiling. Even if I was so sleep-deprived I could sob.

Jenny's actually a life saver.

My mom used to be front of house before. . . .

I sucked down a breath.

I had to get used to thinking about it.

She wasn't here anymore, but just avoiding all thoughts of her period wasn't working for me. It was like I was purposely forgetting her, and, well, fuck that.

She'd always wanted to have a teashop. It had been her one true dream. Back in Ireland, when she was a little girl, her grandmother had owned one in Limerick. Mom had caught the bug and had wanted to have one here in the States. But not only was it too fucking expensive for a woman on her own, it was also impossible with my feckless father at her side.

I didn't want to think about him either, though.

Why?

Because the feckless father who'd pretty much ruined my mother's life, wasn't the only father in my life. My biological dad hadn't exactly cared about her happiness, but once he'd come to know about me, he'd tried. That was more than could be said for the man who'd lived with me throughout my early childhood.

"You look gloomy."

Jenny's statement had me blinking in surprise. She had a ton of dishes piled in her arms, and I'd have worried for the expensive china if I hadn't known she was an old pro at this shit. Just as I was.

We could probably earn a Guinness World Record on how many dishes we could take back and forth to the kitchen of *Ellie's Tea Rooms*. I swear, I had guns because of all that hefting. My biceps were probably the firmest part of my body.

More's the pity.

I'd have preferred an ass you could bounce dimes off of, but, when it boiled down to it, there was no way in this universe I could live without cake.

Just wasn't going to happen.

My big butt wasn't going *anywhere* until scientists could make zero calorie eclairs and pies.

"I'm not glum."

"No? Then why are your eyes sad?"

Were they? I pursed my lips as I let the 'sad eyes' drift around the tea room. I wish I could say it was all forged on my own hard work, but it wasn't. Not really.

"I was just thinking about Mom."

"Oh, honey," Jenny said sadly, and she carefully placed all the dishes on the counter, so she could round it and curve her arm around my waist. "It was only seven months ago. Of course, you were thinking of her."

"I just—" I blew out a breath. "I don't know if I'm doing what she'd want."

"You can't live for her choices, sweetness. You have to do what you think is right for you."

I gnawed at my bottom lip again. "I-I know, but she was always there for me. A guiding light. With Fiona gone and her, too? I don't really know what I'm doing with myself."

This business wasn't something that made me want to get up on a morning. It was my mom's dream, her goal. Every decision I made, I tried to remember how she'd longed for a place like this, but it wasn't my passion. It was hers, and I was trying to keep that dream alive while fretting over the fact my heart wasn't in it.

"I think you're doing a damn fine job. You have a very successful teashop. Your cakes are raved about. Have you visited our TripAdvisor page recently? Or our Yelp?" She squeaked. "I swear, you're making this place a tourist hotspot. I don't think Fiona or Michelle could be more proud of you if they tried."

The baking shit, yeah, that was all on me, but the other stuff? The finances?

I'd caved in.

I'd caved where my mom had always refused in the past.

With the accident had come a lot of medical bills that I just hadn't been able to afford. Without her help, I'd had to take on extra staff, and out of nowhere, my expenses had added up.

Mom had been so proud of this place, so ferociously gleeful that we'd done it by ourselves, and yet, here I was, financially free for the first time in my life, and I still felt like I was drowning because my freedom went entirely against her wishes.

"Is this to do with Acuig? I know they're still pestering you."

Jenny's statement had me wincing. Acuig were the bottom feeders who wanted to snap up this building, demolish it, and then replace it with a skyscraper. Don't get me wrong, the building was foul, but a lot of people lived here, and the minute it morphed into some exclusive condo, no one from around here would be able to afford to live in it.

It would become yuppy central.

I'd rejected all their offers to buy my tea room even though I didn't want the damn thing, not really. Mostly I wanted to keep mom's goals alive and kicking, but also, it pissed me off the way Acuig were changing Hell's Kitchen. Ratcheting up prices, making it unaffordable for the everyday man and woman—the people I'd grown up with—and bringing a shit-ton of banker-wankers and 1%ers to the area.

So, maybe I'd watched Erin Brockovich a time or two as a kid and had a social conscience... Wasn't the worst thing to possess, right?

"Aoife?" Jenny stated, making me look over at her. "Is Acuig pressuring you?"

I winced, realizing I hadn't answered—Jenny was my friend, but she also worked here and relied on the paycheck. It wasn't fair of me to keep her hanging like that. "They upped the sales price. I guess that isn't helping," I admitted, frowning down at my hands.

Unlike Jenny who had her nails manicured, mine were cut neatly and plain. I had no rings on my fingers, and wore no watch or bracelets because my wrists were usually deep in flour or sugar bags.

I spent most of my life right where I wanted it—behind the shopfront. That had slowly morphed where I was doing double the work to compensate for Mom's loss.

Was it any wonder I was feeling a little out of my league?

I was coping without Fiona, grieving Mom, working without her, too, and then practically living in the kitchens here. I didn't exactly have that much of a life. I had nothing cheerful on the horizon, either.

Well, nothing except for next Tuesday, and that wasn't enough to turn my frown upside down.

The money was a temptation. I didn't need to sell up and start working on my own goals, but that just loaded me down with more guilt and made me feel like a really shitty daughter.

Jenny squeezed me in a gentle hug. But as I turned to speak to her, the bell above the door rang as it opened. We both jerked in surprise—each of us apparently thinking the other had locked up when neither of us had—and turned to face the entrance.

On the brink of telling the client we were closed for the day, my mouth opened then shut.

Standing there, amid the frilly, lacy curtains, was the most masculine man I'd ever seen in my life.

And I meant that.

It was like a thousand aftershave models had morphed into one handsome creature that had just walked through my door.

At my side, I could feel Jenny's 'hot guy radar' flare to life, and for once, I couldn't damn well blame her.

This guy was . . . well, he was enough to make me choke on my words and splutter to a halt.

The tea room was all girly femininity. It was sophisticated enough to appeal to businesswomen with its mauve, taupe, and cream-toned hues, and the ethereal watercolors that decorated the walls. But the tablecloths were lacy, and the china dishes and cake stands we used were the height of Edwardian elegance.

Moms brought their little girls here for their birthday, and high-powered executives spilled dirt on their lovers with their girlfriends over scones and clotted cream—breaking their diets as they discussed the boyfriends who had broken their hearts.

The man, whoever the hell he was, was dressed to impress in a navy suit with the finest pinstripe. It was close to a silver fleck, and I could see, even from this distance, that it was hand tailored. I'd seen custom tailoring before, and only a trained eye could get a suit cut so perfectly to this man's form.

With wide shoulders that looked like they could take the weight of the world, a long, lean frame that was enhanced by strong muscles evident through the close fit of his pants and jacket, then the silkiness of his shirt which revealed delineated abs when his bright gold and scarlet tie flapped as he moved, the guy was hot.

With a capital H.

"How can we help, sir?" Jenny purred, and despite my own awe, I had to dip my chin to hide my smile.

Even if I wanted to throw my hat into this particular man's game, there was no way he'd choose me over Jenny. Fuck, I'd screw her, and I wasn't even a lesbian. Not even a teensy bit bi. I'd gone shopping with her enough to have seen her ass, and I promise you, it's biteable.

So, nope. I didn't have a snowball's chance in hell of this Adonis seeing *me* when Jenny was in the room.

Yet. . . .

When I'd controlled my smile, I looked over at the man, and his focus was on me.

My breath stuttered to a halt.

Why wasn't his gaze glued to Jenny?

Why weren't those ice-white blue eyes fixated on my best friend's tits, which Jenny helpfully plumped up as she preened at my side?

For a second, I was so close to breaking out into a coughing fit, it was humiliating. Then, more humiliation struck in a quieter manner, but it was nevertheless rotten—I turned pink.

Now, you might think you know what a blush is. You might think you've even experienced it yourself a time or two. But I was a redhead. My skin made fresh milk look yellow, and even my fucking freckles were pale. Everything about me was like I'd been dunked into white wax.

But as the heat crawled over me, taking over my skin as the man looked at me without pause, I knew things had rarely been this dire.

See, with Jenny as a best friend, I was used to the attention going her way. I could hide in the background, hide in her shadow. I liked it there. I was comfortable there. Sometimes, on double dates, she'd drag me along, and even the guy supposed to be dating me would be gaping at Jenny. As pathetic as it was, I was so used to it, it didn't bother me.

But now?

I just wasn't used to being in the spotlight.

Especially not a man like this one's spotlight.

When you're a teenager, practicing with your mom's blush for the first time, you always look like a tomato that's been left out in the sun, right?

I was redder than that.

I could feel it. I could fucking feel the heat turning me tomato red.

When Jenny cleared her throat, I thanked God when it broke the man's attention. He shot her a look, but it wasn't admiring. It wasn't even impressed.

If anything, it was irritated.

Okay, so now both Jenny and I were stunned.

Fuck that, we were floored.

Literally.

Our mouths were doing a pretty good fish impression as the man turned back to look at me.

Shit, was this some kind of joke?

Was it April 1st and I'd just gotten the dates mixed up again?

"Ms. Keegan?"

Oh fuck. His voice.

Oh. My. God.

That voice.

It was. . . .

I had to swallow.

Did men even talk like that?

It was low and husky and raspy and made me think of sex, not just mediocre sex, but the best sex. Toe-curling, nails-breaking-in-the-sheets sex. Sex so fucking good you couldn't walk the next day. Sex so hot that it made my current core temperature look polar in comparison. Sex that I'd never been lucky to have before, so I pined for it in the worst way.

Jenny nudged me in the side when I just carried on gaping at the man. "Y-Yes. That's me." I cleared my throat, feeling nervous and stupid and flustered as I wiped my hands on my apron.

Sweet Jesus.

Was this man really looking for me while I was wearing a goddamn pinafore?

Even as practical as they were, I wanted to beg the patron saint of pinnies to remove it from me. To do something, anything, to make sure that this man didn't see me in the red gingham check that I always wore to cover up stains.

And then I felt it.

Jenny's hand.

Tugging at the knot.

I wanted to kiss her. Seriously. I wanted to give her a fucking raise! As I moved away from the counter and her side, the apron dropped to the floor as I headed for the man whose hand was now held out, ready for me to shake in greeting.

There are those moments in your life when you know you'll never forget them. They can be happy or sad, annoying or exhilarating. This was one of them.

As I slipped my hand into his, I felt the electric shocks down to my core. Meeting his gaze wasn't hard because I was stunned, and I needed to know if he'd felt that, too.

From the way those eyelids were shielding his icy-blue eyes, I figured he was just as surprised.

It was like a satisfied puma was watching me. One that was happy there was plump prey prancing around in front of him.

Shit.

Did I just describe myself as 'plump prey?'

And like that, my house of cards came tumbling down because what the hell would this man want with me?

I was seeing things.

God, I was so stupid sometimes.

I cleared my throat for, like, the fourth damn time, and asked, "I'm Ms. Keegan. You are?"

His smile, when it appeared, was as charming as the rest of him. His teeth were white, but not creepy, reality-TV-star white. They were straight except for one of his canines, which tilted in slightly. In his perfect face, it was one flaw that I almost clung to. Because with that wide brow, the hair so dark it looked like black silk that was cut closely to his head with a faint peak at his forehead, the strong nose, and even stronger jaw, I needed something imperfect to focus on.

Then, I sucked down a breath and remembered what Fiona had told me once upon a time. When I'd been nervous about asking Jamie Winters to homecoming, she'd advised me in her soft Irish lilt, "Lass, that boy takes a dump just like you do. He uses the bathroom twice a day and undoubtedly leaves a puddle on the floor for his ma to clean up. I bet he's puked a time or two as well. Had diarrhea and the good Lord only knows what else. Just you think that the next time you see that boy and want to ask him out."

Yeah. It was gross, but fuck, it had worked. Her advice had worked so well I hadn't asked anyone out because I could only think of them using the damn toilet!

Still, looking at this Adonis, there was no imagining *that*.

Surely, gods didn't use the bathroom.

Did they?

"The name's Finn. Finn O'Grady."

My eyes flared at the name.

No.

It couldn't be.

Finn O'Grady?

No. It wasn't a rare name, but it was a strong one. One that suited him, one that had always suited him.

I frowned up at him wondering, yet again, if this was a joke of some sort, but as he looked at me, *really* looked at me, I saw no recognition. Saw nothing on his features that revealed any ounce of awareness that I'd known him for years.

Well, okay, not *known*. But I'd known his mother. Our mothers had been best friends. And as I looked, I saw the same almond-shaped eyes Fiona had, the stubborn jaw, and that unmistakable butt-indent on his chin.

At the reminder of just how forgettable I was, my heart sank, and hurt whistled through me.

Then, I realized I was *still* holding his hand, and as he squeezed, the flush returned and I almost died of mortification.

FIFTY-TWO

FINN

GOD, she was perfect.

And when I said perfect, I meant it.

I'd fucked a lot of women. Redheads, blondes, brunettes, even the rare thing that is a natural head of black hair. None of them, not a single one, lit up like Aoife Keegan.

Her cheeks were cherry red and in the light camisole she wore, a cheerful yellow, I could see how the blush went all the way down to the upper curve of her breasts.

She'd go that color, I knew, when she came.

And fuck, I wanted to see that.

I wanted to see that perfectly pale flesh turn bright pink under my ministrations.

Even as I looked at her, all shy and flustered, I wondered if she was a screamer in bed.

Some of the shyest often were.

Maybe not at first, but after a handful of orgasms, it was a wonder what that could do to a woman's self-confidence, and Jesus, I wanted to *see* that, too. I wanted a seat at center stage.

My suit jacket was open, and I regretted it. Immensely. My cock was hard, had been since we'd shaken hands, and her fingers had clung to mine like a daughter would to her daddy's at her first visit to the county fair.

Fuck.

Squeezing her fingers wasn't intentional. If anything, I'd just liked the feel of her palm against mine, but when I put faint pressure on her, she jerked back like she'd been scalded.

Her cheeks bloomed with heat again, and she whispered, "Mr. O'Grady, what can I do for you?"

You can get on your fucking knees and sort out the hard-on you just caused.

That's what she could fucking do.

I almost growled at the thought because the image of her on her knees, my cock in her small fist, her dainty mouth opening to take the tip....

Shit.

That had to happen.

Here, too.

In this fancy, frilly, feminine place, I wanted to defile her.

Fuck, I wanted that so goddamn much, it was enough to make me reconsider my demolition plans.

I wanted to screw her against all this goddamn lace, which suited her perfectly. She was made for lace. And silk. Hell, silk would look like heaven against her skin. I wouldn't know where she ended and it began.

When her brow puckered, she dipped her chin, and that gorgeous wave of auburn hair slipped over her shoulder.

If we'd been alone, if that brassy bitch—who was staring at me like I could fuck her over the counter with her friend watching if I was game—wasn't here, I'd have grabbed that rope of hair, twisted it around my fingers, and forced her gaze up.

Some guys liked their women demure. And I was one of them. I wasn't about to lie. I liked that in her, but I wanted her eyes on me. Always.

It was enough to prompt me to bite out, "Can we speak privately?"

She jerked at my words, then as she licked her bottom lip, turned to look at the waitress. "Jenny, it's okay. I can handle the rest by myself. You get home."

Jenny, her gaze drifting between me and her boss, nodded. She retreated to a door that swung as she moved through the opening, and within seconds, she had her coat and purse over her arm.

As she sashayed past—for my benefit, I was sure—she murmured, "See you tomorrow, Aoife."

Aoife nodded and shot her friend a smile, but I wasn't smiling. There were dishes on every table. Plates and saucers and tea pots. Those fancy stands that made any man wonder if he could touch it without snapping it.

Aoife was going to clear all that herself? Not on my fucking watch.

When the bell rang as the waitress opened the door, I didn't take my eyes off her until it rang once more upon closing.

Aoife swallowed, and I watched her throat work, watched it with a hunger that felt alien to me, because, God, I wanted to see my bites on her. Wanted to see my marks on that pale column of skin and her tits.

Barely withholding a groan, I asked, "Do you often let your staff go when you still have a lot of work to do, so you can speak to a stranger?"

Her cheeks flushed again, and she took a step back. "I-I, you're not —" Flustered once more, she fell silent.

"I'm not what?" Curiosity had me asking the question. Whatever I'd expected her to say, it hadn't been that.

She cleared her throat. "N-Nothing. You wished to speak with me, Mr. O'Grady?"

My other hand tightened around my briefcase, and though seeing her had made my reason for being here all that more necessary, I was almost disappointed. There was a gentle warmth to those bright-green eyes that would die out when I told her my purpose for being here. And her innocent attraction to me would change, morph into something else.

But I could only handle *something else*.

Some men were made for forever.

But those men weren't in my line of business.

I moved away from her, pressing my briefcase to one of the few empty tables. I wasn't happy about her having to do all the clearing up later on, and wondered if Paul, my PA, would know who to call to get her some help.

There was no way I was spending the rest of the night alone in my bed, my only companion my fist wrapped around my cock.

No way, no fucking how.

I paid Paul enough for him to come and clear the fucking place on his own if he couldn't find someone else.

I wanted Aoife on her knees, bent over my goddamn bed, and I was a man who always got what he wanted.

In this jungle, I was the lion, and Aoife? She was my prey.

I keyed in the code and opened my briefcase. The manila envelope was large and thick, well-padded with my documentation of Aoife's every move for the past few months.

It had started off as a legitimate move.

I'd wanted to know her weaknesses, so I could put pressure on her and make her cave to my demands.

Now, my demands had changed. I didn't just want her to sell the tea room we were standing in, I wanted her in my bed.

Fuck, I wanted that more than I wanted to make Aidan Sr. a fucking profit, and Aidan's profit and my balls still being attached to my body ran hand in hand.

Aidan was an evil cunt.

If I failed to deliver, he'd take it out on me. Whether I was his idea of an adopted son or not, he'd have done the same to his blood sons.

Well, he wouldn't have taken their balls. The man, for all his psychotic flaws, was obsessed with the idea of grandchildren, of passing it all on to the next generation. He'd cut his boys though. Without a doubt.

I knew Conor had marks on his back from a beating he refused to speak about. Then there was Brennan. He had a weak wrist because his father had a habit of breaking *that* wrist.

Without speaking, I grabbed the envelope and passed it to her.

She frowned down at it and asked, "For me?"

I smiled at her. "Open it."

"What is it?"

"Leverage."

That had her eyes flaring wide as she pulled out some of the photos. A gasp fell from her lips as she grabbed the photos when she spotted herself in them, jerking so hard the envelope tore. Some of the pictures spilled to the ground, but I didn't care about that.

Leaning back against one of the dainty tables once I was satisfied it would take my weight, I watched her cheeks blanch, all that delicious color dissipating as she took in everything the photos revealed.

"Y-You've been stalking me. Why?"

The question was high-pitched, loaded down with panic. I'd heard it often enough to recognize it easily.

I didn't get involved in wet work anymore. That wasn't my style, but along the way, to reach this point, I'd had no choice but to get my hands dirty. Panic was part of the job when you were collecting debts for the Irish Mob. And the Five Points were notorious for Aidan Sr.'s temper.

He wasn't the first patriarch. If anything, his grandfather was the founder. But Aidan Sr. was the type of guy that if you didn't pay him back, he didn't give a fuck about the money, he cared about the lack of respect.

See, you owed the mob and didn't pay? They'd send heavies around, beat the shit out of you, and threaten to do the same to your family, and usually, that did the trick. You didn't kill the cash cow.

Aidan Sr.?

He didn't give a fuck about the cash cow.

Only the truly desperate thought about borrowing money from Aidan, because if you didn't pay it back, he'd take your teeth, and your fingers and toes as a first warning. Then, if you still didn't pay—and most did—it was death.

Respect meant a lot to Aidan.

And fuck, if it wasn't starting to mean a lot to me. The panic in her voice made my cock throb.

I wanted this woman weak and willing.

I wanted it more than I wanted my next breath.

Ignoring her, I reached for my phone and tapped out a message to Paul.

Need housekeeping crew to clean this place.

I attached my live location, saw the blue ticks as Paul read the message—he knew better than to ignore my texts, whatever time of day they came—and he replied: *Sure thing.*

That was the kind of reply I was used to getting. Not just from Paul, but from everyone.

There were very few people who weren't below me in the strata of Five Points, and I'd worked my ass off to make that so.

The only people who ranked above me included Aidan Jr. and his brothers, Aidan Sr. of course, and then maybe a handful of his advisors that he respected for what they'd done for him and the Points over the years.

But the money I made Aidan Sr.?

That blew most of their 'advice' out of the window.

The reason Aidan had a Dassault Falcon executive private plane?

Because I was, as the City itself called me, a whiz kid.

I'd made my first million—backed by the Points, of course—at twenty-two.

Fifteen years later?

I'd made him hundreds of millions.

My own personal fortune was nothing to sniff at, either.

"W-Why have you done this?" Aoife asked, her voice breathy enough to make me wonder if she sounded like that in the sack.

"Because you've been a very stubborn little girl."

Her eyes flared wide. "Excuse me?"

I reached into the inside pocket of my suit coat and pulled out a business card. "For you," I prompted, offering it to her.

When she turned it over, saw the logo of five points shaped into a star, then read Acuig—in the Gaelic way, ah-coo-ig, not a butchered American way, ah-coo-ch—aloud, I watched her throat work as she swallowed.

"I-I should have realized with the Irish name," she whispered, the muscles in her brow twitching as she took in the chaos of the scattered photos on the floor.

Watching her as she dropped the contents on the ground, so she was surrounded by them, I tilted my head to the side, taking her in as her panic started to crest.

"I-I won't sell." Her first words surprised me.

I should have figured, though. Everything about this woman was surprisingly delicious.

"You have no choice," I purred. "As far as I'm aware, the Senator has a wife. He also has a reputation to protect. I'm not sure he'd be happy if any of those made it onto the *National Enquirer's* front page. Not when he's just trying to shore up his image to take a run for the White House next election."

She reached up and clutched her throat. The self-protective gesture was enough to make me smile at her—I knew what the absence of hope looked like.

There'd been a time when that had been my life, too.

"But, on the bright side," I carried on, "this can all be wiped away if you sell." As her gaze flicked to mine, I added, "As well as if you do something for me."

For a second, she was speechless. I could see she knew what that *something* was. Had my body language given it away? Had there been a certain raspiness to my tone?

I wasn't sure, and frankly, didn't give a fuck.

There was a little hiccoughing sound that escaped her lips, and she frowned at me, then down at herself.

"Is this a joke?"

"Do I look like I'm the kind of guy who jokes, Aoife?" Fuck, I loved saying her name.

The Gaelic notes just drove me insane.

Ee-Fah.

Nothing like the spelling, and all the more complicated and delicious for it.

"N-No," she confirmed, "but . . ."

"But what?" I prompted.

"I mean . . . you just can't be serious."

"Oh, but I am." I grinned. "Deadly. You've wasted a lot of my time, Aoife Keegan. A lot. Do you think I'm normally involved in negotiations of this level?"

Her eyes whispered over me, and I felt the loving caress of her gaze as she took in each and every inch of me. When she licked her lips, I knew she liked what she saw. I didn't really care, but it was helpful for her to be eager in some small way—especially when coercion was involved.

Aidan had called it bribery. I preferred 'coercion'. It sounded far kinder.

"No. That suit alone probably cost the mortgage payment on this place."

I nodded—she wasn't wrong. I knew what she'd been paying as rent, then as a mortgage, before some kind *benefactor* had paid it all off. Free and clear.

"I had to get my hands dirty, and while I might like some things dirty . . .," I trailed off, smirking when she flushed. "So, as I see it, we have a problem. I want this building. You don't want anyone to know you're having an affair with a Senator. Or, should I say, the Senator doesn't want anyone to know he's having an affair with someone young enough to be his daughter . . ."

If my voice turned into a growl at that point, then it was because the notion of her spreading her legs for that old bastard just turned my stomach.

Fuck, this woman, the thoughts she made me think.

Because I was startled at the possessive note to my growl, I ran a hand over my head. I kept my hair short for a reason—ease. I wasn't the kind of man who wasted time primping. It was an expensive cut, so I didn't have to do anything to it. Even mussing it up had it falling back into the same sleek lines as before—a man in my position had to look pristine under pressure. And very few people could even begin to understand the kind of strain I was under.

The formation of igneous rock had less volcanic pressure than Aidan Sr.

She licked her lips as she stared down at the photos, then back up at me. "And you want me to sell the place to you, even though this is my livelihood and the livelihood of all my staff, and then sleep with you?"

Her squeaky voice, putting suspicion into words, had me crossing my legs at the ankle. "We wouldn't be doing much sleeping."

Another shaky breath soughed from her lips, then, those beautiful pillowy morsels that would look good around my cock, quivered.

"This is crazy," she whispered shakily.

"As far as I'm concerned, all of this could be avoided if you'd just sold to me a few months back. Now you have to pay for my time wasted on this project."

"By spreading my legs?"

Another squeak. I tsked at her question, but in truth, I was annoyed at her using those same words I had to describe her with that old hypocrite of a Senator.

I didn't move, though. Didn't even flex my arms in irritation, just murmured, "Small price to pay. And, even though it's ten percent above market price, I'll stick to the last offer Acuig gave you. Can't say anything's fairer than that."

She shook her head, and there was a desperation to the gesture as she cried, "I need this business. You don't understand—"

"I understand that some very powerful and very dangerous businessmen want this building demolished. I understand that those same powerful and dangerous men want a skyscraper taking up this plot of land. I understand that a four hundred million dollar project isn't going to be put on hiatus because one small Irish woman doesn't want to go out of business . . ." I cocked a brow at her. "You think I'm coming in hot and heavy? These kinds of men, Aoife, they're not the sort you fuck around with.

"Take my check, and my other offer, before you or the people you care about are threatened." I got to my feet and straightened my jacket out. "This suit? These shoes? That briefcase and this watch? I own them because I'm damn good at what I do. I'm a financial advisor, Aoife. Take my word for it. You're getting the best deal out of this."

She staggered back, the counter stopping her from crumpling to the floor. "You'd hurt me?"

"Not me," I repudiated. Not in the way she thought, anyway. "But the men I work for?"

Her gaze dropped to the one thing she'd retained in her hand—my card. "Acuig," she whispered. "Five in Gaelic."

My brows twitched in surprise. She knew Gaelic?

"The Five Points." Her eyes flared wide with terror. "They're behind this deal."

I hadn't expected her to put one and one together, but now that she had? It worked to my advantage.

Nodding, I told her, "Any minute now, there'll be a team of housekeepers coming in here to clear up for the night." When she gaped at me, I retrieved the contract from my briefcase, slapped it on the table, and handed her a pen as I carried on, "I suggest you let tonight be your last night of business."

What I didn't tell her, was that my suggestions weren't wasted words. They were like the law.

You didn't break them, and, like any lawmaker, I expected immediate obeisance.

***

Aoife

SO, the beautiful man just happened to be an absolute cocksucker of a bastard.

Still, this couldn't be real, could it?

The dick could have anyone he wanted. Jesus, Jenny was panting after him like a dog in heat. She would have gone out with him if he'd so much as clicked his fingers at her.

But he'd had eyes for me.

Like he wanted me.

He thought he'd bought me. Or, at least, bought my silence, and yeah, to some extent he had. But . . . why buy me, why not just drop the price on the building if he wanted me to pay for the time he'd wasted on me?

The arrogance imbued in those words was enough to make me pull my hair out, but that was inwardly. I was a redhead. I had a temper. But that temper was mostly overshadowed by fear.

Senator Alan Davidson wasn't my boyfriend, my lover, as this dick seemed to believe. He was my father, and as Finn O'Grady had correctly surmised, he was aiming for the White House.

How could I put that in jeopardy?

My dad was a good man. He'd made a mistake one summer when he'd come home from college, one that only some careful digging by his campaign manager had uncovered. Dad himself hadn't known of my existence, not until his CM had gone hunting for any nasty secrets that could come out and bite him in the ass.

This had been five years ago when he'd run for Senator. Now, Dad's goal was the presidential seat, and I wasn't going to be the one who put a wrench in the works.

When Garry Smythe had approached me back then, I'd thought he was joking. I was out on the street, heading home from work. At the side of me, a black car had driven in from the lane of traffic, just to park, or so I'd thought. As he'd held out his hand with a card, one of the car doors had opened up, and I'd been 'invited' inside.

Had I been scared?

At first.

But when Garry had told me my country needed me, I hadn't been sure whether to laugh or tell him to fuck off. He hadn't shuffled me into the car, though, hadn't tried to coerce me. He'd just asked if I'd voted for Senator Alan Davidson in the elections, and because he was one of the only politicians out there who wasn't a complete douche, and that was the name printed on the card in my hand, I'd shuffled into the back of the car.

Where the Senator himself had been sitting.

Now, when I thought about that day, I realized how fucking naive I'd been to get into the back of a limo for such a vague reason. But I'd been fortunate. Alan *had* been waiting for me. Waiting to tell me a story that still shook me to my core.

I'd made a promise to my dad that I wouldn't tell anyone. He'd offered me money, and I hadn't accepted it. I guess I should have, but back then, I'd been haughty and proud, and because the good guy I'd thought him to be hadn't been so good when he tried to buy my silence, I'd told him to fuck off. I'd been disappointed in him, frightened by the lifelong lie I'd been living, and equally hurt that the man who'd sired me was just concerned that I was a threat to his campaign.

I'd walked out of that car never expecting to see my dear old Dad ever again.

Then, the day after he'd been elected, he'd been sitting in the booth of the cafe where I worked part-time to get me through culinary school.

Seeing him, I'd almost handed that table off to one of the other waitresses, but I hadn't. Not when every time I'd passed the table, he'd caught my eye, a patient smile on his lips, one that said he'd wait for me all day if he had to.

Ever since that second meeting, I'd been catching up with him every three weeks.

And this bastard thought he could use our limited time together against my father? The one politician who could make a difference in the White House? One who didn't have Big Oil up his ass, a pharmaceutical company sucking his dick, or any other kind of corporation so far up his rectum that he was a walking, talking lie?

No.

That wasn't going to happen.

Which meant I was going to have to sleep with this stranger.

Before this conversation, hell, that hadn't been too disturbing a prospect. Because, dayum, what woman wouldn't want to sleep with this guy?

Even with an ego as big as his, he was delicious. Better than any cake I could bake, that was for fucking sure.

More than that, I knew him.

And I now knew that the life Fiona would never have wanted for her son was one he'd been drawn into.

The Mob.

The Five Points were notorious in these parts. Everyone was scared of them. I paid protection money to them, for God's sake. I knew to be scared of them, and having been raised in their territory, it was the height of stupidity to think paying them wasn't just a part of business.

Still, Fiona had never wanted that for Finn, and her Finn was the same as the one standing before me here today. In my tea room, which looked far too small to contain the might of this man.

She'd be so disappointed. So heart-sore to know that he was up to his neck in dirty dealings with the Five Points, and as he'd pointed out, the cost of his shoes, his clothes, and his jewelry, was enough to speak for itself.

If he wasn't high up the ladder in the gang, then I wasn't one of the best bakers of scones in the district.

Like Jenny had said, I had five star ratings across most social media platforms for a reason. I was good. But apparently, this man wasn't.

Before I could utter a word, before I could even cringe at how utterly sorrowful Fiona would be about this turn of events—not just about the Five Points but what her son was making me do—the door clattered open.

Like he'd predicted, a team of people swarmed in.

Finn motioned to the floor. "Want anyone to see those?"

With a gasp, I dropped to my knees and collected the shots, stuffing them back into the envelope with a haste that wasn't exactly practical.

Two shiny shoes appeared before me, followed by two expensively clad legs, and I peered up at him, wondering what he was about. He held out his hand, but I clasped the photos to my chest.

"You're making more of a mess than anything else, Aoife." His voice was raspy, his eyes weighted down by heavy lids.

For a second, I wondered why, then I saw *why*.

He had an erection.

An erection?

I peered around at the staff, but they were all men. Not a single woman in sight, well, save for the seventy-year-old with a clipboard who was barking out orders to the guys in what sounded like Russian.

So that meant, what?

The erection was for me?

The blush, the dreaded, hated blush, made another goddamn

appearance, and to cover it, I ducked my head, then pushed the photos and the envelope at him.

For whatever reason, I stayed where I was, staring up at him as he calmly, coolly, and so fucking collectedly pushed the photos back into the torn envelope—it was some coverage. Better than none at all, I figured.

Being down here was. . . .

Hell, I don't know what it was.

To be looked at like that?

For his body to respond to me like that?

It was unprecedented.

I'd had one sexual experience with a boy back in college, and that had not gone according to plan. So much so I was still technically a fucking virgin because, and this was no lie, the guy had *zero* understanding of a woman's body.

Craig had spent more time fingering my perineum than my clit, and every time he'd tried to shove his dick into me, he'd somehow managed to drag it down toward my ass.

I'd gotten so sick of him frigging the wrong bits of me, that I'd pushed him off and given him a blowjob. It had been the quickest way to get out of that annoying situation.

Yeah, annoying.

Jenny, when I'd told her, had pissed herself laughing, and ever since, had tried to get me to hook up with randoms, so I could slough off my virginity like it was dead skin and I was a snake. But life had just always gotten in the way, and I'd had no time for men.

Shortly after *that* had happened, we'd lost Fiona. Then, I'd graduated, and after, Mom and I had set up this place thanks to some insurance money she'd come into after her husband had died. It had been crazy building the tea room into an established cafe, and then mom had passed on, too.

So, here I was. Still a virgin. On my knees in front of the sexiest man on Earth, a man I knew, a man whose mother had half raised me, one who wanted me in his bed as some kind of blackmail payment.

Was this a dream?

Seriously?

I mean, I'd been depressed before Finn O'Grady had walked through my doors. Now I wasn't sure whether to be apoplectic or worried as fuck because he wasn't wrong: you didn't mess with the Five Points.

God, if I'd known they'd been behind the development on this building, I'd have probably signed over months ago.

The Points were. . . .

I shuddered.

Vindictive.

Aidan O'Donnelly was half-evil genius and half-twisted sociopath. St. Patrick's Church, two streets away, had the best roof in the neighborhood and the strongest attendance because Aidan, for all he'd cut you into more pieces than a butcher, was a devout Catholic. His men knew better than to avoid Sunday service, and I reckoned that Father Doyle was the busiest priest in the city because of Five Points' attendance.

"I like you down there," he murmured absentmindedly.

The words weren't exactly dirty, but the meaning? They had my temperature soaring.

Shit.

What the hell was I doing?

Enjoying the way this man was victimizing me?

It was so wrong, and yet, what was standing right in front of me? I knew he'd know what to do with that thing tucked behind his pants.

He wouldn't try to penetrate my urethra—yes, you read that right. Craig had tried to fuck my pee-hole! Like, *why*?

Finn?

He oozed sex appeal.

It seemed to seep from every pore, perfuming the air around me with his pheromones.

I hadn't even believed in pheromones until I scented Finn O'Grady's delicious essence.

It reminded me of the one out of town vacation we'd ever had. We'd gone to Cooperstown, and I'd scented a body of water that didn't have corpses floating in it—Otsego Lake. He reminded me of that. So green and earthy. It was an attack on my overwhelmed senses, an attack I didn't need.

With the envelope in his hand, he held out his other for me. When I placed my fingers in his, the size difference between us was noticeable once more.

I was just over five feet, and he was over six. I was round and curvy, and he was hard and lean.

It reminded me of the nursery tale Mom had sung to me as a child —Jack Sprat could eat no fat, and his wife could eat no lean.

Did it say a lot for my confidence that I couldn't seem to take it in that he wanted *me*? Or was it simply that I wasn't understanding how anyone could prefer me over Jenny?

Even my mom had called Jenny beautiful, whereas she'd kissed me on the nose and called me her 'bonny lass.'

Biting my lip, I accepted his help off the floor. My black jeans weren't the smartest thing for the tea room, but I didn't actually serve that many dishes, just bustled around behind the counter, working up the courage to do what Mom had done every day—greet people.

I wasn't a sociable person. I preferred my kitchen to the front of house, hence the jeans, but I regretted not wearing something else today. Something that covered just how big my ass was, how slender my waist *wasn't*.

Ugh.

This man is blackmailing you into his bed, Aoife. For Christ's sake, you're not supposed to be worrying if he likes the goods, too!

Still, no matter how much I tried, years of inadequacy weighed me down as I wiped off my knees.

"Do you have a coat?" he asked, and his voice was raspy again. "A jacket? Or a purse?"

I nodded at him but kept my gaze trained on the floor. "Yes."

"Go get them."

His order had me shuffling my feet toward the kitchen, but as I approached the door, I heard his strong voice speaking with the old woman with the clipboard: "I want this all cleaned up and boxed. Take it to my storage lot in Queens."

With my back to him, I stiffened at his brisk orders. *Was I just going to let him do this? Get away with it?*

My shoulders immediately sagged.

Did I have a choice?

If it was just him, just Acuig, then I'd fight this, as I'd been fighting it since the building had come to the attention of the developer. But this wasn't a regular business deal.

This was mob business, and it seemed like somehow, I'd become a part of that.

FML.

Seriously, FML.

FIFTY-THREE

FINN

SHE WASN'T AS fiery as I imagined.

Did that disappoint me?

Maybe.

Then I had to chide myself because, Jesus, the woman had just been *coerced* out of her business. What did I expect? For her to be popping open a champagne bottle after I'd forced her to sign over her building to me?

Sure, she'd made a nice and tidy profit on her investment—I hadn't screwed her that way. But this morning, she'd gone into work with a game plan in mind, and tonight? Well, tonight she was out of a job and knee deep in a deal with the devil.

Of course, she hadn't actually agreed to my other terms, but when I guided her out of the tea room and toward my waiting car, she didn't falter.

Didn't utter a peep.

Just climbed into the vehicle, neatly tucked her knees together, and waited for me to get in beside her.

Like the well-oiled team my chauffeur and car were, they set off the minute I'd clicked my seatbelt.

The privacy screen was up, and I knew how soundproofed it was—

not because of technology, but because Samuel knew not to listen to any of the murmurs he might hear back here.

And if he was ever to share the most innocent of those whispers he might have discerned? We both knew I'd slice off his fucking ear.

This was a hard world. One we'd both grown up in, so we knew how things rolled. Samuel had it pretty easy with me, and he wasn't about to fuck up this job when he was so close to retirement. If he kept his mouth shut, did as I asked, ignored what he may or may not have heard, and drove me wherever the fuck I wanted to go, Sam knew I'd set him and his missus up somewhere nice in Florida. Near the beach, so the moaning old bastard's knees didn't give him too much trouble in his dotage.

See?

I wasn't all bad.

Rapping my fingers against my knee, I studied her, and I made no bones about it.

Her face was tilted down, and it let me see the longest lashes I'd ever come across on a woman. Well, natural ones. Those fucking false ones that fell off on my sheets were just irritating. But as with everything, Aoife was all natural.

So pure.

So fucking perfect.

Jesus, Mary, and Joseph.

She was a benediction come to life.

I wasn't as devout as Aidan Sr. would like me to be, but even I felt uncomfortable thinking such thoughts while sporting a hard-on that made me ache. That made my mental blasphemy even worse.

"Why did you let him touch you? Was it for money?"

I hadn't meant to ask that question.

Really, I hadn't.

It was the last thing I wanted to know, but like poison, it had spewed from my lips.

Who she'd fucked and who she hadn't, was none of my goddamn affair.

This was a business deal. Nothing more, nothing less. She'd fuck me to make sure I kept quiet, and I fucked her so I could revel in the copious curves this woman had to offer.

Simple, no?

She stiffened at the question, and I couldn't blame her. "Do I really have to answer that?"

I could have made her. It was on the tip of my tongue to force her to, but I didn't really want to know even if, somewhere deep down, I did.

"You know why you're here, don't you?" I asked instead of replying.

Her nostrils flared. "To keep silent."

I nodded and almost smiled at her because, internally she was furious, but equally, she was lost. I could sense that like a shark could scent blood in the water. This had thrown her for a loop, and she was in shock, but she was, underneath it all, angry.

Good.

I wanted to fuck her tonight when she was angry.

Spitting flames at me, taking her outrage out on me as she scratched lines of fire down my spine as she screamed her climax....

I almost shuddered at how well I'd painted that mental picture.

"When you're ready, you have my card."

"Ready for what?" she asked, perplexed. Her brow furrowed as she, for the first time since she'd climbed into the car, looked over at me.

"To make another tea room. I've had them move all the stuff into storage."

She licked her lips. "I want to say that's kind of you, but I'm in this predicament because of you."

A corner of my mouth hitched at that. "Honestly, be grateful I was the one who came knocking today. You wouldn't want any of the Five Points' men around that place. Half that china would be on the floor now."

Her shoulders drooped. "I know."

"You do?"

"I pay them protection money," she snapped. "Plus, I grew up around enough Five Pointers to know the score."

That statement targeted my curiosity, hard. "You did, huh? Whereabouts?"

Her mouth pursed. "Nowhere you'd know," she muttered under her breath.

"I doubt it. This is my area, too."

She turned to me, and the tautness around her eyes reminded me of something, but even as it flashed into being, the memory disappeared as I drowned in her emerald green eyes. "Why are you doing this?"

"Why do you think?" I retorted. "You're a beautiful woman—"

"Don't pretend like you couldn't have any woman under you if you asked them."

I wanted to smile, but I didn't because I knew, just as Aidan had pointed out to me earlier that day, that Aoife wasn't exactly what society considered on trend.

She'd have suited the glorious Titian era. She was a Raphaelite, a gorgeous and vivacious Aphrodite.

She wasn't slender. Her butt bounced, and when I fucked her, I'd have some meat to slam into, and her hips would be delicious handholds to grab.

If I smiled, I'd confirm that I was mocking her, and though I was a bastard, and though I was enough of a cunt to blackmail her into this when it hadn't been necessary—after all, before I'd told her who I was, I could have asked her out and done this normally—there was no way I was going to knock this glorious creature's confidence.

"Some men like slim and trim gym bunnies, some men like curves." I shrugged. "That's how it works, isn't it?"

Her eyes flared at that. "But Jenny—"

"Would you prefer she be here with me?" I asked dryly, amused when she flushed.

"Of course not. I wouldn't want her to be in this position."

I laughed. "Nicely phrased."

"What's that supposed to mean?"

Leaning forward, I grabbed her chin and forced her to look at me. "It's supposed to mean that you can fight this all you fucking want, but deep down, you're glad you're here. Your little cunt is probably sopping wet, and it's dying for a taste of my dick. So, simmer down. We're almost at my apartment."

And with that, I dipped my chin, and opening my mouth, raked my teeth down her bottom lip before I bit her. Hard enough to make her moan.

***

Aoife

THE STING of pain should have had me rearing back.

It didn't.

It felt. . . .

I almost shuddered.

Good.

It had felt good.

The way he'd done it. So fucking cocky, so fucking sure of himself, and who could blame him? He'd taken what he wanted, and I hadn't pulled away because he was right. My pussy *was* wet, and even though this was all kinds of wrong, I did want to feel him there. To have his cock push inside me.

Jesus, this was way too early for Stockholm syndrome, right?

I mean, this was . . . what was it?

It couldn't be that I was so horny and desperate for male attention that I was willingly allowing this to happen, was it?

Fuck. How pathetic was I if that was true? And yet, I didn't feel desperate for anything other than more of that small taste Finn had given me.

As a little girl, I'd watched Finn. It had been back in the day when his old man had been around and Fiona had lived with her husband and son. He'd beaten her up something rotten. Barely a week went by when Fiona, my mom's friend, didn't appear with some badly made-up bruise on her face.

I was young, only two, but old enough to know something wasn't right. I'd even asked my mom about it, wanting to understand why someone would do that to another person.

I couldn't remember what my mother had said, but I could remember how sad she'd been.

For all his faults, my dipshit stepfather had never beaten her, he'd just taken all her tips for himself and spent every night getting drunk.

Well, Finn's dad had been the same, except where mine passed out on the decrepit La-Z-Boy in front of the TV, Gerry had taken out his drunk out on Fiona.

And eventually, Finn.

Even as a boy, in the photos Fiona kept of him, Finn had been beautiful.

I could see him now, deep in my mind's eye. His hair had been as coal dark then as it was now, and not even a hint of silver or gray marred the noir perfection. His jaw and nose had grown, obviously, but they were just as obstinate as I remembered. Fiona had always said Finn was hardheaded.

When I was little, I hadn't had a crush on him—I'd been a toddler, for God's sake—but I'd been in awe of him. In awe of the big boy who'd been all arms and legs, just waiting for his growth spurt. Sadly, when that had happened, he'd disappeared.

As had his father.

Overnight, Fiona had gone from having a full house to an empty nest, and my mom had comforted her over the loss of her boy.

To my young self, I'd thought he'd died.

Genuinely. The way Fiona had mourned him? It had been as though both men had passed on, except we'd never had to go to church for a service, and there'd been no wake.

As kids do, I'd forgotten him. I'd been two when he'd disappeared, so I only really remembered that Fiona was a mom and that she was grieving.

We'd barely spoken his name because it could set her off into bouts of tears that would have my mom pouring tea down her gullet as they talked through her feelings.

As time passed, those little scenes in our crappy kitchen stopped, yet Fiona hung around our place so much it was like her second home.

One day, my stepfather died in an accident at work. The insurance paid out, Fiona moved in with us, and Mom had started scheming as to how to make her dream of owning a tea room come true. With Fiona living in, I'd heard Finn's name more often, but the notion he was dead still rang true.

Yet, here he was.

Finn wasn't dead.

He was very much alive.

Had Fiona known that?

Had she?

I wasn't sure what I hoped for her.

Was it better to believe your son was dead, or that your son didn't give enough of a fuck about you to contact you for years?

I gnawed on my bottom lip at the thought and accidentally raked over the tissue where Finn had bitten earlier.

"We're almost there," the man himself grated out, and I could sense he was pissed because the phone had buzzed, and whatever he'd been reading had a storm cloud passing behind his eyes.

"O-Okay," I replied, hating the quiver in my voice, but also just hating my situation.

This was. . . .

It was too much.

How was it that I was sitting here?

This morning, I'd owned a tea room. Now, I didn't.

This morning, I'd been exhausted, depressed about my mom, and *feeling* lost.

Now?

I was the *epitome* of lost.

A man was going to use me for sex, for Christ's sake.

But all I could think was: *did I still have my hymen?*

God, would he be angry if he had to push through it?

Should I tell him?

If I did, it would be for my benefit, not his, and why the hell was I thinking like this? I should be trying to convince him that normal people did not work business deals out by bribing someone into bed.

But, deep down, I knew all my scattered thinking was futile.

I wasn't dealing with normal people here.

I was dealing with a Five Pointer.

A high ranking one at that.

It was like dealing with a Martian. To average, everyday folk, a Five Pointer was just outside of their knowledge banks.

Sure, they thought they knew what they were like because they watched *The Wire* or some other procedural show, but they didn't.

Real-life gangsters?

They were larger than life.

They throbbed with violence, and hell, a part of me knew that Finn was cutting me some slack by asking to sleep with me.

Yeah, as fucked up as that was, it was the truth.

He could have asked for so much more.

He'd have a Senator in his pocket, and to the mob, what else would they ask for if not that?

Yet Finn?

He just wanted to fuck me.

My throat felt tight and itchy from dryness. I wanted some water so badly, but equally, I wasn't sure if it would make me puke.

Not at the thought of sex with this man—a part of me knew I'd enjoy it too much to even be nervous.

No, at what else he could ask of me, that had me fretting.

Was this a one-time deal?

How could I protect my dad from the Five Points when . . .?

I shuddered because there was nothing I could do. There was no way I could even broach any of those questions since I wasn't in charge here.

Finn was.

Finn always would be until he deemed I'd paid my dues. Whether that was tomorrow or two years down the line.

Shit, it might even be forever. If my dad hit the White House, only God knew what kind of leverage Finn could pull if my father tried to carry on covering up my existence. . . .

"We're here."

Something had *definitely* pissed him off.

He'd gone from the cat who'd drank a carton full of cream, to a pissed off tabby scrounging for supper in the trash.

"We're going to go through to the private elevator, and I'm going to head straight down the hall to my living room. You're going to slip into the first door on the right—that's my bedroom."

"O-Okay," I told him, wondering what the hell was going on.

"You're going to stay quiet, and you're going to try to not hear any fucking thing I say, do you hear me?"

"I hear you."

"You'd better," he ground out, his hand tightening around his cellphone. "Coming to Aidan O'Donnelly's attention is the last thing a little mouse like you wants."

A shiver ran through me.

Aidan O'Donnelly was in his apartment?

Fuck, just how high up the ranks was he?

CONTINUE
THE FIVE POINTS' MOB COLLECTION
HERE:
www.books2read.com/FilthySerenaAkeroyd

CONTINUE
A DARK & DIRTY SINNERS' MC SERIES
HERE:
www.books2read.com/MaverickSerenaAkeroyd

READING ORDER

WHILE THE SERIES ARE SEPARATE, you might enjoy reading The Five Points' Mob Collection and the Satan's Sinners' MC series in this order:

FILTHY
NYX
LINK
FILTHY RICH
SIN
STEEL
FILTHY DARK
CRUZ
MAVERICK
FILTHY SEX
HAWK

UNIVERSE READING ORDER

FILTHY
NYX
LINK
FILTHY RICH
SIN
STEEL
FILTHY DARK
CRUZ
MAVERICK
FILTHY SEX
HAWK
FILTHY HOT
STORM
THE DON
THE LADY
FILTHY SECRET (COMING NOVEMBER 2021)

FREE BOOK!

Don't forget to grab your free e-Book!
Secrets & Lies is now free!

Meg's love life was missing a spark until she discovered her need to be dominated. When her fiancé shared the same kink, she thought all her birthdays had come at once, and then she came to learn their relationship was one big fat lie.

Gabe has loved Meg for years, watching her from afar, and always wishing he'd been the one to date her first and not his brother. When he has the chance to have Meg in his bed—even better, tied to it—it's an opportunity he can't refuse.

With disastrous consequences.

Can Gabe make Meg realize she's the one woman he's always wanted? But once secrets and lies have wormed their way into a relationship, is it impossible to establish the firm base of trust needed between lovers, and more importantly, between sub and Sir…?

This story features orgasm control in a BDSM setting.
Secrets & Lies is now free!

CONNECT WITH SERENA

For the latest updates, be sure to check out my website! But if you'd like to hang out with me and get to know me better, then I'd love to see you in my Diva reader's group where you can find out all the gossip on new releases as and when they happen. You can join here: www.facebook.com/groups/SerenaAkeroydsDivas. Or you can always PM or email me. I love to hear from you guys: serenaakeroyd@gmail.com.

ABOUT THE AUTHOR

I'm a romance novelaholic and I won't touch a book unless I know there's a happy ending. This addiction is what made me craft stories that suit my voracious need for raunchy romance. I love twists and unexpected turns, and my novels all contain sexy guys, dark humor, and hot AF love scenes.

I write MF, menage, and reverse harem (also known as why choose romance,) in both contemporary and paranormal. Some of my stories are darker than others, but I can promise you one thing, you will always get the happy ending your heart needs!

Printed in Great Britain
by Amazon